The Death (and Sometimes Life) of Barthalamew Buckett

**For Bob. For Joan.
For the best of Amys.**

ISBN-13: 978-1729061190
ISBN-10: 1729061192

PROLOGUE

Even then, in his day, the crag overlooking the eastern tip of Upper Alabaster Bay cast an augural shadow. Even then the hard, gray face of that unscalable wall seemed uncommonly haunted. Even then, it evinced the look of some long-standing tomb, of some ominous marker that forewarned of a thousand ghosts and a thousand more to come. But, of course, no ghost is there, for what ghost haunts a crag!

To see it now is to see it then, for nature is rather constant here. A hundred years, after all, is nothing to such a rock as that. A hundred more will come and go before wind or water leaves a scratch and you will find it looming, still, over that rugged shore below, no less cold or severe or unsympathetic. I suspect it could stand like that until the very end of time.

You will find another rock nearby, a very different sort of rock, but a rock no less. It is comparatively diminished and rather smooth, purposely so, and stands waist high in a hallowed field called Oglethorpe. It is encircled by a tall fence of black wrought iron. Its face is hard and gray and bears the appearance of some long-standing tomb, which bodes well for its intendment, since a tomb is precisely what it is.

This, of course, is his rock, his marker, and beneath it, of course, is he, and there he has been without so much as a sip of rum for six and one hundred years. And at all the appointed hours on all the appointed days, the great-great-grandson of Gilbert Loydford, a fat and flaunting man who is not too far from a rock of his own, will, for a simple coin, stand over that blessed site and commence to tell, as best he can, all about that thirsty fellow resting now beneath his fat and flaunting feet. However, allow me to note that this so-called best of his has always been more for profit than it has ever been for truth.

Still, he knows the names well enough, a few of them at any rate, and he sounds them off in the richest voice he can muster. Then, like blubberous children to candy, the onlookers snap to life, their eyes widening as though they are being hand-fed the most delicious treat of all.

Oh, dear reader, I do recommend it, for I have seen it myself and I do think it a very fine show. It is worth that simple coin, if only to hear that fat man call out those particular names, giving life once more to the likes of dear Jayne Hundley and Janice Littleton and the terribly ill-fated Trudy Bishop. And then, of course, there is the most tempting morsel of all, the mysterious Lady of Oglethorpe, of whom he clearly knows so little but sells so very well.

And on all the anniversaries of St. Barthalamew's untimely death, at the east end of High-Street just after dawn, the privileged few who are selected and who then become, as one, the Sisterhood of the Rose, present themselves in a luxurious ensemble of white and proceed, single file and with great pomposity, to the boneyard ahead of an utterly silenced crowd. These selected few then assemble before his cherished rock and sweetly place his token gift as she first left hers more than a hundred years ago.

It is all accomplished without so much as a word, with nary-a-whisper from the thousands who dare look on. And it is done with such tremendous effect that even the king, there to see it all for himself, was forced to turn away and sweetly dab his eyes and, with remarkable decorum, pretend on some feverish cause.

And then, at sunset, the High-Street church bell tolls exactly forty-two times. I daresay a thousand mugs are filled and drained as that count drones on and thousands more are wetted as the count rounds forty-one, for here begins, and with unconditional delight, the festival that bears his name.

And what a splendid sight it is. That is, of course, when one can see it, if one's eyes are not so bursting with ale by then, as so many are; if one's breath is not so bursting with the wily spices of so much food and rum; if one's back is not so entirely numb from a profusion of neighborly pats and slaps, so often dispersed by the townsfolk who, for three days straight, take to drink and dance as though they might keel over and die without it.

What a spirited affair for the senses! Well, for those four senses, at any rate. I have discounted all reference to the legions of smells. This I do out of respect.

In all, it is a most prodigious celebration, one that is known the world over, for there is dancing, now, in the streets and pubs of more towns than the one. By these jubilant circumstances, it is only too easily deduced that this good fellow, rest his soul, has some unprecedented story, the very sort of story that cannot wait to be told, much less heard. Indeed, good reader, you have chanced upon the quick truth of the matter.

Merely ask that fat and flaunting man and he will tell you, with a wink, the good living he makes. But, a moment please, as I undo for you all this fine cheer and all those fine words Mr. Loydford puts up for sale. A moment, if you will, as I lay bare a largely abandoned truth. I pray you do not mind.

For this, I ask that you observe once more that polished rock. Please do take a second look, a third, a fourth, if you must. Pay no mind, at least not yet, to those many trumpeted angels, in spite of those impossibly beautiful etchings. Ignore, if you can, the forceful but graceful spelling of his name. You must look past all of these lovely intricacies for the truth is not found in these kindly adornments, but it is left, as always, to hide in plain sight.

Perhaps you will permit a clue. If so, let me suggest that the secret beneath that stone awaits you just there, in the numbers. Look closer, my friend. Can you see it now? Can you see that which has so long since been forgotten? Are you sorting it out?

Examine the artwork now. Take in those kindly curves and lines, all the heavenly beings tooting their own heavenly horns. Admire the bold elegance of the letters that herald his blessed name. Review each intimate detail separately, then the scene as a whole. Is it not the most exquisite work? And now, once more, look to the numbers etched upon his elaborate stone.

A journeyman engraver would note it at once. It is not that the dates are incorrect, although we do know the first is but a guess, but that the numbers are of a different style, a very different cut, altogether a different hand. There is no art to this effort at all. There is something plain here. Something very plain, indeed.

So, which, do you suppose, is our champion of truth? Could it be, perhaps, the incomparable craftsmanship that decorates so well this beloved rock? Or, is it those uncommonly modest numbers? Well, allow me to clear up the matter for you: First and foremost, and for almost sixteen years, it was only the numbers that existed.

Can you see it now? Might you now understand this fugitive truth? If not, then I fear I am fresh out of tact. With your permission, I will let loose of my suavity and just say it outright.

Here lies a man who, at the hour of his death, was but a name, and barely that, on the tip of no more than half a dozen tongues. Here lies a man who knew of no family or friends or money, who left behind no lover, who was not at all considered the sort of man who would ever be missed.

Here lies a man who, despite all efforts, went fast in to the grave, who went head first, I daresay. Here lies a man who took his departure early, so young, so broken and so utterly alone. Here lies suffering. Here lies misfortune. Here, by Molly, lies a wretched dog!

Well, that should be clear enough. Surely, you understand there is more to know and see now. As such, my job here is nearly done.

I give to you now the humble tome of St. Barthalamew of Alagood, our treasured patron saint of unconditional love and spiced rum. I give to you all of the pretty as has been rendered famous by history's most drunken and mischievous poets. I give to you passion, virtue and romance as well, for, indeed, there is some of that to account for.

Here, too, you will find all of the ugly that was so tediously removed, rewritten or purposely unremembered, as has been put aside for the sake of a good rhyme or, in the many instances of the tragically unimaginative, a very, very poor rhyme. And yes, good reader, I give to you the mystery of the Lady of Oglethorpe and her unforgettable gift, for her tale, in regard to his, has never been told to any critical satisfaction.

Do hold kindly to these good pages for herein lies the story of the death and sometimes life of Barthalamew Buckett of Alagood. If ever a man hoped for love, it was he. If ever a man tried for love, it was he. If ever a man failed at love it was, without any doubt and in every conceivable way, he above all.

Well, there we have it. I have prefaced the thing as best I can. I daresay it is no easy task to un-build a saint, especially one so commonly adored, but there is the truth to consider. I recognize, of course, that it may be thought an unpleasant truth, and, in the end, you may choose to forego it but what do I care about that! This business of caring, after all, is no principal concern of mine nor, you will come to know, is it any concern of Truth.

Ah, but the great bell calls the hour. T'is coming on a bit late, I suppose. What else is there for an old man like me to do but recommend a proper chair and a hearty glass of rum or two. That is my preference, at any rate. You may turn the page when you are ready.

I am already there.

1

Barthalamew Buckett was an eager man of twenty when he first fell in love for the third time that year. He was the same boyish twenty when he resolved, and with all the usual vigor, that this time, being the magical third time, would be the very last time; that this one, being the magical Ms. Davison would be his very last. And for all his efforts, kind, romantic and otherwise, it did come to pass. The magical Ms. Davison was, indeed, the very last love of his life. That year.

And just how did the magical Ms. Davison, daughter to Dr. Waxon Davison, local physician of no particular achievement or wonder, find herself atop such a notorious pedestal? Was it that she was a young woman of singular beauty? Not so, according to the journal of Mrs. Joan Theryoung. Was it that she was a young woman of singular style or standing? Additionally, not so by the terms of said journal. Was she well liked or regarded by the many of her community? Almost entirely not so and, again by Mrs. Theryoung's blessed account which, as you may have guessed, puts the poor girl in a light that might best be described, and with no charity to spare, as dim.

So, what were these qualities of Ms. Davison that deemed her so magical to young Barthalamew's eye? Well, it is known that she had a full natural count of eyes and arms and legs as well, which was a very fine thing for Mr. Buckett was drawn, and with some ease and frequency, to that simple and none-too-rare design.

It is known that she was a woman of average height and weight; a woman, it might be said, who let loose the very appearance of someone dipped at birth into a whole vat of averages; a woman, it might be said, who took an early fall from some average height out of the most impeccably average tree and hit upon every average branch on the way down to an otherwise average ground; a woman, it might be said, devoid of any particularity but for her golden locks which, though much less common, appeared all the more average for all the average she so averagely was. To the point, Ms. Davison was as plain as plain could be and if that can be considered a quality, magical or no, then, by all means, consider it.

What, then, of our kindly hero? What of his look, his manner, his averages? Well, of course, there were some to count, for we all have touches of average here and there, some more than others being the previous point.

Barthalamew Buckett was no exception to the rule, but his averages were rather unusual. His face, for instance, was no bigger or smaller or rounder or squarer than any you might know or see, but his lips were thin, his nose was sharp, and his eyes set uncommonly low. And his beard, when he thought to grow it, and he only once thought to grow it, was an awkward and patchy mess.

As for the rest of him, the ebony haired fellow had the look of a man not so actively strong, but strong enough for the sake of his youth. He had handsome parts and not-so-handsome parts and parts of him that seemed rather troubled as to which part to be. He was tall and thin, somewhat lanky and known by a less-than-confident gait.

Barthalamew's dress was fair, though mostly poor, commonly dark with black prevailing. His top hat was short and weathered and, like his hair, dark as night in most spots, but some spots were lighter and already hinting at some future sort of gray. He was young when he smiled and old when he cried and at a loss for age when in love. He therefore seemed almost always ageless or aging fast for love was most often what he was in.

It is no secret now, as it was back then, that Barthalamew's courtship of Ms. Davison was conducted (as a number of his courtships were) and concluded (as a number of his courtships also were) at a very particular site, at what has become a site of legend. It is of the crag, of course, that I now speak.

At the time there was only the south end of High-Street to point the way, to try its level best against such unlevel ground to the waiting summit above. Though a trying path, it was commonly agreed that the trek was well worth the effort as the view proved to be something nearing sublime. It is here where one might daily observe the loveliest of all hours as the golden sun takes its bow before the coming night and the cavorting waters below.

I have seen it myself. I can attest to its splendor. In fact, it has been alleged that, if one is patient enough, one may divine by the call of that celestial scene the ever-so-light and heavenly heart of God's unconditional love. However, it is only alleged, for no one has ever proved to be as patient as all that.

To the point, the upshot is that there exists such a view and it was this particular view that compelled young Barthalamew up that slanted path to a waiting bench entrusted to the cause of appraising that exalted stage. How entirely poetic it was! How entirely poetic it remains! And how so very much a miracle that a fellow so romantically challenged as he would ever know of such a place as this! But he did, for there were miracles yet in Barthalamew Buckett.

And so, it was upon that solitary bench, atop that solitary cliff where Barthalamew seated himself. It was late in the day, early in the fall of his twentieth year. He was there to await the arrival of his beloved Ms. Davison, who had agreed to meet with him by some furtive means.

The boy did not have to wait long. The good woman, so far, had proved herself punctual and, true to form, she arrived precisely on time. Not a second too soon! Not a second too late! How so very punctilious! How so daringly ordinary!

As well, Ms. Davison did look, by her fashion, increasingly plain. Vanilla was her color, as it had always been, and there seemed no chance for another. Vanilla was the parasol, vanilla was the bonnet, vanilla was the dress, shawl and all. Vanilla were the shoes though no one ever thought to look, for what would be the point of that?

Vanilla was, in case the point is not yet clear, every little thing about her. Vanilla, then, was her approach to that solitary bench atop that solitary cliff where salutations between the two were exchanged as though it just happened to be the most remarkable meeting of chance.

"Ms. Davison, a delight!"

"Mr. Buckett, indeed."

Together the two then sat with that waiting horizon now before them. By a measure of no more than a dozen feet the governess of dear Ms. Davison stood, doing quite well as it came to pretending on some unexpected distraction. Then, too, Mrs. Butts, for such was the woman's unfortunate name, was instructed to keep a regular view of the High-Street approach so as to advance a proper signal in the event of a passerby. This was typically managed by a fair bit of hemming and hawing, with more hemming than not and thankfully so, for Mrs. Butts, it was learned, had no true talent for a haw.

"I'm afraid we cannot be so very long," said Ms. Davison in her perfectly common voice which resonated, as always, at the very middlest note of the vocal spectrum. "Papa will be very upset if I am not home upon his return."

"Of course, my Daphne."

"But your letter did say it is of the utmost importance."

"Y-Yes, my Daphne."

The wooer's voice wavered but his heart was readily present. His words were as flat as any man's or boy's or whatever two decades of living suggests, but you may be sure his common sound was music to her waiting ears.

"Very well, Burt. I also have—"

"Barth," he softly corrected.

"Yes, of course. Barth. As I was saying," his Daphne resumed now with a smile, "I too have some wonderful news to share."

Barthalamew mustered a smile of his own, for it could only be supposed by his fledgling heart that these important things to be said were pleasantly in league with one another. He looked down at her lap and applied for her average-sized hands, then gazed with all of his being into the average depths of her remarkably average brown eyes.

Oh, what a perfectly splendid moment it was. In all of his life he had not known a moment so splendid as that. It was a moment, he intuitively knew, that would not soon be forgotten.

"I suppose I should go first," Barthalamew offered, as it was recently suggested to him that a proper woman prefers a decisive man.

"I suppose you should," her ordinary reply.

"Yes, I suppose so."

"Yes, that would be fine."

After a blundering silence, Barthalamew dared again.

"That is to say that I should...perhaps..."

"Yes, perhaps."

"Very well, then."

"Yes, very well."

Of course, the moment was made notably less splendid by these ridiculous iterations, but we must allow that the boy was quite new to such perfectly splendid things. How fortunate for him that the sweet calm of the evening remained before them.

Nature's good grace, after all, was readily wanting and whereas Barthalamew was unable to furnish any such grace for himself, it was clear that grace was to be furnished. The sun, ever nearing the horizon, was very soon to set and between this minute and that moment there was only to speak his heart, to free himself from the emotional weight that had, by way of the past many weeks, so profoundly encumbered his soul. It had to be let out and he was certain that the time and place for the letting had thankfully materialized. So, by nature's serendipitous touch, out it came:

"..."

Sadly, what supervened was a maddening rush of nerves. His throat constricted. The words did not surface. But, what of it? T'was to her, bless her vanilla heart, just a slip, a miss, a gaffe, nothing more. Well, there was still time for a fellow to get it right.

And so, Barthalamew closed his eyes, then widened them again and proceeded to try once more.

"..."

His lips would not have it! Not a bit! Oh, how he practiced those words to unquestionable perfection and yet, there he sat, his eyes and mouth and heart wide open, but not a syllable to be heard, barely a noise at all.

Barthalamew looked away and then back to his Daphne's waiting eyes, inspiration now at every turn. This time he managed to force a lonesome word down the stiff dry plank of his tongue:

"I..."

"Yes," from his Daphne, who was quite curious, but she could not help but look a little bored, for looking bored is what looking average means.

"I..." came his next attempt, his fourth now by count and no better than the previous three.

But then, something broke the spell the poor boy had placed himself under. From a dozen feet away a hem was sounded, the pronouncement of a passer-by. Within the minute a well-dressed gentleman of High-Street stepped up from the path and noted at once the young miss and her governess seated on the bench and a quieted young man now at a distance and staring awkwardly at some faraway thing. All the man could do was give a casual shrug, then surrender the scene, at which point Barthalamew and Mrs. Butts once more took up their respective positions.

With the coast now clear it seemed as though, now more than ever, that the thing had to be done lest the fair reputation of his dear love face the slightest touch of ruin. Thus, with his Daphne again beside him and her eyes still quickened to his, still wide and waiting and so impossible to interpret, Barthalamew put himself once more to the task at hand.

"I..."

Again, those lips, those cheeks, those locks and all set the boy back a bit. It was all so much vanilla to anyone but him. Such is the spell that befalls a man who intends to take a knee before the one he loves. It may be rather simple to imagine and only slightly less simple to decide upon, but when it comes to performing the actual deed, any lad who has chanced it well knows that there is much more to it than a gentleman's blush and a handful of words.

And therein lies the rub. The romance that thrived in the depths of Barthalamew's heart could not at all be doubted. That it was panicked to the point of collapse as it came into possession of his lips…Well, I need hardly point out that we have hit upon that critical fact.

Without reservation I concede that there are greater tragedies about the world, albeit not so numerous as you might think. Imagine, if you can, a heart so gravely crippled, so daily shattered, so perpetually in ruin. Consider a heart so continually undone by its own unforgiving hand, and you will understand as grim a curse as any one man should be forced to bear. It is a wonder, then, that the boy ever took up the courage to speak at all. But, he did, for there was courage yet in Barthalamew Buckett.

"It's just that," the lad bravely pursued, finding some traction at last, "I have a great deal to say."

His Daphne could only shrug for this seemed obvious enough.

"I see," came her simple return. "A great deal to say about what?"

"A-about you, my Daphne."

"About me?"

"Well, about me too," he said thickly.

"About me…and you?" she said thinly.

"About us."

Oh, but what a crowded topic it so suddenly was! And yet, Ms. Davison appeared neither more nor less affected. Her eyes maintained their vacancy. Her modest cheeks gave not a twitch. Her smile remained every bit as undistinguished.

"I see," she said, which only meant she did not see at all. "Well, Burt—"

"Barth," he softly corrected.

"Yes, of course. Barth. Whatever it may be, it does seem to weigh quite heavily on your mind."

"Yes, my Daphne. I suppose it is quite a weight."

"Then, perhaps I could guess," his Daphne kindly offered.

"Guess?"

"Is it about my dress?"

He shook his head, as it was not at all about her dress.

"I see. Has it, perhaps, to do with Pudgie?"

Pudgie was her pony, a gift from her dear father but, much to her dismay, it had not to do with Pudgie.

"Well, then, perhaps it is to do..." and here Ms. Davison appeared nearly at a struggle, "with the weather?"

Well, it is too common a topic not to try but, no, it had not so much to do with the weather.

"Not so much?" Ms. Davison said, as nearly aroused as her unarousable soul would allow. "Well, that does sound like progress."

And yet, it was nothing like progress at all.

"It is to do," Barthalamew started again, in spite of all the starting that had already commenced, "with us."

The boy loosed his most boyish smile as his fingers roamed the lining of his coat pocket, till they wandered across a fine little trinket made of something like gold.

"I would like to know," he now said with a swelling confidence, for the feel of the ring provided a small jolt of encouragement. "I wish to ask—"

"Oh!" came the interruption and with better than average force.

"Oh?"

"But...!"

"But...?"

"That smell!"

"That...smell?"

But then it struck and, indeed, what an appalling smell it was.

"Burt! Burt! What is it?" his Daphne's voice screeched, yielding now to a rather uncommon pitch.

Barthalamew's nose gave chase to the scent and hit upon it at once.

"I think...I think it's the..."

And, in fact, it was the dog. Without any doubt whatsoever, it was the dirtiest, nastiest, scabbiest, brown-haired, one-eyed runt of a flea infested mutt that ever drew breath from the well of life and it was now lying just beneath the bench, now chewing on something at the foot of the bench, chewing on a dead...on a dead...well, on something quite dead at any rate. It was the stink of that miserable beast and its unfortunate snack that, together, so violently assaulted the air between them.

"I don't...I don't...I don't..." his Daphne squeaked, trying and failing to finish the thought and then, quite anxiously, begging and failing on another. "I can't...I can't...I can't..." and then, finally, "I...may be sick!"

"Of course, my Daphne. It is only natural for you to be sick, only natural to—"

"What does it matter if it is natural or not?"

"Well, I suppose," he tried after a moment's thought, "it doesn't really...matter—"

"Walk away! Please, please let us just walk away!"

And so, as it was only natural, Ms. Davison stood with her parasol at her side, tugged a bit at her shaw and awaited Barthalamew who was at once eager to lead her away and did so with all possible haste.

To the edge of the cliff they quickly stepped and there they stood, rather content to be upwind from that horrific dog, and from that rancid beast left to that dog's horrific hunger, that doomed and disfigured thing that was formerly one but now two distinct...now three distinct parts. From that simple distance Barthalamew was fast pleased to see the return of some color to his Daphne's face. She was beginning to look herself again, which is to say she was on the verge of looking as plain as ever.

"I am much better now, thank you," she offered by way of a more pedestrian voice.

"I am most grateful to hear it," he said, and, indeed, he was.

Just then a salty breeze pushed from the pounding surf below and gave many-a-playful turn as it whirled about his Daphne's bonnet and dress and made a curious circus of Barthalamew's hair. The boy pressed for her hand once more and renewed his want of a smile.

From its spot beneath the bench, that ratty brown mutt let loose the treat and, for a moment, looked on, as though there was now before it some framed bit of art that was just beyond the bounds of interpretation. It was sunset over Upper Alabaster Bay and there, at the near edge of that cliff, was young Barthalamew in his tattered black coat and tails and fading red cravat, standing tall before the woman he loved, holding dearly to her as though the kiss could come at any moment.

"It is quite lovely!" she just then said of the setting sun.

"It is like…a wedding day," Barthalamew happily added.

"Only that it is no longer day and there is no wedding," his Daphne sadly subtracted.

"But…perhaps…perhaps…"

Wretched tongue! So fine the dreams that come and go as it lays there stuck in place. To the west, all the while, the sun was setting, setting, setting.

"Oh, have I mentioned," his Daphne started.

"Have you mentioned…what?"

"Cousin Catherine is to marry. The announcement was in today's Gazette."

Well, to be sure, this so-called mention did not sit well with the lovesick boy and for two considerable reasons.

"Yes, my Daphne. I know."

"Oh, but of course! I forgot you know Cousin Catherine."

Being the first of reasons.

17

"Yes, my dear," Barthalamew said softly, so as to conceal the touch of a wound. "Also, I wrote the announcement."

Being the second of reasons.

"Did you?"

"Yes, dear. It is my job."

"Is it?"

"Yes. I have told you this."

"Have you?"

"Yes," Barthalamew said rather forcefully, for it was just too peculiar that she so commonly forgot the very simplest of things about him. His name. His occupation. "I work at the Gazette. I prepare the social announcements for Mr. Loydford."

"Do you now? Well, I must say that sounds like devilish fun!"

And yet, it was neither devilish nor fun.

"Well, I suppose it would be if, perhaps, we were to one day announce...to announce our own—"

"I cannot stay long," his Daphne said rather abruptly with a telling glance to her governess. "You did say it was an important matter!"

Oh, how could it all be going so wrong! Why was the boy destined for so much interference!

Y-Yes," Barthalamew fumbled. "It is important."

"Very well, Burt. Please, tell me."

At that moment, a burst of purple blasted the sky as the sun began its melt into the coming night. It was quite clear, by nature's good show, that it was now or that it would never be. Placing a hand into his coat pocket to assure the offering was still there, Barthalamew took a slow knee before the immutably adequate foot of Ms. Davison. From this position, the good lad looked up with his softest eye and spoke with his softest voice yet.

"My Daphne—"

"Oh, Burt! Have you dropped something?"

"...?"

How odd was this bit of art to that curious dog now! How so very abstract, indeed! And so, back it went to its rat or its bird or whatever it was, that fallen and gutted thing between its front paws with maybe a tail or a wing or who could really say at that point, for it being as chewed and chomped and crunched and gnawed as it so entirely was.

"My Daphne," the boy tried again, only to find himself suddenly in an unexpected competition with the sound of a very fitful cough plying from the direction of the respectfully distant governess. The cough came again and again, and, for a moment, the good lady seemed to be either at the point of exaggeration or nearing the point of death.

"Burt," his Daphne said with a flush of her cheek and a twitch of her nose, "I truly must go. I do wish I could be of some help in your search but I'm afraid you'll have to find it yourself. You should hurry, though. It is getting quite dark."

And so, what else could that luckless fellow do but to pretend to comb the ground and feel about for...something.

"Yes, of course. I have nearly found it," he said, at once despising the lilt in his voice which he knew to be no less than the sound of surrender.

Pretending to have recovered it, Barthalamew then stood and gave himself a proper dusting, only to realize that his Daphne was already stepping away. It was quite clear that she was rather in a hurry to return to her governess who, by the grant of some perfectly unaccountable miracle, was just then fully restored to health.

How ridiculously unfair was that chance of his! How could it be so unfair! Could it possibly be more unfair than that! But, of course, it had nearly been forgotten.

Burt," she called out and with a swift turn stepped back a bit in his direction. "I had nearly forgotten."

"Yes, my Daphne?"

"I am to depart just after Cousin Catherine's wedding."

"To...depart?"

"Yes. The following day."

"The following day?"

"Yes. I am promised."

"You are...promised?"

"To a banker."

"A banker?"

"A banker in Kent."

"In Kent?"

"Where I am to be married."

"To...be...married?"

"It is quite odd that you keep repeating what I say!"

It was quite odd, indeed. Remarkably odd. Disturbingly odd.

"Yes. Quite odd," Barthalamew said, realizing then that he was still at it. "It's just...that I usually have a fair warning about this sort of thing."

"Yes, well, it's been a bit of a secret."

"Yes," Barthalamew had to accept. "I suppose it has.

There was nothing to say of the silence between them now. They seemed as perfect strangers before that infant night, as though two people who had not yet met and somehow never would. How crippling it all was to that simple man who could only stand there with his trembling hand still in his pocket, still reaching for that now worthless band of something like gold.

"I have only met him once," she resumed, as though it was her duty to do so. "A little less than a year ago. He's fat and old and as dumb as hay," and here she loosed an impeccably average giggle, "but he is apparently quite taken with me, which is rather sweet. And I suppose it cannot hurt that he has some family wealth. A good deal of it, as it turns out."

No...I suppose not."

By now Barthalamew had taken to staring at the ground for it seemed the only thing before him that was true. And yet, he found himself hoping so very much that it might also prove false, that it might, at that moment, open up at his feet and swallow him whole and never return him to the torturous light of day.

"You...must have known that I..." he started, gawking now at the unyielding ground, "I mean to say...I do wish you might have said...something..."

"But it was a secret! Papa insisted. Don't tell a soul, he said. But when Cousin Catherine announced, that put Papa in quite a proper mood!"

"A mood?" Barthalamew repeated, kicking now at the ground beneath, all but begging it to open and let him in.

"Yes, in a very fine mood."

"I see," but he did not see.

"Besides," his former Daphne continued, "I did not want to spoil your fun."

And here were the most cutting words of all. Oh, why would the ground not just give a little. He felt plenty small by now. A mere crack would do the trick.

"That is not to say," she thought to amend, "that I did not have my share of fun as well. I just adored your secret letters. They were all just so adorable!"

Any crack would do. His very soul for the slightest crack of all.

"And I am sure that I speak for Mrs. Butts," his former Daphne persisted, "when I say that she too is terribly fond of our little sunset chats. It has all made a perfect spy of her which, I must say, is particularly agreeable, as she is otherwise," and here a bit of a whisper, "the very dullest sort of creature. Oh, I do believe she will come to miss it all so very much, perhaps as much as I will."

Damned ground. Stupid, blasted ground!

"It has all been a very good bit of fun," his former Daphne continued. "I am so very pleased that I've had the chance to know you these past few weeks. I will not soon forget you, dear Barth."

"Burt."

"Yes, of course, Burt. Well, I must surely hurry now. It is quite late and I'll soon be missed. Do wish me luck."

And with that went the Maiden of Middling, stepping plainly away from poor Burt, who did not wish her luck, who spared not a word in parting, who only stood in place and stared at that cruel and constant ground and wondered of all the rum in the world.

But then there came the most unexpected shriek from the nearby bench.

"AAAHH!"

And with it, the very last words the young boy would ever hear from those impossibly ordinary lips of the magical Ms. Davisson.

"Where ever did that wretched thing come from?!"

Despite the sudden volume, the dog was not stirred for his ungodly meal still ruled the day.

Barthalamew, however, could not help but blink, for that particular yelp had a fast and familiar sort of sound.

2

"Where-ever did that wretched thing come from?"

There was hardly a room in the world that could well receive the fast, metallic shriek of Sister Josephine and that particular room, so cramped and crumbling as it was, was clearly not one of them. The screeching elder echoed that age-old sacristy with unmatchable fervor, bouncing her voice from one wall to the next before striking the floor with a trebulous snap at the piteously sandaled feet of Sister Marihanna. For her part, the graying Marihanna, lost at that moment to the most extraordinary mood, had only a smile to give. And so, it became her silent reply.

To even the novice eye it was clearly an unpracticed smile, unused, perhaps, for a number of years but now recalled with remarkable ease. Her sheepish grin was blissful and buoyant and sweetly suggested the pleasure of some forgotten memory or long-ago dream. And as the old, plump gal let it unfold across the width of her wrinkled, apple-like face, she could not help but feel the magic of her youth reaching out and up from some beautiful far-away place. There was heaven, dear reader, alive in her eyes, and notwithstanding that shrill, metallic cry, Marihanna appeared to be a woman at peace with all the world.

The good sister was standing in the far corner of that formerly sacred room, turned from the entrance where a door once was but once was stolen, taken, presumably, by a needful band of doorless thieves. At the end of her reach, in the large, olden sacristy sink where only the great instruments of religion were once cleansed, was the wretched thing in question, was the impossible baby boy enjoying, consequently, his impossible baby bath. He was a chubby and a decidedly happy babe with a struggling patch of black hair atop his little baby head. He was naked and squirming and at the start of a giggle when Sister Josephine stepped into the room and let loose that hellish squawk.

And what a trauma it was for such fine, young ears. Baby's eyes widened. His tiny fists clinched. Baby took on the look of some unholy baby terror. Only the charming smile of his warm-hearted bather kept him from a passionate scene. The squawk, however, was quick to come again.

"Sister Marihanna!" this time with gasps, staggering as her temper now was. "Where! Did! That baby! Come from!"

Sister Marihanna could not help that she was as literal as she was. To the point, she had a very plain approach to the notion of language. The question now, as she perceived it, was rather awkward, all the more so before the little angel.

Perhaps, she conceded, Sister Josephine was at an advanced age. Perhaps she was the sort of woman to forget such things. Perhaps she was in need of a refresher.

"Well, Sister," Marihanna started, but then paused so as to allow for some sense of propriety, "when a man and a woman love each other very much—"

"Sister Marihanna! You will not talk of such things!"

"But, you asked."

"What I asked, sister, is where! Did! You! Find! Where did you find! That baby?"

Well, that did seem a more sensible thing to ask. The answer now was far less involved, comical by comparison. She turned quickly about, smiling still, hopeful, even by the start of a laugh, but found the steadfast elder not so pleased. She was, in fact, as severe as ever and seemingly braced against every possible joy.

There Josephine stood, unbreakably rigid, arms crossed, lips pursed, eyes wickedly afire with all her usual tempers. But it was her hair that told the story best, those hard, gray strands so firmly locked in place, so tightly packed atop her shriveled head, so entirely compressed as though to give the uneasy impression that it was all on the verge of some cataclysmic reversal, as if, at any moment, it might all violently unbind and explode through walls. By all accounts, there was plenty to fear from a head of hair like that and, indeed, fear was the stock response.

Sister Marihanna turned back to the task at hand. She tucked away her smile. She elected not to laugh.

"Well, Sister, if you must know, I found him out back in the mop bucket."

"In the…" a pause and then a pause again, followed by a number of nearly inaudible gasps, concluded with yet another pause before, finally, "…bucket!?"

"Yes, Sister, he was left in the bucket."

"*In* the bucket," Josephine said, stressing at first the preposition as though, perhaps, only some other preposition would do, as though, perhaps, that it was only reasonable to abandon one's infant child under or near or, possibly, on a bucket. "In the *bucket*!" now placing emphasis on the subject, as though a bucket somehow inspired someone to go about leaving a baby on, under or near it. "*In the bucket!*" she said finally and this time equally stressing each syllable, amazed now by the complete sounding of those three simple but clearly unexpected words.

"Yes, sister, in the bucket."

"Why, it's…that's…" the elder sister faltered, stupefied nearly to the point of pursing her lips. "It's just…unheard of!"

"Well, yes, sister," Marihanna could not help but agree and turned about to say so. "I suppose it is."

"What kind of person goes about leaving babies in buckets?"

"I'm sure I don't know."

"Well, sister, perhaps you should have left it in the bucket!"

"But, it was needed for mopping."

"There is another bucket! Did you not think to look for it?"

And here Sister Marihanna now had to stop and wonder for the argument, as much as it was expected, was off and running in a most peculiar direction. Sister Josephine, so passionately bound to all her usual states of denial, seemed rather fixed on the matter of buckets and not so much on what some might consider to be the more essential matter of the baby. It was, therefore, Marihanna's decision to redirect with a question of her own.

"Should I not have saved the baby?"

"To save! The baby! From a bucket!?" Josephine was gasping still, gasping now like a dying fish. There was only to fall to the ground and flop about to complete the effect. "It is for the baby to save itself!"

Yes, this was more in line with what was expected. There was only to accept the silliness now as Josephine's tantrums, so nonsensical as they commonly were, simply had to be accepted.

"Him," Sister Marihanna asserted with a soft smile and a playful splash of water. "To save himself."

"Him?"

"Him."

Him!

"Oh, dear God," Josephine whooped, cutting loose the matter buckets altogether. "You've gone and let a man into our home!"

"Well, sister, he's not quite a man just yet."

"A boy then! And boys are well known to grow into men!"

"Indeed, I have heard as much," Marihanna rejoined.

"And this one will, too!"

"I think it more likely than not."

"Well, if we both agree that it is to be a man, then I cannot help but feel it is my distinct duty to remind you, Sister Marihanna, of the core principle of the order!"

"Well, sister, if you cannot help it—"

"Men are not welcome! Are not allowed! Are not tolerated here! Are not! Are not! Are not!"

Each exclamation was augmented by a stomp of a foot but as Josephine's shoe was such an old one and attached to such an old foot, the two together had only a diminished effect against that firm floor of ingrained brick. Regardless of the efforted stomp, Marihanna had no care or interest in

Josephine's simple duty. Her full attention was now taken by the magnificent snicker of that darling baby boy.

"He seems to really enjoy the water," she then said, with all the pride of the most curious of mothers.

"Sister Marihanna, have you not heard a single word I have said?"

"Yes, yes, Sister Josephine. All about men and so forth and so on."

The boy was performing a joyful wiggle now, practically a dance in her matronly grasp, but there was, by the tone of Marihanna's reply, a trace of impatience, the soft suggestion of the dream coming apart before her eyes, of some unwelcomed reality ever-so-slowly drifting back into view. Oh, nothing suffers like a dream in that forgotten place! Such was her thought as she lifted the boy from the old sacristy sink and prepared him for a proper drying.

But then the most curious thought prevailed.

"Barthalamew!" her voice lifted at once.

Josephine was not so quick to follow.

"A what!" the spinster screamed with a quick glance about the room as though she was expecting a Barthalamew to emerge.

"His name."

"Whose name?"

"His."

Only then did Josephine understand. A Barthalamew was already there.

"But...you cannot name it!"

"Surely, I must," said Sister Marihanna.

"You cannot! You are not allowed!"

"Not allowed what?"

And here was a different sort of voice, another voice altogether, one so absolutely calm that it could not be any other than Sister Marilyn. The soft-footed woman had chanced upon the scene, as she most often chanced upon them, inadvertently and without much in the way of notice.

This was the custom if not the very definition of her character.

Sister Josephine turned at once to the slightly younger Marilyn so as to be the first to press the argument.

"She has named the baby!"

Marilyn eased a more curious voice now as looked to and noted the babe in Marihanna's arms. "But, Sister Marihanna, wherever did you find the time?"

"He was in the bucket," was Marihanna's fast reply, "He was left there."

"And for excellent reason, I suspect," Josephine thought to add, for it seemed, she decided, in need of adding.

The remaining women, however, did not seem to hear a word of that, for their focus remained entirely on the baby. Sister Marilyn resisted, but then stepped quickly to the freshly dried boy and gave his toes a fast wiggle. This eased a boyish laugh, which, in turn, put a soft mark on Marilyn's nearly forgotten heart. And just like that, another rare smile in that dreamless place was surfaced.

"Do you feel Barthalamew to be a proper name?" Marihanna then asked of Marilyn.

"As good as any, I suppose," was Marilyn's gentle reply.

"T'was the name of my good uncle. Uncle Barth was a dark-haired fellow, too, also raised as an orphan. The similarities are quite telling."

"Well, if that be the case, it is most agreeable," Sister Marilyn allowed.

"But there is to be no name!" Josephine charged, needing her voice to be heard now more than ever. "Do you two hear me! Put that child back in the bucket at once!"

"Back in the bucket?" Marilyn said, finally acknowledging, in her quieted little way, those queer grievances of the anxious elder. "Don't be silly. He has just had his bath."

"He may be in want of a nap," Sister Marihanna said. "I think I shall take him to my room. Perhaps, Sister Marilyn, you can find something in the vegetable garden for a proper snack. He does look a bit peckish."

"As any bucket baby would," Sister Marilyn said with a last wiggle of baby's toes.

"No! Not to your room! I forbid it!"

"Come now, Sister, how ungodly you are being," Sister Marilyn said and then stepped, with all the ease in the world, from the room and made way for the garden.

Bolstered by Marilyn's kindly support, Sister Marihanna also stepped to but not before Josephine, with firmly crossed arms, made her last claim.

"This will not stand!" said she with as much conviction as she could muster.

"Oh, but it shall," was Marihanna's simple reply.

"Not if I have anything to do with it!"

"Then I advise you to have nothing to do with it."

This seemed as good a thing to say at the moment as could be said. And so, having said it, Sister Marihanna, with baby Barth in her arms, took her step from the sacristy and made way to her room where the dear boy was fed and then put down for a peaceable nap.

3

As most any crow flies, for I do not presume to speak for all crows, Alagood must be something of a marvel to see. I daresay it is like no town most crows might ever know or have ever known before, which does make me wonder, and more than a bit, what a crow might think when one first comes upon it.

Were you to make your approach to Alagood from Lower Alabaster Bay, as all boats and most crows do, you would see rising up before you the most irregular creation ever devised by the hearts and hands of men. From west to east the incline runs and at such a remarkable slant as to seem almost silly.

This is the landscape, so bent as it is, that first grabs the eye and likely gives a crow as good a reason to laugh as any crow might ever have, assuming, of course, that crows have any reason at all to laugh and that evolution has, by some kind fashion, devised a way to permit it.

But then that crow-smile, I suspect, would fall to wonderment for what fool, I believe that crow might think, would choose to build on such lopsided land as this! What fool would even think to pave a road on so unnaturally wicked a slope! What fool would hoist up such a strange row of buildings to attend the cruel stretch of that slanted street!

And how does it all stand? Why does it not all fall down on top of one another? Why does it not all roll down that ponderous hill to the lowly west side port where the fishing boats gather and wade at what seems to be gravity's most plentiful point!

And then that crow-wonderment, I can only assume, would fall prey to pity for any bit of livestock that might be forced to step up and down that peculiar ground. What horse, after all, would give a damn for that west-east run knowing, especially, that by its return it would have to walk the most devilish sort of walk! But then, upon second glance, the crow of Barthalamew's day might note that horses were hardly used at all, that walking, not riding, was the chief mode of transport for those ridiculous folk and lucky thing too, as humans are much more ably designed for all the products of their own absurd imaginings than any poor horse might ever be.

At this point, it could be guessed, that poor bird might put an end to all these musings. This, after all, would constitute a rather exhausting day of emotion for the everyday crow. And so, I imagine that it might choose to ferry on, repressing as best it could every memory of having ever come across such a place as Alagood. That is, of course, until it sucked in the hard and penetrating air of the fisherman's wharf, which would surely bring it fast about and place it heartily in love with the west end there.

In his day, this was where all smells, but a good smell lived, where the poor and the humbled and the artisans perched, where the beggarly gathered to plead for their scraps and to cast up their eyes in awe of those east side folk who, every so often, stepped down from their High-Street lofts and lowered themselves to market.

It was here where a lesser soul's only chance was to sit and stew and sell one's wares in the hopes of inching one's way up that increasingly prosperous road. It was here where as many could be born would soon enough die and with more dreams in their hearts than coins in their purse, for it was and continues to be the business, you see, of the rich to stay rich and of the poor to stay poor and for those about the middle to keep ever-so quietly to the middle.

And that is how it was on Port Street in his day. There was the devilish low, the enviable high and that necessary spot about the center where the road did, for a moment, level a bit, as though to reconsider its course before slithering on. And it was near that level spot, albeit a bit more west than east, that is to say more poor than rich, that is to say west enough to be thought quite poor, that a public house rose by two simple stories and gave residence to a handful of men and, on occasion, a working woman or two.

Altogether known as Jasmine House, where no Jasmine was known to have ever lived, that particular abode was bedecked with the very smallest of apartments for let. The rooms were situated above a larger, insufficiently furnished public chamber where the residents often gathered to sup or drink or smoke or chat or grunt or silently gawk or stare or glare or gloat or wear down their eyes on some window pane upon the other side of which the circus of life so proudly (though so poorly) passed.

Jasmine House was predominantly peopled by a worn and weak and hungry folk, an unproductive bunch that swore no pride for all the moaning and groaning and growling and spitting that took up so much of its otherwise empty days. It was here where those lesser denizens stewed, where their lives sustained before an unavailing cycle of debt and depletion, before absolute stockpiles of misfortune and mischance and before as much disagreeable hygiene as any one room could possibly contain.

Here unhappiness was bred, it seemed, for the very purpose of continued unhappiness. To be sure it was not the sort of place one aspired to but, quite certainly, the sort of place one aspired from. And yet aspiration had not a breath to give in the confines of that singular house of Jasmine.

Of course, the house no longer stands, but if one was to seek out Barthalamew Buckett in his final days and years, that would have been the place to start. Up those rickety stairs and then to the end of the hall, one would have found upon entry as black a room as could be imagined, a room so dark as to render its walls like the chamber of one's heart; not so much seen as felt, not so much felt as understood.

Beneath an awkwardly low ceiling one would then find a ragged frame and mattress put up against a corner where a window might have been but never was. And then one might, with squinted eye, spot a fireplace of simple stone and the afterthought of a mantle just above, supporting with effort a sconce and two volumes of constantly read fiction.

And perhaps, one would spy nearby, for it could only be nearby, a creaky old chair and an uncommonly old desk, the sort of desk one keeps about for the sake of thinking or writing or thinking of writing but mostly for the sake of thinking; a second-hand desk (on its very best day) replete with a number of second hand drawers, each assigned, by a measure of its hold, a very particular worth.

Here, and sadly, lived all things related to the boy and it is here that we now find said occupant in his natural state, seated alone, seated in misery and only vaguely aware of the sound of some distant knock. Distant as it was soft, soft as it was the knock of a woman and unrelenting as it was the knock of a very specific woman. It was a tapping so steady, so constant and so often peppered with the hurried call of his name that it could not, by any chance in the world, be ignored.

"Mr. Buckett!"

Again, with the knocking. Once more with the call.

"Mr. Buckett! I know you're in there!"

How awful a thing knowing can be when knowing is such a plague.

"Mr. Buckett, please! There seems to be something wrong with...with...this..."

Dog. There was no doubt it was Dog. And there was no doubt that something was entirely wrong with it. However, it had been Barthalamew's longstanding intention to avoid any and all discussion with that particular woman about that very particular dog.

"Mr. Buckett! Please, I need__"

But what else could he do? The knocking, he knew, would continue without end. There was only to concede. And so, with a dreadful spirit, Barthalamew stepped to the door, grasped the knob and gave it a slight pull.

"Oh, Mr. Buckett, there you are."

Dog was in at once; when the devil demands mischief, he only needs an open door.

For her part, Mrs. Lora Dean simply stood her ground and offered a most disingenuous smile.

"Barthalamew, you mustn't keep a good lady waiting," said she, and with as much good will as could be spared. "Especially a lady that is owed. The rent is due!"

"Yes, ma'am. I shall have it," he barely answered as he was barely in want of saying much of anything before that particularly discomforting woman.

It was not that she was the landlord's wife. It was just barely that she was the landlord's pretty wife. It was mostly that her strangely gray eyes had such a mesmerizing sway. They were as an orchestra under her direction, playing wildly through the emptiness of some great hall, playing despite the emptiness, playing, in fact, all the more for it. Hers was the sort of lunacy that put the boy's nerve on alert.

"As for your pet," she continued as she brought her smile to a close with a near audible snap.

"Oh, no ma'am, the dog is not my pet."

"Well, I shall leave it to you to decide who is the pet among you, but if you must insist on keepin' a dog—"

"But, t'is not my dog, ma'am."

"Oh, Barth, it matters not to me. I won't say a thing to Mr. Dean," she offered, though this was hardly a sacrifice on her part since she had not said so much as a word to Mr. Dean for more than a month now. "Please just keep it outside as often as you can! That creature," now with a sly eye towards its imagined location within, "was born to the streets. Let's agree that's where it belongs."

Let's agree, he thought to say, that it belongs in a boiling tar pit of endless fire, but Barthalamew, good lad that he was, held his tongue and turned instead to the simple language of Mrs. Dean.

"Yes, ma'am."

At which point the dog surrendered the room and at once gave chase to some new order of play. It took to the hallway, to the stairs, to the common room below, then out the door to the lamp-lit street where it decided to squat and lift its leg and put its tongue to some joyful use. Satisfaction for the dog, like any such dog, came fast and by all of its usual marks.

"See?" the landlady delighted. "It's in a much better way now. I think the little fellow knows his place well enough. You might have yourself a smart one there."

"But, I don't…" Barthalamew started then stopped. It was, he decided, all the answer he needed, the only words, in truth, that she would bother to hear.

"Well, Barth, I'm pleased that is settled," she said as the orchestra played on. "I shall expect your rent by this time tomorra'?"

Though served as a question, the answer was clearly in waiting.

"Yes, ma'am."

"Oh, I do wonder," for now the landlady's symphony stepped upon a wandering course, "have you heard about Cousin Catherine?" for everyone had come to call her that.

"Y-Yes, I have," Barthalamew stuttered as objectively as he could.

"It seems she is to wed."

Indeed, it seemed.

Mrs. Dean's eyes now darted, the two together and all at once focused on every little thing; his chin, his nose, his lips, his eyes, first left and then right and then together. Such was the great industry of the landlady's curiosity, conducting itself now into a frenzy as it quietly composed the most satisfying sort of hymn. That he said something or nothing at all was no matter to her but simply a part of the show.

"Yes, ma'am," he finally said.

"Well, I do believe she found her a good one in this fellow," said she with a curious wink which easily suggested that Mrs. Dean had no idea of this supposed fellow but simply wanted to say as much. "Don't you think so, Barth?"

"Yes, ma'am."

With that defeated response there appeared the start of a tear though Mrs. Dean was too uncouth to know why. She only knew to carry on in all her usual and curious ways, and carry on she did, reciting to him the arrangements as listed in the Gazette, as written, in fact, by his very own hand. Barthalamew made no effort to comment, but only lowered his gaze as though to give his forehead in reply.

After a moment, the minuet was completed, and the symphony changed its tune.

"There's some raisin porridge left," Mrs. Dean said, for she just then remembered he had passed on his supper. "Should I keep it for you?"

Barthalamew declined with what was an attempt at grace for he had no love of porridge and less love of raisins; it was therefore well beyond his wits to even pretend on a love for raisin porridge.

"No thank you."

The landlady's gray eyes, still darting, now tried to reach further in, tried to find any corner of his undersized room.

"Mr. Buckett," she then asked, suddenly formal again, "are you in need of candles?"

"No, ma'am," Barthalamew said.

"Are you sure? It's just so…dark in there."

"Yes, ma'am," he parroted and then, with a touch of courage and a gentle smile, he put the door between them.

Barthalamew returned to his bed in the dark. At that moment it seemed to suit him. Tonight, there would be no rum. The rent was due and with a good bit of luck, he would just be able to meet it.

There was only to sell his Daphne's ring. A buyer, he knew, would be easy to find but his desperation would not allow for even half what he paid. His poor soul loved too much, too fast this time. It proved to be his most costly season yet.

And then, he knew, the sharp breath of winter would follow. By his own heart's measure he knew winter was the most desperate of seasons, a dreadful stretch of nights and weeks where all the loneliest of hours were kept. Once more he would know the icy stare of those innumerous stars so clear in the chill of that nightly sky, each blinking intolerably, each counting from its own unique corner of creation, each looking back at him as though it was his number and not theirs that was so impossible to grasp.

At times like this Barthalamew did his best to find comfort in the simple dark of his room, in not seeing, in not being seen, in knowing only the sky-less night of those low hanging beams and begging against the clamor from the public chamber below. And yet, try as he did, he inherently knew that peace, by those hours, would never be his.

A candle was soon lit. It took but a moment for the whole of the room to illuminate. Shadows then emerged and danced about, revealing the second-hand desk nearby.

Here, comprised in no short order, was all that made the boy up. Here was his lawless empire of tasks and debts, his mindful thoughts and sometimes drunken scribbles that framed the starts, middles and the very worst endings to all sorts of reckless and unreadable poetry. Here was a vast citizenry of pages, a population of paper, all folded, or crumpled or ripped to bits, then ranked and stuffed accordingly into this or that drawer, each madly overrun and each in a state of revolt.

And to the middle of that beastly prop, among the madness of those second-hand drawers, there remained one drawer that was clearly apart and the only one that had a proper second-hand lock. It was a lock more nimble than not, but a lock no less and faithful to its charge before the eyes and heart of that frequently melancholic fellow.

And beyond this simple lock was kept the vanguard of his worth, a fortress unchallenged and nearly well-kept, the quiet aristocracy of all that rowdy second-handedness. These were the papers that ruled them all, the pages of sweet nobility, the very kings and queens of words. And at the bottom of each magical sheet, there was inscribed the most blessed of all possible names.

These sacred nobles were kept in a modest box, bound by a single, loosely tied knot of once-red-but-faded pink ribbon. Only the slightest tug was required to release the pages and raise the curtain on those hallowed and waiting memories. Here lay the play of his heart, the one and only thing in Barthalamew's life that was ever truly his to have and hold.

There was only to reach for it, but there were nights, so many nights such as this, when the effort proved too much, when Barthalamew found he had only the strength to lay across his lumpy bed, to stretch his legs and let sleep have its way, to dream the quiet and hopeful dream of some other day in some other life, of some other love, of some other smile, of some other pair of dear green eyes, of some other...

But, oh, what was that infernal smell? What was that unsavory mess steaming now upon the wrinkled mass of his bed?

Oh, that dog! That damned, damned, damned dog!

4

"I say," Toby said, "I've been meaning to ask," for he had been meaning to ask, "what is with that dog?"

Just what was it with that dog? Barthalamew turned to it, to sneer at it, to put once more to himself and for the hundredth time that very question and for the hundredth time no answer dared surface.

"It follows," he finally said with some unease.

"You?" for it seemed an unlikely answer.

"Yes."

"A pet?" for it seemed even more unlikely.

"No," Barthalamew replied. "The damned thing won't let me near it."

The damned thing was stretched out on the nearby lawn, atop the cool and giving grass, clearly taken by the gentle wealth of its surroundings, seemingly smiling at its predicament. It was, at that moment, as well off as it had ever been, as well off as it would ever be. To either side of it, Toby's dear daughters sat, young and playful and with no less than a million giggles and shrieks. They prodded and petted the happy dog with their usual childlike curiosity as their unhurried father looked on.

"Well," a hesitation, "but you do feed it?"

At that point, a number of unwelcomed visions surfaced. Barthalamew winced as he answered.

"Not a bit. It rather enjoys feeding itself."

"And still...it follows?"

"Yes," was Barthalamew's tired reply. "Day and night. It sleeps at my door."

"How very odd, Barth. How very monumental! What do you call it?"

"By God," Barthalamew started, but then kept his voice as the children were near. "I call it nothing! I want nothing to do with it."

"And still it follows?" Toby's interest could not help but peak and so peak it did. "Truly monumental! Do you suppose," he then asked as an afterthought, "that the girls are safe?"

Young Amy and Lee Ellen remained intrigued, rolling about the lawn as though at the start of some silly convulsion, playing whereas the dog had only want for rest, drawing freely from that near infinite chorus of giggles and shrieks. By their nature, their youth, especially their gender they were simply too quick to love anything at all that played host to so many fleas and a tail.

"Quite safe. He doesn't seem to mind anything or anything but me."

"Mon-u-men-tal!" Toby repeated, now enunciating each syllable for effect. "What a queer pup. Well, queer second. Ugly first and foremost. Ugly as all the devils of Bazre!" for the devils of Bazre were reputed to be quite ugly. "How delightful that it found you!"

And with that said, the mystery of the dog, as known as it may ever be, was gently retired. From his kingly chair atop his kingly porch and his bent straw hat atop his kingly head, Toby lit his pipe and eased a smile as he looked to all that he owned, to his home and porch, to the barn nearby, to his happy daughters and the grass beneath and the fifty family acres that quietly boxed it all in. Life, by his rested heart, had been most kind.

Toby then pushed back his head as though to consider some heavenly thought. This motion was followed at once by a determined and musky scent, given rise to by the smoke that billowed forth from his pipe and then chased up and away, beyond the quiet comforts of that kingly porch and toward the unreachable blue of that morning sky. The young patriarch, already a reputed man of reflection, decided then and there to reflect.

"Barth, good fellow, I have seen a thing."

As it was assumed, by tone, texture and simply the timbre of his voice, as well as the fact that when Toby thought to announce that a thing had been seen, it was generally his way of suggesting that it was an unpleasant thing, Barthalamew reached for the mug on the table between them and braced himself with a hearty swig.

"It seems Cousin Catherine," for everyone had come to call her that, "is to be married.

Yes, it seemed.

Barthalamew took another quick drink and then pressed, "Why is it that no one can remember what it is that I do?"

"Ah, yes, well then, a' course you know," Toby said with a contemplative breath. "Still, you did love her rather...vigorously. So, I was a bit worried." Another breath, another contemplation. "But, how I do forget," and here he turned up a most obliging smile, "it is the good doctor's daughter for you now. What a dear comfort she must be, eh?

Oh, how heavy the silence that so swiftly pounced! It was as though nature itself gave pause and dropped all of its constant doings so that it could hear what might next be aired. Barthalamew, however, gave not a sound, said not a word; in that shared moment his hesitation was more than enough.

"I see," said Toby, looking away to the open fields and the break of the town beyond. He let out a soft puff from his pipe. "Saw it comin', saw it comin'. But you're better off for it. Monumental, even. An undistinguished girl like that! And, I suppose I can say so now, not entirely handsome. Not so handsome at all."

There came not the faintest sound of objection from Barthalamew. His words were quickly lost to the mug still before him.

With his eyes still town-ward and his pipe once more leading the way, Toby thought to repeat what had been said so, so many times before.

"Don't worry yourself, Barth. There are still plenty of fish in the sea. Sure, there might be one fewer but plenty, still!"

Looking to his mug as though it was the rum that had said it, Barthalamew finally rejoined but with the sound and sway of a seasick man.

"I don't have the heart for it anymore."

"Nonsense, good fellow. The problem is that you haven't the heart for anything else."

Which was true, and which was honest and which, having been so confidently said, encouraged the pipe, then Toby, to forge ahead.

"A fisherman you've always been, a fisherman you'll always be, until ya' put yourself to some better use," and here seemed the start of some wayward sermon but Toby hastily concluded. "What ya' need, my good man, is something in the way of a hobby."

Barthalamew looked again to the mug in hand, to the muddied rum within.

"But, I've got a hobby."

Pipe. Toby.

"Poetry is not a hobby, Barth. Poetry is an affliction. Poetry is the merciless work of a hundred-thousand demons retching down the throat of a godless soul," which, despite all of its unseemly language, seemed a rather poetic thing to say. "T'is high time you give up this romance business. Nothing good comes of it, ya' see."

But Barthalamew did not see.

"Nothing good?"

"Nothing! Good!" Toby said, twice tapping his pipe on the table, once to the sounding of each word.

"But…this comes from it!"

"This?"

"Yes," Barthalamew insisted with a tapping of his own. "This!"

By this, of course, he meant all the favored colors of nature, all the favored sounds of those laughing children and the favored sight of a beautiful wife picking vegetables in the garden nearby. By this, he clearly meant the house and the kingly porch and the barn and the grass and the pipe and the rum and the curiously constant scent of peaches and hay and puppy breath. By this he meant love. This!

"This?" Toby repeated rather stupidly and without much conviction. "You don't want this!"

"But, it is exactly what I want!"

"No," Toby persisted. "You don't want this."

"But I do! I *do* want this."

"No, you don't!"

"Yes! I do!"

How impossible it had become to move the thing forward!

"Do you?"

"Yes, of course!"

"Are you certain?"

"How could I not be!"

Toby picked up his pipe and took a long and proper puff and this time with the air of a fellow in pursuit of some critical thought. His nose and chin were now decidedly raised as though he was the mightiest of captains sailing fast and free on the wild and wily seas of high thinking.

A thought came to him, like a rogue wave, perhaps, cresting and then breaking with a satisfying crash across the bow of his simple-minded soul. His forehead wrinkled. His eyebrows went up. His pipe came down.

"Barth, good fellow, I remember quite well a voice from our beloved past. Do you remember that voice?"

He remembered the voice.

"Monumental," Toby said in response to the boy's keen memory or, perhaps in response to that long-ago voice or who knows, really, as he was so clearly fond of the word and only too pleased to serve it up at nearly every turn. "She said, and said often, as I recall, that good things come to those who wait."

Oh, what a useless pearl. It was heartless, in fact, for it was precisely the sort of thing generally esteemed by those who were only too happy to wait for all the good they already had. An answer came quick to Barthalamew, but he struggled to say it. It was therefore up to the rum.

"But you..." said the rum with some difficulty, for rum can be a difficult speaker.

"But I what?"

"But you didn't have to wait," rum concluded. "You met Joan right away," rum said quite truthfully. "You were married within a month," rum continued. "And her father was dead within a week of that," which was sad enough, but true and which meant business, which meant money, which meant property, which meant house and porch and barn and grass and pipe and rum, and peaches, hay and puppy breath and all without the slightest bit of waiting.

Rum's point was well made. Rum's point was strong. At once Toby's pipe was back in place. Puffing. Sailing. High thinking.

"Oh, but Barth, a week in the life of a married man," puff, puff, puff, "is not the same as a regular week. It's a very different sort of week altogether. I dare say it's almost like one of your years."

Which seemed an absurd thing to say.

"That's an absurd thing to say."

"But Barth," puff, "It could not be more true."

"Ha! What I'd give for just one of your weeks!"

"Ha! What I would give for one of yours."

And here was a common truth. No man, it seems, can live without envy for another. No man, it seems, has thought to try. And so, Toby puffed. And so, Barthalamew sipped. And so, the world happily carried on.

Again, in the grass before the porch the two girls giggled and shrieked, while the dog breathed all of his easiest breaths and finally committed to rolling about, with his head so happily tilted and his paws put up in the air. Toby and his pipe gave a smile to the scene and then turned back to his brooding guest.

"Barth, m'boy, it seems your drunk."

That was not entirely untrue. His mug, though half-empty, was not half-empty for the first time that day. Nor the second.

"I'd rather be drunk," was the boy's simple return, for the accusation from Toby came often enough.

"Yes, of course," puff, "but it seems an awful waste of time, all this drinking' ya do."

"I disagree. T'is a perfect waste of time."

"I suspect I should cut you off forever."

"Absurd," said Barthalamew with something nearing a smile. "Besides, it makes me happy."

"Does it?" puff. "I rather think it makes you stupid."

"I'm not so sure of the difference."

Puff.

Drink.

"Papa!"

It was young Jack now who stepped from the front room of the house and onto the porch and with a very worried look on his face. He was a simple boy of five and growing fast into his father's mold. His nose and eyes and easy blond hair gave them both away and Barthalamew, for reasons he could not resolve, was uneasy at the sight of him.

He was a man, of course, with hopes for a wife and a child of his own, but he was often quieted by the thought of a son. Barthalamew was never too sure why this was, but part of him held firm to the notion that it was because he was once a son himself.

"Papa! Papa! Papa!" the five-year-old persisted.

With a parental glance, the boy was answered.

"The goldfish," was then Jack's urgent reply.

"The goldfish?" said Toby, braced now for the worst.

"T'is on fire!"

Puff. Pipe down. Drink down. Everything down. By Molly, what is this but the most unexampled predicament of all! Here now is the wail of a boy about his pet fish, a thing, by the very nature of its keep, that is very hard-pressed to catch fire.

Barthalamew was sure he heard wrong, but Toby appeared unstirred. No longer braced and suddenly the ever-wise Papa, he tendered his reply and with remarkable ease.

"Well, Jack, m'boy, just drop it back in the fish bowl. That should do the trick."

"Yes, Papa!" Jack yelped, elated by this command, then trotted happily away.

Pipe up Drink up. Puff.

"It's been dead for two days now," Toby explained. "The boy's taken quite a likin' to dead things."

"But, on fire?" for it was beyond Barthalamew to overlook the point.

"Oh, that," puff. "Well, he's taken a likin' to fire, too. It's just a phase. I'm sure it'll pass soon enough."

"But…it's dead."

"What's left of it, yes, and thank the stars for that. I don't think I could take it if the boy was burning his pets alive."

At that moment, a slight tremor marched upward Toby's arm and gave his pipe hand a bit of a shake. There was something like a flinch, as though the young father suddenly found himself at the edge of some wayward truth and had no choice but to carry on. His words quickened but remained anchored beneath the weight of his breath.

"I don't sleep so well these days, Barth. By Molly, what I'd give for one of your weeks."

By Toby's tone alone, this thing said had all the sounds of a confession, a measured clue to the married soul. As well, it had all the sounds of a warning, but to the impractical ears of the impractical man there was nothing more to it than a sad little string of words. And so, the impractical man gave it no mind.

Another minute came and went before the visitor stood and announced his leave. There was a bit of puffing still to be had but Barthalamew's mug was empty and put down and his hat was picked up. His eyes were now forward, already on that country road that led south and then twisted west into town.

"I should go," he said calmly and with a bit of a wobble.

"You should eat!" was Toby's hurried reply. "Joan's expectin' ya' for supper."

But it was not Barthalamew's intent to stay. He was drunk, and it was more his want to be drunk than fed. His excuse then came, and still with a wobble, that his appetite was not so good.

"Well, I should say not," puff. "I suspect an appetite might be rather confused when one dines on so much rum."

Barthalamew said nothing but made for the steps of the porch that led to the grass and the girls and the giggles and shrieks and, of course, the curiously gratified dog.

"By Molly, take it all," Toby said as he grabbed the corked bottle and gave it an easy toss. "Ya' might as well make a full course of it."

And with this their good-byes were had and Barthalamew, cork, bottle and dog in tow began the short journey home. The two girls waved and called and waved some more as though it was a matter of practice for the two to have a friend to wave and call and wave to. The dog, however, gave no reply but only walked the walk of a busy brute with his day's work yet to be done.

"Monumental!" Toby's word lingered as he sat and watched and puffed away.

"What is?"

And here was Joan, his darling wife, just then returned from her garden nearby, attired, from head to toe, in a working dress and her favorite apron that was smartly embroidered with a wealth of pockets. A worn, blue field hat sat atop her head holding, but barely, her chestnut curls, which, when loosed, framed her youthful eyes and able smile with a fast and natural charm.

Joan placed her basket, laden now with vegetables for the evening meal, on to the table before her husband, and instead of bringing the question again, turned her attention to the parting guest.

"He's leaving?" she said, noting the girls and all their waving and calling and Barthalamew now nearing the road.

Toby lowered his pipe and looked to Joan and then back to the road.

"Aye."

Joan's heart gave a small rise. She was not too terribly upset.

"The doctor's daughter?" she then asked, for it was a question that was foremost on her mind.

But no answer was given for silence, again, was answer enough.

"Saw it comin'," Joan concluded but then pursued a more pressing observation. "But, dear husband, what is that wretched little thing walking behind him?"

Pipe up. Puff.

"That, my dear wife, is the devil's bare ass."

5

In the early spring of his twenty-second year, after Danielle, after Kimberly, after Edith and Kate, after Holly and Candace and Holly once more, there was Jayne. Sweet Jayne. Beloved Jayne. Entirely embraceable Jayne!

Jayne Hundley was no simple rose. She was, in effect, all the petals of a rose, of every hue and style of rose, of every thickness and texture and scent of every possible rose. She was love at first sight and at last sight and at all sights in between. She was physical, tangible, substantiated grace, a young woman, by all accounts, of inimitable beauty.

Jayne was fondly regarded by those who were fortunate enough to know her as the Jayne of Charm, the Jayne of Elegance, the Jayne of Thoughtful and Unending Heart, the Jayne of Sweet Nothings and Sweet Somethings and Sweet Everythings as well. She was adorable Jayne, happy Jayne, winsome Jayne. She was Jayne with the buoyant cinnamon-brown hair; Jayne with the bright, lively blue eyes; Jayne with the most remarkably tender smile. She was lovely, lovely, lovely Jayne and with all the wealth of Alagood to boot.

Such was Jayne. Underlined. Exclamation point. Jayne!

"Jayne?"

But Jayne was a busy gal, for at the moment of that very particular call, desperate though it was, she had found for herself the most curious new friend.

"Jayne?" again from the portly Mrs. Crabtree who owned, it must be said, a peculiar voice, who possessed, it cannot be denied, an assertive voice, who had, in truth, a way of screeching more than saying and who screeched in a manner most often described as something quite nearing the sound of pure agony.

Jayne called back with a voice of her own, with what was obviously a song of a voice. Hers was not at all like the wild and wretched shrill that erupted from that grumpy old cow. Of course, she never once thought her governess to be neither grumpy nor old or even so much of a cow, for Jayne was an angel who acquiesced only to angel thoughts.

"I am over here, Mrs. Crabtree," she sweetly said.

And, indeed, there she was and whatever was she doing there? Behold Dear Jayne, the lone and unforgettably lovely daughter of the venerable Lord Mayor Mumford Hundley, so well dressed by daddy's finest money and standing tall in all the colors of her youth and as courageously and as beautifully as can be done before so savage and barbarous an affair as the Fisherman's Market.

On the West End! On Low Ground! By the docks! For shame! What infamy! Had she not been, by the sheer reputation of her beauty, so very much above all possible scandal what a sensation it would have caused! What a sensation, in truth, it may cause yet!

"I have found you!" and she had and what a lush look of gratification this afforded the Screecher.

"Yes, but have you lost Mr. Crabtree in the process?"

"Well, it seems…yes!" came again the governess and with all the vocal pleasantries of a feral herd of starving cats.

And with this the Screecher spun her grumpy old head from left to right and then from right to left and then likewise and likewise again until all futility proved itself. She could not make out her own husband amidst the husbands of so many as they were, no doubt, deep in the stew, occasioned at every turn by every possible sight and sound and unfortunate smell of the industry now at hand.

All about was the constant show of fish and bait and nets and rope and crusted men, old and young and short and tall and drunk and drunker, calling out their numbers, making their deals, dancing and stomping and cussing about (as though this would affect the very greatest of fortunes), closing, finally, their business, handing over, finally, their monies and most often for the sake of a dead and smelly fish which was then wrapped in whole by some thick cabbage leaf or week-old page of the Gazette and taken off to nearby households and kitchens to be prepared at once for supper.

But the industry did not stand alone, for those in the boisterous fishing trade were forced, by fiscal necessity, to share the west end with the ever-emotive artisans who were entirely as determined to make a deal of their own. Their curious wares were always on display, always for sale and were almost always in some shape or support of some sort of fish.

At any time and by any turn one could find, and with abundance, sketches of fish, colorings of fish, portraits of fish, emblems of fish, fish pendants, fish earrings, fish bracelets, fish lockets, fish chimes, fish carved from shiny wood and knotted wood and rotted wood alike, fish made from blown glass, fish made of silver or copper or pewter or cork or flotsam or jetsam or whittled from some variety of scrimshaw or any sort of debris that was sizable and solid enough to support a good bit of whittling, all which sold quite well but which made no one rich.

This was the mess, the crowd, the mayhem in which Dear Jayne was lost, then found, in which a husband was then lost, in which the Screecher, by the very looks and sounds of her, seemed not at all unlikely to misplace an entire population of husbands and wives and children as well and each of them one at a time.

What a frantic gal she was! What a plump old maid, so hardened and grayed and perhaps fattened a bit by an egregious diet of distress and constant mistrust. Here was uneasiness born to the world in human form and given as a heart something like a pebble, something like a small clod of muscle that barely knew to stir, much less beat. And here was all of that uneasiness primped more like a husky pilgrim than a governess and brought hesitantly, unhappily to market.

By sight alone, it could not be more evident that Mrs. Crabtree did not take well to crowds. It was not her place to like them or love them or even to know them; it was only her place to love and know Jayne. This was, of course, a prodigious job, but Dear Jayne had quite recently come to enjoy a crowd, which, in turn, had become sadly trying for the Screecher and which, also, in turn, brought her screeching to agonizing new levels, as was exampled when Jayne again spoke.

"I've found a new friend," she said with a smile, always with a smile, bless her impossibly dear heart.

And there at Jayne's dear feet, amid that crowded marketplace, was the new friend in question and what an ugly friend it was. Oh, but for the devils of Bazre, how could life ever take so ugly a turn as this!

"BAAAAH!" the screecher screeched and in such a way that turned more than a few heads and turned one head in particular. "A DOOOOG!"

"I wonder, good sir," offered Jayne as sweetly as ever, "is it yours?"

"…" said the particular head for, of course, you know it was he.

And how wide were Barthalamew's eyes now! How so very wide, indeed. Here, after all, was all the beauty in the world smiling now at him (at him!) and asking now of him (of him!) the most remarkable question, as any question of hers, he then and there decided, could only be thought remarkable. What else could he do but stand there in place and widen his eyes to their very limits?

"He's adorable," came again that heavenly voice.

"He's wretched!" came again the other voice, the voice which twice now made Barthalamew flinch.

"He's…mine," Barthalamew finally managed, much too stunned, much too amazed to realize the fallacy of his own words.

"Well, he's just delightful."

It was a preposterous summation, to say the least, one that did not bode well for beautiful things, one that, for but a moment, jarred Barthalamew from his awkward state of wonderment. He glanced at the governess in want of a clue, but found instead the narrowed, beady eyes of a mad griffin readied and waiting for the chance to pounce and devour the enemy of her young. In this moment it could not be more clear that the young was Dear Jayne and that the enemy was the owner of any dog that Dear Jayne deemed delightful, especially a dog so positively undelightful as the one before them now.

The dog, for his part, was incurious. He only sat there and scratched and licked as only dogs can and, therefore, do. He seemed almost bothered by the attention, as though this highbrow doting was but an obstacle to all the scratching and licking that remained and, by the looks of it, a good bit remained.

"I am most curious, sir, of his pedigree," dear Jayne pursued.

Remarkable again, Barthalamew decided. Can someone be this ignorant of dogs? Well, if so, then how entirely beautiful the ignorance! The boy looked to the dog and then to the Screecher and then, finally, to the lovely young maiden. It was a quick and curious ascendancy from the very ugliest to the very prettiest of all things.

"Rat," was the answer Barthalamew wanted, but instead he humbly answered, "He is a rare breed of... hunter."

"Well, I am quite sure, sir, that he is the most splendid hunter," said Jayne with what was clearly a good deal of misplaced conviction. "Do tell, what is his name?"

And here the poor fellow stumbled a bit for the idea of a name had never before come to him. Many adjectives had indeed surfaced from time to time, but never so much as an actual name.

"Well, he...hasn't a name just yet."

"Just Dog, then?"

At once this seemed the most remarkable answer as any answer of hers, he then and there decided, could only be thought remarkable.

"Yes, that's it. Just Dog."

And thus, the beast was named.

Barthalamew, realizing now his lacking manners, finally thought to remove his hat and make his simple bow and introduction. Dear Jayne, in reply, gave her curtsy and offered her name in return which immediately struck a chord.

"Hundley? As in…Lord Mayor—"

"Yes, Mr. Buckett. He is my father," Jayne offered with all possible modesty so as not to appear to boast.

"Miss Jayne!" from the Screecher who had, by now, seen quite enough of this and who could not, by any effort, contain herself another moment. "It is not proper, not at all proper for a good lady to take up so freely with…with…" and here she seemed rather stuck on a word, "strangers…in the street!"

"Well, Mrs. Crabtree, I do appreciate your counsel on such matters, for you are, by the merit of my father's good word, the very best governess in all the world. However, I am obliged to point out that this is hardly a street, but a market place and that Mr. Buckett, who has been so kind as to provide his name, as well as the name of his dear companion, is no stranger to me. Not anymore, at any rate. I therefore request that you address him with due respect and not openly berate the good man as you have just done. I must admit that I am rather embarrassed for the gentleman, as well as for myself."

What an absolute pile of words and what a sensation this little speech caused. There stood the Screecher with her mouth wide open, with her cheeks quite flushed and her forehead wrinkled and with those narrow, beady eyes quite suddenly throttled. There she remained, rendered speechless, and thereby screech-less, for she could not find even the start of a sound and how so very satisfying that was to Barthalamew's ears.

And there he stood, with his hat in hand and his heart aflutter upon his sleeve, forever smitten with the dearest of Jaynes, for even in chastisement the angel had a voice so soft and so impossibly pleasant. Oh, how he reveled just then in the sweet art of her sound, of her look, of her entire being. Could there be any doubt of a God in Heaven before such an absolute beauty as this?

And then, of course, there was Dog who, just moments before, was otherwise blessed with a pleasing occupation of his own. This was all quite astounding to him as well. Although you may presume he could not have possibly understood any of what was said, it was rather clear that the sounding of those many words greatly appeased him. And so, with his remaining eye, he gave Jayne a very firm look of one-eyed delight and made for her a fast wag of what was left of his raggedy tail.

Barthalamew's attention was then put once more to the Screecher for he sensed, by his periphery, something that had the feel of imminent danger. Mrs. Crabtree, having let go her look of surprise, was gathering fast a great deal of steam. How so very pressed were her lips and how so very red were her cheeks and how narrow and beady were her eyes, narrowed now to the very smallest possible bead!

Curses, he knew, were coming his way, but what did he care for that! The very angel of life was standing before him and had effectively taken his side and it was her heavenly voice that rose once more to the occasion and very nearly put him to a knee.

"I cannot be too sure of you, Mr. Buckett, but I have been at the market all morning and must admit to a bit of exhaustion. Perhaps we can take a bench."

It was as direct an invitation as had ever been issued from the Heavens to him, but Barthalamew found himself almost too stupefied to form a sensible reply. And yet, a reply was clearly wanting.

"Miss Hundley," he tried, unsure of his words. "I believe...I mean to say that I am more than happy to find for you a suitable—"

But Dear Jayne stopped the boy with a smile so sublime as to be supernatural. "Mr. Buckett, if we hurry I do believe one is already found."

Indeed, she was correct. From that very spot in the market place the entrance to the cobbler's shop was just in view and it was to the side of this particular door that was spied an unoccupied bench. It was seemingly waiting and just for her and there was only required but a bit of navigation through the market's busied crowd to claim it. Dear Jayne was at once underway.

"Perhaps from that spot," she kindly offered her governess in passing, "we shall catch sight of your beloved Mr. Crabtree."

And with this now said, all the beauty in the world sallied forth, leaving Barthalamew to the mercy of the angered and the ugly. Dog, in the absence of the good angel, was only too happy to put his tongue once more to some practical use while the Screecher continued to murder the boy with her unblinking eyes.

Though it was but a moment, it seemed to Barthalamew the full run of an hour. He was entirely confused. The votes were in and tallied and it was clear that he was every bit as invited as not and yet what was he to do before such a formidable audience!

The boy may have been dumb-lucked from the start, but that alone did not make him a fool. The deciding vote was his and you may be sure he cast it well and with the full backing of his dumb-lucked heart. And so, with a respectable showing of courage, Barthalamew provided his most agreeable bow and waited for that queer-eyed Screecher to lead the way.

Dear Jayne was the first to the bench. The clever girl perched herself to the middle, assuring her new acquaintance a very prosperous seat. The Screecher, forced to an opposite side and looking rather slighted for it, plopped down with as much disdain as she could possibly muster. To further demonstrate her contempt, the governess dived, head first, into an ill-mannered silence, lending not a word to the proceedings, not a screech, barely a sound at all, aside from a sporadic "Hmmph" which seemed to serve as her notice of disgust on the rare occasion that her opinion on some matter was sought.

"But, what of Dog," dear Jayne pondered as Barthalamew politely took his place beside her. "Will he not join us?"

Barthalamew was genuinely astounded. Dog did not follow. Indeed, Dog did not emerge at all from the crowded marketplace.

"Well, Ms. Hundley," the boy started with pleasure, "I leave Dog, at times, to be his own master."

Dear Jayne, much to his surprise, was quickly pleased with this half-truth.

"I must say, Mr. Buckett, that is a very spirited approach. It shows a good deal of respect for all of God's little creatures. I am certain Dog relishes his freedom."

Of that Barthalamew had no doubt whatsoever.

"Don't you think so, Mrs. Crabtree," dear Jayne resumed with hardly so much as a pause. "Hmmph!"

But Dear Jayne heard no such thing.

"Are you a breeder of dogs, Mr. Buckett? I only ask because your good temperament suggests it."

Was that a compliment? It did seem a like one or, at the very least, something much like it. Barthalamew could only stagger his reply as the question was quite unexpected.

"Umm…well, no, Ms. Hundley, not…not so much."

"Well, that is a shame. Don't you think so, Mrs. Crabtree?"

"Hmmph!"

Jayne, again, heard nothing of the sort.

"So, what is it that you do, Mr. Buckett?"

Barthalamew was rather pleased with the question as the answer was all but waiting to spring from his tongue.

"I am a writer. I work for the Gazette."

"Oh my," said Jayne with widened eyes. "What a wonderful thing. Did you hear that, Mrs. Crabtree?"

"Hmmph!"

"An honest to goodness writer, and with the Gazette, no less! And what a charming building. It must be such a joy to work there!"

But, it was not! It was most definitely not such a joy to work there! Barthalamew was perplexed! Here now beside him was a woman with all the beauty in the world and yet she thought to call Dog delightful and the place of his employ charming. What odd heart was this? How could such a lovely thing have it all so entirely wrong!

"I do wonder so much about that little place," she continued. "It has my utmost attention every time I find myself walking by."

"Well," Barthalamew dared, "I am there most every day so, I suppose, the charm has worn off a bit for me."

"That is a shame. Don't you think, Mrs. Crabtree?"

This time Mrs. Crabtree proffered no reply as her attention was quite diverted. Before them now stood the old man, a cadaver-like fellow with queer, bulbous eyes and six, make that seven radical strands of ghostly white hair, each standing atop his skeletal head, each sadly secluded from the other, each seeking, it seemed, some mad attempt at its own particular direction. Barthalamew immediately deduced that this was the wayward Mr. Crabtree, for his appearance was greeted with a good deal more cheer than the boy ever thought likely.

"Why, sir!" dear Jayne rejoiced. "How good of you to find us! We had all but given up."

"Hmmph," the griffin now added and this time for good measure, for it seemed as good a way as any to annunciate her displeasure to the ashen form of her husband.

Mr. Crabtree, however, said nothing in response to either greeting. For the moment it seemed his very calling in life was to merely stand before them, with his bulbous eyes and those ghostly strands, as though he was rather busied by the idea of a good haunting. But then the ashen fellow made effort for a word and the good occupants of that bench leaned in so as to give a fine ear to the failing whispers of that impossibly old man. Barthalamew, for his part, heard nothing whatsoever.

"Yes, Mr. Crabtree, we should go at once!" the Screecher then said, only too pleased to reply to whatever was said.

Dear Jayne turned to Barthalamew with her never-ending smile and relayed the words to him.

"Mr. Crabtree has concluded our business here and has loaded the carriage."

"I see..."

But the boy could no more see than hear, for he was equally as blinded by the relay of this announcement as he was deaf to the idea that any announcement had been made it all.

"It was such a delight to meet both you and Dog. Truly, it was."

Barthalamew's heart then skipped a beat for it was all too clear to him now. Dear Jayne was preparing to leave. Oh, what a fast and wicked turn. His new love was on the verge of stepping away and there was nothing he could say or do to prevent it.

"And you, Ms. Hundley." he said, his voice weak and weary. "I do not believe I could have found a lovelier companion for the day."

"You are most kind, Mr. Buckett. I would like to think we might be such good friends."

"I would be honored if you think it so."

"Jayne!" came the screech and how cruel the name sounded from those plump and heartless lips.

And with that Dear Jayne stood and turned to go, but not before she gave to Barthalamew her most unexpected and secretive voice. How sweet the words came when they came only to his ears!

"Will you be at your work tomorrow? I would like to send him to you. It will be a surprise, I think."

What blessed eyes, what blessed kind things, comprised Dear Jayne!

"A surprise," Barthalamew whispered, for the word was so sweetened by her tongue that he could not help but try it for himself.

6

"A surprise?" for the word was so new to his tongue that he thought to try it for himself. "Yes, Barthalamew, a surprise."

Still, the young boy seemed unimpressed, seemed, in fact, more baffled than pleased.

"Come, Barth," Sister Marihanna said as she led him out and away from the front of the church and to a waiting stairway in the back. "You must have faith."

The boy was but five, as far as anyone knew, when the good sister took him by the hand and helped him ascend those rickety stairs for the first time. The old bell tower led them up to the flattened roof of the run-down church where a blanket was put down next to a crudely patched hole that overlooked the nave below. Before them now was a dead drop of some twenty feet and, yet, together the two sat beside it as though this curious gap was no more than scenery.

"There's nothing to see down there," Marihanna said on that first night. "The trick in life, Barth, is to always look up."

Therefore, the boy followed the trajectory of her pointing finger and turned his eyes skyward.

Sister Marihanna taught what she could teach when she thought to teach it, which was little more than half the time. Some nights she called out a litany of names, pointing out, as best she could, the planets and stars and the stick figure constellations. Other nights, she barely spoke a word, as if there was a far greater lesson looming in all that was left unsaid.

She was a learned woman, in fact a teacher in years past. She also harbored a friendly passion for the nighttime sky. However, Sister Marihanna gave no lesson on the singular moon, offered no excuse for its blistered and battered skin. From her came no account at all for its place in the world. It was, therefore, always the moon for him, always his want to point and press her for a proper answer.

"Oh, that old bug," was her constant reply, soft even, as though it was her need to avoid an answer altogether.

And yet, young Barthalamew was entranced. That old bug was just so fat and full, so incurably bright. And so close.

But then so alone. And unattainable. And unknowable. As such, the boy's earliest and most vivid childhood memory was one of cosmic frustration.

By those many evenings it was no accident that they sat where they did. The hole in the rooftop beside them played its own little part in those formative outings. Through it, a registry of voices called up from below, announcing some occasion or another.

"Sister Marihanna," came the cry from the raspy throat of Sister Margaret, dry and cracked and as old as the dirt, "supper!"

"Sister Marihanna," Sister Marilyn beckoned, her voice always so flat and stale, enough to bore one to tears, "study!"

"Sister Marihanna," bellowed Sister Josephine, forever determined to be the loudest of all, "prayers!"

And on the occasion of those entrancing full moons, up from the nave came the serenading call of Sister Maribeth, the youngest sister by far and, therefore, one habitually given to unaccountable fits of delight.

"Sister Marihanna, assembly!" came her gleeful, out-of-place call.

Early on, it seemed an abuse of the word, but in the year that was Barthalamew's fifth, in the year that began those rooftop meditations, the Order of Cecilia found itself braving the most unexpected dilemma. To the point, there was a curious increase in its otherwise inconsiderable number.

"Come now, Barth," Sister Marihanna said with all the kindliness of the loving mother that she decidedly was. "You can sit in the back with the others."

Others.

It was such an unexpected word, particularly new to the child's tender ear. There was an element of romance in its sound, of this the boy was sure, but when he thought to repeat it to himself, he divined at once the realization that some extraordinary turn was at hand. And turns, extraordinary or otherwise, had thus far proved quite traumatic in his little life.

The last one, as little of it as he could recall, involved himself and a mop bucket. Therefore, it occurred to him to suspect this word; at the very least, he had to entertain some proper fear of it, but oh, how it seemed to please Sister Marihanna.

In a moment, they were both up and dusted, and the blanket was folded. Barthalamew had but a second to sneak a whispered goodbye to his friend the moon before he was escorted back down those rickety stairs and back in through the front of the church. There, he was directed to a back pew and deposited alongside the aforementioned others.

Sister Marihanna gave a quick matronly lecture, given to one as though given to all: "Now remember, no talking."

Barthalamew was listening, with his face turned up, his eyes wide, and his mouth half-closed.

"No noise, not a peep," she concluded with a cursory smile.

And with that she was gone, leaving the boy to the others and the others to the boy and the lot of them as one, uncomfortably united in nothing at all but that sacramental call for quiet. All the while, Barthalamew never let Marihanna go. He looked on as she made her way up that dimly lit aisle to the front of the nave. He watched in silence as she took a pew of her own before what was once an altar but was now only a rise, vacant save for a sizable candelabra and a tattered table and two chairs.

Here were the sisters, Josephine and Maribeth, sitting determinedly before the so-called assembly. Their expressions were miserable and happy, respectively, as they surveyed the many worn and scattered pews, anxiously and happily, again respectively, awaiting the last of the herd. At that moment, she finally arrived.

Sister Margaret emerged from the vestry, so monstrously old and so monstrously slow and as excitable as an entire legion of the walking dead. Garbed in black from head to toe, the typical attire of the order in those early years, Margaret, bless her undead heart, floated ominously into the room like a dirge, like the white-haired widow of a thousand deaths.

Her every step to reach the foremost pew seemed as insurmountable as the last and the last, by all accounts, had all the qualities of a dozen magnificent miracles heroically bound into one. By those supernatural efforts and by all the time in the world, Sister Margaret was ultimately seated and accounted for. Only then could the assembly commence.

"This assembly of the Order of Cecilia is hereby called to…" Sister Josephine troubled herself for another word but to no avail. "Called to order!" She raised the makeshift gavel and the old table was given a fast and thorough thrashing. "Sister Maribeth, have you noted the day and time?"

Sister Maribeth, with her hair so straight and black and nearly half-way to the ground, with her fat brown eyes and steadfast smile, merrily confirmed that, indeed, she had noted the day and time.

"You may then proceed with roll call."

"But, of course, Sister Josephine," came her sing-song reply. There was a moment's pause as she readied her pen. "Sister Josephine?" she then called out.

From mere inches away came the confident return, "I am here."

"Very well," Sister Maribeth chirped as she put the pen to ink and made her mark for the record. "Sister…?" After another pause, there was a pleasing realization, "Oh, that's me!"

Another triumphant mark for the record.

"Sister Marilyn?"

A bored and awkward sigh broke out from the pew behind Sister Marihanna, followed by a keen silence.

"Sister Marilyn?" came again the buoyant call.

"Here," was her drab and awkward reply.

"Thank you, Sister," the caller said, then made a slightly less than triumphant mark upon the record. "Sister Marihanna?"

"Present."

"Why, bless you sister," so sweet and sisterly and with a happy mark upon the record. "Sister Margaret?

But here the bouncing pen went down for Sister Margaret was quickly unkind and her reply was not at all for the celebrated record.

"Ignorant cow!" was her answer and with no volume to spare.

"Sister Margaret!" Josephine startled.

"It is for the record, Sister," Sister Maribeth added, curiously unaffected by the suggestion that she was both stupid and bovine.

But Sister Margaret was in no hurry to comply for the record. After all, it was no record of hers and she felt much too old to sacrifice any of her remaining precious minutes to this ridiculous sounding of names. When she spoke again, she did so with the very coldest air of contemp.

"Are you insane?"

Sister Maribeth could only offer her reply which was utterly and inexplicably true: "Oh, not at all, Sister. I'm perfectly wonderful."

"You're a dingbat!"

"Sister! Margaret!" Josephine charged, her gavel high and ready to pounce. "Are! You! Here?"

"Of course, I'm here! Ask the dingbat. She'll tell you."

From behind Sister Marihanna, a fast chuckle escaped but was quickly withdrawn. Marihanna herself had to lower her head to bury a near smile of her own.

"I do believe," Sister Josephine finally submitted, "that Sister Margaret may be...unrested."

"Perhaps so," at once and with pleasure from Sister Maribeth.

"She seems a bit...delirious."

"You may be right," again with near unrestrained glee from Maribeth.

"Ignorant cow!" once more from the white-haired widow.

Another stifled chuckle from the pews, another projected silence.

"Shall I note it for the record, Sister Josephine?"

"Yes, Sister Maribeth, I believe you must."

And so, it was merrily noted.

"Let us dispense with the reading of the minutes, Sister, as it has been a long and trying day."

For a moment, Sister Maribeth was nearly given to something not entirely like a smile, perhaps even like the start of a frown, but the sheer tightness of her face all but promised some painful, scarring result. The smile, therefore, held, as did her sprightly spirit. "Is it a motion?"

"It is," said Sister Josephine.

"Is it seconded?"

At first, there was no second. Instead, Maribeth heard only the trailing echo of her call.

A full moment passed, and then another came and went. A third dallied and was nearly gone before Sister Marihanna finally conceded, "I will second the motion."

"Why, bless you, Sister Marihanna. Such a kind gesture."

And so, Sister Maribeth noted, with the magical charge of her pen, that Sister Marihanna did indeed second the motion and that she was very kind for doing so. Thus recorded, and with luminous joy, the happy clerk turned again to Josephine.

"To old business then?" her query.

"To old business," the answer.

And so, off to old business they went, with the three sisters in tow: Marihanna abiding, Marilyn resisting, and feisty Margaret already before the gathering fog of a much-needed nap.

Sister Maribeth, her bobbing pen now rested, combed the exalted record and happily recited her findings. What followed was a catalog of sisterly concerns that required, much to her delight, a variety of motions and nods and yays and nays, all of which, over the course of a simple half-hour, was easily put to rest until one last item remained. Sister Maribeth brought it gently about.

"There was," she started, then amended, "still is, I should say, the matter of the roof. To be patched."

"Yes, of course," Josephine said, glancing now at the roof, at the fair-sized hole that had, thus far, defeated all of their womanly efforts at repair. "And what of our notice in town, Sister?"

"Well, Sister Josephine, I am glad you asked," and indeed she was. "It has produced inquiries from two well-referenced roofers."

"And?"

"Well…" and here a pause, for bad news was to be given and it seemed beyond Maribeth's nature to know how to go about giving it. She looked up. She looked down. She smiled all about. "…they seem like very fine fellows.

So unfortunate was the sounding of that very last word.

"Men!" Sister Josephine gasped as if she had just gobbled some hideous poison.

"Yes, Sister, it is my sad duty to inform you that they were," she said, pausing again to amend, "uh…still are, men. I know we were hoping otherwise, but as it turns out, for I did think to ask, there is a considerable shortage of women in this business of roofing. In fact, there are none."

An uneasy silence broke out, during which Josephine broke into a curious fit. With reddening cheeks, she appeared at that very moment to be holding her breath. Only Maribeth looked on: Sister Marihanna had not the heart, Sister Marilynn had not the interest, and Sister Margaret, bless her soul, was well beyond the cares of all business, old, new or otherwise, as was just then indicated by a ripening snore.

Josephine's tantrum quickly subsided, and she quietly exhaled, the fleeing air taking with it the color from her face. "Not unexpected, I suppose," she softy conceded.

"Also," Maribeth continued, as it seemed the time to say so, "there remains a shortage of women masons, carpenters, glaziers…"

"Yes, Sister Maribeth, that is fine."

"…plumbers, blacksmiths, whitesmiths…"

"Yes, yes, Sister. Well noted."

"…limeners, refurbishers…"

"Sister! Mari! Beth! That will do!" Josephine wailed, then softened. "That will do, I believe, for old business."

And, indeed, that did it as far as old business was concerned, except for-

"Chimney sweeps."

It was swiftly added, whispered even, but Sister Josephine was beyond Maribeth now, beyond hearing that last bit of old business. Instead, she was already caught in the grip of some brand-new plan.

From out of the blue, an idea had reached out and grabbed her. The grays of her wooly brows suddenly arched, her forehead creased, her eyes sharpened to a point, and the sharp end of her nose even seemed to give a wiggle. She gripped the gavel again, as if it alone had the power to complete her thoughts. "Sister Marihanna…" she started in an easy but assertive tone.

Sister Marihanna's attention was all forward.

"I say, Sister Marihanna," she repeated for the effect of civility, "perhaps that boy of yours can be of some practical use."

"Well, Sister Josephine, I don't think of him as entirely my boy. I like to think he is part of us all."

"Yes, I like that, part of us all. Write that down, Sister Maribeth."

Instantly, Sister Marihanna realized her mistake.

"It seems to me that he is familiar enough with that roof," Josephine continued. "Perhaps the boy can patch it properly. Actually, I rather think he should."

It was known, had always been known and had never doubted, that Sister Josephine was incapable of any sort of humor, be it good or bad, low or high, or blue or dark or light. She was deaf and dumb to it all, to the whole spectrum of wit and jocularity. She had not a care in the world for a laugh, and it was generally agreed that she never would. Still, the words rushed to Marihanna's lips before she could even think to stop them: "You must be joking!"

But, of course, she was not.

"We all do our part, Sister. Why not him?" came the readied reply.

"But he's only 5 years old...or so."

"I barely see your point."

"B-But how can you not?!" Marihanna barked.

Marihanna's eyes darted at the sound of her own voice as it bounced off the ghostly walls of that old and once forgotten room. She was quickly embarrassed. She did not care in the least for loud people, and it was never her intent to add to their numbers.

"What about the other one? He looks a bit older."

"Sister Josephine," came a glad reminder from Sister Maribeth, "I do believe this...other one falls under new busi—"

"Well, he is older, yes," Sister Marihanna interrupted, though his age, at this point, could only be guessed and the guessing placed it near ten. "But they are only children!"

"They're men!"

"They are not men!"

"Sister Josephine," again from Maribeth and gladly, still. "I believe we should close out of old business first."

But Jospehine was all a-tremble. It was clear that the very idea of men, that the very word itself, ate up every last bit of her patience and left her kicking and screaming before the ungodly altar of misery.

"They! Are! Men! Men, under our roof! It goes blatantly against our principles, even those you agreed to, Sister Marihanna. And do not, for one moment, think I have not noticed all the time you spend with...with that one!" for Josephine only once called him by name.

"But I am Barth's teacher. It was voted that I would—"

"Always together, always! You two are like…" Josephine paused so as to find the right word, then settled on a continuance: "Like…"

"Peas, Sister?" from Maribeth, who was only too happy to help.

"Yes, peas!"

"In a pod, Sister?" again and happily from Maribeth.

"Yes! Peas! In a pod! And I will not have it!" Josephine shrieked and with such a daring grip on the gavel that, even at a distance, Marihanna thought to flinch. "From here on, there are to be no peas and no pods! Write that down, Sister Maribeth!"

"Yes, Sister. No peas, no pods." But then a brief and glorious pause. "Should we not… I mean, I believe we should vote on it."

Which was true. Which was preposterous but, in fact, true.

"Sister Maribeth, please. It has been such a long day. Let us just…table the vote."

That news was delightfully received.

"Is there a second to table the vote on peas and…" Maribeth paused briefly to consult her notes, "and pods?"

But, of course, there was not, for who had ever heard of such a thing.

"Sister Mari! Beth!" a harsh but persuasive whisper.

"Well, then," was the joyful reply, "I will be more than happy to second the mo—"

"New business!"

With that declaration, the gavel came down and the old business was out with a bang. Up shot the eyes of Sister Margaret, heavy and uncaring and so very out of focus, only too eager to turn down again. And so, down again they went, every bit as heavy, every bit as uncaring.

Sister Marilynn, looking as if she was on the verge of some vast and random dream of her own, came to as well and actually stayed to, indicating, for the first time that night, an interest in the proceedings. Sister Marihanna, for her part, was unchanged, keeping her attention glued on Josephine's grip.

"It seems," Sister Josephine started with a cutting glare to the back pew, "that we have been mistaken for some sort of...religious fold!"

The last two words were forcibly pressed, so as to assure all those within earshot, especially those who now occupied the last pew, that this was precisely what they were not. The aforementioned others, having no real understanding as to where they were or why they were there, had no more idea what to make of this than what to make of the rest of their fate. Per Marihanna's previous instruction, they made no move. They said no word.

"Perhaps it is thought we are a convent," Maribeth submitted with an elfish smile.

"Which we are not!"

"Or perhaps something like an orphanage," she said, not losing her grin.

"Which we are most *definitely* not!"

"But I suppose, Sister Josephine," said the elf, unable to help it, as she never could, "it is thought that we are."

"But we are not, not, not!" Josephine screeched as her gavel pounced at each explicit syllable. "Who are these people," Josephine continued, her temper now fixed and ready to spring, "these inbreeding jackals?"

Even in her sleep, unsettled as it was, that remark begat Sister Margaret an easy smile.

"Who keeps dropping off their...their...their..."

"Children, Sister Josephine," said Marihanna, who apparently stood alone as the lone champion of that simple fact.

"Children! Who keeps dropping off their children at our doorstep?"

"And in our buckets," clarified Sister Marilynn who decided, for the moment, to champion a fact of her own.

"Yes, and in our buckets!" Josephine rejoined.

"Well, actually, the boy," Marihanna began, then paused to revise, "that is to say, the other boy, was left in the… Well, he was found in the privy."

"In! The! Privy?"

That shocking revelation even astounded young Barthalamew. At that moment, he turned to his right and looked the boy over and saw at once a thick layer of soot and grime. The other boy was dressed in tattered rags, rotted nearly beyond use. His hair, so unlike his own, was very full and very blonde and very, very dirty.

It was not that the boy was poor, for who could even think to doubt it, but that he looked as mean as he did grim and that was particularly daunting considering all the grim he already was. He was eight or nine, quite possibly more, but Barthalamew couldn't be sure, as he'd never seen another boy before; for all he knew, the child could have been any age at all.

"He's much abused," Marihanna insisted.

"What do I care about that? What do I care about dirty boys standing about in naughty places? I suppose, if you had your way, you would insist on calling him little Oliver Outhouse or some such nonsense."

Well, it was nearly funny, as close to a joke as Sister Josephine ever dared, but her voice only bounced as Marihanna's did before, then evanesced into the quieting walls.

Marihanna seemed equally indifferent to the slight. Her reply was intentionally modest. "He's old enough to have a name of his own or to choose one of his own liking."

More was implied than said. Once again, it was the unfortunate, but familiar predicament: The boy's name had not yet been determined, but one would surface soon enough, and it, like the boy, would not be going anywhere anytime soon.

Sister Josephine cringed at the thought, but what she could do! A vote on the matter would prove futile. Even

Maribeth would yield to the cretin. It was her intention, then, to put the boy to some use.

In the meantime, the elder, for once, dismissed her temper, and an eager frustration filled the void. "We cannot live like this. We are not an orphanage. Why do they think us one?"

"Well, Sister Josephine," answered Sister Marilyn, who had taken it upon herself to champion yet another fact, "we do live in a church."

To be sure, it could not be denied. Even though it was an abandoned church it was a church, no less. And even though the nearby town of Adelayde did not actually own the church or the vacant stretch of land on which it stood, the newly established township was only too happy to consent to their particular occupancy. And even though a record of previous ownership was sought, but conveniently never found, the neighboring mayor was only too pleased to draw up a deed of sale, so as to oblige the sisterhood. As such, it was irrefutably true that they did, indeed, live in a church.

"And we also wear black," allowed Sister Margaret, who was quite suddenly and inexplicably more awake than not.

"Always black," Maribeth mirthfully affirmed.

"Perhaps we should consider some other color," from Sister Marilyn who had, for some time, embraced the idea but never found the courage or occasion to suggest as much.

Josephine quickly turned to face her, with teeth bared, with nostrils flared, with eyes of lava fire, when the wisdom of this thing said found an unexpected depth. She pursed her lips and understood at once the dilemma as it was proposed. There were either to be more colors or there were sure to be more children. It was then and there decided that more colors must win out.

"Perhaps so," Josephine yielded, confounded now to the point of exhaustion.

"Perhaps so," Sister Maribeth repeated and then, with Josephine's permission, gaily declared the matter open for discussion.

What followed was the most unexpected discourse on the merits of the rainbow itself, of this color and that, of every thinkable hue in regard to the purpose of the order and, all too importantly, the remembrance of dearest, fairest Cecilia for whom black was worn for in the first place. With their idol so sweetly invoked the assembly was quickly given to good humor and for the first time in a very long time the sisterhood had the air something rather sisterly. In the end there was a vote of unanimity. The issue was tabled for further consideration. Sister Maribeth, with her mighty pen and ink, made her mark for the record and with all possible cheer.

With her gavel still in hand, Josephine gave every indication of bringing the assembly to a close. There was calm now among the sisters, a rare peace, but as she glanced again that rearward pew where the others remained in waiting, she felt her temper, still. She had no want of these ridiculous orphans and she would, no doubt, have chased them out and let them starve and then, for her part, slept as well as ever, were it not for the very littlest one with the bright red hair and the wide green eyes. Josephine tried to shake it but had to admit a proper curiosity.

"What of the girl?" she finally thought to ask.

All eyes turned to the child.

"She is young, quite young," Sister Marihanna replied with a soft smile "but she seems very unselfish. I believe she would make a fine—"

"Addition?" Josephine concluded with all haste.

"Well, yes," Marihanna said through gritted teeth, as if though it pained her to say it.

"Yes, I like that," Josephine said. "She may provide the order with something of a future. What is her name?"

Barthalamew turned to her, to his left now, and wondered now of her age, for he had never seen a girl either. The question apparently took shape in his eyes and the girl seemed to know it.

As she turned to him she said nothing at all but only held up her hand and showed him three of her fingers, each as tiny and starved and as dirty as the rest of her. He, in turn, held up his fist, then opened his hand for her. Five.

So dear, so sweet and without a sound between them. Well, do be sure, this was all her little heart required.

"I don't know her name at all," Marihanna answered. "She... Well, she hasn't said a word."

Which was true, sadly true. The little girl had yet to say a word and, in fact, never would.

"Lydia!" from Sister Margaret, who was again awake and now quite determined to be of help for the topic of the little girl did strike a good note with her as well.

"Lydia?" from Marihanna who was sure this was not it.

"Lydia!" parroted Josephine, as she was quicker to understand than Marihanna.

"It was the name of my mother, of Cecilia's mother," Margaret offered boastfully. "If the girl is our future, I believe she would do well to have it."

Well, who could say no to that! Not a one could, not even the little girl who sat in happy ignorance of the vote, who was oblivious to her now being Lydia, who was disregardful to everything but the boy to her right with the wide-open hand.

"I daresay that was easy enough," Josephine said, as it proved to be the most pleasant and uncontested of any vote the order ever knew. There remained, though, the boy and the matter of his name, and it seemed as good a time as any to settle that. "What about you, boy?" she said sharply. "Give us your name, or I'll name you myself!"

"Shut it, ya ol' hag!"

Which was what the boy then said, which was, perhaps, the most villainous thing a boy could say under the circumstances (under any circumstance, really), which nearly brought the old church walls down, and which brought fast tears to the now wide-opened eyes of Sisters Josephine and Margaret, though it must be said for entirely different reasons.

Young Barthalamew's jaw was exactly in his lap. He could not help but stare, and at some length, at the burning sun that was now before them all as the center of some unexpected and very unholy universe.

"What 'er you lookin' at?" to Barth from the boy and with a mouthful of wrath.

But Barthalamew had no chance to answer, for there was blood at once. The elder boy turned and swung hard on the child who had never seen a fist before and who, until then, had no clue as to what it might be for.

Hands to the faces of the sisters of the order, and a fast tear down the cheek of their tiny, green-eyed recruit. Indeed, there was shock enough to go around, shock enough for dozens more, for the cold and naked face of violence was suddenly loosed before that flat-footed assembly.

"My name," the boy then bellowed, as young bellowers so often do, "is Toby!"

7

Upon the following morning dear Jayne's surprise made its appearance at the illustrious Hamm and in the precise, archaic form of Mr. Crabapple. Having alighted from the great Hundley coach and having then stepped into the building and then to Barthalamew with all the warmth and ease of the recently exhumed, the cadaver, flaunting still, those bulbous eyes and those seven unyielding strands of gray, extended his arm and, by consequence, his cadaverous hand, in which was found a rather large and decorative envelope of the most elegant color pink.

Barthalamew obligingly accepted the colorful gift and, by his good nature, was preparing to return a tip when the wraithy fellow turned about and, without word or sound, made his retreat to the waiting coach. In short, the envelope was sent and, by this fashion, received.

By the lonesome light of his office, which looked more the part of a closet and which contained, and just barely, the very littlest writing desk and chair, Barthalamew looked to this curious parcel as one might look to all the jewels of the world. Upon it his name was inscribed, so sweetly added, he had no doubt, by the touch of Dear Jayne's own hand. How blessed the effort. Such charm! Such style! Such wondrous cheer!

His heart could not have been more pleased. Had a thousand gold chips fallen from the sky, the boy could not have possibly noticed. Had all the angels of Heaven appeared before him, what chance had they to be heard? Dear Jayne was now his soul for Dear Jayne somehow chose to be.

So fanciful was the moment that it took him nearly a full minute to realize there was a bit more to it than some fine bit of cursive. Only then did the boy note the flap on the back sporting the great Hundley seal. Indeed, there was something inside that had the look and feel of a proper invitation, though Barthalamew was rather naïve as to what proper invitations looked or even felt like.

And yet, he had only to give a tug. The seal gave way and the envelope opened where upon a notice of engagement was then revealed. Oh, wicked fate, what new pleasure was this?

Barthalamew gave the beloved parchment a hearty stare, for he was unable to do much less. There was only to admire that thick and fancy placard, all adorned with as much ribbon and color as any ten men could ever think to devise. By Molly, how did such a lovely thing as this ever pop into existence! And whatever was it doing before his curious eye!

Barthalamew's heart then and there committed to a good deal of lettering, to the many rows of glorious words, all printed by some magnificent hand, all put before him in the richest of all possible ways. Consonants and vowels flowed seamlessly from this side to that, spilling about the page as though by the stroke of some impossible wizardry. In all his life and by the way of a thousand lives more, it was the most remarkable piece of paper that might ever be found.

But what did it all mean? It proved too dazzling a penmanship to take in at once. A proper study was required. And so, Barthalamew allowed the words to fall into focus and their proper meaning was finally revealed.

There was to be a ball. It was to be in Dear Jayne's honor. It was to be that very evening at the Hundley Mansion. There was to be feasting and music. There was to be dancing!

Barthalamew leapt to his feet, nearly breaking the tiny chair and table that bound him to his tiny work. He stepped boldly from his tiny office and made haste, past the tiny heart of Mr. Loydford who, in that moment, simply stood in awe of the boy's clear and present departure. In a blink, he was gone.

By the matter of a brisk yet somewhat lengthy walk, Barthalamew found himself once again at the waiting door of the Theryoung's home. His hand was quick to the wood and gave a fast rap. Young Jack was first to the door, just ahead of Joan who greeted the boy at once and invited him in.

"Barth, you're all aglow!" she noted with a broad smile upon her face.

To be sure, the missus was overly kind, for she saw that the boy's forehead was beaded with sweat. As well, he had the look of a man stuck in time, ruined by the notion of being unstuck. To the point, his panic was palpable.

"You are quite…colorful today," she said, her voice oozing with kindness. "Are you looking for Toby?"

But the boy could not answer, for he was not sure at all what he sought. All he knew was the color pink, as was made clear by the glorious request that now extended from his hand. Joan glanced the invitation and then relieved him of it. She gave it a fast read.

"Well, sir, would you look at that," she said with a glaring smile as the meaning of the card was absorbed. "You have been invited to Jayne Hundley's birthday ball!"

Joan nearly fell over. It could not be more unexpected. It was, after all, the grandest ball of the season and she immediately thought to say so.

"It's the grandest ball of the season! How did you ever—?"

Joan glanced back to Barthalamew who simply stood before her in an obvious state of terror. At once, she understood.

"I can help you, of course!"

Such softening words had never fallen upon his ears before. Barthalamew thawed and immediately surrendered. Help was precisely the thing wanted. Hope, it seemed, was to allow an easy breath.

Joan then dragged the boy to a back room where he was instructed to wait. There was a good deal of clamoring about from the next room over before she returned with a solid black suit and a dark red cravat. Blessed be this inexplicable sight!

"It was my father's," Joan explained.

And with that, the suit was left with the boy, but it was not like anything he had ever seen or worn before. There was a fortune of buttons and loops and curious slipknots and whatnots and how could he ever tell one from the other from top to bottom and left to right! What a tangled mess it so quickly became! A struggle ensued and frustrated the boy and, before long, his confusion overwhelmed him.

Upon hearing his cry, Joan rushed back into the room and managed to contain her wanting laugh. The boy made a mockery of proper dress. She stepped around him, turning and twisting, unbuttoning and rebuttoning, untying and retying, unlooping and re-looping, until Barthalamew was properly suited.

It was barely a fit. It was a bit tight. It was, in fact, quite tight. Barthalamew had want to breathe but found it rather trying. He stepped and realized the obvious tension now in his legs.

"I-I don' know," he started with a gasp.

Joan simply smiled. "We have a few hours. I can loosen the stitch a bit."

The boy tried again for his breath.

"I know how to do this," Joan again affirmed with a comforting smile.

From the corner, Jack and his sisters looked on. Though that sequence of events remained an easy mystery to them, it was rather clear that it fell in the realm of the comical. Smiles were pressed, and laughs were lightly had until Joan turned and begged away.

"There's nothing to see here. Go outside and play with that damned dog!"

The children, still giggling, scurried from the room and fled outdoors, where Dog was waiting and more than pleased for some proper attention.

"An hour," Joan said, examining the hem, "at the most."

The woman was rather precise with the needle as well as the clock. By that hour's end, a number of stitches were corrected, and Barthalamew was fitted once more. Other than the reach of the jacket, the suit was better fitted. The pants remained were still a touch short of the mark, but all in all, it would do.

"Better?" Mrs. Theryoung asked with a knowing smile, quite pleased with her quick-served alterations.

"Better," was his simple reply.

"You're invited to Ms. Hundley's ball, sir. To be sure, that is a considerable accomplishment for a man of Port Street."

That was said with a good deal of pride as Mrs. Theryoung clearly meant it. She looked upon the young lad now and beamed for the sight of him in her dead father's clothes. Somehow it made absolute sense to her.

"I suspect Ms. Hundley will prefer dancing," she merrily continued.

"Aye," said Barthalamew.

"Can you dance, sir?"

The question bore straight to Barthalamew's heart. In all of his life he was never more sure of an answer.

"Yes. I can."

8

Hundley Manor was just north and then east of town and occupied a good many acres. It was a most prosperous piece of land. This was made evident by the well-paved entrance to the estate which was both extravagant and protracted. To simply approach, one had to traverse a good mile of cobblestone, and that alone impressed poor Barthalamew as he calmly walked the most curious trek of his young life.

It was not that a decent stead was not offered, for Toby tried to persuade him, but Barthalamew had not once ridden a horse, had never been taught, and was rather decided that it was not the sort of day to take up new habits. To be sure, the boy's cup was quite full. To add a near thousand pounds of uncaring beast to the mix was simply a burden that would not serve him well, so he kept to what he knew best: He simply put his feet forward and made his way.

Upon approach to the estate, Barthalamew was passed, time and again, by a number of wealthy carriages. Not a one of them slowed for his sake, but that barely bothered the boy at all. His spirits were quite high and though his suit was old and a bit out of style and something that just barely fit, he walked the walk of a man of great wealth, for love was in his blessed heart.

As the manor came into view, Barthalamew was stunned. It was an impossibly beautiful estate. Never before had he seen such splendor, such rise, such wealth! The land, the home, the whole of it was simply overwhelming. The boy held as best he could his absolute wonderment and stepped forward as though a man somewhat blinded in place.

It was, of course, a peculiarity for the servants to note Barthalamew's approach. The boy was on foot and, by the expectations of that particular tract, his arrival was more than awkward. The question arose at once.

"Invitation, sir!"

The servant was curiously tiny and featured a curiously tiny voice. It caught the boy off guard. When no answer came, the little fellow, dutifully cried out once more.

"Invitation, sir!"

Barthalamew then looked sharply to the servant and offered his pink summons, which was quickly recognized and ceremoniously accepted.

"Right this way, sir."

And so, Barthalamew was led from the front door into the foyer where his life was inexplicably changed forever. At once, his soul was struck by the constant measure of white marble and wealth. He breath was halted. His mind was trapped. His heart nearly failed. How could such a place ever be!

Barthalamew was then led through a series of impeccably crafted double-doors and then down a curious number of wide and impossibly tiled passages before the Hundley Great Room was finally reached. Each and every step was more grand than the last and yet no step prepared him for what was beyond the archway ahead. The last great door was opened and breached and, in that moment, Barthalamew's infantile notion of wealth was unexpectedly shattered and born again.

Below him now was a dazzling room of gleaming white. A small legion of crystalized chandeliers unveiled a population of the most remarkably well-dressed people imaginable. Even the stairs at his feet begged against his lesser step as it all but promised of some unspeakable affluence. And yet, this was merely what sight provided. Other senses quickly stepped to.

Music was then noted. Barthalamew's ears perked at the start of some symphonic sound. His eyes then charged to the opposite end of that impossible room where a slight stage ascended, and a formal band held court.

The boy's soul was entirely lost to the pressing notes that stretched the full run of that room. His heart sank and rose again with every measure, every beat, every bar. How could such a place like this even begin to exist!

Barthalamew's immediate want was to leave his jaw to the floor where it clearly belonged and which he nearly did, but for the sake of the old fellow now before him. Crabtree stood in waiting though Barthalamew was hard-pressed to understand what the elder might be waiting for. But then the cadaver made a fast reach for his invitation and, just like that, the matter had come full circle. That which was given was now removed.

Crabtree gave the pink paper a slight glance before turning to the crowded room below and pronouncing in the most daring of voices, "Mister! Barthalamew! Buckett!"

The boy was certainly rattled. Never before had anyone made such a ruckus of his name and most assuredly not before such a crowd as this. It was Barthalamew's thought to hide at once, but he found quick comfort in the notion that hardly a person in the grand room below seemed to take much notice, except, of course, for her.

To the bottom of the stairs Dear Jayne stood and sent a smile upward as though on wings. Barthalamew was so quickly struck by the sheer magnitude of her radiance, of her dress, of her hair, of her unstoppable beauty that he was entirely oblivious to his descent. In a moment, he was in the grand ballroom and standing before her and begging time to halt and hold forevermore.

"You came!" she said, with unexpected glee.

"Of course," his reply, though it required some volume so as to rise above the symphony.

"I do hope you will save a dance for me."

"Yes," Barthalamew tried, then pressed his ear forward. "Wait. What?"

"I do hope you will save a dance for me," the kind girl repeated.

"I believe it is you who must save one, milady!"

"Ah! Yes, of course. Then it shall be done!"

And with this Dear Jayne was called away by Mrs. Crabtree who, under the circumstances, looked almost womanly. Another caller was waiting, another dance to be had. And yet, Barthalamew could only smile. It was clearly the most precious moment of his young life.

A treasure had been found. A new love was at hand. A promise was simply waiting to be had. And all in the most splendid of—

"Mr. Buckett, is it?"

The voice was a bother at once. It was a muddied sound, as though a sack of wet sand had somehow poured into the room and called out. Barthalamew turned and acknowledged its owner, a terribly handsome man, similar to his age and build but clearly dissimilar to his station in life.

"I am Gaylord of House Littlewick," the wet sand then said with an extended hand.

Barthalamew was immediately distrusting for the spindly fellow was dressed beyond all riches and his demeanor seemed to swoop down from some impossible height so as to make this little effort to greet him.

"Yes, sir," Barthalamew said as he gently accepted the man's greeting.

The wetted sand then looked to the retreating Jayne and offered a proper smile yet the words to follow seemed entirely against the grain of what was, for that moment, a pleasant sort of look.

"I suspect you are here for me."

But, of course, this was the most unimaginable thing in all the world to hear.

"Sir?" Barthalamew pushed, even though he had no want at all to do so.

"It has been arranged, you see, but she is a rebellious cur."

The last word was loud and, at once, unkind by the boy's waiting ear. He was much too stunned to apply a response. He therefore stood mute before this House of Littlewick, begging against the continued sound of his wretched voice.

"She likes to make me jealous, you see," continued that wealthy lot of wetted sand. "It's harmless, I suppose. Am I right?"

And with a pat to the back Littlewick was away, stepping grandly from one corner of the room to the other as though all the white in the world was now his to know and love.

Indeed, it was a bothersome exchange, but what could the boy say or do? The wetted sand had its weight, but the boy remained buoyed. After all, there remained the promise of a dance and Barthalamew's heart was entirely focused on the kind promise of that very particular gift.

And so, Barthalamew put his eye once more to the moneyed crowd before him and spotted her at once. Dear Jayne was all about the floor, caught in a curious dance with a fatted fellow who clearly sported two equally fatted feet.

Well, he was barely a dancer at all! Clearly, he pulled against instead of with the music and yet the dear girl smiled all the same. Such a blessed and beautiful heart!

A nearby servant with a tray full of wine stepped to Barthalamew and made an offer. The boy, however, waved the man off, for his want was for the girl and not so much for the grape. Focus, above all, was now his king!

The song concluded. The band came to an abrupt and telling stop. It was a rather amazing to see and hear, this notion of live music. Barthalamew was staggered by it all that he was nearly caught off guard by Dear Jayne's approaching voice.

"Perhaps, good sir, you may entertain me for the dance that follows the next."

Before Barthalamew could accept, dear Jayne was whisked away, led to her next waltz. And so, the boy looked on again as he stood oblivious to the wealthy many who stepped by with their many wealthy stares as though to wonder who would allow such a straggler before them. But Barthalamew saw none of this. His eyes, his heart, his very soul was only for her.

The band played on. The music was now strong and passionate and exquisite and with each beat Barthalamew could feel his legs, his feet wanting for the occasion.

He looked on as she again danced the most regular of all possible dances. And he counted the beats and measures and the rising and falling tempos. Though the song had a particular length, patience was easily his. Time, in that moment, was a proper friend to him.

And then it was ended. The band held. The conductor took a proper moment before he again lifted his wand and eased the next song into play. Jayne, by her dear word, stepped quickly to Barthalamew and reached for him.

"Our song, sir."

To be sure, Barthalamew never knew the name of the song that so suddenly became his and hers. By the full run of his short life he never heard it again. And yet, it played over and over and over still, a hundred thousand times again in his always wanting heart, for the boy now had a song with a beautiful girl and that was nearly all he ever wanted from life.

Her hand was quickly taken, her back kindly secured, and in that moment, dear Jayne was whisked to the floor as never before. The dance was underway, and not a soul in that remarkable room would ever forget it.

The tempo was kept rather handily. Barthalamew moved as though on a thousand impossibly simple clouds. The song sounded with ease in his ears and the rhythm was absorbed like air into his lungs and he breathed his dance into Dear Jayne's legs and swept her across that heavenly room as though she was the Queen of all possible Hearts.

The floor cleared itself of the many other dancers for not a soul could take their eyes from that singular demonstration. A master was at play and the world had need to see. That curious boy in his tight and unusually cheap suit exhibited the most fanciful sort of step. He danced as though a king before them all.

His grace was clear. His strength of step was exquisite. Jayne was at once taken and then twirled and twirled again with such masterful ease that she had no choice but to be his beautiful gift to music.

Never before, nor ever again, would dear Jayne know such a dance as this. It was perfect. It was enchanting. It was well past heavenly. It was all the things she knew she would love and want.

Her smile was wide, her feet were golden. Her movements, by the boy's gentle guidance, were nothing short of art. She tried to stifle a girlish giggle but simply could not, for her life was suddenly staggered with the happiness of a thousand proper and telling steps.

And so, the two floated across that magnificent room as though there was no other room in all the world. There was not, nor would there ever be, a more perfect moment in either life. The music was pulsing. The dancer was brilliant. And the maiden was charged with absolute happiness.

From one of the many corners of the room, the young wetted sack of Littlewick looked on and was slowly affected by the idea that he might have something to worry about after all.

9

Barthalamew's weekly dinner with the Theryoung's became a fast tradition. Upon his arrival at Alagood, he took up with the happy family for the length of two days until his accommodations in town were established. He was then off to the Jasmine House, where his small, windowless room awaited.

Within the hour of his simple move to Port Street, a courier arrived bearing an invitation to return to the Theryoung's for dinner. Thus, the boy returned the next day; the weekly tradition was kept from thereon.

To be sure, the dinner following the Hundley Ball was highly anticipated. Mrs. Theryoung was nearly beside herself with excitement. And so, the good wife sat upon the porch and looked to the simple road that led the way across the field and awaited his arrival. At the usual hour, his approach was noted.

"He's coming," she said to Toby as she stepped quickly into the house.

"And ya' thought he wasn't?

"I'm just so nervous for him! He went to the Hundley Ball! Have you ever heard of such a thing!"

"I admit," Toby started with a nod, for it was a peculiar notion even by way of his heart and mind, "it was rather unexpected."

But the dear wife barely heard this. Tales of the Hundley's were now at hand. Her smile was wide, her heart was begging.

"*She* invited him!" she then added with proper amazement. "Can you believe it!"

"Well, the boy is due a bit of a break."

To which Joan openly laughed.

Just then Barthalamew stepped through the front door donning a smile so perfectly reserved yet so entirely from the heart. Joan saw it at once. She could not help but so clearly see the changed man before her. Oh, how he had a new shine all about him!

Even the children, who were well accustomed to teasing Barthalamew to no end, who so routinely thought to point and scream and laugh and make as much noise as could be made and all at his expense, were immediately hushed by the arrival of this new and confident soul. There seemed in him now such a touch of grace as to make the whole room blush on his behalf.

"I say," Toby said, with his good pipe at the ready, "there is a change in you, Barth."

Barthalamew, however, was rather shy in his reply. It did not help that Joan was on him at once, saying nothing on her behalf but simply grinning as wide a grin as she could muster. Her arms were around him in that first moment of greeting, holding him as a mother might grasp her own pride and joy. She seemed near tears.

"I wonder of your adventure, sir," Joan then said with a widened smile.

"It went quite well, Mrs. Theryoung," was his hushed reply.

"Of course, it did. I can see it in your eyes. It must have gone splendidly."

The boy had not want to brag and made a valiant effort to refrain from such behavior, but his ego needed a little room to breathe.

"I suppose it did," he pushed with untried confidence.

With this Barthalamew gave a knowing glance to Toby and Toby returned a proper smile. Joan, for her part, nearly fell over for the sake of such outrageous news.

"Blessed be all!"

A smile then launched from her face that seemed to nearly halve it and, in fact, looked more than a bit macabre, but such was the good woman's smile when it reached and then nearly surpassed its limits.

"Let's sup," Toby then said, aware that he would have a long evening of it ahead.

And so, with Barthalamew at the head of the table, Joan and Toby and the three young children each sat down, and a proper blessing was then offered. Bowls were then passed, and plates were then filled, and simple courtesies were exchanged. The meal was well underway and yet Joan could not take her eyes from this new boy now beside her.

There were clearly a thousand more questions waiting to burst from her face. She held them until she could hold them no more. Her voice erupted.

"Did you dance?"

Toby's face lit up.

"Aye," from Barthalamew's proud eyes. "We did."

"And there's a fellow who can dance!" at once from Toby, who knew he would have little to contribute but was pleased for this early chance.

"Can you, Barth?" Joan eagerly asked.

"Can he?!" Pipe up, pipe down. "By Molly no one in all a' Kirkland knows how ta' dance as well as he!"

Joan gave her spouse a cursory glance, for there seemed by these words some telling ghost of her husband's past. She then turned back to the boy who was only too pleased to follow through.

"I learned from the sisters."

Joan's interest found a new gear. "I am so curious of these sisters!"

"T'is hardly a thing to be curious about," from Toby.

Joan was adamant for the matter was now pressing and some new perspective was at hand. "But, who were they?"

Barthalamew glanced Toby, wondering what it was that he was or was not to confess. Toby gave not a clue. The boy then offered as best he could his reply.

"They were our mother's, I suppose."

Joan could not have been more pleased for the answer. She was almost squeamish with joy. "I am most pleased!"

"Are you?" from Toby.

"You have never said as much."

"I have said plenty enough."

"How could you possibly think that?"

"Have you not been satisfied with my answers, love?"

90

"Your answers have never suggested that these women were mothers of any sort!"

Puff. Pipe down!

"Because they were not!"

"But surely, they were!"

"They were slave masters, no more!"

Pipe up and with absolute confidence, but Barthalamew sat now in wonder of this assessment.

"We were given to a proper home," the boy tried.

Joan turned from one to the other and back again. It seemed odd that neither could agree upon the matter.

Pipe down. "What does it matter! Barthalamew danced. I assure you, the girl swooned!"

Joan finally pushed her glare back on the boy, all but begging for the details.

"Dear Jayne?" were now the words from her lips with a quieted sort of want.

"It was a very good dance," Barthalamew then said with certainty, but neither confirming nor denying any hint of a swoon.

It was the children's turn now to contribute to the conversation or, more to the point, around it. A quick squeal launched from Jack's face followed by the girls who, in that moment, thought it only proper to offer a squeal in return. This was followed by a quick burst of yelling and then the most random medley of noises. And then, most curious of all, a perfect silence.

By Barthalamew's ear it was all a tremendous discomfort. He had want to hold to his ears, but Joan's questioning was only just under way.

"What is the home like?"

Squeals. Yells. Calm.

"I have never seen a thing so large and so—"

Squeals. Yells. Calm.

"—so white."

Joan offered a bowl of greens before pressing on.

"Was she pleased to see you?"

"I believe—"

Screams. Yells. Calm.

"Shut it!" Toby quickly admonished.

The squeals were then held. Only the silence remained.

"I believe so."

Joan was very pleased!

"I am very pleased!"

"Of course, she does have a number of potential suitors," Barthalamew thought to add, for the image of Gaylord Littlewick then struck.

The good wife was hardly impressed. "Of course, she does, Barth. She is nearly a princess. But she invited you and that alone was her personal gift to you. Do not ever forget that!"

Barthalamew pressed a smile, pleased for Joan's kind words.

A nearby squeal was building. Toby quashed it. He then looked back to Joan and then to the boy and quickly found himself bothered by the notion of his smile. This, he knew, would not do. It would not do at all.

Pipe down, "Joan!"

His voice resonated with purpose. Joan quickly turned to her husband, bothered by this unexpected volume.

"Let's not say as much as all that!"

Pipe up. Stern look.

Joan was rather displeased for the reprimand.

"As much as what, sir?" for her voice also promised of some coming rise.

Only then was Toby aware of how quiet his children were and how so suddenly loud he now was. The whole of the table had his attention, including Barthalamew who was confused beyond all doubt.

Toby looked away, nearly ashamed for his outburst but certain that he was right to say as much. Still, he had said his peace. There was only to finish his dinner and beg his wife's rotten glare away.

For her part, Joan said not another word. She completed her meal in silence, then excused herself and the children to another room, leaving the men alone, just as they were at the end of every day by way of their earlier years.

"It's just that," Toby started and then stopped and then started again, "she shouldn't put thoughts in your head like that."

Barthalamew looked to his near empty plate, wondering how he could pretend upon the meal that was almost no longer there.

"Thoughts like what?" he asked, displeased by the tone of Toby's suggestion.

At once, Toby realized he had backed himself into a corner. It was not his want to say as much, but he knew it had to be said. He pushed his own plate away and leaned back into his chair and looked directly to the boy.

"Jayne Hundley will not marry beneath her station. Frankly, even if she wanted to, it would not be allowed."

Barthalamew quietly recoiled.

"Remember where we come from!" Toby continued. "Abandoned to buckets and outhouses."

Barthalamew finally looked up. It was his want to look Toby in the eye, but the boy was fearful. And so, he turned away and focused on the room around him and it's simple wealth.

"But you married above your station," was the boy's softened return.

"Aye," Toby conceded. "Joan is above me. But a Hundley cannot be reached by any of us, under any circumstance."

"She likes me."

"She has a reputation for liking everyone."

"She invited me."

"And her family invited everyone else."

Barthalamew pushed his eyes down once more to his now empty plate. He begged against ever looking up again.

"Barth, it is the job of her father to make sure that she marries well. Be assured, the mayor will not fail in his duty!"

Toby's heart suffered for having to say as much and for having to say it without a proper touch of compassion, but he was fairly certain that it had to be said and in exactly that way.

Barthalamew stood uneasily from his seat and stepped to the door. He calmly reached for his hat and coat. Once dressed, he turned back to his life-long friend and offered a simple, fragile smile.

"You were not there," were his words, was his heart. "You were not!"

The boy then turned and took to the door and made his kindly exit.

Joan emerged from across the room. She had heard all. Her soul hurt. Her heart reeled. Her want for the pleasantry of a unique and exciting meal had been directly taken from her. Her eyes bore through the back of Toby's head as she announced her absolute displeasure.

"I will forgive you, sir. I shall always forgive you! But I will not forgive you tonight!"

10

In the early days of Alagood there was erected on Port Street, nearing the middle of town, the most inelegant and ill-considered example of accidental architecture that ever dared for the sky. It was thankfully limited to two of the shabbiest stories ever constructed, but the idea that it was able to stand at all was, by some, considered nothing short of a miracle. Most, however, refused to attribute such a squalor to anything so grand, but, instead, chalked it up to all the unintentional consequences of gravity, mortar and luck.

Oh, it was not so much to look at but the trick, you see, was not to look, for the building did seem as though it was in need of a good deal of attention. As well, it appeared, as much as a building could, to be more than a bit drunk. It slumped. It swayed. It had the look of something that slept till noon. On rainy days, it assaulted passersby with a raffish stench. For these reasons, and a good number more, it was easily agreed that, as far as buildings went, it was not a building to be trusted.

To make matters worse, it was constructed of the most hideous shade of brown. It cannot be strongly enough implied what an unkind shade it was. That any one brick would be stained a shade so awful as that seemed an almost unforgivable gaff for, clearly, it could not have been intended. But, that so many bricks were made of that abominable hue, well, what could be said of it! By all accounts, it seemed an unconscionable act of villainy. And yet, very much to the dismay of those early settlers, the building was put up and not a soul was arrested for it.

The benefactors of the Hamm, for it is of the Hamm that I now speak, were rivals, were brothers, were twins, no less, who were rarely seen together and could not be told apart and who confused the poor architect to the absolute point of madness and who were, in case you had not guessed it, so entirely blind to color as any two men could be. It was their intent, by this curious construction, to establish the Hamm's Bros. Dry Goods Store which might have turned a very fine profit were it not for the unfortunate fact that neither of the Brother's Hamm could see anything of the color of a brick or the quality of a brick but merely the price of a brick. Well, I dare say, that is all you need to know as it pertains to the manufacture of the notorious Hamm.

Now then for the consequence as, indeed, one was had, and it was a dire one at that. It was but a matter of days to the completion of the Hamm when there came to the ears of the twins a good bit of heckling. Public opinion, it seemed, had come up against them. The Hamm, it was said, was a dump. The Hamm, it was said, was a misery. The Hamm, it was said, was no more than a lean-to in kind need of a good wind.

The words were never put directly to either brother but only passed around them until, by the nature of so many whispers, the meaning was had. They were, by their investment, to be snubbed and each was fast determined to blame the other.

By that particular week's end, the rivalry peaked and as the final architectural touches were applied, the siblings, in a mad drunken fit, achieved at the very same moment very much the same thought which, as may be presumed, is not so much the anomaly among identical twins.

A duel was quickly declared, to which each brother showed with polished pistol and to which each brother took his paces, turned and fired his shot and to which each brother was then affirmed the victor for the other losing. In the end, when the smoke cleared from that bloodied scene, the simple truth was affirmed. There would be no Hamm's Bros. Dry Goods Store, after all. There was only to be the Hamm.

With its debt to society paid in full, the Hamm was given no more derision but allowed its place in peace. There would only be pity now for that orphaned pile of ugly bricks. By the end of its woeful first year it was bought and sold twice and before the breach of yet another year it was bought and sold twice more. To the point, the deeds of sale throughout its youth are said to stand well against any ten buildings in town.

Its story, of course, is legend now but it was, by the track of its start in life, quite accustomed to neglect. Still, the Hamm served, as best it could, as home to three poorly received pubs, a doomed clothier, a luckless chandler, a hapless attorney, two very ill-fated doctors of medicine, a regrettable collector and seller of some fine (and not so fine) books, a miserable cartographer and, most unsettling of all, though for no more than half a year, the town mortician.

Beyond that, the Hamm was leased to the local artisan's guild, but the members could not, by any means, purge from its walls the unsparing smell of Alagood's most recently deceased. It was then, by their abrupt departure, that the way was finally cleared for the most distinguished tenant of all, that being the mighty voice of all decorum and truth as was established, written and put to print by the very good people of the Alagood Gazette, of which Barthalamew Buckett, at the time, was one.

The Hamm, of course, finally came down and there is little debate these days as to why. Its timing, after all, was more than remarkable; even I must concede to that. And yet, you might be surprised to know that, at first, there was no accounting for it.

Only by the passage of a good many years was the revelation had and the miracle decreed. And not until then was that wretched brown brick raised again, figuratively speaking, of course, and placed with great joy into the fold of worship. Such is the history of the illustrious Hamm. Despised at birth. Ignored by life. Esteemed in Death. Admittedly, it is a curious parallel.

But, I digress.

In its bloom the Alagood Gazette was a weekly of fine repute. That is to say it had not, in those early days, all the fussy bother of a rival to properly disrepute it. There was only the Gazette. And whatsoever came to the mind of the Gazette was put to the mind of the people. And whatsoever was put to the mind of the people by virtue of the Gazette was briskly championed as incontestable fact.

You are welcome, however, to presume that the notion of fact was quite removed from the scene. To be sure, it was no nearer the Gazette than the sun itself, such the rascally animal that is fact. Not all the ink in the world could round it up and hold it down for even a moment's worth of print. I daresay, it is hardly worth the effort to try, for what good…

"…comes of a fact! What fact, I ask, would anyone choose to know or hear or read or share. A fact is nothing, Buckett, nothing to all the world but a bleeding nuisance, a blister and botheration, a dreadful pox that haunts, and without relent, those who let it. It is a money-less scag that has no place by me, that has its own time and place which, I most vehemently add, is not here and not now!"

Barthalamew, for his part, was rather startled by the lesson at hand.

"But are we not to print the truth?" he asked of Mr. Loydford and from the clear discomfort of his impossibly tiny desk.

Gilbert Loydford was a man who was both round and proud and who very well could have been more round than proud but only at a considerable risk to his health. As well, the man had a notion for money and, like most, chose money over most anything else.

As such, it was Loydford who, in time, perfected the business of news into a good many profits, mostly for himself and at great expense to an entire galaxy of truth. He was therefore quite staggered by this dogged persistence from the boy, for his point, he was sure, was as made as any point could possibly be.

So, what was it the boy was not hearing? How was it that any question at all could be fielded from so definitive a lecture as that? How might one possibly proceed from here!

Loydford looked up, looked down, looked all around as though the hunt was on for some legion of words, some more effective testimonial to his thoughts on this awfully important matter, as though all the testimony in the world was at his command, just waiting for his call to charge, to pour through those seemingly unsound walls of the Hamm and leap into battle on his fatted behalf.

"Bah, the truth!" he started, for the legion was slow in coming. "What need has anyone for something so...so...so idle!" ah, the legion at last, "and impractical as the truth! What need has anyone for something so common and crude as all that! My press, indeed no press in all the world, calls out for this wretched little runt you call truth. We print the news, Buckett! The NEWS! How can you not see the difference?"

How, indeed! The good editor, for his part, had run fresh out of places to look, so he put his eyes back to the boy. Clearly, the legion had done its job, the battle waged, the war won. There was no more for him to do, he was sure, but to quit the field. Any yet...

"But how can we write such things about the deacon?"

How had so much been said and not heard!

"T'is the news, Buckett," Loydford pressed. "It must be written. It is precisely my job to write it."

"T'is no more than rumors, gossip at best."

"And what is gossip but news! Gossip is the word of the people, the thoughts of the people, the will of the people, Buckett, that is what makes for a profitable press. How would I ever feed my precious wife and Junior if I turned my eye from the wants and the words of the people? What good would the Gazette be if I was to write anything less or more than their beautiful and necessary gossip! Seriously, I'm beginning to wonder whose side you're on!"

Barthalamew took a moment to consider this unexpected possibility of sides, for it seemed entirely unlikely, by way of his budding career, that a side was to be had. There was the truth. And there was not. Surely, it was not Mr. Loydford's intention to...

"But to suggest that the pastor had an affair with...with..." Barthalamew found no comfort in the word, "a prostitute. It is unfounded. It seems a bit...unfair."

The fatted editor was nearing a sweat. Beads were topping his forehead. How many legions were required to set the boy straight! And now the notion of fairness!

"What has fairness to do with it at all!?" Loydford yalped. "I daresay, Buckett, I do not object to the truth, not entirely, but it's not worth a copper. It can't be given away. Just try and suggest some truth into any old circle of talk about town and you'll never see so many yackety mouths snap shut! Just you try, Buckett, and you'll find yourself on the run or seeking other employment at best! How's that for fair! The truth! Ha! By Molly, nobody wants it. No one has use for it. As such, it will find no quarter here, except, from time to time, as it accidentally slips in."

How proud now the fat man, for that last bit seemed a comfort, seemed as though he had confessed what ought to be confessed, as though he was only human and only too pleased to admit that such things will slip by, from time to time. After all, he was no more, no less than as God intended. A touch of a smile came about and distended across his chubby face before being swallowed up by the folds of his constantly fatted cheeks.

"We must move forward," he then happily continued. "We have a deadline and I shall print what needs printing. And this, Buckett, is in need of printing."

"But...t'is hearsay, no more..." from the boy who seemed now quite tired of the topic and had the sound of retreat by his giving voice.

Loydford's voice softened. Victory was finally at hand. And so, he gave up his last bit of wisdom on the matter, as though a master rewarding a learned pet.

"Hearsay, my boy, is as good as the truth and a thousand times more profitable."

Barthalamew's surrender was complete. The boy was sure he was right, but the battle was simply too uphill. He returned the article to its beaming and bulbous author who was, at that moment, on the verge of snatching the page away.

"By the way, your words on the Hundley affair were top notch! Top notch! Well done."

"Thank you, Mr. Loydford," was his hesitant reply, and then, "it was factual."

"It was a dance for a little girl. You have another assignment?"

"Yes, Mr. Loydford."

"Very well. I shall expect your words within the hour," concluded the victor with a snap.

Loydford then made as quick a turn as he could and began a brisk wobble back to his office, where he charitably allowed another full hour of gloating before continuing with his day. Barthalamew had only to turn back to his tiny desk and sort through the notices that awaited his attention, for his assignment, at that moment, was nearly concluded.

And so, he sorted for a number of minutes until there was no more sorting to be done. After all, the notices of engagements and balls and other social affairs were not so many in those days and the boy had, from his early experience, learned to prioritize and prepare with wondrous efficiency. The result was that his workday had hours to go with, at best, mere minutes of work to account for. It was a typical dilemma.

Another experience learned early in his career was the matter of pretending to work, a talent that took some getting used to. Barthalamew had never been faced with such an issue but, in time, he came to realize the solution. All that was required was a paper and a pen which, as it turned out, was all he was ever given.

And so, the boy began to write. At first, his pen could barely give a wiggle as he was rather confused as to what to write about. Aside from the trivialities of his routine assignments, it was all rather new to him. There was a want, a need to express and yet his initial efforts were no more than random doodles, circles and squares and triangular shapes that filled a paper with misguided abandon.

It was like that for many months. The boy's heart was committed, but ill-prepared for the effort. Well, it is a common problem. Even the greatest of writers can attest that, no matter the stage of one's career, a proper word is no easy thing to come by. And yet, the boy persisted, for there were miracles yet in Barthalamew Buckett.

And so, his pen dipped and dallied and tried for a voice and soon a number of thoughts surfaced and formed and begged for his page. In those kind moments, a slow sense of direction kindly made its advance. It was as though Barthalamew was quietly, unexpectedly finding the start of some purpose.

He was on the verge of that comforting practice when there appeared at the door of the Hamm a very cordial sort of courier. He was young, as the best of couriers tend to be, and he was entirely polite, clearly the sort who made his turns by way of the less challenged in life. In short, his was a client of some obvious wealth.

Mr. Loydford stepped to the door and accepted the visitor with a tip of his hat.

"A notice for the Gazette," the lad announced with the most blessed of courier voices. "Hoping to make the deadline, sir."

"Yes, my good fellow," Mr. Loydford said in return. "And what sort of notice is it?"

"An engagement, sir!"

"Very well."

And with that, Mr. Loydford kindly accepted the notice, waved the courier off and stepped to Barthalamew with the paper in hand.

"Well, sir, t'is to be a wedding!" he announced with a quick and jolly laugh, for weddings were typically quite jolly and the business of their announcements was the easiest of all possible profits. "I am sure it is chock-full of fact, sir. Precisely what your silly heart craves."

Barthalamew accepted the notice and immediately found a frown for there, in his trembling hand, was an envelope affixed with the beautiful but suddenly defiant Hundley seal. All the pink in the world seemed suddenly upon him and ready to pounce.

"I want it within the hour!"

Barthalamew waited for Mr. Loydford to step away before he gave the seal an uneasy tear and read the notice. At that moment his misfortune was revealed. Dear Jayne Hundley was to wed in a month. Her intended was no other than that impossibly wetted sack of sand, Lieutenant Gaylord Littlewick.

11

Spring was unremitting. It was, and always is, as unlike the broken-hearted as could be! After all, it is the most desired of seasons, the constant and imperishable champion of winter, the very breath of so much hope and life. It is loved entirely and without question and it shall always be. It has no cause to flinch or fade or grieve or want of more and it is the very sort of thing that readily, happily chews upon the heart of the openly wounded man.

For Barthalamew Buckett, that particular spring was all teeth. It gnawed upon his soul without mercy. It wrecked his want for day and made him all but weep for the simple darkness of his cramped and windowless room.

And then night would become day again and Barthalamew was forced from his harbor and put to the street once more where he kept his eyes to the dirtied ground as his broken shuffle slowly kept him forward. He made no effort or want of the people but only to know the push of his blackened shoes as they impolitely moved him from home to work and back home again. His life was only for the black, for only the black would do.

And it was all for the cause of Dear Jayne, dear, blessed, impossibly wonderful Jayne. There was a part of the boy's heart that accepted the simple fact that he was loving rather selfishly. Well, that could not be denied.

And then there was the part of his heart that savagely cried out against the idea that the battle was lost to some impossibly snobbish and boorish fellow such as Littlewick. And, again, Barthalamew was more than aware that this, too, has a self-serving touch.

And then there was the matter of the sun, which he found to be too bright. And the sky, which he found to be too blue. And there was almost always some gentle breeze which was decidedly too soft and almost immediately reminded him of her.

And there were constant, ruining delusions of a kiss that would never be, unshakable dreams and apparitions that came to him by the shape of her eyes, of her face, of the merciful ease of her smile. He was taunted daily by the phantom touches and smells of her cinnamon-brown hair.

And then, of course, there lingered the melody of her laugh, so sacred to him now, so dreadfully missed. He feared he might forget it. He knew, in fact, he soon would.

And by the sounding of any music at all, Barthalamew was startled and then assaulted with the remembrance of a perfect dance, of her hand in his, of some dearly unspoken vow that suggested the moment would never end. But, of course, there remained the obvious and agonizing fact that it did.

It was all part of that fractured dream that he was so ashamed to have ever dreamed, for a fellow like him, he now knew, had no business to dream it. And yet, how could dear Jayne ever be undreamed? Indeed, it could not be done!

Damnable season! Why could it not be fat, glorious sheets of unending rain! Why could it not be suffering for all! Oh, the agony of that awful unremitting spring.

And with this fresh misery came a good deal of work and, by Molly, Barthalamew continued to hit his mark, though he did not go about doing it was well as he could. It was his pen, you see, that was suddenly an enemy to him, that made no effort in his hand, that begged across the page as though an extension of his darkened soul, with nothing kind or keen to offer.

Every day battles were waged and lost to the very smallest army of words. Every day Barthalamew tried for the high ground and every day he was routed by some unfinishable sentence or thought.

And as deadlines rapidly neared, the boy would give some careless shrug and surrender his budding skill to something far less befitting. The assignment was then passed up to Mr. Loydford whose agitation by those efforts was clearly on the rise.

As one might imagine, the Hundley wedding announcement, per Barthalamew's deed, suffered a miserable fate. As submitted, it was an atrocious wreck of errors and misspellings that, when overlooked, read as more like an elegy. It was haunting. It was dismal. It was enough to make a grown man collapse to his knees and openly weep in the streets.

To the point, it simply would not do! Clearly, the thing had to be undone. And so, by his own pen, Mr. Loydford undid it, put it right and into print.

But the matter was far from over. More deadlines came and went and more of Barthalamew's elegies were placed upon his desk and the editor-at-large, being a reasonable man, could not help but wonder if his fair associate was beyond all reasonable help.

Loydford's spring, then, was no good either. Ever since that Hundley debacle, for he had come to think of it as no less than that, his workload all but doubled. Everything young Barthalamew wrote had to be reworked and there was only himself to do it.

And when Barthalamew chose not to write, which was often enough and which, at that point, was practically the same as writing, he sulked about his little room without so much as a word and made a misery of the day. It would be this way, Mr. Loydford knew, until it came to pass. But, oh, how to make it pass!

Early on and after some consideration, a sermon was devised and delivered to the boy in which all of the warm and sometimes cold matters of the heart were taken up and put before him in a more conversant light. It was done, however, to no avail. Despite its smartly worded bits, despite its hours-long rehearsal, despite its masterful recitation, Mr. Loydford's grand effort was received as though by a ghost with no understanding of the language at all.

Barthalamew raised not an eyebrow, gave not a look, said not a word, but only stared down the inkwell on his little desk as though it was brimming with some poison he was now firmly committed to drink. Loydford, feeling rather small for his failed effort, lowered his head and stepped away and took to his office where he spent the rest of his day thinking upon some pretty face from his clouded past and pondering an inkwell of his own.

And then summer stepped up in its quiet little way and with it came a whisper of salvation. Word had found its way to the Hamm that a new man was about town. The word, I admit, had not so far to travel as the man was only next door, but travel it did and what satisfaction it brought to those spring-wearied fellows of the Gazette.

He was a wiry man, it was said, with thin, shiny hair and a thick, shiny beard and fat, shiny

piles of money. A purchaser. An investor. A new owner for the King Robert Arms! Oh, what news! What an absolute bundle of news!

Loydford decided at once that no less than a special edition would do. The inn, after all, was to shut down, to close for a number of weeks for extensive renovations.

A story!

Scores of local craftsmen and artisans were to be contracted for the work.

A story, indeed!

The local economy was to be soundly affected.

An absolute saga!

As well, the new man, this champion of money by the name of Littleton, was in need of proper introducing and who better for the job than the fine, industrious fellows of the Alagood Gazette! Oh, a special edition was just the thing!

But a good deal of writing would have to be done, a great deal, in fact and all within a matter of days. It was too much to do, Loydford knew, for any one man. He would have…he would have to…

Yes, but of course! How did he not think of it before? It was not just an idea, but the notion of a fix, a cure, a remedy, for sure! Barthalamew was merely in need of something else to love. By Molly, the answer was truly at hand!

"Buckett!" Loydford called out, bellowed actually, for he then and there decided it was high time for a good bit of bellowing. "I say, Buckett!"

There came, however, no reply to his call.

Urged by a mix of curiosity and surprise, Mr. Loydford stood from his desk and stepped busily across the puddled floor. The Hamm, on that particular day, was putting up with a fair bit of water, the result of an early summer's rain and a number of architectural nuances that forbade the downpour from staying out of doors.

Barthalamew was found easily enough, sitting quietly at his tiny desk, deaf and dumb to all the world, apparently in deep contemplation of his navel.

"Buckett!"

The fat man's roar rattled the walls which, in turn, rattled the boy. Barthalamew leaped to attention provoking a number of splashes as he did, for the rain, it seemed, favored his little room.

"Yes, Mr. Loydford," his timid reply.

"I heartily congratulate you, good sir," the editor said, this time by way of a more common voice, "on your advancement to the position of Gazette reporter!"

"Re-reporter?" Barthalamew stammered, clearly surprised by this inconceivable string of words.

"Yes, that's you! Now gather your things!"

"My...things, sir?"

"By God, Buckett! Don't stand there and play stupid with me! Get your ink! Get your parchment! Get your pen, most of all! Make haste, dear boy! A story has no patience! It waits not for some laggard fool. A thousand words await! Gather and go! Your first subject is merely a door away."

And so, Barthalamew, with his mind so suddenly occupied by the menace of those thousand words, went about gathering his things, though it did prove a curious task as he had never been asked to gather those things before. With the task then complete, there was now only the matter of confirming...

"Am I to speak with Mr. Littleton, sir?"

At once, Mr. Loydford was pleased. The boy's face was fresh with a curious color. The boy was suddenly smart and willing.

"Mr. Littleton," was the kind confirmation.

A cheer for convenience. Within the minute, the boy was there. He looked up to the ornamental door of the King Robert Arms and, after a quick adjustment of his many gathered things, balled his fast and offered a hearty knock.

A bald man quickly answered, as though his entire day and night was to stand to the other side of that door and beg for a knock. He was a taller, older fellow, thinned to the point of something not too far from starvation and yet surprisingly strong by his look. His aged voice was slow to sound.

"Yes," a pause, "sir?"

"I am Buckett. From the Gazette," Barthalamew said, as though to announce.

"Yes," a pause, "sir."

"I am here to request an interview," he then said with a blossoming poise.

"Yes," a pause, "sir."

"With Mr. Roy Littleton."

"Of course," a pause, "sir."

And with this, Barthalamew was finally let in and, by the old man's lead, marched across the large tavern room which seemed rather nice and not so much in need of any sort of renovation, as far as his unqualified eye could tell.

But then there launched a fast and telling racket. To a far corner a team of men busied themselves with the tools of more trades than Barthalamew could account for: hammers and saws and gimlets and gougers lined the floors amid an assortment of other contrivances that were entirely new to his eye.

Strips of perfectly good wood were being ripped from the wall and cast away as though rubble. Thick, attractive tapestries were brought to the ground and tossed aside with the very best of rugs. The old bar, being quite old and, thereby, quite rich, was in the process of being made young again and, somehow, all the more rich for the effort.

It was an absolute slaughter of the finest things Barthalamew had ever seen, and the fact that so prodigious a room was being so entirely undone hinted at some nearly unimaginable thing to come. Already, the novice reporter's first one hundred words were leaping into play.

At the far end of the tavern room, the bald man held and reached for an ornamental red rope that dangled just before him. He gave it a forceful tug and, though, Barthalamew could not hear from the mess of that busied room, some far away bell presumably sounded. With this bit of custom completed, the bald man then stepped forward through a double door and led the boy to a small but luxurious study where he was quietly prompted to sit and wait.

And so, the boy quietly eased into a nearby chair and end table where he thoughtfully assembled and placed his gathered things. Ink. Parchment. Pen, most of all.

The newborn reporter then considered the kindness of the room around him. Without any doubt whatsoever, he had never seen such a wealth of books and leather in all his life. The mere idea that Port Street could ever yield such a room as this startled the boy's imagination nearly to tears. And, just like that, another hundred words leaped into play.

"The Gazette?" the voice now called from a few feet away, firm but gentle.

Barthalamew turned at once to note his host. By first sight, Roy Littleton, Senior seemed something of a devilish man. The clothes were of obvious wealth but so very tightly pressed upon him. As well, he walked an impossibly quieted walk. This was evidenced by his entry which failed to yield a single sound at all.

"Yes, sir."

The return was pressed with a respectful glance upward as Senior Littleton was also a man of some fair height and weight, height especially. To the point, he towered.

Barthalamew stood in greeting and was immediately put back a bit. Never had he seen a man rise so high against him as this.

A hand was proffered. The boy accepted and looked on in quieted awe as his own hand was then devoured by what seemed to be ten pounds of fingers and flesh. Was there nothing at all little about this man Littleton?

"Roy Littleton, Senior!"

Buckett, pushed a smile as upward as he could and fought to send his voice as well. "Barthalamew. Buckett."

The greeting was generously accepted. The towering fellow then issued a smile that eased the boy at once. The boy would soon discover that this was the common greeting offered to those of his newly elevated position. Blessed be the man who was to be the reporter! Good tidings seemed at his command.

Barthalamew was directed to sit, which he did, and then directed to commence with the interview, which he also did. With eye to eye and pen to pad, the two were happily underway. The questions came and went with such ease that the boy hardly noticed what he was doing.

The first inquiry regarded the nature and timeliness of the renovation. The answer was quite happily given.

Mr. Littleton was then asked about his overall ambitions for the King Robert Arms. The reply was cheerfully provided.

More questions were asked about his ideas, his history, his experiences, his education and family, his thoughts, thus far of Alagood, about his politics and his religion. Barthalamew was unstoppable. The words all but raced from his lips and the answers were kindly returned.

"By Molly, it is a true joy to talk to the likes of you," said Mr. Littleton, Senior, so clearly pleased for the occasion to speak so much about himself.

"Thank you, sir. T'is my first interview," Barthalamew calmly confessed.

"I dare say, you shall have a thousand more!" delighted Littleton, Senior. "It is your gift!"

111

The compliment found its depth at once. The boy was struck happy. Life be pleased, was his quieted cry, for here was something to do, here was everything to do and what a comfort it was to his hungering soul to know that he could do it well.

Do you wonder what thought of Dear Jayne came to him from that moment forward? Not so many as you might think Not so many at all!

And now, with the interview concluded, there was only the matter of some simple salutations.

"I am much obliged, Mr. Littleton."

"Have you all that is needed?"

"Quite enough, sir."

"Very well, then. I shall have Button see you—"

But then came the sound of something like love.

"Father?"

The voice, sweet and slow as though molasses, arrived well ahead, announcing itself from around the corner with a quick and decidedly feminine tone. By the aid of his notes, Barthalamew gave a quick determination. It must be the daughter! And, indeed, it was.

"Janice, my pumpkin," Mr. Littleton said, with his head now as high as his lofty hopes. "Do step in for a moment. I would like for you to meet a very clever young man."

"A man, father?" again the voice and only the voice, for the daughter was particularly slow in her approach.

"Please, dear. Do step in."

And with this, the daughter finally arrived. At once, there was noticed a pile of hair, stacked quite high and as black as coal and all of it atop a tilted head of lovely feminine curiosity. The dear girl's eyes were a fatted brown and ever-widening before the boy, as though it was her intent to bore right through him. As well, she, like her father, was entirely tall and dressed entirely well.

"Who is it, father?"

"This, my dear, is a reporter. Mister Buckett, this is my lovely daughter Janice Ellen Littleton."

Only then did Barthalamew apprehend that his chance to be gentlemanly had come and was already on the go. He made a quick effort to salvage the situation by quickly standing and accepting the introduction with as much grace as he could possibly muster.

"I am most pleased to meet—" the boy tried but was quickly cut off.

"I am to be featured in a special edition of the Gazette. Can you believe it, my pumpkin?" Mr. Littleton said, taking from Barthalamew a bit of the moment.

"I can believe it quite well, father. Did you say," the daughter then paused, for she seemed affected by something in the way of a recollection, "Buckett?"

"Well, yes, love. Barthalamew Buckett. He is a man of considerable skill, I must insist!"

And here the young woman's eyes turned quite favorably upon the boy and, in that moment, that tall and handsome head of hair was a hundred thousand cakes and dear jayne was no more than a floor-bound crumb. How loving were the words just then as they slipped her ever-pretty lips!

"And a dancer, Father. Word about town is that Mr. Buckett is quite the dancer…"

12

"Quite the dancer."

By the sound of her voice and the gleam in her eye, there was clearly a good bit of motherly pride. Sister Marihanna turned from Sisters Josephine and Maribeth so as to place her smile once more to the nine-year-old boy who was standing as gravely as ever beside her. Just beyond the patched roof of that candle-lit nave, the kindly glow of yet another full moon hovered.

"Quite the dancer," Marihanna sweetly concluded.

"Sister! Marihanna!" Sister Josephine intervened with gavel in hand, as brooding and anxious as ever to strike out and knock down this ridiculous bit of business. "What do I care about all that!? What do I care if the boy can float in mid-air at the mere sound of a tune? It is not! Nor has it ever been! Nor will it ever be! The business of the order to care at all about any sort of…dancing!"

"But, Sister Josephine, with all due respect, it would be such a welcomed addition to our educational curriculum if—"

"Bah!" Sister Josephine blurted, as blurting had become, in her passing years, a foremost enjoyment for her.

"But the children," Sister Marihanna resumed, for she was rather determined in her cause. "They are gifted with a variety of talents that must be recognized and explored. It was by mere chance that I thought to teach Barthalamew to dance and it is quite remarkable what he has accomplished and without so much as a note of music."

"But, how is it done?" Sister Maribeth then pressed and with the very happiest sort of curiosity and all, of course, for the glorious record.

"She counts," Sister Marilynn explained from her usual pew and with the ever-placid green-eyed Lydia sitting quietly at her side. "She counts out the steps and sometimes hums along. Barthalamew has learned a good many dances." And here the typically flat and incurious Marilynn came very near to a smile of her own. "I have danced the Stratford with him and it's a perfect joy."

"Is it truly?" rejoined young Maribeth, who was quite suddenly beyond herself at the idea of it all, for she had never known a dance and had succumbed to the idea that she never would.

"Well then, sisters," Josephine again intervened as her own point seemed to have been made and she was only too eager to say so, "it seems that humming and counting is more than enough. It gets the job done, insofar as the job is in need of doing, which, I maintain, it is not! So, what need have we for anything like a piano?!"

Sister Marihanna was quieted at once. Although she was decidedly prepared to advance her cause against a good number of objections, as a good number were expected, there came a fast and simple logic by way of that particular return. She found herself rather ruined for a response, rather lost to a whole train of thought, aching to press on but abandoned by her wits, her words, by all sensibility. There was only the hope, and a weak hope it was, that someone in heed of her bumbling silence might think to chime in and say something, say anything, say anything whatsoev—

"Cecilia!"

Well, it was something, at any rate.

"Bah!" Josephine blurted yet again for blurting had become...but, of course, you know. "Who said what?"

"Cecilia!" again the hardy reply.

Six heads in all (for young Toby was not there, was typically in defiance of these full moon affairs) turned to face the eldest sister who was still known to wake from time to time and utter such things before collapsing back into slumber. That this old and wearied woman knew what to say and when to say it and almost always from the wily depths of what seemed a perpetual sleep, forever amazed young Lydia. The mere sound of that rustic voice brought the child's eyes fast to life and put in motion all the freckles about her adoring face.

Here, you might conclude, was the look of a good daughter's love. Well, there is the truth of it. A daughter, it had been decided, she was. Oh, how sisterhood would become the likes of her.

"Does anyone wish to know what I mean when I mention my dead sister's good name?" Sister Margaret said, having yet to open her eyes as it was a thing she gladly did less and less.

"Bah!" Sister Josephine blurted.

"But, of course we do," Sister Maribeth entreated, for the record was patiently waiting.

"I believe," Sister Josephine rejoined, "what Sister Margaret means to suggest is that Cecilia once played the piano."

"Once, you say? You know as well as I that she played it always, and she played it beautifully. Lest you forget, Sister Josephine, the piano was Cecilia's first love."

The very prompting of this memory, so sacred as it was, stole a coming blurt directly from Josephine's mouth. It could not be helped. Even her gray and wretched heart was not immune to the recollection of it all, to the remembrance of so much beauty, of so much music and laughter, of those spectacular days of a long ago, forgotten youth recalled to life and loved, oh, so loved all over again.

Josephine's mind was then lost at once to a parlor room, so finely furnished and well-windowed and forever lavender-scented; to a large, scenic bay window so thickly dressed in velvet red so as to temper the oncoming light of day; to the olden upright piano nearby and the young girl seated before it; to her always white dress and always black shoes and sometimes cerulean blue ribbons; to her flowing, raven-black hair and her tiny, nimble fingers playfully dancing across the black and white of those delighted piano keys. Dear Cecilia, so beautiful in so many ways but in music most of all. Oh, sweet friend, could you possibly be missed more than this?

"A piano is what she would want," Sister Margaret resumed, speaking, still, as though from the far side of a dream. "To be quite honest, I am rather curious as to why, in her heavenly name, it was not considered before."

A silence again prevailed as there seemed among the sisters a want of approval by some ethereal means, by some ghostly sight or sound that might only be seen or heard, one can only assume, by the very quietest of hearts. Even Lydia and Barthalamew considered the air above them all as though some thing or someone was simply waiting to be breathed into the room.

And then a voice pushed but it was merely that of Sister Marihanna as she firmly resumed her cause.

"I have spoken to a good lady in town with a piano for sale. Her name is Patsy Brinda. Her husband John has just passed. He owned the tavern which is to be closed—"

"A tavern piano!?" Sister Josephine objected, for though her spirit was now inclined, her nature could not be refused.

"Yes, sister, a tavern piano."

"And, have you even seen this…this tavern piano?" the objecting Sister pursued.

"Well, of course not, Sister. It is in a tavern."

"Where men lurk!"

"Yes, I suppose. Where men lurk…"

"And drink! And spit! And sin! With this-this piano!"

It was Sister Marilynn who then spoke up, who then put in for some much-needed clarification.

"I think it not so much that they sinned with the piano, Sister Josephine, but that they sinned near the piano. Respectfully, I believe it a difference worth noting."

This pleased Sister Maribeth to no end. And so, for the record, it was happily noted.

At any rate," Sister Marihanna continued, "Mrs. Brinda assures me it is in fine condition and I have found that the townsfolk do consider her to be a woman of very good repute."

"How much?" snapped Sister Margaret, for she was not in a mood for so much recreational chatter.

"Six gold, five."

That prompted from Sister Josephine another blurt, her most guttural yet.

"For that, she will have it delivered and properly tuned." Marihanna concluded.

A favorable hush echoed across the nave. Sister Marihanna put a hand to Barthalamew's shoulder as she eased a confident smile. There was no doubt in her mind that Sister Margaret's interjection would win the day. The piano would be had and, by Margaret's next words, it was all but confirmed.

"Send for it."

Sister Maribeth, however, being eternally for the record, felt immediately obliged to try for an objection of her own.

"Well, yes Sister Margaret, it seems a wonderful idea, but I do believe such an expense requires a motion followed by a proper vote…"

"No, it does not. It only requires my consent. And I consent."

"Well, yes, but—"

"Sister Maribeth!"

There could not have been a more unexpected outburst than that devilish cry from the old widow of a thousand deaths. Such life now from the old maid and with such wide open eyes! Such volume! Such animus!

"Lest you forget, I shall remind you! I shall remind each of you whose gold it is that you are dealing with here. It is my inheritance! And it is Cecilia's inheritance forfeited to me that sustains us, that shall always sustain us! Do not, at any time, suggest to me that I cannot do with it as! I! Please!"

Those choice words were clearly meant to be the very last on the matter and, indeed, they were. Not a soul stirred. Not a one hoped to. Even Josephine knew well enough to hold her blurting tongue. The record, you may be sure, was promptly retired.

"Sister Marihanna," Sister Margaret calmly repeated, "you may send for the piano."

All of this so that a boy could dance. Well, I daresay it rather terrified the boy. Barthalamew, after all, knew very little at the time as it pertained to the shape or size or sound of music. He was aware, of course, of a number of household tunes and Godly hymns as were passed around by the sisters from day to day, but those songs were never too well sung and, by his young ear, not so very soothing.

As well, it could not be helped that the boy was entirely oblivious as to what a dead man's tavern piano was, as to whether or not that man was dead as a result of this tavern piano and, if so, as to whether or not this tavern piano thing was likely to go about killing again. The promise that it was somehow musical was nothing at all to the unknowing boy. The notion of some coming violence was now his first and only concern.

Oh, how he begged against so much fuss, so much bother, so much death and gold! What did he care about dancing? It was only, to him, something to do and he would have been just as happy to do without it. However, the boy was much too afraid to offer up a word of his own.

And so, the gold was produced and the very next morning the piano was sent for.

The job, of course, fell to men, three of them to be exact. This was to be expected. It could only be expected. Only men did such things.

Still, the Sisters of Cecilia spent much of the day pretending against it, as had become their habit of so many years. To the point, if it was not brought up from the ground or up for a vote, the order, by its usual wisdom, was only too pleased to think around it. The delivery of the piano, therefore, was given no mind at all until word was soon received that the it was forthcoming, that it would arrive by week's end and that a number of men were entrusted to the task.

And so, on the appointed day and by the appointed hour, the men arrived, and the sisters were no longer able to pretend against it. There was only to quietly, collectively gasp and beg for the end of the day.

For the children, however, the tortoise-like approach of the horse-drawn ox cart was decidedly enchanting. Visitors and horses and ox carts and all were exceedingly rare to their eyes. These curious three had no choice but to look on, for their minds and hearts were too overwhelmed to allow for anything else.

Once the cart halted at the front of the church, the three men, each clearly unbathed but thankfully candid in their speech, unloaded the cargo, allowing Barthalamew his first wide-eyed sight of the now infamous man-killing tavern piano. Though dented and dinged and clearly more than a bit worn, it had a quieted, boxed look about it and right away the boy knew it was nothing to fear. It was curiosity that now raced to mind, for he was quickly in want of understanding how such a thing might bring about anything like a dance.

The men were quick to move on with the chore of placing the piano indoors where Sister Marihanna represented the order as best she could. By her kind direction, the instrument was centered atop the altar in merely a matter of minutes. There was then the swift but mindful matter of a proper tuning.

The three men remained entirely focused on the task at hand. Barely a word was exchanged, nary a glance was favored. The sisterhood was quite pleased for those quieted efforts. Even Josephine appeared more at ease than usual, which proved remarkable considering the usual.

The job, in its entirety, took barely an hour and before the children could even think to ask what had happened, the men were readying their leave. Their tools were quickly gathered as the instrument was given to one last wipe of the cloth. There only remained the passage of a number of sheets of music, as promised with the price.

And so, Sister Marihanna, having received the sheets, offered her gratitude and, as a party of one, waved the men off as they mounted the ox cart and directed themselves back to town. She then stepped inside and then to the altar and took her place upon the piano bench with a fast and excitable pride.

Those first few moments were hers alone as it seemed only right by the others. As well, there still remained a number of chores so it was only too easy to fall back to work. Lydia, however, with so little to do, was soon to emerge. She made her quieted steps to the altar where her deep green inquisitive eyes considered the piano with all her muted attentions.

"Don't be afraid," Sister Marihanna assured with a smile.

And with this the young girl tried for a number of curious faces so as to express anything other than fear.

"T'is all tavern music," said Marihanna as she evaluated the pages now before her. "I suppose we can omit the lyrics. None shall be the wiser."

This was offered with a wink and a smile to sweet Lydia, who had, at so early an age, developed an instinctive love for collecting secrets. It could not be helped. It was, after all, her very nature to keep them. And so, they were only too easily kept.

It was not until after supper when the piano was given the full attention of the order. Marihanna again resumed her seat before the instrument as the sisters gathered about, each in her own way and by her own state of curiosity. Barthalamew kept to his back pew, shyly wondering what, if anything to make of such a thing as this. He would be called forward, though. This he knew. And so, he was.

"Barth! What say we try a number?" from Marihanna who now had that sinful sheet of music laid out before her.

And so, Barth stepped up to the altar where a space was cleared, took a simple, though silly pose, and waited for the counting to begin. This time, however, there was to be no count. Marihanna, instead, struck a key, a wonderfully thick and beautiful note that made the boy turn and forget his place. Another note followed and immediately another.

The whole of the nave was suddenly filled with a legion of notes that instantly became as one and, in that moment, Barthalamew instinctively knew. These were the numbers now. This was how the dead man's tavern piano worked. And so, he took a step and began a quiet count of his own and in that moment, the boy prodigy was well into a dance.

It was Sister Josephine who first coughed up a smile but then quickly recanted and gave a quick glance of the room so as to make sure no one else saw. No one did. No one could have.

All eyes were glued to the dancing boy as he made his soft steps and spins and flipped about that hardened church floor as though all the world was a mile beneath his tender boy feet. All ears embraced the tavern song which was slowed a good deal for the sake of a more agreeable sound. All hearts were lost to the moment at hand which, though a bit silly on its own merit, offered a number of forgotten kindnesses to the otherwise ailing souls of those sitting before that prancing boy. Even Toby, though for only a moment, took his mind from some critical thought and decided right then and there that music just might be something worth knowing.

As the song came to an end and with only a few notes shorted, an examining silence could not but be helped. Not a one in that church room had any idea how to respond. There seemed a want for applause but before a response could be collectively considered, Sister Marihanna put forth another idea.

"Lydia."

And sweet Lydia sallied forth from her seat beside Sister Marilyn and with all the smiles in the world, for this sound of music and this sight of Barthalamew were at once her two favorite things in the world.

"Perhaps, you and Barth should try together."

The dear girl's smile went as wide as it could go. And even though the boy made no true effort to return a smile of his own, her heart could not have been more content.

"Like I showed you," Sister Marihanna offered in encouragement.

And in that moment, Lydia stepped to Barthalamew and assumed a pose of her own. It was now up to the boy to match her stance, to reach for her hand, to put his other to her back and to wait once more for the count. And again the count came and again by the sound of some old tavern song which was eased once more to some kindly tempo.

Barthalamew took his step, and Lydia magically followed. And in that moment, all the hopes and dreams of that quieted girl poured forth from her tiny but remarkably abled heart and were met at once with everlasting bliss.

13

Love, that ancient drifting vessel, had found for itself a strange new sea, had set adrift, it seemed, before some freshly wetted horizon. Life was entirely anew.

What was once, and barely just, a blundering lump of heart now soundly beat within Barthalamew's chest, buoyant with purpose. All that was previously thought to be so deep and dark was quite suddenly as light and bright as the best of all possible days. How sweet and engaging was that new season in the boy's wanting life, for it brought with it so kind an endorsement as the most precious of innkeeper's daughters!

Janice Littleton, however, was not so much like Dear Jayne, not so entirely a rose. One might say she was something like a rose, perhaps something very near it, perhaps something in the process of some wonderful bloom, a woman seemingly on the verge of something, perhaps, like beauty, but a beauty, permit me to say, still in the coming. But what did that matter to Barthalamew Buckett? It was all beauty and always beauty to the boy.

To the point, whereas the girl was clearly rigid, Barthalamew saw her as statuesque. Whereas she was a bit pig-headed, he thought her resilient. Whereas she was evidently proper to some very annoying degrees, the lover chose to call that virtue.

None of it, not a bit of it could be second guessed by his wanting heart. That is how love is for the unseasoned fellow. Inasmuch as he adored, Barthalamew did so in the face of all possible reason.

To further the point, there was the matter of Ms. Littleton being overly tall. At first, it was something of a peculiarity, for when the boy did try to stand next to her, he found her always standing more. As well, there remained her towering pile of hair that absurdly advanced the matter to a dizzying height. The issue, however, was not long lived, as Barthalamew was fast to embrace that singularity; in fact, he was soon all the more drawn to her for it.

It was clear that Ms. Littleton was decidedly firm with her womanly style and choices. Her style of dress was overwhelmingly girlish. Her abilities to charm, to smile, to smirk, to flirt, were only exceeded by her capacity to want and dismiss and, in this, it must be said, she displayed prodigious skill.

Moreover, those keen feminine charms were accentuated by the most captivating pair of voluminous brown eyes. In no time at all, there emerged the widely agreeable truth that Ms. Littleton's real draw was neither her coming beauty nor implied wealth but her solicitous glance which was commonly rendered and renounced with a confounding sense of urgency. Hers was a leer that took a fast toll on her mark, one that made the simple man feel suddenly complex and the complex man unexpectedly simple.

As well, she possessed a similar sort of smile. It was offered only when least expected and, like her eyes, it quickly found its depth. These feisty flirtations were her gift to mankind and she enjoyed providing for that gift though, let it be said, it was rarely offered, if ever, without a proper price.

As such, Barthalamew's heart and mind were then and there committed. Every last bit of his love's desire was now for Janice, for her eyes and for that ever-threatening smile that dared but rarely came and then, of course, for that magnificent pile of hair that so easily defied much in the way of imagination to say nothing, I might add, of gravity.

Indeed, he could only dream of having twice as many hands, for it would require at least that many, to run one's fingers through those many wanting tresses. That is, to say, on those seldom occasions when there was not so much ornamentation involved.

Over the course of the next two weeks, the boy did not go hungry. Three separate invitations lured him to dinner at the King Robert Arms, and, by the passage of each evening, he could not help but notice her heaping pillar, rising more and more and given to an increasingly generous bit of decoration. Such baubles and knickknacks and who knew what teetered and dangled and ran amok in all the places where amok had no business of running. It was, in a word, mesmerizing. Barthalamew could not help but look, could not help but wonder…

"Mr. Buckett?"

But how could he possibly hear for all that he had to see. His eyes were affixed, as though glued in place. That fantastic hill of hair and all of its stunning gadgetry—

"I say, Mr. Buckett?"

And what could Janice Littleton do but render some fast and easy smile, for the boy's eyes were so clearly for her.

"Mr. Buckett!"

The spell was finally broken. Barthalamew, nearly ashamed, looked to his host, fearful of a coming scorn. His behavior, he knew, was obvious and low. Mr. Littleton, Senior, however, was all pride.

"What say you to your potted roast?" he asked with a senatorial smile.

"Entirely remarkable," the boy replied, though with more thought to Janice than the content of his plate.

"Junior," Mr. Littleton then said to his younger self, "is it as remarkable as Mr. Buckett says?"

"Doubly so," the Junior answered, for the Junior, like his father, was as agreeable as could be.

"What about me father?" Janice's voice came up among the men as something so very different, something heavy and burdened. "Do you not care about my thought on the roast?"

Barthalamew tried not to look, but he could not help himself. And so, he looked and once again he was stuck.

"Well, my dear, the consensus is in," Roy Senior said. "Your opinion is rather beside the point now."

"Fah!" came the syllable, as unique and as loud as her hair. "I say t'is a dreadful roast. The poor beast died for naught! Its whole life was lived so as to sit on our plate and make for a miserable dining!"

Barthalamew could only look on, wowed by the slapstick bob of Janice's head and, by consequence, the shiny circus that bobbed along with it.

"And this is why a woman's opinion is so rarely sought!" Senior replied with a masculine huff.

"Fah!"

How alarming now was the sound of that wayward syllable! Whether it was meant as a noun, verb or some unruly adjective the boy could never tell, but for the length of those three unforgettable meals, the one thing that could always be relied upon was the chirp of that curious call.

"Fah," she said again, apparently in want of driving home the point of her preceding fah's. "I dare say a woman's opinion is not wanted for a man has no need of a right one. Don't you think, Mr. Buckett?"

Barthalamew was dumbstruck. The jingle-jangle of Janice's hair had reached a new level of distraction. His heart begged for some focus as his mind raced for an answer.

"I believe," he started, then halted, being, in that moment, acutely aware of how thin the side of a coin can be, "that all opinions have value and degrees of right and wrong."

A considerable pause gave chase. The boy thought perhaps he had fumbled a bit and said it all wrong, but his fear was thrown asunder by the start of a lengthening smile across Roy Senior's face.

"Brilliant! Here, here," Senior said with widened eyes and a glass raised high. "The lad has as good a tongue as he has a pen and there is something to be said for that!"

Junior followed, for Junior seemed doomed to do nothing but follow. He was succeeded by Janice, who consented with a kind glance of her own and a slow tilt of her glass, allowing for the impression of a wink, though not just by eye alone.

Truly, the woman was at the start of a flirt as it could not be more clear that her father's praise directed almost entirely the sails of her heart. A kind wind, therefore, was starboard and pushing. What more could the boy do but proffer a smile in return! And so, he smiled.

Thus, the courtship was decidedly afoot and was eagerly supported by Senior and, by consequence, Junior. Senior, in fact, was intrigued by the idea of the match. His darling Janice was clearly the jewel of his eye and Barthalamew was a talented fellow on the verge of wonderful things.

Senior's support of the boy was all but cemented following the successful run of the Gazette's special edition. By way of Barthalamew's clever prose, the Littleton's quickly found themselves the toast of the town, celebrated at both ends of Port Street, at the high end especially. It was quite clear that the restoration of the King Robert's Arms would attract as much business as was needed to succeed and Roy Senior, inasmuch as he was pleased with himself, thought to share this wealth of self-joy with the clever lad. A second dinner, he decided, was just the thing. And so, a second invitation was sent and received.

Oh, sweet bliss. Barthalamew had never known such kindness and by way of such considerable wealth. His heart was fluttered and fattened to the point of exhaustion. The boy could barely breathe for want of knowing her sight again, for the idea of being invited once more to the inn where she stood happily, knowingly in waiting.

Indeed, the matter required some better effort on his behalf. And so, Barthalamew put himself once more before Joan Theryoung and her dead father's trunk and was sent back to Port Street in a faded but more tolerable fashion.

All confidence that night was his. It was spotted with ease by the look of his eye and by the stride of his gait as he stepped again to that blessed door and rapped once more upon that good and waiting wood. And when the old man finally answered, Barthalamew gave not a thought in the world as to whether or not he remembered his name or whether he had ever been made aware of it.

"Old man," was his greeting, fast and kind and as sure as ever that such a salutation would easily do.

"Yes," pause, "sir."

"Roy Senior sent."

And with this Button dutifully stepped aside and let the boy and all his wayward hopes back into the King Robert's Arms, where his dreams now freely roamed, where he hoped, at every turn, to find and know that tall and proper girl and her waiting pile of embroidered hair, where he simply begged to find the ease of her kindly form and smile. Oh, what a blessed child at heart he was, for heart was so dearly new to him!

Barthalamew was then led to the library where Senior was found, standing before Junior, each with a proper pre-dinner smoke in hand, each pleased for the wealth of the room and, of course, for the wealth of the house. The camaraderie of men was clearly at hand and the boy, being rather new to the idea, took his awkward seat.

There was quick conversation about a good many topics such as the weather and the church and the poor misguided Deacon who had been thoroughly ruined by so much word-of-mouth that Barthalamew could not help but wonder if he should just give in and add to the heap. But then the topic once more changed and changed ten times more before Button returned and, as though a tired rooster, cleared his throat and made his obligatory call for dinner.

The three men then adjourned to the dining room and it was here Barthalamew finally found Janice and her nearly impossible hair in waiting. With a good deal of rattle and prattle, she stepped up to greet him and then invited him to sit across from her just before the head of the table. It was clearly a favorable placement, made all the more obvious by Junior's fast look of unease for, in that moment, he was inexplicably displaced.

It was Senior, then, who took his own seat, who sat ahead of them all and signaled for the feast to begin. Thusly, dinner was underway. All the familial courtesies and formalities quietly surfaced. Every kindness was applied to every passage of food, every smile afforded to each and every request.

It was so impossibly foreign to the boy and yet, his heart was quickly comforted by the sight of it all. As that second meal was underway, the boy realized that his love was no longer just for the girl. His adoration of those kindly moments at the King Robert's Arms was about the notion of home, permanence, and the one thing he always wanted but never had.

Family.

"Mr. Buckett," from Roy Sr. "What say you of your potted stew?"

"It is a delight," Barthalamew eased with a grateful smile.

"Junior?" the question was then redirected to the uprooted lad. "Is it as excellent as Mr. Buckett suggests?"

"Yes, father, delightful," though Junior's lacking enthusiasm was easily noted.

A curious silence then held as Senior again omitted to advance the question to his waiting daughter. At this point, Janice had only to extend her begging syllable.

"Fah!"

Fah, indeed!

And so, the meal proceeded with little variation from the previous dinner. Between courses and bites and courtly chews, Senior engaged in a good deal of men's talk while Janice continued with her monosyllabic dissents. Bathalamew, clearly so in love as he was, simply agreed to agree with all possible sides while he enjoyed his much better-than-average stew.

As the second hour neared, the dinner was completed, and the stately affair drew to a close.

Senior was all smiles. Janice was all fahs. Junior was all flustered by his curious displacement before that inexplicable boy, a concern that was quietly disclosed by a number of telling glares.

Of course, Barthalamew gave it no notice. There was only Janice, now, for his wanting eye. There was only the sound of her many fah's and the baubles that bobbled about her heap of hair whenever she glanced to him or from him but, especially, to him. There was only the unrelenting thirst to find, to capture, to hold and provide for whatever she was after.

As well, Senior's consent was all but irrefutable. Barthalamew appeared to have the patriarch's absolute stamp of approval. That unexpected notion of acceptance gave the boy's heart a good jolt. Could life be more blessed for all that it so suddenly was!

And so, with the evening done and farewells given, Barthalamew was escorted to the door where he took his leave once more of the King Robert's Arms. Port Street was now at his feet. Dog was at his heel. That old bug was overhead, calling him west to his dark and scanty room.

"Mr. Buckett!"

As the hour was nearly late, the common room of the Jasmine House was mostly cleared.

"Mr. Buckett!"

But, of course, she remained. How could she not! Mrs. Lora was rather vigilant as it came to the comings and goings, though mostly the comings, of her varied tenants. This proved especially true after dusk.

"I say, Mr. Buckett," she persisted, for it was her very nature to persist. "There is raisin porridge left over."

Barthalamew gave a quick smile and a tip of his hat but nothing more. He was well fed. He was well pleased. He was readied for a candle, for his room, for his sleep. It was only his intention to pass and make for the stairs ahead, but her voice came again and this time with something like a shrill.

"Mr. Buckett! Have we not spoken about that…dog?"

Barthalamew quickly glanced his feet. Dog was in. Dog was at his heel. Dog was clearly intent for the stairs as well. Barthalamew considered and then confidently gave his answer.

"Yes, ma'am. I believe we have."

The boy's surefire tone gave Mrs. Dean a bit of a shock. It was her want, her absolute need to press back but Barthalamew and his wretched companion were already past, were at the stairs and then up the stairs and gone from sight before she could even begin to mount her protest.

A gasp was let, followed by the start of a word that was never quite formed. Her mind raced. Her heart pulsed. Something was so very different! Something was so very...

By Molly, was her fast and curious thought, what the devil is in that boy!

14

From time to time, Barthalamew agreed to accompany the Theryoungs to Sunday service at High-Street Church. This was done with some reluctance, as the matter of church-going was decidedly not a good fit for the boy. It was to a church, after all, that he was abandoned, and it was from a church that he was literally expelled. Therefore, the notion that some God or another had anything to do with such a place confounded him entirely.

And yet, Mrs. Theryoung's occasional invitation was accepted for the boy could not deny a request from such a proper heart. Thusly, Barthalamew made his periodic steps to the furthering heights of Port Street where the aptly named High-Street crossed and made a perfect chancel of itself. The boneyard alone trumpeted an obvious wealth, with its formal fencing and high-standing stones, each lined in its perfect row, each atop its perfect ground and all before the exceedingly rich doors of that exquisite house of worship.

Indeed, it was nothing like any church Barthalamew had seen or known before. The exterior was unusually bright and overly ornate. Its many eye-catching angles and curves and architectural feats were fierce and vaunting and unbelonging to all the canons of practicality. It begged one to scoff and look away, but who could ever turn from something so imperious, so terrifying, so wonderfully overdone!

The interior was no less pretentious. Here thrived gaudy cuts of hued glass, patterned slabs of windows that fractured the incoming light into a thousand different colors before firing it off into as many directions. As well, the spacious nave was lined with rich looking pews of remarkably rough wood where the whole of the congregation sat as though upon a legion of solid brick. To the front of it all was an altar of unusual design. It was daring in its fashion, unrelenting in its wealth and openly begging for some Godly attention.

To be sure, the ceiling was vaulted, as church ceilings tend to be. And yet, Barthalamew had never seen anything quite like it. He was startled at first. How could he not be? The roof was untouchable and, thereby, entirely unpatchable! By his own account, it seemed a remarkably impractical height.

And beneath it all, the aggregate wealth of Alagood gathered and systematically devoted its Sunday mornings to some kindly thanks and praise and, of course, a good deal of singing. To better underscore the point, allow me to suggest that song was foremost on the docket and seemingly without end.

At first, it seemed agreeable. By the boy's own limited experience with churches, music was all but expected. And so, Barthalamew settled into the hymns and even made an effort to lend his pitiable voice.

However, a curious pattern then emerged. The first song was promptly followed by a second. The second song was pursued by a third. A fourth immediately prevailed. And then, inexplicably, a fifth.

A silence was then courted as the collective was allowed its breath before another song launched from the floor and, again, cleared the high rafters. And then another was signaled and completed. By Barthalamew's mind, it seemed more than enough for any sort of God who happened to be floating by at the time and yet another song was then piled on, apparently for good measure.

And then a miraculous break. Silence succeeded once more and was happily extended. The singing was concluded. There was now only for the plump and pleased middle-aged pastor to effort his way to the podium as though he was being anointed with each and every step. He then looked to the those many before him, offered his thin-lipped smile and raised his fatted arms.

"Good people," he started, for it was only too kind to suggest that the people, being there for so much singing to their invisible and, likely, uncaring God, were remarkably good. "Today, we offer our praise and many thanks!"

Well, to be sure, the many good people were only too happy to offer as much.

"Praise be to Him!" the resounding reply.

Once more, the many voices died and gave way to an echoing silence. In that simple moment, the church proved its softened, more romantic side. Though fleeting, it was Barthalamew's favorite part of the service. The pastor then continued.

"I speak to all of you with a heavy heart as we face the many dangers of lower society."

Well, to be sure, higher society is always quite flummoxed by the lower.

"We stand before hard times," the pastor pressed, "and we call upon our God to guide us, to provide for us a passage through the many months and years ahead." Hard times, indeed! "Sin stands before us all and takes many forms. We have seen it strike down and take from this very congregation!"

The passion of the pastor was quite clear. The temper of his voice could not be more focused, more purposed. Sin was obviously upon the better people by way of the lesser.

"Hear me as I command our God to save us from the wretched evil that corrupts those better fellows among us!"

Indeed, there was only to hear.

"I speak of our fallen comrade!" whom he dared not name, until he did. "Dudley Doyle!"

And then a pause for effect and the pause was fully appreciated. A good deal of murmuring stepped to and flitted about. Words were tossed as though bullets; targeted, sharp and piercing. The pastor then raised his arms again and the nave fell quiet.

"Wickedness is unforgivable!"

Murmuring. Bullets.

"Sins of the flesh are abysmal and ungodly!"

The congregation erupted. The fervor was quickly discomforting. The boy was nearly shaken from his rock-hard seat. At the time, Barthalamew could hardly put a finger on it, but allow me to suggest it quite clearly. Here was the great and spirited sound of Hypocrisy.

135

"God forbids the notion of improper congress before and especially during the course of marriage." the pastor said before his incensed crowd, then quickly corrected himself. "Outside of your beloved spouse, of course!"

But, of course. Improper congress. Beloved spouse. By Molly, every syllable was as though a whirlwind of Godly command!

"Our former Pastor Doyle fell prey to the devil's grip and was submerged into a life of lust and want. He gave into the advances of wrong and evil women. He allowed these women to touch him in places that were not theirs to touch. And he, in turn, touched them very much in a number of places that are not acceptable in the eyes of his marriage or before the heart of our God!"

To be sure, those words were rather stifling and for a good many reasons. To start with, Barthalamew had not been properly versed in such matters by the sisters. The notion of sex was briefly glanced upon during his last year among with the order, but this notion of touching seemed, to his uninformed heart, immaterial. In fact, it was all rather confusing until the boy took note of the quieted crowd around him. The men, in particular, had an eager look about their eyes, as though there was some distinctive need to hear a good deal more about these very specific touches of Mr. Doyle.

"He and all like him," the pastor yelped, yanking his audience from its whetted trance, "will burn in the pits of the devil's never-ending Hell. So, let it be said, so let it be done!"

The crowd echoed in kind and with splendor.

"So, let it be said, so let it be done!"

And with that, another song was pursued and put to those high and waiting rafters. Three more hymns were then called for before the congregation was seated and asked to offer some kind but silent prayer for the many fallen souls whose greatest crime, more oft than not, was more before man than it could ever be before any God.

After a full minute, the silence was broken one last time.

"Love and be loved!" from the pastor.

"Love and be loved!" from the congregation.

Well, to be sure, this had a contrary sound to the pastor's previous rant which, to Barthalamew's ears, was not so much about loving or being loved as it was about judging and being judged. Indeed, the idea of religion at this point was an absolute conundrum to the boy. If the pastor and the assemblage was to be believed, there existed a God who promised forgiveness for all sins but only after a lifetime of torment and condemnation by the many who smugly championed his cause of unconditional love.

What a misery was this thing called church! Why would anyone consider it? How could such a God and such a people possibly account for one another?

At that moment, the boy was resolved. There was only to leave it, to simply walk away, to be done with a church once and for all.

"Bart!" was the pastor's greeting as he stepped from the nave to the waiting midday sun.

"Barthalamew," was the boy's quieted correction.

But the pastor had no need to hear it. It had been and would always be Bart, for Bart was barely a man worth knowing before so many. And so, the preacher pressed on, for it was his very job to do so.

"Joan!"

Of course, he would have her name correct.

"Pastor, it was a lovely service."

That seemed by the boy's good ear an unusual descriptor.

"Well, God speaks to me and through me!" was the jovial reply. And then, "Toby!"

Of course, he would have his name correct.

"Thank you for your good words, pastor."

"They are not my words, but the words of our God."

Bart was all the more dizzied by the pastor's need to constantly say as much and with such a vacant smile.

"It is an awful thing that has happened to Mr. Doyle."

Joan's choice of words struck Bart's ears poorly. The boy had want to say something on behalf of Mr. Doyle, but the pastor was quick to turn the dagger.

"For the many years that I have known him, I have always sensed some evil on the surface."

"Even when..." Bart started, then stopped.

The many around stopped along with him. A small crowd held, curious of the boy's voice as it seemed on the verge of a challenge.

"Even when what?" from Joan who, despite her query, offered a supporting tone.

Bart was clearly caught off guard. His voice surfaced before he could check it. He looked to Toby as though to apologize but then realized that the apology was not his to give but to have.

"Even when," he softly continued, "he raised over ten-thousand silver to build the children's hospital in Bourg?"

A fast and telling pin drop could be heard. Barthalamew pursued, more confidently now.

"A councilman in Bourg claimed that Mr. Doyle's selfless effort has saved the lives of nearly a hundred children so far and hundreds more will be saved in the coming years."

Another dropped pin. Mouths agape.

"Was he evil," Barthalamew pressed and with building volume, "when he opened his home to an impoverished, terminally ill woman and her child so that she would not have to die alone on the streets? Was he evil when he paid for her proper burial and then continued to raise that child as his own and even sent him to university?"

Pins! Pins! Pins! An absolute racket of pins!

"By my accounts, sir, which are documented and according to actual fact, if Mr. Doyle is evil, then we should all strive for evil!"

The pastor's smile was vacant no more. It was, in fact, in ruins and begging for a proper fix. Bart placed his own smile accordingly as he efforted his final words on the matter.

"When you pray for *my* salvation next Sunday, sir, please note that my name is not Bart."

Joan squashed a fast smile and Toby gave up a quieted grin as Barthalamew turned and stepped away from High-Street Church, never to be admitted again until, of course, well, you know.

15

The third dinner invitation arrived at the Hamm and was promptly placed before Barthalamew who simply looked to it as though there were a thousand more to come. Such a head was unlike the boy. Mr. Loydford was stunned, to the point of being inquisitive.

"Mr. Buckett, this seems to be the start of a habit."

"Aye," was Barthalamew's reply, now as a man with more confidence than sense.

And, in that moment, Loydford knew. The boy was hopelessly in love. The editor held his tongue as he quietly considered a proper challenge to the Barthalamew's sensibilities.

"By the week's end," he then said, "I shall need a thousand words on the state of the wharf and the fisherman's life!"

The assignment was accepted with barely a nod.

"Aye."

Loydford's annoyance quickly swelled. Barthalamew was not in step. Indeed, the most useless words ever put to a page were at the very brink of invention. The boy's pen was clearly lost to a girl!

In Barthalamew's defense, the deadline was handily met, and the article was submitted but it could not have been less inspired. In fact, it was something nearing rubbish, but what could Loydford do? There was only to beg against the boy's good spirit, to hope for some coming suffrage.

It was not so much that Loydford was an evil man, but a man of profit and practicality and he knew, above all, that it was neither profitable nor practical for his writer to go traipse about life as a man happily in love. After all, to satisfy a writer's heart is the death of a writer's art. If love was to be provided for the boy, it would forever be the enemy of the Hamm!

"I am to my dinner," Barthalamew said with a slighted smile.

Loydford barely had the want to look up. The miserable thousand words were now in his hands and he had no more use for it than all the devils of Bazre. There was a want, a need to seethe. And so, he seethed.

"So be it."

Barthalamew stepped once more to the neighboring door of the King Robert's Arms and made his presence known. Again, the old man answered and greeted with his many pauses. Again, the boy was led to the library where he was greeted by Senior and given to some manly small talk. Again, all were summoned to dinner where, again, Barthalamew was greeted by the lovely Janice and her ever-rising mast of hair.

Her smile, her curtsy, the sweet sound of her voice kept his heart high and ever-beating.

Barthalamew was now as sure as ever that love was all but a given but, of course, love is no such thing at all.

The boy was again directed to sit next to Roy Senior. The meal was then brought forth and the dining portion of the evening was once more under way.

"I say, Buckett," again from Senior, for it always seemed his want to ask, "what say you of that rib?"

It was quite remarkable and Barthalamew thought to say as much. The question was then put to the displaced Junior, who had not the heart to say anything other than all of the most agreeable words. The question was then, again, not put to Janice, but her answer came nonetheless.

"Fah!" was her response from the shadowed face beneath that glorious and unstoppable head of hair.

"My dear, you and your mouth must learn some restraint," Senior said with aplomb.

"Of course, I must. We all must, father. All women must know restraint, must know their tiny little place in the world."

It was as clear as could be for Senior and Junior that hers was the simple sound of ladylike abdication. Barthalamew, however, was not as convinced. He sensed some touch of daring and adored her all the more for it.

Love, after all, remained his cause. No word of hers could be considered less than remarkable to his ears. And so, the boy stared and without any care in the world as to who might take notice.

"My dear Barthalamew," Senior then pressed, "you do have some eyes on you!"

With something nearing absolute certainty, Barthalamew pulled his captive gaze from his beloved and offered Senior a smile. "How can a man have eyes otherwise before such company as this?"

Senior smiled. Janice beamed. Junior had only the inclination to smirk. It seemed the dinner had found its high-note almost at once and it was only too easy for it to proceed accordingly.

The evening ended as well as the others, but this time there was a noted difference. To start with, there were fewer fahs and by a good measure. For this, Barthalamew was quite pleased as it allowed him a chance to become better acquainted with the many other words and sounds Janice thought to espouse.

As well, Senior prompted Junior to join him in the library, leaving Barthalamew at the table with Janice. It seemed a rather unusual gesture. At once, the innkeeper's daughter thought to say as much.

"I think my family is rather fond of you," she offered with a fast and telling bat of an eye.

"I think I am fond of your family," Barthalamew said with ease, "and with a certain daughter in particular."

Janice played along. Coyly, she jested, "A particular daughter? But there is only the one!"

"Yes, there is only and forever the one."

Barthalamew's heart was aflutter. His eyes were fastened to hers. His want was clear. His love was begging.

Janice leaned ever closer, and closer still, her smile pressing.

"I wonder," she teased.

"What do you wonder, my dear?"

"If you dance as well as they say."

"Perhaps better," the boy said without hesitation.

Clearly, he was bolstered by the closing distance between the two, her smile now so warm, that towering head of hair shadowing anything and everything that ever made him feel lonesome or bitter or lost to the world.

"I wonder…" from Janice again, who was suddenly just a bit closer. "If you are as good…"

The words lingered as her lips neared. The want for a kiss was inexplicably at hand. Janice closed her eyes and eased her advance until her lips finally met his. Softly. Sweetly.

Barthalamew's heart exploded at the touch. The boy jolted in his seat. Fear gripped his soul but was then immediately quashed by the most euphoric sensation he would ever know. For the first and only time in his life he knew the proper touch of a woman. It was, to be sure, nothing short of—

"Excuse me, madam!"

It was the harsh voice of the old man that descended and destroyed. The butler had returned to clear a setting. Janice staggered, suddenly aware of her own impropriety. Her syllable launched at once.

"Fah!"

It was so suddenly loud and uninviting and then followed with a fast and furious hand. Her slap reached Barthalamew's helpless face with a reddening pop.

"You, sir, are a foul and debased man!"

You may be sure those words were quickly confusing. Barthalamew looked from Janice to the old man, then to Janice again. It was his want for some safe and proper harbor but none, clearly, was to be found. To further complicate the matter, Senior was in the room at once.

"What has happened here!" was his fatherly charge.

Janice replied at once and with venom to spare. "He has molested me, father!"

Senior put a soured face to Barthalamew and at once demanded, "Be free of my house, sir. At once! And pray that I do not have you arrested!"

"But, sir…" Barthalamew tried, for he had to try.

"Father!" Janice screamed in what was clearly a specious attempt to emotionally reassert her case.

"You sir," Senior then accused and with the most damning voice of all, "are a scoundrel and a rapist!"

It was as though a sledgehammer was blasted deep into his failing chest and crushed everything in him that was alive. At that moment, the boy instinctively knew. The word was fatal.

There was to be no recourse. There was to be no truth. There was to be no family for him.

And there was never to be a return to the King Robert's Arms.

16

Autumn was over. Winter promised and delivered. Barthalamew, again, kept to his windowless room and drank, again, from so many bottles of rum. He had little need of the day or night, but for going to and coming from work and, when the mood struck, which was not so often, stepping to his lonely seaside bench where he would sit and sadly dwell on his so-called rapist ways.

He took no notice of Dog who, in turn, took no notice of him, and together they noticed not at all the unusually hard gray skies and the curious northerly winds that raced in from all the coldest of places.

Alagood, being coastal and ordinarily thought tropical, was not too often answerable to such northerly conditions, but that year there came a telling chill, the very sort of chill that made naysayers of yea-sayers and yea-sayers of naysayers, that generally brought about a good deal of havoc to that silly business of standing about and saying at will, and without a care in the world, any sort of nay or yea at all.

And every fellow who thought to have a trick knee (for there were far more fellows who thought it than had it) suffered entirely it as it came to sitting or standing or walking about or doing much of anything on account of all that forecasting going on between their unsuspecting hips and feet.

A proper rain was expected and, indeed, it came and stayed the season through. It was not so much an everyday sprinkle; rather, it was a mischievous sort-of stop and go patter that left one neither drowned, nor dried but uncommonly wretched and cold and with an unkind regularity. Barthalamew, however, was immune to it all, for not a bit of it, for not all of it at once, was nearly as wretched and cold as he.

With the slow passing of each miserable month, the boy did little more than wake and work and stumble home and sit and drink and try for sleep. And when the bad dreams came, they came in waves. They drowned his nights in sorrow and all but made him beg for the light of day. And when day stumbled upon his broken world, he found it to be no better than his dreams, which, in turn, made him sick again for night. To the point, he wanted neither and was sadly stuck with both.

It went on like this for weeks on end, for what seemed at great length some other life to which he did not belong, some ghost of a shadow of a shell of a man that was not at all himself but the barren outline of some shamed and needless thing. It was as though he had been purged from the land of the living, as though his heart was remanded to some ethereal plane where it could do no more but look on through the eyes of a soul that once was but was now no more than a wretched and lurking brute.

There would be no mercy for him from that dreadful season of grief! The loss of Janice was ruin enough, but Senior's word found its depth. It scraped bare the absolute bottom of his heart.

Being thus affected, Barthalamew was, by all accounts, a frightful sight. He seemed barely conscious of the day, of any given hour, of his bloodshot eyes and of his rum-filled breath and his tasseled and dirtied hair, of his barely adequate dress, of his constantly muddied shoes and of Dog who remained throughout as wet and as rank and as inexplicably present as ever.

He almost never spoke, almost never looked up. He almost never smiled and when he did, the effect was strangely off-putting. His was not the smile of a pleasant fellow, but that of a man well-dead to all the world. All of this, of course, afforded Mr. Loydford all the usual worries. Work, he was sure, would suffer.

And yet, there emerged, by degrees, the telltale signs of a remarkable, if not altogether unexpected, sort of genius. The boy's misery, it seemed, played out on paper and in the most unusual of ways. Barthalamew fell into his pen like never before. There emerged, to his journalistic efforts, a progressive flow, a decisive rhythm, a veritable dance of words and punctuations that brought about a certain delight to the eye of the reader, that brought about, at any rate, quite a bit of delight to the eye of a very certain editor-at-large.

Barthalamew's simple announcements, once bland and too much to the point, were quite suddenly buoyant and daring. By that long winter's end, the social column had come to life with all the lyrical qualities of a fast-reading novel. As well, there was penned, and seemingly with no thought at all, a rather commanding article kindly regarding an emerging west end artist who had, at the time and by his own good fortune, become exceedingly trendy.

Words had never been so adored. The story was beloved. It was gobbled up. On that particular day the Gazette did something it had never done before. It thoroughly sold itself out. It was gone, entirely, by the stroke of noon. As was the next edition and each edition thereafter for the run of a month.

Barthalamew, it seemed, was writing his way through a dream and Mr. Loydford, for one, had no intention of bringing the boy about. The office of the Gazette was quickly declared a tomb. A moratorium was enacted on every conceivable sound. There was put a sign to the door of the Hamm, as glaring as one could be, forbidding all knocking, all tapping, all talking of passers-by.

Loydford even sacrificed of himself. He managed his footfalls more carefully, walking ever-so-gently and only in his softest shoe and only when he absolutely had to. His voice was respectfully hushed. His typically charged speeches were abandoned to frenetic whispers that he no longer imposed upon his morose but suddenly abled reporter, but only upon himself and only by the use of some distant wall or corner. What did he care if it all made him look like a loon! This, he determined, was his path to riches and by Molly he meant to walk it.

By the full course of those water-logged months it all seemed as though some stretch of time tied to a history all its own. The season played itself out not as a season, but as an epoch. In the end, however, winter rolled over, threw up its feet and took to all its usual deaths. Those far-reaching north winds finally ebbed. The sun revived, the many puddles dried up and there emerged with vigor all the customs of spring.

Oh, how life did come around! Oh, how it so nearly burst at the seams, so anxiously pressing itself into place, clamoring for its inch, for its foot, for its ever-crowding mile. Alagood, by nature's kind brush, was so slathered in green that particular spring that not a soul in town could help but feel reborn, not a single soul, that is, but one. Young Barthalamew was so lost to the dark that he barely understood the sudden presence of light.

And then, one day, he did.

It was the dryness of his socks that brought him about, that awakened the poor boy to a promising change. For the full run of the previous winter, his feet were so continually soaked that there was only to believe that they would always be so. And yet, he stepped to the Hamm one particular morning, beneath the kindest of skies and the most sensible sun with the driest toes in all of Kirkland.

Indeed, what a difference that made, for there was discovered, just then, something like a spring in his step. And there was felt, just then, as inviting a breeze as had ever been felt. And there was heard, just then, such a medley of songs by as many birds as any one morning could possibly hold.

And as Barthalamew made his way up Port Street was he not just then assaulted by the enticing smells of Dusenberry's fine bakery? By Molly, he was and how was it, he asked himself at once, that he had ever lost hold of that glorious scent to begin with!

And was not that bulbous fellow, who was just then crossing the street and tipping his hat to old Mrs. Kinsey, his over-eager boss? You may be sure it was. And was not Mr. Loydford just then coming to the door of the Hamm at precisely the same moment as he? Well, one may hardly call it coincidence for it happened often enough. And yet, was not that the very same door to the illustrious Hamm that Barthalamew was now walking past and was not that the solicitous cry of Mr. Loydford giving chase?

Indeed!

"Buckett!" were not these his very words? "I say, Buckett! Where are you off to? The Gazette is waiting! Deadlines hold for no man! Buckett!"

And did not the fading sound of that agonized voice reach his ears like a song, like the most pleasant lullaby as could ever be imagined? And did not the King Robert's Arms seem quite suddenly invisible to him as he ambled past!

Well, I daresay he took no notice. Not in the very least. It was as though the damnable building was never built. It was as though there was nothing whatsoever for the great Alagood Rapist to see in its place.

And did it not appear that Barthalamew was a bit taller with each and every fugitive step away from those lower, lesser steps? Well, I suppose we must chalk that up to Port Street's rather dramatic rise, but for anyone who might have thought to look on, not that anyone did, the consensus very well might have been that the boy was climbing more than a street.

And so, climb he did, for he knew where he was going, for he knew the way quite well. Past the Great Raff Pub he spryly stepped, past Hender's cobbler shop, past the fancy clothier and its window dressed with all its fancy cloth; past the high-end boutiques and the high-end homes that fancied the top of that first big hill; past the High-Street churchyard, as green and dead as it had ever been, alongside High-Street church; past the simple road that ambled north to Toby Theryoung's porch; past Port Street's cobbled end where was found the worn and waiting path that urged him on and upward still; past all the things that could be passed until that peak was reached and that view was had and that waiting bench was found.

However, on that particular day, at that particular moment, the boy was to be denied.

"Good morning to you, sir!"

A woman! Upon his bench! A dear girl fast at work on some dainty project of her own! Barthalamew could not help but be astonished. Her words came fast. She barely made effort to turn about.

"Good morning," the boy stammered. "My apologies. I did not know—"

"Oh, but what is there to apologize for? It is as much your scene as it is mine. It is as much anyone's for that matter."

With that said, the woman turned in greeting and demonstrated the kindest of smiles. For the first time in months, Barthalamew realized a smile of his own. His soul eased as his eyes absorbed the woman's kind presence. At once, he realized there was much to appreciate.

A colorful bonnet framed her modest face. She was dainty, mousey, smallish in nature, in voice, in everything about her. The poor boy's heart could not help itself. At that moment, it was hers.

"You may sit with me if you like, sir. I am always fond of good company."

There could be no doubt of the impropriety of her suggestion, but it was so kindly a proposal and from so kindly a face, that Barthalamew could hardly consider refusing. A casual glance quickly provided for the fact that she was rather busied, needling away with vigor, doing who knew what to what seemed the start of some poor hat. In a moment he understood.

"You are the milliner's daughter?" for he had seen her before at market and there was word about town that she was more than a bit outspoken.

"Indeed, sir. Gretchan Coopersmith at your service." And with that, the woman launched. "T'is always a pleasure to make a new acquaintance and I always make it a point to try why I hardly think there's a soul in town that I do not know by some means or another except for you of course but I am

150

guessing by your looks that you must be that fellow what works at the Gazette who prints the socials and whatnot am I right?"

All of this was said with the most forceful sort of rhythm and without the notion of any pause or punctuation. By comparison, the boy's reply was remarkably slow.

"Yes, ma'am. I am Barthalamew—"

"Luckett or Puckett or some such?"

"Buckett."

"Yes, that's it! Mr. Buckett of the Gazette a fine name and a fine print my father does say and therefore so do I for father is as wise as a dozen owls on all literary matters why there's not a book that I have heard of that he has not read and I daresay the first thing he thinks to read at the start of each and every week is the Alagood Gazette and that is as fine a thing as can be said of your good paper Mr. Buckett. Please do sit. It's quite concerning with you standing over me like that."

And so, the boy took his seat next to the milliner's daughter and together they shared a good number of smiles as she needled away and talked away what remained of that fateful morn. Barthalamew, for his part, could barely take his eyes from her kindly features, from her dainty nose, from her attentive smile.

How precious were those waiting gifts! How exquisite was her voice with its simple call and its unending catalog of words! How divine the look and sound, of every little thing about Gretchan Coopersmith! The boy could hardly imagine loving anything more.

Time surrendered the scene. The hours sounded retreat. There seemingly remained nothing now between day and night but for the charge of her constantly coming words.

"...so bothered was I that I could barely sleep for a fortnight, a fortnight I tell you, and what a long stretch of endless days that turned out to be..."

Barthalamew looked on in quieted awe, cherishing the kind form of her lips as they rapidly waged everlasting war on all the established principles of brevity. The stories of her life came and went with such alacrity that the boy had no choice but to try and keep up.

"...the headaches that caused, I tell you. It was just so curious what he thought to do then for no one ever expected so much as all that, it just wasn't like him you see not like him at all to even think to do half as much as all that and to so unsuspecting a person as my dear old father who in truth isn't all that old but is every bit as dear a man as any dozen or so..."

What a curious kindness was that constant sound! It was so light and crisp and came to him as though across some heavenly stretch and for the sake of his very own ear. It was, to him, the whisper of an angel, albeit an angel with a great deal to say.

"...for what sake I ask you? Well, you may be sure it was for no sake at all for he had no business in the affair, in any affair for that matter and he could no more see reason than a dozen blind men could see a barn door and I don't know any one blind man much less any dozen that could possibly see any such thing..."

But what did he care about so much prattle! That she was there at all was a quick kindness to the boy, having suffered such a dull and quiet winter. It was as though three months' worth of voices were finding him at once.

As the morning kindly passed, the boy could not help but feel more and more drawn to Ms. Coopersmith with all the smiles and winks and her hundred words a minute! How sweet the day proved to his wanting heart and ears!

"...for what was father to do under such a circumstance such as that? Well, you may be sure he did the right thing but sometimes the right thing doesn't feel as right as you might like it to, as anyone might like it to because the right thing can sometimes be a trickier thing than a dozen blind monkeys in a barrel..."

The morning collapsed into noon and noon began its gentle slide into mid-day and the words kept piling on. All the while the milliner's daughter needled more and more until the thing in her lap appeared more like a hat until it actually was a hat and even a proper hat at that, for all the punishment she seemed to give it.

"I am done," she finally stated.

And, indeed she was and, in more ways than one, for the coming silence, noting its chance, finally let loose a long and satisfying sigh. Gretchan Coopersmith completed her hat and likewise completed her chatter. She stood and offered up her hand to Barthalamew.

"Goodbye, Mr. Buckett."

"Goodbye, Ms. Coopersmith."

"Perhaps we shall meet again," said she with a subtle smile. "I enjoy the view on occasion. Shall I send word when I step this way again?"

It was a rather bold suggestion from the young milliner's daughter, but the notion of her good company immediately gladdened the boy's soul.

"Yes. I would like that very much."

"So it shall be, sir."

And with that, the Gretchan offered a kind curtsy and departed the scene, leaving Barthalamew behind to tend to his suddenly awakened heart.

17

"So it shall be!"

And with that the gavel came down and, per usual, the vote of the order was cheerfully noted. There was to be built a new maintenance shed at a slight distance behind the church. It was to replace the barely standing shed which, at the time, was more in need of pity than renovation. A number of men, for only men did such things, were hired for the task and in a matter of days it was done. The old shanty was put down and a new one was put in its place.

It was, however, only new by its look. The good sisters of the order chose against much in the way of expense. The result was something new that easily appeared on the verge of becoming something old. Nonetheless, it was concluded that this new structure, in addition to providing storage for tools, would also serve as a new home to Barthalamew and Toby, for the boys were fast coming upon a certain age that was, by unanimous vote, decidedly dangerous.

To the point, while the two had grown to be nothing short of champions of propriety, their simple blankets in the nave would no longer stand. They simply could not remain quartered under the same roof as so many women. And so, as the finishing touches were applied, the young lads took hold of their meager belongings, routinely kept beneath their respective pews, and walked them from one building to the next.

Clearly, it was something like a banishment and yet it was very much like a gift. After all, neither child had anything like a home for themselves and, quite suddenly, one was there. Though it was not a lively sort of room at all and, though, a good number of cracks ran about it, allowing, with ease, as much weather as weather wanted, it was, by their minds and hearts, the most impenetrable realm.

That the whole of the shed shook when the winds commanded made no difference to them. That it seeped all sorts of rain was no matter at all. That it tried and tried to fight back the cold and lost on every front was barely a concern.

That shack was now their home. Those were now their walls. That was their dirted floor and just above was their flimsy roof. And while not a bit of it could be considered majestic, by any stretch of the imagination, it was, to the boys, exactly so.

Barthalamew was assigned the small corner opposite the door, and while it could not have possibly amounted to anything more than something just above homelessness, the boy embraced his little spot on the floor with as much heart as he had to lend it. The tiny spot was cherished and without reservation. The boy finally had a true space to claim.

For his part Barthalamew had little more than a hay-stuffed mattress and pillow, beneath which was kept a book by the title of "Pirates, Scamps and Scallywags, Too". Indeed, the title sounded rather treacherous, but Sister Marihanna allowed it, as it provided wondrous tales of life on the high seas. By her blessed heart, it seemed a boy should have as much. And so, Barthalamew had it and treasured it, for the nature of those youthful years allowed little else to treasure.

The boy's blanket rounded out his possessions and, to be sure, it was just barely a blanket. The failing cloth had more holes than not and was so terribly faded as to give no hint of its original hue. As well, it had no true chance of providing for any degree of warmth from any sort of weather that happened to wander in.

And yet, what a dear thing it was to Barthalamew's heart. While it was not anything one would normally think to want, it was entirely his for the wanting. And so, the boy wanted it. By way of the coming years, he would come to know other blankets, newer blankets, even warmer blankets, but none would be so adored and remembered as his first.

By comparison, Toby lived a life of luxury. He quickly claimed the remaining corners of that rackety shed for himself and likewise cluttered them with a scattering of his own personal effects, things made to look like things,

155

youthful attempts at woodwork and whatnots. The more valuable the effect the more immediate their proximity to Toby's mattress, which stretched out across a makeshift bed that allowed an easy rise over Barthalamew's tiny, floor bound world.

From his throne of blankets, Toby beamed and ruled the room as any good king would, but Toby was no fool. Soon, he knew, he would be forced to advocate. His time with the order was drawing nigh.

As mentioned, that cramped little space, boasting its cramped little kingdoms, was not entirely their own. It was shared with a variety of remarkably rusted tools, most of which were aged beyond use but used no less for there was always a need. Hammers, saws, axes and augers each had a spot of their own, either hanging by some equally rusted nail or placed upon the workshop bench that lined the nearby wall as a neighbor to Toby's domain. Ever quietly but ever present, those old tools resided, as though some bit of art, some rustic décor.

Privacy, being now truly allowed, put the boys in a more sociable mood. By the confines of that suddenly removed shelter, a good many night's discussion allowed for a proper bond. The matter of the order and the ever evolving, often conflicting, tales of Cecilia were targeted most, closely followed by a number of very critical opinions with respect to Sister Josephine. The old bird made for an easy target as it remained her constant insistence that each child was to eventually be evicted from their shiny and happy new home. As such, the old bird was not spared a villainous word.

Sometimes a lighter mood prevailed. On those nights, Toby spoke of his past, of some aunt who took him in and made effort to provide for the both of them. He spoke highly of her good spirits and then lowly of her failing health and then, with a tear, of her final words which, though once promised, were not of the whereabouts of his parents but of some love long since lost.

The story, often repeated, had a curious effect on Barthalamew. There was always this mention of a thing called love. It struck the boy as something worth knowing and, very soon, it became his want to know. And so, one night he thought to ask.

"What is love?"

"Love!" Toby said, almost yelled, openly offended by the simple sounding of this dry and daring syllable. "Love is nothin' to know!"

"But you said...your aunt..."

"Shut your trap!"

Clearly the word did not sit well with Toby. This was emphasized by the start of a tear which was concealed at once with a blow to his candle. Silence prevailed as the three corners of that shack fell into darkness.

Confused by the outburst, Barthalamew's attentions were then put to his own wavering candle and to the howling of the nighttime winds that eased their songs through the waiting cracks of that pitiful shed. His mind was racing. His heart was trembling. His sleep, he knew, was now ruined by the curious power of that seemingly uncomplicated word.

In the morning the boy was wearied from thought. He made no effort for breakfast. By noon he was at a stumble. He moved through his chores as though nearing a slumber at any moment.

Lydia, of course, was the first to notice, as noticing Barthalamew was now her specialty. At the kindly age of nine, the dear girl was still years ahead of her heart, but her want to comfort the boy had already become an inherent part of her nature. And so, with only her ever-sweet smile to give, she stepped to and proceeded to give it.

Of course, Barthalamew made no effort to accept it. He was young. He was ignorant. He simply lumbered by and carried on with his labors, allowing the girl no more than a simpleton's glance.

Late afternoon finally stepped in. With his chores now completed, the noy was most anxious for supper. He had only just then realized that he had not a thing to eat all day.

And so, Barthalamew made effort to the sacristy where he found Sister Marihanna giving a number of vegetables a vigorous cleanse. She was alone. No one was about. It seemed an ideal time to try once more.

"Sister Marihanna," he ventured, "what is love?"

Although the question was asked with ease, Marihanna was startled by the boy's quieted, unsuspected presence. A number of carrots were fumbled about and then re-collected and put back to a wash.

In that moment, the boy witnessed the power of the word. He saw it in her eyes. He heard it in her voice as the syllable broke from her lips like an evasive rogue begging for the cover of night.

"Love?"

It seemed, by the anxious look on her face, that an answer was both quick to her lips and quick to retreat. The struggle brought about another worrisome look as, once more, she tried to push a reply and again surrendered. By her own heart and, especially, by her inexperience, Marihanna was hard-pressed to know how to provide a proper answer for herself, much less for an eleven-year-old boy.

"Well, Barthalamew..." she tried, with barely a clue as to how to proceed, "Love is what you choose to make of it."

The boy wasted not a second. "What am I to make of it?"

"Well," she started once more, still striving for some traction, "you should make it your want in life. Love is what you should always strive for."

Marihanna was quickly satisfied. The answer was both right and appropriately vague. She was on the verge of turning back to the chore at hand when the boy, as boys do, prolonged the query.

"But...what is it?"

Marihanna dared not turn back. The boy's eyes were a bother. They were sleepy and confused and awfully pressing.

"It is..." she said, then paused. "It is..." she said and paused once more. "It is like the sun, Barth," Marihanna eased with a thankful tone, for she was grateful for this new direction. "On a good day it fills your life with warmth and wonder. On a bad day, you are sad and cold, and you miss it and the sky lets loose its tears by its absence."

Oh, what a blessed response! It was the very perfect thing to say. So affected was Marihanna by her own answer that she could not help but look up through the small window of the sacristy and gaze upon the beautiful blue of that loving sky and give to it her softest smile.

"So, love is like the sun?" the boy asked, every bit as confused as when he began.

"Yes. Love is like the sun," Marihanna happily affirmed with a nod and a shake of a carrot.

"But the sun is so far away," Barthalamew pined.

"And yet how warm it keeps the whole of the world," Marihanna then said with her apple-faced smile. "Perfectly so."

"Yes, Sister Marihanna," was his reply, though it was clear that he deemed the answer unsatisfactory.

Having properly cleansed the carrots, Marihanna placed them towards a cutting board. She then reached for a large potato and put it in the sacristy sink and went about her business of preparing it. It was not her expectation that the topic would persevere.

"But, it's cold here."

Sister Marihanna was stopped. She looked sadly to the potato in hand. The metaphor was rather cutting.

"Aye, Barth," she said, then paused, for there was a part of her that was forced to accept that unkind truth. "Sometimes, yes," she tried with a teacher's patience, "but the cold needed so that we may know to properly celebrate better days."

Yes. That seemed, by her good heart, a fitting thing to—

"But, I don't like the cold so much."

Marihanna glared at the potato.

159

"No one much likes the cold, Barth."

"So, when it's cold, there's no love?"

"Don't be silly. There can always be love. It's just not so common as you might want it to be. That's all."

"Why not?"

Why not, indeed! What a frustrating inquisition from such a daring young boy! Sister Marihanna was overwhelmed by the simplicity of the question and, by consequence, all the more displeased by the difficulty of the answer.

"Love," she then tried, "is like money. "One does well to hold on to it as best one can, for as long as one can, until one finds just the right person to spend it on. That is why, Barth."

That did not clear the matter at all and, in fact, only muddied it all the more. Barthalamew had no choice but to revert to the original example.

"But, you said it's like the sun."

"Well, yes...it is," Marihanna stumbled.

"Is it more like the sun or is it more like the money?"

Marihanna quickly understood how far behind she was on the topic. It occurred to her to bring the thing back under control. She dared not look up from that damned potato.

"Love is a gift for all people," she rebutted. "But for one person, it is the greatest gift of all!"

And that seemed to sum the thing up as well as it could be summed. But, of course...

"But for which person?"

The question, again, was both childish and brilliant and Marihanna could not have been more pleased with her star pupil's line of inquiry. However, another concern just then mounted. All this talk of love could invariably lead to a far less suitable topic. At that moment Marihanna knew she had to arrest the topic and bring it to a fast and tidy conclusion.

"The person most deserving. You will know her when you meet her."

"How will I know?"

"I cannot explain it, but to say that you will," Marihanna replied, realizing just then how impossibly clean was that potato in her hands. "Your heart will leap at the first sight of her. Then and there you will know."

"And I will love her?"

"Yes, you will love her."

"And she will love me?"

"Without question," Marihanna concluded with a confident smile for this, she was sure, would come to pass and, in fact, she was equally sure it already had.

The subject, no doubt, had run its course and to further signal its end Marihanna turned from the sacristy sink, placed that impossibly sterilized potato in another nearby basket, and made her step for the nave. She dared not look to the boy for his eyes, she was sure, were blazing with questions she could no longer answer.

But Barthalamew was quieted now, clearly lost to a mountain of thought. These many answers had a hopeful sound, but the grand mystery remained. How and, more pressingly, where might he know such a love so promised as this? What blessed face, what splendid touch, what impossible girl awaited him?

After all, he had never known a woman outside of the order and he was hard-pressed to understand how he might ever come to meet one. It all seemed so ludicrous, so painfully absurd.

And yet, the most curious of all possible seeds was planted. Its depth was ideal. Its soil could not be more fertile. Its light, by way of the boy's unchecked heart, was as bright as could be. Oh, indeed, that seed would prosper but, in that moment, it was merely the seed.

Barthalamew left the sacristy that day with a virgin sense of longing. It suited him. It felt right. Sister Marihanna, after all, could not have been more assuring. There was only to love. And to be loved. How could there ever be any more. Or less.

The boy then stepped into the nave and was greeted almost at once by the sisters and their obedient rush for dinner. In spite of his emptied stomach, he gave them no mind. It was his young heart that was hungry now, that begged for sustenance. What care had he for the notion of food when the promise of love was suggested!

Barthalamew then stepped from the nave and exited the church where he was greeted by Toby, who was just stumbling to with an allotment of cut wood. The boy gave not a word to the other. The whole of his mind and soul was otherwise committed and to a very specific direction.

Barthalamew continued to the backside of the church and up the bell tower, and then to his favored spot on the roof before that constantly patched hole. The boy then sat and put his eyes skyward to the waiting heavens, to the fading blue of that curious day. At once, the slivered moon was spotted, easing its way westward, as though there was no other way to ease.

There was his old friend, so tired, so distant, so terribly alone, forever forced to march across that thankless sky by the uncaring dark of a hundred-thousand million nights and without so much as a whisper or hope for any such thing called love. There floated the quieted mask of solitude, that impossible beast, glowing yet begging against its lonesome life and death.

That damned rock would never taste the world of love. It would never exist outside of its own friendless orbit. It was only there to rise and fall from the sky and for no one at all. Its very purpose was to be without purpose.

Barthalamew leaned back and put his head against the thatch of the roof and eased a buoyant smile. He was not that old bug. His orbit would change. He was to love. And he was to be loved in return.

The universe, he was assured, would allow nothing less.

18

For all that the effusive Ms. Coopersmith could not think to say, which was, you may be sure, not so very much, the dear woman did effort to write it down. One may therefore presume, by the immutable nature of her talk, that, perhaps, she wrote down very little.

Well, I daresay, rare is the case when one can be as right as one is wrong. While it was true that the milliner's good daughter authored very little, it was equally a truth that she authored quite a lot. That curiosity was daily examined by as many as a dozen letters, each composed, and diligently so, by the start of breakfast so as to make the morning post.

"Dearest Mildred Alice," one such missive began. "Goodness gracious, how are you today?" it then proceeded. "Your very humbled friend and servant, Gretchan Annabell Coopersmith," it then handily concluded.

Well, now, how does that rate for brevity? Top notch I should think. Such a letter as that should have been the very easiest in all the world to receive. However, short and sweet as her notes were, they came so often and to so many that it quickly proved awkward, to say the least, to the many of her list.

To the point, an unusual conduct emerged. To send any response at all only encouraged the girl to answer with another. And so, in time, her many beneficiaries, by varying degrees, tapered off their replies in hopes that she would taper as well.

It was then quickly discovered that to not reply was, in fact, all the same to Gretchan Coopersmith. And so, much to the botheration of her father, who might have been a man of considerable wealth but for the cost of so much postage, her missives continued unabated.

"Dearest Ms. Dolly, is it not the loveliest day ever to make way for the market? Your very humbled friend and servant, Gretchan Annabell Coopersmith."

"Dearest Marian, I do believe I saw you yesterday walking Port Street, and how delightful you looked with your new plum bonnet. Your very humbled friend and servant, Gretchan Annabell Coopersmith "

"Dearest Mr. Bingham, it has come to my attention that Mrs. Bingham is unwell. Please give her my very kindest regards. Your very humbled friend and servant, Gretchan Annabell Coopersmith "

"Dearest Mr. Buckett, what a delight it was to meet and sit with you on what is now my most favorite bench in all the world. Very much your humbled friend and servant, Gretchan Annabell Coopersmith "

It was upon the morning that followed their destined encounter when that last note was delivered to the Hamm. It was found inside a perfectly plain envelope, tightly squared and addressed with a very spirited sort of penmanship.

Upon its unsealing, the note was produced, and those blessed words revealed. A smile never formed so quickly as the smile that came to Barthalamew that day. The rapist's heart was at once aglow and pining.

Unfamiliar with the proclivities of Ms. Coopersmith, the boy could not help but offer his most charming reply. From the depths of his inkwell, the tip of his pen emerged and was put to paper. His scratch was applied. The letter was sealed. The courier was off at once.

Before the hour's end the courier appeared with her retort. Still innocent to the cause, Barthalamew replied once more, every bit as happy to do so. The courier left. The courier returned once more.

Astounded by the kindness, the boy submitted his pen anew. The courier was away. The courier was returned. By the day's end, the boy found himself more than a bit indebted to that wearied fellow who, by that hour, delivered eight of the very briefest letters ever written, much less received.

It was somewhere in the midst of the second day when it occurred to Barthalamew to let go a bit on his replies. Much to the agreement of that wounded-looking courier, he withheld. And yet the courier knew that which the boy did not. Her sweet letters persisted.

Six more letters were received that day. Seven letters were delivered before the following evening. Eight letters arrived at the Hamm the day thereafter. By the week's end, Barthalamew found himself besieged with a legion of pages containing the impossibly concise words of the milliner's overly-communicative daughter.

The more readable letters, being those that were kind, those that suggested nice things about him, about his hat, his eyes, about the good curve of his gentle smile, about his voice, and keen skills as a proper writer were itemized and placed with care atop his second-hand desk in his dark and tiny room at the Jasmine House.

Those letters of a lesser nature, bearing details about her hair; her countless bonnets; her father; her many shoes and the many colors of her many shoes; about her fat cat Piper; about Piper's shoes, which she crafted and presented to her cat and without much success; about the odd rash on her arm and then about its odd dissipation; about her freckles, which were not so many except by her particular count; about her nose; about her toothache; the swelling of her fingers; her knitting with said swollen fingers; her replies from other correspondences as well as the lack of replies; and about every other conceivable and inconceivable minutiae that could be squeezed into as few words and, thereby, as many letters as possible, were summarily abandoned to a bucket of his own before he could offer a second thought.

It was not that he did not love Gretchan or her many, many letters. To the contrary, his heart pined for both. Her letters mattered immensely. There remained, however, the issue of prioritization. It was not truly his wish to dispose of a single word but, for the first time in his young life, the boy came to understand that there can be, by love's youthful nature, such a thing as too much.

Nearly two weeks came and went since their fateful meeting when the milliner's daughter extended her invitation as promised. A task was at hand. She was to do a bit of crafting and was in need of a more inspirational view. The pleasure of his company was requested.

That simple missive was enthroned at once, put to his room and into that waiting second-hand drawer, next to the Hundley invitation and the dinner solicitations from Senior Littleton and just above those now nearly forgotten words wrapped in that ever-fading red ribbon.

And so, on the morning of the intended day, Barthalamew feigned a peculiar illness. A letter of his own was crafted and sent to the Hamm, claiming that he was besieged with "throat cramps". Loydford was rattled at once. It seemed an unlikely suffrage for anyone of the profession, for what writer had need of a throat, cramped or not!

The trick, then, was not to walk Port Street and before the wide-open windows of the Hamm. Barthalamew was forced to try a number of unfamiliar backroads until High-Street was reached. At this point, he resumed the usual path to that entirely beloved cliff where he was greeted at once by the loquacious Gretchan Coopersmith.

"Two weeks, sir. To the day. Do you not find it a splendid day for a proper anniversary?"

Barthalamew was allowed little room to think or say. The answer was given at once.

"Of course, all days are good days for something so kind as the anniversary of our meeting."

"But, of course," he ably replied and then dared, "my dear."

Gretchan was sweetly affected. Her hands halted on the near-bonnet in her hand as she put her eyes towards his and gave him a proper smile.

"How delightful that you call me dear. It has always been my want to be called dear especially from a man of renowned skill a writer even an artist a handsome fellow a proper gentleman and all."

Barthalamew nearly had time to blush.

"Father likes your Gazette so very much and has espoused many great things about your articles and such and I hear nearly every other morning some announcement or story with your name attached and it brings him great joy to read and share these words of yours. It seems you are quite the name in the town with all sort of talk of writing and dancing about and I am rather envious of your adventures sir and I am told I should be envious of your skills with the pen. I have heard your stories are quite delightful."

Gretchan allowed for a rare pause as the boy considered that last thing just said. There was a sting to these words as they reached his ears. His voice returned, gentle but confused.

"Have you not read any of them?"

"Of course not, good sir. That is man's work, reading papers and articles and taking on all the news of the world well it's no place for me to go about reading what you write. I daresay I would not be so inclined to understand it all."

"But," the boy tried, for it was his absolute want for her to know his words, "it is not really the news that I write…"

"Which means it is more than news and what business have I for more than that?"

Barthalamew was stumped. His heart was halted. His want was for some immediate correction on the matter.

"I would really like to have you read something of mine. It would mean a great deal to have your thoughts and heart attached to some word, to some paragraph or page from me. I have a number of poems I could pass on."

Gretchan's working hands came to a fast stop. Her smile suggested some coming kindness, but her voice was just barely amenable.

"Well, sir, that would be silly, and I am not so sure I have so much time as all that, what with all the knitting and letters that I must send out each day. I have a good deal of writing myself, you see, and I mustn't let down my friends nor you, I suppose, for writing is what keeps me in touch with them and, hopefully, always in touch with you."

"Perhaps, I could write you a proper love letter or some story," Barthalamew tried with a dash of sincerity.

"Don't be foolish, sir. I suspect some love letter might be quite sweet, but my time is more precious than all that."

"I see."

And yet, Barthalamew did not see at all. He did not hear at all. His soul was bruised. His only want in all the world was to be read by the woman he loved but the woman, it seemed, was simply too busied. What else could the boy do but press on? And so, with a lowered head, he pressed.

"How has your week been, my dear?"

The inquiry was music to her ears. In a flash, Gretchan's indifference was gone.

"It has been a wretched week as father has made some daring choice if you can believe it and surely I cannot, not at all, not in the least. He swears now that beige is the new style but what do I care about a color so dull as that and yet he has made his orders for the coming months and I am to knit accordingly and life, it seems, is to be all beige all the time no matter what I say or think or want. Beige, beige, beige, beige! I mean, who truly cares about a color that is not really a color. Its beige! Its only beige and will only ever be beige. I think it rather…"

It was a rush of words that quickly swamped the boy's soul. His heart was fractured. His patience was faltered. Gretchan's rant about a colorless color was lost to the wind and the want of his mind to wander with it was quite strong. And so, his mind wandered.

"…Was all just so preposterous. That's what I said, at any rate and you may be sure he heard me well…"

The salty, clean scent of the sea suddenly reached Barthalamew. His senses were taken with the notion of those raging waves below and he found himself rather determined to smell, to hear, to know them all the more.

"…was the silliest thing said in the history of all the kingdom. I mean, how does one even think to go about being so silly as that? You can be sure I had no want to know or hear of such tomfoolery as you may well know I don't deal well with neither Tom nor foolery but only with…"

It was the southerly winds now that took him, that purchased the boy's heart and moved it forward and away from Gretchan's impossibly one-sided chatter. His begging mind raced across the waiting sea, in search of some distant island where, perchance, he would discover some sweet island girl who might at once be enraptured with the idea of knowing some good word of his, some kind note, some loving passage that was crafted from him and only for her. Blessed maiden, so real and yet so fictive…

"…But this, you may be sure, would not stand, would not stand at all before my eyes and you may be sure that I put my foot down loud and hard and upon the floor and with such a force that it gave Little Girl a bit of a fright. Little Girl is my new baby kitty in case you thought to wonder but wondering aside I was most displeased and thought to say as much with every bit of my being…"

…with such lovely island girl eyes and such sweet, precious lips! What kindness by that blessed smile! What promise by her gentle reach…

"…was not father's want but was my want and be sure that my want exceeds father's want entirely that much is sure and yet all of my world this season is beige and nothing but beige and more beige. I am drowned in it and miserable for it, I tell you…"

…and the sparkle of her look, the kindness of her touch. She stood before the boy as though a perfect dream, as though a proper and wanting love, as though the very gift of the universe itself…

"Mr. Buckett!" came the most unusual shriek, only to come again and with a fast touch of stringency. "Mr. Buckett!"

The boy's retreat from the island was underway at once. His mind charged from that happy place and raced across that distant sea and found, once more, the tails of that southerly wind which led him back to the high-standing crag and the bench upon which it sat and to the milliner's clearly dissatisfied daughter who was beside him now with a much-bothered look.

"Have you heard a word that I said?"

Had he? It was a question that seemed rather appropriate, far more appropriate, the boy had to admit, than the actual answer. Barthalamew had heard some words but, clearly, fewer than he cared to admit. There was mention of her father and his need for some color or another, for some legion of hats. Something was preposterous. Something was beige. There was a curious mention of a little girl—

"Why bother!" Gretchen blurted but then, as though a miracle, she seemed out of words. However, the miracle, like most, was short-lived. "Why bother asking me about my day when you have no intention of listening to me discuss it. Why make such a fuss at all about father or Little Girl or anything whatsoever?"

Yes! Little Girl was the ridiculously named kitty! Well, now, that made some sense.

"How dare you just sit there and daydream about...about...about whatever you daydream about while I tell you the most important parts of my days and nights! Why did you come at all? Why would you even bother to pretend to love me when you so clearly do not?!"

"But I do love you!" Barthalamew tried but what chance had he before the charge of that remarkable tongue!

"You do not!" Gretchan screamed, for now it was clear she was in need of a scream. "You know nothing of what it means to love someone, you silly dreaming boy!"

Barthalamew was stopped, put on his heels. Was she right? Was he no more than some silly boy? It did not help that she chose to echo the sentiment and with a good deal of volume.

"Silly! Boy!"

The silly boy was critically wounded. His heart was well below the line. The sounding of her voice was now ruinous, and more sounding, it seemed, was to come.

"Have you nothing to say?"

Barthalamew was stupefied. He had nothing to say.

"You are a bothersome child, after all!" Gretchan said with a huff.

The milliner's daughter then stood and looked away as though to further her disapproval of his presence. It was clear that she wanted him gone. The broken fellow had no choice but to leave.

And so, Barthalamew raised from the bench, made effort from the crag to the waiting path and sadly plodded his way back to Port Street, where the full weight of his black, though thankfully quieted, windowless room awaited him.

19

For Gretchan, revenge was not served cold but swiftly and often, the best way she knew how. Her pen was put to parchment with a resolute sense of purpose and was then mercilessly tossed to post.

"How dare you sir!" her exclamatory was, then curiously followed by the standard signature. "Your very humbled friend and servant, Gretchan Annabell Coopersmith."

And then a thousand more like it.

"You are a very foul man, indeed! Your very humbled friend and servant, Gretchan Annabell Coopersmith."

"I am sure you snore like a wildebeest set to fire! Your very humbled friend and servant, Gretchan Annabell Coopersmith."

The maiden was unrelenting. The letters arrived at the Hamm most every day and even by a good many nights when not a soul was there to receive them. It was therefore Mr. Loydford's unexpected pleasure to stumble across them by way of the following morning.

To be sure, he was rather curious as curiosity was the very nature of his industry. As such, the editor-at-large thought to secretly take hold of one and have a look for himself but his better side prevailed. And so, he bequeathed the many sealed letters to Barthalamew's desk where they awaited the boy's miserable arrival.

"Truly, sir! You are a scoundrel! Your very humbled friend and servant, Gretchan Annabell Coopersmith."

"I cannot imagine what awful measures caused your ridiculous soul to be created! Your very humbled friend and servant, Gretchan Annabell Coopersmith."

The letters kept coming, a constant volley of vitriol, as direct as they were unkind, and yet, there were a number of curious entries that were more vague than not:

"Astounding, sir, just astounding! Your very humbled friend and servant, Gretchan Annabell Coopersmith."

"I can barely believe it at all. Your very humbled friend and servant, Gretchan Annabell Coopersmith."

"How dare you even breathe? Your very humbled friend and servant, Gretchan Annabell Coopersmith."

And then, without any rhyme or reason, the letters stopped. A full week came and went without so much as a barb or a jab. It seemed as though the misery of Barthalamew's misstep was finally at a pass. There was only to breathe again, to move forward. To try for some new—

"You are but a child after all. Your very humbled friend and servant, Gretchan Annabell Coopersmith."

And just like that, the barrage was returned.

"I am baffled by your silly, childish ways. Your very humbled friend and servant, Gretchan Annabell Coopersmith."

"You are a terrible boy who does not deserve the air he breathes. Your very humbled friend and servant, Gretchan Annabell Coopersmith."

"You are a weak fellow. And your writing is as weak as any child's. Your very humbled friend and servant, Gretchan Annabell Coopersmith."

"Truly, you should be ashamed to present yourself in the public eye. Your very humbled friend and servant, Gretchan Annabell Coopersmith."

"You are not such an attractive fellow after all. I am embarrassed to have thought so to begin with. Your very humbled friend and servant, Gretchan Annabell Coopersmith."

It was all more than a bit personal; in fact, it was intentionally ruinous and seemingly unending. By the arrival of the second week since he last saw her, on the one-month anniversary of their meeting, the notes truly began in earnest:

"Detestable! Your very humbled friend and servant, Gretchan Annabell Coopersmith."

"Ugly boy! Your very humbled friend and servant, Gretchan Annabell Coopersmith."

"Stupid, stupid man! Your very humbled friend and servant, Gretchan Annabell Coopersmith."

"I do wonder how you ever thought you might be a likable sort of fellow. Please know that you are not! Your very humbled friend and servant, Gretchan Annabell Coopersmith."

And then finally, "Please never mention that I ever met you. It would be a most troubling embarrassment to me and my family. Your very humbled friend and servant, Gretchan Annabell Coopersmith."

That particular correspondence was the most hurtful of all. It cut well beyond its intended depth. Though the arrows had finally ceased, the boy knew that a good deal of bleeding remained.

And so, to the rum it was.

With a brutally wounded soul, Barthalamew barely maintained his work by day but by night he easily maintained his drink. The misery of those lesser hours was inexorable. In between each and every breath the boy fought for some touch of noise, some proper voice to step up and forgive him his trespasses.

And so, the boy tried for a voice of his own. Beneath a constant faltering candle, Barthalamew took to his secondhand-desk and desperately tried for one of his silly, secondhand poems, but all the starts, middles and ends were clearly lost in one another. His mind, like his heart, was too dipped in ruin to give his pen a proper hearing. There was only to…There was only to…

The boy was struck. Indeed, there was only a single recourse! There was only to reply! His pen! His ink! His paper!

"You are a wretched cow. Your humbled friend and servant, Barthalamew Buckett."

"Your hats are gaudy and silly. Your humbled friend and servant, Barthalamew Buckett."

"The mere sound of your voice is enough to frighten small children into hiding," a lie, of course, his worst to date, but the boy's spirit was eased by the mere presence of the words. "Your humbled friend and servant, Barthalamew Buckett."

"You are a tiresome hag with no chance at all of landing a proper husband. Your humbled friend and servant, Barthalamew Buckett."

And nearly a hundred more like it and all before dawn and what a difference it made. Of course, not one of those missives made the post. Barthalamew's heart was not like hers. It only had want for a voice, even if it was his own. His callous pages were simply left to the waiting candle.

And though the boy's heart was far from healing, it did allow for its beats and, between them, Barthalamew entrusted himself to a new diversion. The two books upon his sagging mantel now looked back as though to cast some new and daring shine. The wanting writer within leaped at the chance to put new eyes to those all too familiar pages.

And so, Barthalamew studied the intent of each book. He embraced the plots, the arcs, the thoughtful endings. He noted and considered the rhythm and sway of each properly chosen word, of each sentence as it caused itself into a paragraph. He considered the characters, their faults and failures and their impossibly poetic speak. He openly wept as he realized and accepted the wanting beauty of each of these remarkable stories.

And when Barthalamew finished the first book he turned to the next. And when he finished the next he reverted back to the first. He even considered the idea of purchasing a third, but, deep in his heart, he knew that two was more than was needed. In fact, it had always been his want for only one.

And so, each night Barthalamew kept to his room and to his books, and to his candles and rum until the suggestion of sleep kindly intervened. The boy then stepped to his mattress and put his head upon his withered pillow and, for the first time in a long time, counted his meager blessings.

A pen. A book. A bottle of rum.

But for these three things, the onslaught of that uncharitable spring nearly had the boy beat.

20

Summer tipped its hat. To be sure, there was the promise of a coming heat and, by way of Alagood's climate, a fair bit of humidity was expected as well. And yet, Barthalamew temperament was curiously cooled.

Of course, the boy's heart still suffered. To be sure, love is no easy thing to know and miss and though it was not his want to admit as much, the company of Gretchan's voice, tiresome or not, was dearly missed. But what else could he do? Soon enough he knew, there was only to step up and press on!

And so, Barthalamew shook off the spells of his nightly rum and returned to his little space at the Hamm where he reached for his pen and his inkwell and fell back into his work. Mr. Loydford was initially pleased by the sight of him until the third day when Barthalamew's next deadline was met. The work was common, at best. Considering the circumstances, it was not at all the sort of thing Loydford was expecting.

The editor was therefore pleased to note some curious gossip before the start of the following day and was only too happy to pass it on to his uninspired hand the first chance he had.

"It seems that Coopersmith is to leave town with his tail between his legs!"

Barthalamew had only just entered the Hamm. He was quickly caught unawares by the words of that conspiring editor-at-large.

"To leave?" the boy managed before Loydford pounced again.

"Seems he is overextended. Word is that he is moving to an Aunt's home in Fleming. Well north of here where the winters are much more bleak and, I suspect, the post is a little less…flexible."

"But, I…? Who will…?" Barthalamew tried but failed to get hold of a proper question.

"The whole family is to be misplaced," Loydford said with a well-timed smile. "Or, replaced, as it is. Young fellow steppin' in. No mouthy daughters to squander his fortune."

Barthalamew was stunned. Though Gretchan's letters made for his most unpleasant memory to date, his heart was bothered by the sudden notion that…

"I rather think you had a good deal to do with it," Loydford quickly affirmed, "what with her legion of letters that came and went as though some storm blasted them through our very door!"

"Yes, sir," the boy said more as a whisper, "there were some letters."

"Some!" Loydford loosed a harsh and telling laugh. "More than some, Mr. Buckett. Two couriers are put out as well. Washed up! Begging for coins in the middle of the road now that girl is done! Two!"

The last syllable echoed the walls of that brownish, brickish Hamm. An awkward silence then followed. Barthalamew's soul was at a loss for words. He looked away, begging against the coming guilt. As he turned back to his editor, he found himself face to face with the final blow.

"I want a thousand words on those ridiculous fellows by the end of the week!"

And with this said, Loydford turned and opportunely stepped back into his office. There was only to wait for the coming sound of his victory and in a moment, it was had. The door of the Hamm was opened and then quickly closed. The boy was gone, clearly in retreat.

The Hamm was rather quieted by way of the coming days. There was only Loydford and his own deadlines and musings to fuss with. On occasion, he stepped to Barthalamew's tiny desk and raised an eyebrow as though there was some touch of guilt trying to surface but it was all so easily squashed by the simple assurance that the boy was a misery and profitable times were once more at hand.

And so, Barthalamew sat in his blackened room before his second-hand desk where he conjoined his heavy heart with his duty and his waiting rum. He attacked his guilt with his pen. A thousand words launched with ease. The courier's miseries were eulogized, glorified, beautified. The boy's own heart burst over their demise and bled out on to the page in spectacular form.

At the end of the week, the assignment arrived at the Hamm delivered, can you believe it, by one of Gretchan's former couriers. A tip was called for, granted and the indigent fellow was sent happily away.

Loydford then returned to his office where he unfolded the pages upon his desk and commenced to read. At once, he was struck and, by the article's end, he genuinely and openly wept. The excitable editor went to press at that eve. By noon the following day, the Gazette was swallowed whole.

In the coming weeks, Loydford sent more assignments but never with a sense of urgency. After all, the genius of a ruined man is not to be rushed. As well, he knew, more than anyone could, that the boy had to pay his rent. The assignments were therefore dutifully accepted and returned by the end of each week.

What else could the boy do? There was simply to provide for the many usual social announcements. Some sense of art or commerce or politicking came up once or twice, along with a request for social commentary. It was all a blur to him, mindless ink to mindless page, just silly scribble from what remained of his dark and lonesome heart. Yet, the result, as always, was extraordinary.

The Gazette could hardly keep up. Barthalamew's fluttered heart sold as many papers in a month as was commonly sold in a year. His words, to the eyes and souls of Alagood, simply rang true and with an unexpected and telling depth.

And then, a most curious day dawned, though dawn was far from a common hour for the boy at that point. A quick and rapid knock fell upon his door. By his waking eye, he could tell it was not the rap of his landlady. As well, it was very unlike Mr. Loydford's usual courier. It's sounding was quite distinct. And then it was gone.

Barthalamew stood from his bed and reached for a candle and put it to flame. At that moment, he could not help but notice the letter beneath and just beyond the threshold of his door. The seal was larger than what he was used to. It was involved, curiously artistic, drawn out. It was clearly not from the Hamm. It was definitely not from some milliner's daughter.

It was from…

"Auggie Day, sir! It is a true pleasure to make your acquaintance!"

A hand was pressed forward at once. It was a small hand for it came by way of a small man, a fellow perhaps just shy of thirty and already balding.

"The honor is mine, sir," Barthalamew returned with a slightly hushed voice, for his interest was hushed as well.

"Welcome to Papa Jack's!"

Barthalamew eased a quick look, for a quick look was all that was needed. Papa Jack's was a curious box of a room. It was as plain as could be and supported a plainly impoverished clientele. Though the hour was not quite noon, the pub was clearly in the throes of something more like night. It was an unusual for the boy to note that far more patrons than candles were lit.

"Have you been here before?" Auggie asked with great eagerness as eagerness was seemingly his only gear.

"I…have not," Barthalamew eased with a touch of modesty as he felt more than a bit displaced by such an excitable fellow.

"I took the liberty of reserving a space," Auggie said, gesturing to a small table in the opposite corner which, at that

179

moment, was occupied by a man who looked every bit as old and reserved as the table itself. Auggie corrected at once. "Not to worry of Mr. Barksdale. He is as deaf as he is drunk and right now, I assure you he is quite drunk."

Barthalamew tried for a reply but was immediately confused. By way of this curiously auspicious introduction, the boy was unsure as to whether poor Mr. Barksdale was meant to be celebrated or pitied. And so, he held his tongue and politely followed as his kind host led the way.

"Pubs are the life of a proper community," Auggie offered as the two were seated. He then thoughtfully added, "You can use that if you want."

"Pardon?"

"A quote, sir. You are welcome to jot that down, so long as you attribute it to me. As an artist, I support the community in all ways possible. Please feel free to suggest as much."

It was a proper clue. The interview was under way. And so, Barthalamew placed his ink and well upon the table and produced his parchment.

Mr. Barksdale looked on, pleased with so much attention and then suddenly very displeased, for a man who drinks so well by day or night most often possesses an absolute fortune of moods.

"Blek!" was the drunk and deaf man's syllable as his body tightened, clearly concerned by the immediate colonization of his space.

It was Auggie, then, to the rescue. The community-happy artist merely placed his kind hand upon the man's shoulder and provided an assured smile. Mr. Barksdale settled and eased a smile in return.

The old fellow then looked at Barthalamew as though he'd found a long-lost brother. And then, he sneered. And then, he started to cry. And then, he laughed. And then, he stood from the table and chased off to a nearby corner, where he proceeded to gaze upon a potted plant with all the intensity of a new-found lover.

Barthalamew looked to Auggie, confused and more than a bit bothered before he was provided with a proper distraction that brought him back to center.

"You did a nice write-up for me," Auggie said with a quick and kindly tone.

The boy could not help but remember. "Aye."

"Local Hero Does Good and all."

"You were commissioned by the prince."

"His likeness hangs by the king's in the great hall of Castle Bourg."

"T'is a remarkable accomplishment."

Auggie Day, of course, could not agree more. "Indeed."

"Should you not celebrate by way of some more…reasonable means?" Barthalamew challenged, for even his broken heart appreciated that Auggie Day's reputation alone could afford a thousand Papa Jack's.

"I have had my successes, but the West End is my home. Always was and will be. And it is for my pride of the West End that I call you here today. A young and talented creative has evolved who requires the attention of a man of your caliber."

Well, to be sure, Barthalamew was intrigued. "Please do tell, sir. How may I help you?"

"It is I who seeks your help."

Her voice could not have been more unexpected. Though clearly feminine, it was raspy and gritty and immediately had the sound of something both haunting and yet so impossibly beautiful. The boy put his eyes to the source now before him and, in that moment, his dead heart was born anew.

"Sir," from Auggie, "I present Ms. Becca Fox."

Barthalamew was caught, trapped, stunned and waiting for some word or hope to guide him but no word dared. It was as though the sun had somehow breached his soul and shattered his grief into a million harmless pieces. It was his need to blink. And so, the boy blinked.

And then he looked again. Becca Fox stood over him now with a pressing sort of seduction. There was a pleasing want in her eye, sweetly coupled with a smile that took as well as it gave. Her hair was then noted, deep black and running swift across her shoulders, as though a mountain stream flawlessly plunging from some unimaginable height. She was exactly his age, and, in that moment, he knew she always would be.

"Ms. Fox," he heard himself say, as though some distant, buoyant voice made the call.

"Mr. Buckett," was her hardy reply.

Oh, how the sounding of his name eased from her to him. It descended as though the call of an angel, lowering itself from on high to its simple-hearted target well below. The boy was struck with wonder.

"Ms. Fox," he repeated, for it was his heart's want to repeat and his lung's need to exhale the very echo of her name.

Barthalamew then looked to her lips, waiting once more for her voice, begging once more for the call of his name. At that moment, he was rather surprised by his want of a kiss. It was not that it was so much a new sensation but that the boy then and there realized the sweet bitter depth of genuine, unrelenting passion.

To put it plainly, this was something far more primal. To the point, it was lust. Obviously, the woman was no angel. Even by Barthalamew's naïve eye, Becca Fox was an easy tell, more debased than not, more wanting, more willing, more charged than any thousand women before her. She was the most beautiful and obvious trap he had ever known or seen. And despite the simple fact that the woman pressed her sexuality as though some flippant card upon the table, Barthalamew's heart and mind held tight to the first and foremost fantasy at hand.

A kiss was clearly wanted.

21

A kiss was clearly wanted.

But, of course, the kiss never came. It failed to be realized for a number of simple reasons. To start with, Lydia was impressively shy. This was easily fueled by the obvious fact that she had never said a word in all her life and she knew she never would. By the age of ten, her curse was simply accepted and put to rest.

As a result, the child, like any child and, let's face it, most adults, had too little practice to even know how to go about expressing such a want. Love was all about her mind and soul, but how could she ever say as much when she could not possibly say at all? Her heart, thereby, seemed every bit as tied as her tongue.

Quite often the poor child was frustrated to the point of tears, but she never once let on. Lydia was only too happy to go about her chores, to serve her good sisters and to quietly hope for some proper distraction from her young and silly heart. She begged for quiet. She begged for hope. In time, she begged for new choices. And so, new choices were made.

The first of which was her voluntary dismissal from Sister Marihanna's daily lesson. The choice was not very well received. Sister Marihanna erupted at once! Her immediate thought was to properly punish the child, but the good sister, being once a girl herself, easily intuited the problem.

And so, Lydia was given to an evening class following dinner as the boys were given to the sacristy sink and the sister's dishes before they retired to their waiting shack. With distraction no longer the rule of her heart, Lydia absorbed all Marihanna had to give. In no time, the girl discovered her true voice in the most unexpected of ways. By Molly, that child could write.

Another inkwell and pen were then sent for and gifted to Lydia as she took to writing with a fast and obvious joy. A fresh new world was now literally at her fingertips. For the scope of more than half a year, Lydia's sweet heart belonged entirely to her new love.

Her letters were dispatched daily. She wrote most often to Marihanna and Maribeth, though sometimes to Josephine but only as occasion allowed. Her smile widened with every answer received.

For the first time in her young and beautiful life, Lydia felt as though she was truly heard and understood. For the first time ever, she discovered what it meant to simply ask for and then receive.

Her soul glistened. Her life was anew. Devotion to the order was clearly sustained.

And so, the dear girl made no effort to protest Toby's coming expulsion. She took her seat by Maribeth during the course of those weekly meetings and observed, with a kindly smile, all that was discussed. And when it was proposed that Toby's final day was near, she agreed with a nod and Sister Maribeth made a happy note for the ever-present record.

And the two boys simply looked on from the pews, curious of this thing that seemed a touch like betrayal. The orphaned girl now had her family, now had her wish. There was only to discharge the men, one at a time.

"Women!" Toby huffed and then continued. "The lot a' them are rotten! Mark my word!"

To be sure, the words were marked.

Barthalamew sat in his cramped corner of the shack and looked on as the soon-to-be-evicted, soon-to-be man paced that impossibly small room. By the boy's account, Toby seemed steeped in some curious thought, as though he was counting the many memories of that beggarly shed, but, in a moment, he was proved wrong.

"Damn this place!"

Thus, it was damned.

"Wherever I get to in the world will be far better than this ridiculous room!" Toby said, all conviction. "I s'pose it's yours now, Barth, for a while, at any rate. Don't get too attached though. They'll toss you soon enough."

That he might one day be tossed was not at all what Barthalamew heard. That the room was to be his and his alone was the thunder that first reached the boy's wanting ear. Indeed, what a curiosity! By Toby's dismissal, Barthalamew was advanced from his one little corner to the majesty of all four. The mattress and the pillows and the many blankets would all serve him now. The full space and wealth of his remote life tripled in size and bounty. And yet, it came at a cost.

"Aye," was his simple reply, for there was grief in his heart.

Toby glared. He needed to glare. He wanted to glare for another full day and night, but he knew the boy was not to blame. He knew that his glare was reserved for another.

And so, he softened and reflected and eased a smile. He stepped to Barthalamew's corner which required barely a step at all and kneeled before him. His apology was slow to come but never forgotten.

"I'm sorry..." he started, then swallowed and finished, "that I hit you that first day."

Blessed was the silence in that moment between two good and proper friends. Toby looked away and then looked back again, as though to elaborate but he stopped himself. He then reached for his tightly bound rucksack and ambled to the door. Barthalamew stood and followed and, in that moment, the two stepped together from that ridiculous shed one last time and made for the church.

But then there was a flash of brown. A faded garment, dotted with a touch of red and those ever-green eyes. Lydia! It nearly appeared as though she was coming right for the shed, but she quickly stepped off by some other direction.

"She's an odd bird that one!" Toby shrieked and with a deliberate volume.

Lydia's step hastened, as she was clearly embarrassed by the encounter and all the more so by Toby's insult.

185

"She'll rule th' order someday and all by her damn'd lonesome," Toby said, pushing his voice all the more. "The witches will be long gone, and she'll just fester in this damn'd place alone til she's an old prune herself!"

Barthalamew kept his eyes on the girl till she rounded the corner, out of sight. As he did, he wondered on Toby's assessment.

"If they all die, maybe she'll leave," he said, eager to provide for some kind word on her behalf.

"And go where?" Toby said with the flash of a smile. "And do what with that useless tongue a' hers?"

"She's good on the piano," the boy tried.

"Mark my word, there's nothin' for her in this damn'd world. Not any damn'd thing a'tall!"

Just like that, Toby's rant was over. Never again did he spare a thought or word for Lydia. There was now only to make way to the church and face off against the waiting Sisters. And so, the church was reached, and their entry was made, and the Sisters were found standing upon their blessed altar.

With Barthalamew to his rears, Toby made his approach and set his rucksack to the dirted ground.

"Good sir," Sister Maribeth started, "it is with great regret that we inform you—"

"Let's dispense with all these notions of regret and formality." Sister Josephine was rather telling with the boom of her voice. "So long, bastard."

The room chilled, as though assaulted by an arctic blast. Hardly a soul knew how to reply but then a proper soul made effort.

"I believe what my esteemed sister is saying," said the ghostly figure of Sister Margaret, "is that we are obliged to you, sir, and grateful for your many fine deeds."

The chill then thawed, though not without some unkind glare from Josephine who appeared as though she was nearing a very improper rebuttal. Margaret quickly pressed on with her better voice.

"We have secured a room for you in Adelayde, then in Kent."

Sister Josephine blinked several times, apparently the only sister who was startled by this decree.

"You! Have! Not!" was her fast return, and then, for good measure, she stressed herself once more. "You most certainly! Have not!"

But Margaret had neither want nor care for Josephine's tantrum. Her decision was long ago made and so her reasoning pursued.

"It is taken care of. It would be Cecilia's wish. We beg you well, good sir, in your travels."

Though it was clear she had a very strong want for words, Josephine was stunned into silence. The remaining Sisters, however, were all smiles.

"I-I don't think…" Josephine stuttered.

But then, it was all Toby.

"I would like to say something before I take my leave."

The sisters were stopped. Barthalamew was stopped. It was as though all the air in the world came crashing down into the nave and sank well beneath their feet.

"I want to thank," Toby said, slowly, methodically and with a frightening sort of smile, "my friend Barthalamew." Toby paused, as it seemed a proper place to do so. He then continued with what was now an obviously failing smile. "And not another Goddamned soul in this ramshackle of a miserable hovel. You will all die slowly and alone and without a friend in all the world to know or care that you ever lived to begin with! I pity you all. My adventure is anew. Your adventure never was."

Jaws to the floor. Minds and hearts followed. It was as though words could never again be spoken in that nave, so blasphemed as it now stood. Barthalamew looked back to Toby, clearly shocked, more shocked, in fact, than he was the first time he heard Toby speak those many years ago. There was only to wait for the coming fist. Of course, it did not come. What was returned to Barthalamew in that scandalous moment was something more like a wink and a smile.

Toby then grabbed his rucksack and turned to leave. He made a number of steps toward the exit before he spun about and gave Barthalamew a kindly farewell nod. He then recommitted. A few more steps were all that was needed and, just like that, Toby was gone.

Silence begged for more but was quickly denied. It was Sister Margaret who was next heard, and it was by way of the most unexpected noise imaginable. Barthalamew turned back towards the altar where the elder was spotted, almost doubled over and in a curious state of hysterics. Her laughter was golden, was blessed and so wildly out of place. The boy wanted to smile for that rare burst of happiness and even thought to try before Sister Marihanna abruptly disarmed him.

"Barthalamew," she barked, wielding now the very rare sounding of his full name. "Please return to your chores!"

But, of course. The dreadful deed was done. There was now only to pretend that it never happened to begin with.

And so, Barth left the curious scene in the nave. At once, he went for his ax in the shed and applied it to the nearby wood pile so as to provide for the coming winter. He adjusted a crooked chair that was in need of some straightening. He patched that unstoppable hole in the roof where again a slight leak was noted.

He went about clearing the front of the church with the simple push of a broom. He toiled in the vegetable garden and pulled up some weeds and a number of ripe carrots. He cleaned the altar. He dusted the pews. He helped prepare dinner, then washed the plates in the sacristy sink. He then stepped back to the shed for the evening, where he was finally confronted by the undeniable realization of Toby's absence.

By Molly, that little room was so much larger than before. As well, the silence now boasted a magical softness that both amazed and discomforted the boy at the same time. He could hardly believe his eyes and ears. All of it was his, each and every corner, each and every blanket and pillow and...

Toby's mattress! Barthalamew had never seen such a comforting thing in all his life. His rest had never known such luxury. Indeed, he missed his friend quite dearly but there was a proper night's sleep now to consider.

And so, Barthalamew quickly stepped to the mattress and was nearly upon it when the letter was spotted precisely to its middle. The boy was halted. His eyes widened as he noted the calm, deliberate printing of his name across the first fold.

What was this? How did it come to be here? Why was his name...? Barthalamew then reflected upon his day and easily recalled that earlier flash of brown nearing the shed.

At that moment, he understood. It was from...

22

"Her!"

The voice was clear, loud, and daring. Though the theater was empty but for a sparse few, Barthalamew was rather taken by Becca's obvious volume. He was additionally pleased, if not amazed, by the way she stormed about the stage.

"Her!" she repeated. "Always her!"

Another actor then appeared, quickly on the defensive.

"It has never been her!"

"Then how can you explain?" Becca pressed, though she failed to suggest what it was that was to be explained.

"I can!" the fellow belched, though he made no effort for any explanation at all.

Barthalamew was both entranced and baffled by all the yelling and gesturing and marching about, calling for explanations that were clearly and curiously not forthcoming. Auggie was quick to note the boy's confusion.

"They have to yell," he said. "When it's a full house, they must project to the very last man in the room."

Well, to be sure that made some good sense, but then—

"You despicable cur of a man!"

It was additionally loud, additionally harsh, additionally dramatic.

"She's quite good, isn't she?" whispered Auggie.

"Yes, indeed," Barthalamew answered.

Of course, the boy had no clear idea of the level of Becca's skill. How could he? He had never seen anything like a rehearsal, like a play, like an actress, for that matter, but he was clearly decided on the issue of her remarkable volume.

"Damn you, sir!" her voice shrieked to the rafters above. "Damn you straight to hell and back again!"

And then the most peculiar thing of all! Becca fell to tears on the stage. True tears! By Molly, Barthalamew was clearly moved. He wanted to rush to the stage, to comfort her, but then the most curious thing happened: Becca stood and smiled.

Auggie lifted his hands and soundly applauded her as she took her bow and exited stage left. The artist then looked to Barthalamew and fully expected to see exactly what he saw. The boy was stunned. He could not speak. He could not find the word.

Barthalamew turned to Auggie and loosed a careful breath. "I do not understand. How did she…?"

"Indeed, sir." Auggie said with the smile of a proud father. "Indeed."

"Did you like it?"

Barthalamew was only too easily distracted from the question. At that moment, Becca's dressing room had a tight grip on his attention. It was not that it was more than a bit cramped. Given his usual state of residency, such a thing was hardly a bother, but it was a confusing space, dizzying even for all the flash and color.

To start with, those four close knit walls were overrun with a bothersome number of mirrors. So many reflections bounced about as to suggest a dozen more walls to come and each one more confining than the other. As well, homemade racks cluttered the corners, busily holding to a veritable mob of props and masks and bits of unusually colored wardrobe. It was as though one could live here for the rest of one's life and never see the same thing twice.

"Did you like it or not?" Becca begged once more and with a telling smile that all too easily suggested that she needed the answer to be yes.

"Yes, of course," was Barthalamew's gracious reply.

"Truly?" Becca urged once more, for it seemed she needed the answer to be even more than a yes.

"Truly," Barthalamew sweetly affirmed.

"Are you certain?" Becca nearly cried, for it now seemed she needed the answer to be well beyond yes and with a great deal of certainty to boot.

"Of course," was Barthalamew's tired response.

Finally, a smile lifted the corners of the dear actress's lips. At that moment, she was most pleased.

"I am most pleased!"

Becca lunged forward and gave Barthalamew a considerable hug. The boy's heart was enlarged on the spot. She then pulled back and pressed her own fast and strong opinion. "Sometimes I worry about Auggie's words."

"Do you?" Barthalamew asked, but his question was barely heard.

"I mean to say that he is an exquisite writer, but his female characters are so very shameful."

Unfortunately, Barthalamew was only given a moment to think, and when he tried to say something, he was discounted at once.

"I mean, they suffer a good deal and for the silliest of reasons. I feel as though he intends them harm as he writes his scenes."

Here Becca paused as though to consider Barthalamew's thoughts, but he was quickly caught off guard. The boy could not begin to know how to form a response. And so, he quickly glanced that curious room, hoping some answer might be found among the colored chaos before him. He begged to try, to agree, to succeed before his beautiful new love and was on the verge of doing so. The words were at the surface.

"I think—"

Becca pounced. "He aims to exploit the weakness of women. Truly, I cannot say I blame him. We are a frail sort, to be sure. The thing is, men are just as frail, yet he writes them as if they are beasts of vigor and perfection. Can you imagine such a man ever drawing a breath? It's a myth, the whole lot of it. Yes, Auggie has a brilliant mind and pen, but I'm afraid he is faulted by the nature of his own fiction."

Becca held on that point as though it was Barthalamew's turn to nod and agree. What choice had the boy but to say as much?

192

"Of course."

Her eyes immediately pressed to his. Her smile shot forward as though to suggest that the many thousand hurdles between her heart and his had just been cleared. What a curious flutter! What a blessed moment!

"You, sir, are an old soul!"

It was said with such a telling confidence that Barthalamew had no choice but to believe it. He was an old soul! Becca then leaned in as though to kiss but held her mark and in a way that clearly hungered the lad.

"A beautiful old soul!" she reaffirmed with what seemed a treacherous whisper.

Barthalamew quivered. A proper quiver, it seemed, was called for as her words echoed deep within his begging heart and nearly found some much lesser depth.

Oh, how he cared so much for the kind sound of it all! His life, by her eyes and by that impossible moment, was altered. He was gripped with purpose, with excitement, with an advancing want.

Her lips now before him were so close to his, and yet the boy now knew to practice restraint. And so, he held, as she held. Her smile widened. Her voice then deepened.

"You are the very sort of man who is worthy."

Indeed, it sounded very much like a compliment, but the boy was rather confused by her meaning.

"Worthy?" he tried.

Becca's lips moved closer, her smile so near he could all but taste it. It seemed like a full year came and went before she spoke again. "You, sir, are a better man than most."

Another quiver was called for. Another quiver was had. Barthalamew could not help but be overwhelmed by the coming and going of these many exquisite syllables.

"I like talking to you," Becca continued. "I like that the things that matter to me matter to you."

"Of course, they do," he replied, for all things Becca mattered to the boy at that point.

"No one hears me like you do."

How could that be? He heard her so plainly, so clear! How could she not be heard otherwise!

"Do you know what a woman like me does to a man like you?"

But, of course, how could he possibly know!

"A woman like me loves a man like you. Do you think you could love a woman like me?"

"I-I..." the boy stammered. "I am sure that I do."

Becca's voice now neared a whisper. "Such a kind thing to say."

Indeed, it was. In fact, Barthalamew was quite sure of it: It was entirely a kind thing to say. In fact, it was beyond kind, considering the circumstances or, more to the point, the lack of them.

"I..." the boy stammered once more, "suppose it is."

The actress turned back to her mirror as though her simple war of words was won. She never offered another thought on the matter. She never had to. It was simply her want to extract the words from the poor boy's heart.

Barthalamew was quickly distressed by the silence that followed. There was only to look on, confused and begging, wanting more of her thoughts on the matter of a man like him and a woman like her. His beautiful old soul all but demanded it. And yet, it was clearly not her intent to care a second further.

And why would she? After all, her prize was claimed. Her goal was achieved. From that moment forward Becca's smiles were all her own.

23

The West End Theater had never hosted such a crowd. By way of most any occasion it was no more than a simple herd of artisans and fishermen and the like. It was whatever fellow could make a sneak by way of the back door. It was almost always dark and silly and barely afforded by those who chose to barely afford it. At best, it was a poor man's stage; almost always, it was something slightly less.

However, on the night of Becca Fox's blessed debut a more colorful audience gathered. High Street descended and offered its kindly coin and with such a pretty sort of fashion. Here was pomp. Here was circumstance. Here was more chatter than the simple walls of that lowly theater had ever known or heard.

The show was sold out for the week, much to the dismay of the barely afforded and especially those sneaking by way of the back door. There was to be no reprieve for them but only what could be heard by way of the relatively thin walls of the typical West End architecture. And what was heard, to be sure, was not nearly enough.

The eager crowd was the result of the many good words of the Alagood Gazette. An article was pushed forth citing a remarkable talent. It was nothing short of absolute poetry. It gratified. It excited. It inspired. Barthalamew's gift was all ashine before the advent of his bursting heart and his audience reaped the benefits of his glowing words.

To be sure, it was a daring step. After all, the boy had no real clue as to Becca's true potential. Yes, she was rather pretty. And yes, she danced about the stage with what seemed an obvious confidence. And yes, the dear girl could fall to her knees and weep on command, but was she anything nearing the talent that Auggie suggested?

To the point, the boy had no clue. Barthalamew had never known, much less seen, anything by way of a true performance. It was all so new to him and it all seemed so grand. Grand, as a result, became the absolute charge of his pen and quill.

And so, the tickets sold. The seats were filled. There was hardly room for so much as a breath as the drape went up and an actor took the stage before some very profitable applause. The show was now at hand.

"It is a bit cozy in here," whispered Mrs. Theryoung who, despite her tone, was pleased to attend and, thereby, support the West End event.

"There is a certain...scent," said Toby with an inflection that suggested a quieted distaste for the environment. A fast glance from the misses changed his tune. "Of course, that allows for a very certain sense of authenticity," he quickly amended.

Barthalamew sat to Toby's side, dressed once more in Joan's dead father's threads. Yes, perchance, the seating was tight and perhaps a scent did follow, but how could the boy possibly notice? By his particular standards, the room proved rather stately.

After all, there was a good deal many seats and kindly patrons to fill them. There was light. There was a window. There were several windows though each of them heavily curtained. And then there was the matter of his dear love who would soon take that blessed stage. By way of his humbled heart, it was as splendid a room he had ever known or seen!

"Behold!"

The words were loud, were bold and reached the gallery at once. An actor miraculously appeared center stage without any sort of introduction. His lonesome word echoed the cozy room and brought some fast attention to himself.

Now fully noticed, the young actor pressed on. His voice was strong. His heart was dear. His tone was nearing ominous.

"What chance has the fair man before the brutality of love!"

At once, the words resonated. Barthalamew was struck by the obvious truth and simplicity of the message. What chance, indeed! Huzzah, to the writer! Huzzah, to the stage! Huzzah, all around!

But there was no huzzah. There was only the quieted crowd, looking on as though the play was the thing and the thing, indeed, was the play. The audience was enraptured. The first act was underway.

And what an act it was! Oh, blessed pageantry! How kind was her introduction! Midway through, Becca was brought to life and in a way that could not have been more enchanting.

At once, the room was charmed! Her raspy voice was exquisite. Her performance was compelling. Her smile, her frown, her cry launched from the stage and pulled the crowd ever-forward. Gasps were openly heard. Laughter then followed. And then, can you believe it, tears!

By Molly, the moment was hers. Barthalamew's heart soared as he looked on, so proud of his love for her, so pleased for the words of his article which were now so easily justified. The boy was basking in the presence of her skill, her purity, her very soul!

The second act followed. The conflict was now at hand. Love was wanting and patently denied. Of course, it was the most common of all possible themes and yet Becca's ability dared the obvious limits of the genre. The audience was enraptured.

To be sure, the final act would be triumphant. It could not be doubted. Up to that point, the play was wonderfully laid out and Becca's performance was absolutely riveting.

Barthalamew's heart was as full as it could be. He turned to Toby and then to Joan for he felt dear to that very moment and wanted to share it accordingly. Joan was especially pleased to return a good smile which Barthalamew sweetly acknowledged.

And then, Becca's voice sounded the most telling four words the boy had ever heard.

"I have failed you!"

The audience was halted. Barthalamew put his eyes back to his beloved who now held the stage with the most demanding sort of presence. It was clear her skill was nearing its peak. What drama! What tension! What absolute love for—

"I beseech you, sir," the actress called from the very tip top of her lungs. "I beg you, sir!"

So much begging. Such lovely beseeching. And yet, there was only a huff from the supporting actor. He stepped quickly to exit stage left as Becca sounded her next lines, those that would be fully heard and never, ever forgotten.

"Then, sir," she yelped as she made a grab for her own bosom, and gave her bodice a fast rip, "it shall be as you like. My body is yours!"

At that moment, her breasts were bared, and it seemed her want to bare even more. The actor turned and consented, and the kiss that followed was more than expected. It was strong. It was passionate. It was downright indecent!

Oh, dear reader, you may imagine the awe. Of course, West Enders were no strangers to that sort of playful art, but all of High-Street was rather struck. Hearts stopped. Gasps launched. Hardly a breath could be found as a wave of shock rocked the room.

Whispers then became murmurs, and murmurs became words, and those words, as they so often do before the failing light of lesser hearts and minds, progressed into something suddenly cutting and harsh.

"For shame," came the first cry, a man's voice nearing the front row.

"For shame!" from another to the middle, a woman's voice now, passionate and aggressive.

A silence then held as the production was halted. Neither actor on stage knew what to do but it was Becca Fox who carried on, who pressed her lines like the professional she was. The show, it seemed, had to go on and so it went on, much to the dismay of the unyielding audience who, at this point, heard no voice but its own.

"For shame!"

"For shame!"

"For shame!"

All in unison now and each so very determined. To be sure, those High-Streeters were a sanctimonious bunch, with their crushing calls and their wizardry of hate. Pointed fingers were their want, were clearly their way. And so, their many fingers pointed.

But there was one who gave no voice or finger. There was one among them all who chose to hold to his silent heart. There was one who only looked to the floor and slowly lost his smile to a number of loosened tears, who bravely accepted the suffrage of the beautiful woman before him and accepted her fate as his.

"That was spirited, to say the least!" from Toby, who was clearly wide-eyed and even encouraged by the performance.

Joan, of course, lacked his enthusiasm. "You're a damned wicked man, sir, for even suggesting as much!"

Together, before the falling moon, the three walked the slope of Port Street. Barthalamew kept an easy distance behind the arm-linked pair. His eyes were cast down. His heart was put lower.

"I suspect there will be a proper review of that sort of show," Toby offered, more over his shoulder to Barthalamew than to his waiting wife. "The acting was quite convincing."

Barthalamew, of course, said nothing at all. His heart could barely support the want for words. He only had want for his room and his rum, both of which were thankfully nearby.

"I suspect that slut will be run from town before she knows her next breath."

Joan's words were particularly foul in nature. It was clear that she had a staunch opinion on the matter of the talented Becca Fox. Toby, of course, tried for another course.

"I am pleased for the notion of the theater. Perhaps, we should consider..."

"Perhaps we should not!" was Joan's immediate rejoinder.

The quip was accepted. And then, Toby thought to push it. "Well, I'm sure Barth has a proper thought on the matter!"

Joan was stopped. She turned quickly about. Indeed, her heart now pulsed for the notion of the boy's opinion.

"Yes, tell us, Barth," was the start of her pointed query. "Are you pleased with…the notion of the theater, sir?"

At once, Barthalamew shied away. The question was as though a slap across his face. Toby was first to note. The boy's quieted wilting was answer enough.

"Surely, t'is a shocking sort of thing ta' see but it might be said, and with some agreeability, that this is what art is."

"Most certainly not!" Joan retorted at once. "That was nothing like art! That was heinous and evil. Why, it was… It was just…"

Joan frantically searched the recesses of her mind for the proper word. It seemed all but at the tip of her tongue until she, like her husband before her, realized the true depth of the wounded boy before her. The good wife regrouped and retried.

"But, yes, I see your point," she suddenly encouraged. "Art is… Well, it is art, I suppose."

Barthalamew raised his eyes and gave his kind acknowledgment to Joan's better words.

"I suppose it is, Mrs. Joan," though by way of his failing tone it was clear he was not so sure anymore.

"Well," dear Joan pressed and this time with a look to her husband so as to garner some support, "she's a lovely…actress, nonetheless."

Toby provided. "Yes. Lovely, to be sure. A fellow would be lucky to know a…talent like that."

The kindly couple now looked to Barthalamew with a curious eye. Indeed, it was their need for the boy to be healed, but an obvious shame had gripped his simple heart. Though his words eased in reply, they clearly lacked conviction.

"Yes…lucky."

"Lucky, indeed!" Toby championed before he thought to catch himself.

Joan flinched at the sounding of her husband's unchecked voice, but then quickly corrected for the sake of the boy. "Maybe to know her is a different sort of thing than to...see...her."

"To know her, yes," Barthalamew tried with a failing eye.

The boy was clearly wounded. Toby wanted to try for some other word of support, but he failed too many times already before his wife. It was to her now, he knew, and her coming words were the very sort of thing he once tried himself.

"Barth, there are plenty of other fish in the sea."

Barthalamew looked directly to Toby, as though offended and not knowing how to properly say so before the good wife. His words let out as a shaded whisper.

"There are no fish. There have never been any fish. It's always been dead to me."

At the mere sound of the boy's corrupted voice, Toby's heart darkened a bit. He turned to his wife who then turned to him and together the two quickly understood. It was not that misery was once more upon the boy, but that it was now reaching up and taking hold from some new and perilous depth. Joan quickly turned back to Barthalamew and made her try.

"Barth..." she said with an efforted reach.

But the boy was away, quickly between them with a haunting step and toward his waiting room. In a moment, he was upon Jasmine's door and swallowed whole.

24

How many times had he been here? How many more times would he be here yet? It was all the same sort of misery but, in so many ways, it was now much worse than before. To his lonesome room he once more fled. To his bed and bottle he once more kept. To his tattered soul he once more begged.

Barthalamew smothered himself with sheets of darkness that were, to him, as thick as some hundred-thousand nights. Such is the fate of a heart so chronically bruised as his and his was a fate made all the more wretched by the rum he continually craved.

To rum, then, was his nightly prayer, that is, of course, when the boy could pray. There were a good many nights when he could not, when he did not know to pray, when it seemed as assured as it could possibly seem that he was as dead as any good man could be and the notion of any sort of prayer was well past needing.

By way of the many stupored days and weeks of what remained of that hapless winter, Barthalamew made no effort for his door save for the need of his meals or for the want of his rum or some other candle. His needs were easily met. His wants, however, required some greater effort. And so, a greater effort was made.

The proprietor of Fearnhead's Dry Goods Store being, of course, the elderly Mr. Fearnhead, came to expect the boy almost every day, more often for the rum than the candles though, on occasion, for both. Scarcely a word exchanged between the two, between anyone, really, as Barthalamew's presence about town commanded, by those days, a fair degree of silence.

This was for the simple fact that some folks in Alagood came to see the boy and his wretched dog in a strange new light. After all, Mr. Buckett was now considered a man about town, a gifted writer first and then something of a reputed

202

dancer. Of course, that new light also cast a number of shadows, as other things were also considered and quietly passed along.

His genius, it was proclaimed, required a good deal of rum. His appearance, it was voiced, was grubby and off-putting but could not be helped for such was the appearance of genius. His melancholic mood, it was decided, was precisely as required for a man of his particular direction and skill. His lacking humor was thought perfectly fine and, in fact, somewhat pleasing, if not entirely complimentary to the expected disposition of a man of his work.

There were some who wondered if he was a mute. There were others who considered that he might be partially deaf. Perhaps, a few even thought, he was cursed by some witch. At one point, it was suggested that he was abandoned at birth to some lowly tribe of dogs and raised in some far away wood.

Well, it is only too common for some rumor among so many to accidentally near itself towards a truth, but no one in Alagood ever thought to ask of the boy. Asking, after all, is a bother. Asking requires effort. To judge and presume, as we all know, is less tiresome and far more rewarding.

And so, the dark and daunted writer came and went amidst those many lowly murmurs, those many passive whispers that stalked the boy to and from his lonesome room and, in time, to his curiously crowded grave. They were voices all in one, neither old nor young, rich nor poor, woman's nor man's. It was a singular cry, distantly curious and curiously cruel, but the boy had no ears for all that chatter. He could only hear the call of his crying heart and its constant want of rum.

Winters pressed as winters do and though spring eventually neared it seemed, to Barthalamew, a thousand worlds away. Time shifted around the boy in the most vexing of ways. Hours passed like weeks. Weeks came and went as though hours. Minutes and months could not be told apart. Emptied bottles and full moons ebbed and flowed alike. Life, by those simple measures, was entirely harrowing and yet, it was as though the boy was somehow accustomed to it all.

Barthalamew's absence from the Theryoung's home finally took hold of the patriarch's brow and raised it up a notch. It was typically Toby's way to let the boy be during those moody times, for moods were not exactly his specialty. As well, it seemed only natural to let a man tend to his own emotional wounds.

However, that particular wound, so public as it was, and so personal as it was noted, was clearly more concerning than usual. And so, on a crisp, late winter day Toby Theryoung stepped his way into town and down Port Street way in search of Jasmine House.

On arrival to Barthalamew's door, Toby could not help but note the dark and firm wood that awaited him. The door was curiously daunting, as though it all but dared someone to knock. And yet, he knocked. What more could he do? The knock, in turn, was answered.

It was no more than the boy's eye that pressed through that slight crack and yet Toby knew at once the matter.

"So…dark," Toby said, as he caught a small glimpse of the inexplicably black abyss just beyond.

"I am low on candles," was the boy's reply, but his tone was hardly convincing.

An unusual silence prevailed as each man waited for the other to say something, anything at all. It was Toby who finally pushed.

"May I enter?"

Barthalamew acquiesced. The boy eased back and allowed the door to fall open. Toby entered and was immediately struck by the continuous lack of light. Nothing could be seen. Nothing at all. But something could surely be smelled! Toby looked to where he supposed the boy would be and made his simple inquiry.

"Does Jasmine House yield a proper bath?"

"Out back," Barthalamew answered. "But if costs five copper."

"Happy to pay, sir!"

It was a spare room. Small. Dark. Windowless. It took nearly half an hour for a servant to fill the tub, but Toby insisted on holding court, fully intent on submerging the boy the moment the last bucket was poured.

The two sat on a barely capable bench and looked on as water was continually added.

"I daresay, the writing has improved much!" Toby said with a kind smile.

"Mr. Loydford sends by courier, lets me write as I please now, on any subject I wish. It's hardly news anymore. It's just rambling, hardly worth the paper it's printed on."

"Yet he prints it nonetheless, and people still take the paper. That should tell you something," Toby encouraged. "Joan was particularly moved by your last piece about the fisherman's tax. I did think, though, that it seemed..." Toby took a moment to consider his words carefully. "Well, it was a bit more poetic than need be, in my humble opinion."

Barthalamew, for his part, had nothing to say in reply to the compliment or the critique.

"Not that it was at all bad. It just seemed a bit much for a story about taxes. The point, Barth, was well made. I daresay, you'll find a good many friends at the wharf."

Barthalamew was quickly affected by this notion. His want for a glare was met with exhaustion. He nearly gave up the point as the words passed from his lips.

"I can't imagine why."

"Well, of course you can't. How can you find any sort of friend at all when you keep yourself tucked away in that cramped cell! The world awaits, Barth. The world thrives by a man of your skill."

"The world thrives well enough without it."

Toby gave pause to this thing said, for it was not that it was said but how it was said. There seemed nothing left at all of the boy he once knew. There seemed only a blackened spirit before him, discharging words with a demon's hiss.

205

"We must get you out of this place," Toby quietly begged.

Barthalamew's reply was more nearing a whisper. "I have work."

"Surely, it can wait. Loydford will understand. You need some light, friend. You need some proper rest."

"I believe he prefers it this way."

It took Toby only a moment to understand the possibility of that truth. "Perhaps. But that doesn't mean you should prefer it this way as well."

"It doesn't matter what I prefer. It never has."

"Stop it! You're a better man than this, a good man, with a good heart. You deserve the love you seek, and by Molly, she's out there waiting for you, but you'll never find her in that hideous cave you call home!"

Toby stopped. He was pleased with the sound of his pitch. It was a perfectly reasonable pitch, even a winning pitch.

Still, the boy's rebuttal was firm.

"Love is a disease! Every time I love, I feel sick!"

"Well, if love is the disease," Toby replied quickly and in equal measure, "then I believe I know the cure."

The word struck the boy as though a brick to the head.

"A cure?"

"Your bath, sir," from the servant who had made his final pour.

Toby eased a smile, for his plan was quickly forming. "Yes, your bath, Barth," he said with a pleasing touch of confidence. "Then, I'll escort you to a proper pub for a proper drink."

"I don't want a pub."

Toby's smile widened.

"T'is not the sort of pub you want," he then said with a telling wink. "T'is the sort of pub you need!"

25

The Great Raff Pub was not at all like Papa Jack's. To start with, there was a good deal more room for one to stretch and drink and take in the many sights and sounds. The walls were well apart from one another, and the many tables and chairs were easily and impressively spaced.

The other issue was the matter of headroom. To the point, the rafters were much higher than Papa Jack's, a good deal higher than any the boy had ever been under, aside from that godly ceiling of High Street Church. It was an impressive reach and the very first thing to catch the boy's eye as he and Toby entered.

"'Tis a better place than most about," Toby assured him with a smile.

As Barthalamew lowered his gaze, Toby's claim was quickly confirmed. Indeed, it was an impressive sight. Tapestries and sigils of some forgotten time ran from high to low. Sconces were aplenty, lining each wall, happily illuminating three of the four corners, the fourth falling to darkness but, at the time, the boy was hard-pressed to notice it.

And what a colorful lot of folk! Barthalamew had never witnessed such revelry. By spirit and attire alone, his heart was rather struck and most pleased for the distraction.

"A drink and then a surprise for you, maester of the pen," Toby said as the two intuitively stepped to the long bar at the near-side of the room.

"A surprise?" from Barthalamew, who was immediately displeased by the notion of any surprise, for surprises, by the full run of his life, had never served him well.

"Aye, something proper for a proper man!"

It was clear that Toby's spirit was rather lifted. To the point, Barthalamew had never seen him like this. He knew well enough Toby the child. He was most pleased to know Toby the man, husband and father. And now, there was Toby the buoyant and curiously blithe. His friend's voice was more than raised. It was shrill, bordering rowdy and more than a bit refreshing.

"A rum for my friend!" Toby pitched as the bar was reached. "And a proper ale for myself!"

"No proper ale here, chap," said the deeply gingered man across the bar, wearing a curious look of severity before breaking into a more agreeable smile.

Toby and the barkeep, a fellow kindly known as Big Red and for two very obvious reasons, fell into a boisterous laugh that caught the full attention of the room from start to stop. Clearly, Mr. Theryoung was no stranger here. This was quickly affirmed by another.

"The good Mr. Theryoung!"

The mere sounding of the voice widened the smile on Toby's face. He gave a quick turn and greeted it.

"Pastor   Doyle!"

At once, Barthalamew flinched.

"Former Pastor, good sir," Doyle pressed with a curious smile.

Toby immediately turned to Barthalamew and proffered the introductions.

"Mr. Doyle, this is my good friend Barthalamew—"

"Buckett," Doyle intervened, in a tone bordering on unkind. "Yes, I am more than familiar with the lad's work!"

Barthalamew held his ground, begging his heart for some proper word. But all he could come up with was…

"T'is a pleasure, sir."

"If ya say it is, then ya say it is."

What choice had the boy but to shrink from the infamy of that awkward introduction! He quickly turned back to the bar where his rum was found waiting and put it to use at once.

"Barth!" Toby then called out and with needless volume as the two held but an inch from one another. "You remember your landlord, of course!"

The boy faltered, nearly collapsed. Here now was the suggestion of another troublesome encounter but what could be done! And so, Barthalamew quickly retired what remained of his newly poured rum and eased his turn about.

"Mr. Dean," he said, with much effort to be kind.

"Barth! What a fine surprise," from the clearly intoxicated man. "How is your good friend?"

At once, the question was off-putting. Barthalamew hesitated to answer as he barely understood the question.

"The dog," Mr. Dean clarified. "Lora goes on and on about that animal of yours."

Barthalamew glanced the nearby door, half-expecting the mutt to appear. "I assure you, sir, he's not my dog at all."

"What do I care whose dog it is? So long as it remains a bother to her, I am as grateful as grateful can be!"

And with that, Mr. Dean surrendered all interest in the boy and quickly put his attentions back to Mr. Theryoung and the former pastor.

"Where's Paps?"

Toby's jubilant voice was nearly put to the rafters but Barthalamew was quite uncaring and, in fact, more than a bit fearful as to the notion of meeting anyone else, especially some fellow with such an unwitting name. His sudden need was to be a good step away from the infamy of that gathering circle and another step in the direction of his next drink of rum.

And so, Big Red was signaled, and kindly provided. Another pour was put before the boy and the boy was put before another pour. Barthalamew sipped again.

The rum was decidedly remarkable, clearly not the sort one comes across in a dry goods store or by way of some West End dive but something rather exquisite. It had the taste of the tropics, of some unexplored nature. By its flavor alone, Barthalamew felt as though removed from that immediate world of former pastors and landlords and whatever a Paps might be.

The room was now his to know. It was his to absorb. The boy happily turned his back to the company at hand and put his gaze once more to the many high walls at hand.

The spacious pub and its bannered splendor appeared all the more amenable. Barthalamew examined the many sigils that draped from rafters to floor. Though he had little knowledge as it regarded the great Houses of the land, Sister Marihanna had instructed him well enough to know a few by sight.

Most prominent of all was the House of Haggett, easily recognized by the sheer golden sword upon a darkened field of gray. The House of Boon nearby was dotted with many laurels and coins. The House of LeRoy was easily noted by streaks of burgundy and gold; that one was far more common. Barthalamew had seen it before upon his visits to the King Robert's Arms.

And then there was a draped sigil that was not so familiar. It was a short black banner with bits of silver, displaying a horrid looking sort of castle. This one baffled him. This one he could not—

"Barth!" from an overjoyed Toby.

And just like that, the boy was dragged back into a most unfavorable bit of conversation.

"Yes, I heard it was…quite a performance."

"You more than heard it, sir," said Milford Dean, who pressed the former pastor with a menacing eye. "You saw plenty for yourself!"

Mr. Doyle was checked and humbly conceded the point. "Aye. I did."

"Twice," said Mr. Dean, not about to let the former pastor free of his point.

Mr. Doyle looked away, rather ashamed and even, can you believe it, bothered for all the hurt he felt he might be causing the boy. "Twice, then. I'm sorry for that, but it could not be helped."

"A sold-out show a week in advance?" Mr. Dean snickered. "Not only could it have been helped, but you went out of your way to secure a ticket for a second show, sold your own sword to do it!"

It seemed nearly an insult, which, of course, was Mr. Dean's design. The former pastor pushed back the only way he knew how.

"Well, what use have I for a sword anyway?"

"A family heirloom, was it not?"

Toby and a slightly embarrassed Barthalamew looked on as the argument among obvious friends had found a curious new gear.

"What business is that of yours?" charged Mr. Doyle. "Or anyone's, for that matter!" he added and with some volume so as to properly secure his point.

"All for a slag's tit!" Milford Dean rested for a moment on that obscene point before realizing Barthalamew's shallowed eye. "Apologies, sir. I am sure, by some degree, that she is a maiden worthy of a stronger heart than ours alone."

To be sure, it seemed the start of something like a compliment. Barthalamew wanted to accept it but was unsure how to go about it. The only thing sure in his blood at that moment was the quality of the rum. And so, the boy turned back to Big Red and signaled for another.

Mr. Dean then pushed forth with a more kindly sort of voice. "An artistic woman is a good woman, Mr. Buckett. She is most often a strong woman of heart and character! But, I daresay, there are times when a woman of the arts forgets her place before proper society."

Barthalamew's pour was accepted from the bar. He then had his sip and turned to Mr. Dean and was pleased to find the eyes of his landlord to be amenably fixed on the subject. By look and sound alone, the boy was struck with the idea that some effort at compassion was being advanced. And yet, his heart was nearing his sleeve.

"I loved her," he heard himself say and with all confidence.

A proper hush descended. Even Toby was gripped by the confirmation of Barthalamew's words. Mr. Dean was quickly impressed and thought to say so.

"Love is a wise thing for a better man."

A second hush as the words batted about the ears of the many gentlemen present. Even Big Red considered the pleasantry of these words. And then—

"Bah!" from the former pastor, for the notion was nearly insulting. "No man is wise in love! You, sir, are the example of that! As is he! The boy loved a harlot, after all!"

"Aye. As did you, sir! Your heirloom is across the seas, is it not?"

Well, it could be said, that the argument was won on that point alone, but what argument ever properly dies before midnight and before a fully stocked pub.

"Well, damn, Milford! Do you think I gave that up for love?" Mr. Doyle said with a quick step, so as to push his words forward. "Do you think I sacrificed all I had for this so-called wisdom of yours?"

A third hush, for all good hushes come in threes. A proper silence held. The whole of the room now turned and wondered. Dudley Doyle, realizing his volume, decided to give his audience its due.

"I am as any among you," he openly declared. "A calling doesn't take the want away. Like a million men before me, I have desires. Like a million men to come, I hurt, and I grieve, and I will die alone with a fast tear in my soul." The former pastor then turned to Barthalamew. "That actress is a lovely lass, as lovely as any I've ever seen. I would've given a dozen swords if only I had a dozen to give."

Oh, blessed confession how your words can so quickly echo a room and secure so many hearts. It was quite clear that the former pastor still had a bit of pastoring left within him. It was as though the whole of the pub was lost to the consideration of that singular plea. And then, the most remarkable voice stepped up.

"Here, here!"

Barthalamew's eyes darted about, as he yearned to know the author of that remarkable toast. But then, another rang out.

"An angel among women!"

It was an elder this time, with his mug raised high. Barthalamew saw him at once and his heart was healed.

"To a dozen swords!"

Another voice. Another call. Another high mug. And then the chant began. Three chants, in all as the whole of the pub pressed the most unexpected chorus.

"A dozen swords!"

"A dozen swords!"

"A dozen swords!"

It was as sweet a song as any former pastor might ever hear and all the more pleasing for the boy. And then, as though some candle put out, the many of the Great Raff Pub turned back to their business of thriving about, leaving Toby and Barthalamew and Misters Dean and Doyle to what remained of their own thoughts and drinks.

Barthalamew could not have been more overwhelmed. In that precious moment his love, his want, his appreciation of Becca was renewed, validated by an entire room of impossible strangers. By Molly, his rum had never tasted so good!

The boy looked to those formerly infamous men before him and kindly raised his own mug, then said the first thing that came to his waiting lips:

"T'is strange to think that I have never been here before."

26

T'is strange to think that I have not been here before."

Her last words to him.

To Barthalamew's way of thinking her words were not nearly as strange as the fact that she was there to say them. But, she was. From the very moment she stepped out of the cold of that wintry night and into his shed and closed the door behind her, the boy intuited an extraordinary presence; haunted, yet calm; old yet young; ghostly but alive. By the dark he could not see, but by his heart these things he knew.

Of course, he was awakened at once. It was the door that brought him to, for it, like the shed, was particularly old and let out its moans and cries at a touch. Barthalamew sat up beneath a weight of blankets and cleared his eyes. From the dark there emerged, he assumed, the form of Marihanna.

He looked on as best he could as the womanly figure fumbled about for a chair, which was found with some ease at the foot of his bed. After all, it was a remarkably small room and there was little else to do but stand or sit or make effort to sit. And so, the effort was happily and easily made.

Nothing was said at first. Nothing, it seemed, was going to be said until, at long last, there was the sound of her voice, a voice he could not make out, a voice that was not belonging to Sister Marihanna at all.

"I believe a light would do us well, Barthalamew."

It was a sensible request, no doubt, though it could not have come at a more insensible hour. Barthalamew had no way of telling how long he had been asleep, but he knew right away that it was well past the point of being late to the point of being quite early. It therefore occurred to him that something was terribly wrong, but, so far, there seemed no urgency by the sound of that curious voice.

He reached for and found his candle and, with his nearby flint and stone, made his light and in that moment the darkness fell back to the immediate wall and the extraordinary visitor was revealed. The elder woman was sitting up straight, as poised as he had ever seen her, looking not at him, but directly ahead to the door from which she had just entered.

She was dressed, per usual, in her defiant black, dotted now with wetted spots of snow, and when she spoke again it seemed to him that she was not so old, not nearly as old as she had always been but a woman, somehow, from a younger day.

And then there was the cough. It was a constant for the last month. It shadowed her every step and was sounding more grave by the day. Sister Margaret let it out and then composed herself for the boy.

"I do apologize for the lateness of the hour," she said with great sincerity. "It is not proper, the hour, nor that a lady should..." and here she paused to reconsider the point. "Well, I am too old to be thought a lady and, besides, I never much cared for all of this so-called propriety. Good will, Barthalamew, is easy enough to come by without these legions of rules and regulations." Her eyes searched downward as she continued, as she slowed her speech and intently added a touch of haughtiness. "You can't do this! You can't do that! It's all so much bunk. I believe in rules, of course. T'is good to have rules. But there are too many these days and too many is far worse a thing than none at all."

Barthalamew could not help but be captivated by this thing said, not just for its sound sense, which was quickly admired, but for the notable fact that in these thirty seconds Sister Margaret said more to him than in all of his first sixteen years. As well, her younger, unshaken voice was a curious new song. Having lived the whole of his life by the prattle of no more than half a dozen voices (seven, if his is to be counted) any new voice at all seemed a miracle to him.

Another fit then ensued. Sister Margaret yielded and then looked once more to the door as though there was a need to truly consider it. At that moment the old woman seemed oddly at peace, as though her deep and troubling cough had simply become another forgotten part of her day.

Barthalamew was more awake now, less bothered, more concerned. He had never been so close as this to the aged sister. Though it was more dark than not, the boy could clearly see her thinning white hair and the run of her wrinkles, but her hair now seemed unkempt and the lines of her face appeared deeper, more intimate than ever before. She looked so entirely old, as old as time, as old as anything that had ever been or might ever be.

"I have come here," she started again, with her focus still to the door, with her speech still slowed but kindly tempered, "to say thank you. People don't say it as much as they should. In the past, I suppose I was one of those people and I am truly sorry for that. Please don't ever think that I didn't care. Will you remember that, Barth? Will you remember that I am grateful?"

It was the first question she had ever asked of him, and it took nearly half a minute for him to consider his lackluster answer. "Y-Yes, Sister Margaret," he stuttered.

"So, you accept my gratitude?" the old maid said with the ease of a smile.

"Yes, Sister Margaret."

The old maid nearly flinched.

"Please, just call me Margaret."

Which seemed the most impossible thing in all the world to do.

"Yes…Sister Margaret."

Margaret's smile eased away. By his candle's simple flicker, she seemed a prisoner shadowed by all the walls of silence and regret. Another minute nearly passed before her voice surfaced once more.

"You are thought to be how old?"

"Sixteen, Sister Margaret."

"Yes, sixteen. It must be rather odd not to know your own birthday."

But what could Barthalamew say, for it did not seem a question and Sister Margaret appeared all the more content without the answer. The subject, then, was given up and silence, again, succeeded.

As though on cue a snappy wind pushed up against that tiny shed and coursed its way through a number of cracks, causing the candle's flame to sway and dip and fend for its place in the chilly quiet of that shivery night. Barthalamew, though, had no worry. He knew quite well what sort of wind it took to put that candle out. Those cold airs and giving cracks were no stranger to him.

"How cold it is in here, Barth," Sister Margaret said, noting just then the mark of her breath.

Again, Barthalamew said nothing but began to undo from the pile of his bed one of several blankets he had appropriated over the years. He then made effort to pass one along but was quickly denied.

"Oh, no. I will be fine, Barth. I won't be but a minute longer. It's just that you have never said anything of the conditions here."

"No, Sister Margaret," Barthalamew said, wondering if he was expected to say something about it now.

"My dear boy, don't be so prudish. You must ask for something better than…" and here she allowed for a cursory glance of that cold and tiny room, "…this. Truly, you will never get what you want out of life if you don't speak up." But then came a curious retraction. "On the other hand, no one likes a whiner. After all, Barth, a little suffering is good for the soul."

"Yes, Sister Margaret."

Another fit of coughs. Another recovery. Sister Margaret pressed on.

"Still, you are so very quiet. You always have been. Oh, I don't fault you for that. There's too much noise in the world as is. People want to be heard at every turn, but have nothing ever to say. Such an awful, endless racket. You have noticed, I am sure, that I say very little, myself," and here, again, Margaret eased a smile, "so I know what you mean, Barth. Indeed, I do."

217

At which point Barthalamew was quite surprised to find that he meant anything at all. That he was a quiet soul there was no doubt and he knew this well enough. That his silence somehow came to mean something was an entirely new thought to him. What else could the boy possibly say to that but...

"Yes, Sister Margaret."

"It's just so strange, though. You can say anything you want and won't, and she..."

She!

Oh, how soft the word on her lips! Sister Margaret made no effort to finish but, instead, resigned her voice to a single tear that she could not, for one more second, keep from her cold and reddened cheek, so pretty was the moment for that dear old maid. Barthalamew noted a new sort of smile, surfacing from some deep and tender place, as her tear was left to run its course, as it was let to fall as though a pearl to her waiting lap.

"It is so sweet how she loves you," Margaret continued with a strangely regretful tone. "What makes it even more remarkable is that she doesn't say it. Of course, well, she can't say it, but it's just so...so beautifully unsaid. I only wish I could say what she can't half as well."

Barthalamew shuffled and looked about. He was before an awkward pause. Here in the dead of night, by the cold of that season and his little room, before the struggle of that ignorant flame and in the company of so unexpected a guest, the image of young Lydia came to life and flourished before his mind's tiring eye. Had he heard right? What was this talk of...?

"Tell me Barth, do you know what true love is?"

But how could he possibly answer. How could he possibly know!

"It is perfectly fine if you do not know. You may say so. You may say you don't know."

"It's..." Barthalamew started, but he knew at once the words would not come. "I...I don't know."

"Perfectly fine," Sister Margaret said, as she put down another fitful cough. "Our mother used to ask it of us, of Cecilia and me. We were so young at the time. Oh, Barth, we were just children. We had no idea what she was crowing about. What did we know or care about this love or that love or any sort of love at all! We were tomboys, the two of us. Always playing about in the mud or chasing after stray pups, doing as poor girls do when they think they would rather be boys..."

Barthalamew was awed by the sudden sound of her laugh. Blessed be the stars, it was not at as he had always imagined. It was not the wretched cackle of some dead-hearted witch but something unexpectedly kind and winsome.

His eye was on her now as never before, poring over those aged lines, imagining them away, begging of her likeness at that long-ago age when puppies and mud-pies ruled her little world. He could not help but stare, so as to truly consider the thing, but Sister Margaret seemed not to mind. She only carried on, as though she always would.

"...but mother knew what she was doing. She knew the seed of wisdom must be planted when one is young, so that it may grow into one's mind as one's mind grows into it. It is not meant to be understood until...well, until one is meant to understand it. Still, it must be there. It must be planted."

The boy had little understanding but it seemed, by his young soul, a wise, elderly thing to say. After an obliging pause, he kindly submitted.

"Yes, Sister Margaret."

"Does this...does this make sense to you Barthalamew?"

"Yes, Sister Margaret."

"Does it? Or are you saying 'Yes, Sister Margaret' to everything I say?"

"Yes, Sist..." Barthalamew started and then, with a stumble, made his correction. "Yes...I mean that it does make sense, Sister Margaret."

The old woman's posture eased as she placed her hands on her knees and closed her eyes to the words that came next from her mouth.

"Very well, then. I am pleased that you understand. Sister Marihanna does go on about your mental acuity, that is to say, your cleverness. Perhaps she brags a bit in that regard, but I am satisfied that her pride is not so entirely misplaced."

By the kind tone of her words, the boy was sure this was something like a compliment. His heart perked. His voice pushed. His interest in the topic was renewed and wanting.

"Sister Margaret," he prodded.

"Yes, Barth?"

"What...what is the answer?"

"The answer, Barth?" for the question had already been forgotten.

"Yes, Sister Margaret." It could not be helped that the boy was so very shy, for it was no easy question for any boy to ask. "What is...true love?"

And here again came the eyes of Sister Margaret, wearied now, but once more looking to the door straight before her. She seemed, at first, quite afraid to speak and so, for a moment, not a word was offered. But then came her extraordinary answer, spoken as though each syllable was no less than God's own choosing, as though it was no less than the treasured gospel of a hundred-thousand ages.

"True love, Barthalamew, is that which loves and does not speak."

And that was it. That was exactly all she said. The boy was sure that it was not nearly enough.

"But...what does that mean?"

"All that it implies," was her soft reply.

"But...what does it imply?"

"Only what it means," softer still.

A sweet silence then descended, allowing in that moment, a curious knock about the shed, as though the cold of the night had a thought of its own on the matter. Sister Margaret closed her eyes and then, with some effort, opened them once more. A slighted cough rose up but was then batted down.

She appeared engrossed in thought, clearly wanting to say, but debating the idea of saying it. Her lips parted, then closed, then parted again. Finally, she surrendered and committed at once.

"I will tell you a story of a woman who was loved as such. She was a woman of great beauty," Sister Margaret gave pause as though to call the memory closer. "But she was careless. She broke the heart of a good man. She turned on his kindnesses. She ridiculed him. She mocked him behind his back, knowing that her words would soon find their mark. And so, they did. And that good man succumbed to his wounds and fell into an early grave. And she soon after."

"She died?" the boy asked with whispered concern.

Margaret was clearly affected by the question. She barely had want to answer it. And so, she barely did.

"She did love the man, but hers was a young and silly heart. And she did not know, until it was much too late, what low words can do to a good fellow such as him." Again, a pause as Sister Margaret reflected. "And yet, he never said a word against her. He died with her name on his lips. He died with a smile, he did. Love cut him. And then it saved him. I think he always knew it would."

Even out of context, the story proved remarkable to Barthalamew's wanting ears. He had to know more. His heart all but begged to ask.

"Who was he?"

Margaret passed on the question. "He was a man, no more, no less."

Well, this was not the answer he wanted. And so, he pressed another.

"Who was she?"

At that moment, the boy knew he lucked upon the mark. Margaret's eyes were alive with thought as she slowly eased the sound her confession.

"She was my sister."

Cecilia! But how could that be! For the first and only time that night Sister Margaret put her eyes to Barthalamew. At once she noted the fast nature of his confusion. Her next words were carefully chosen and then put to the boy with a proper sort of weight.

"The heart remembers what it needs to remember, Barth. It does not want for truth. The truth lies forever at the bottom of a well!"

Barthalamew held his tongue, clearly unable to muster a coherent thought, let alone a proper word. His eyes remained locked on hers. His life was frozen in the moment.

"No matter our choices," Margaret persisted, "no matter our wants, our realities shall never prevail. We shall all die, alone and wanting more. Do you understand, Barth?"

Did he? How could he! And yet, he knew there was and would only be his one true answer.

"Yes, Sister Margaret."

Satisfied, Sister Margaret looked away, looked, seemingly, passed the hem of her ever-blackened dress to the simple mess of that dirt covered floor. Another cough rose and was put to rest.

"You have always heard that Cecilia died of a broken heart."

"Yes, Sister Margaret."

"You may continue to believe it. It is still something of a truth."

"Yes, Sister Margaret."

Barthalamew's mouth held open as though he had the idea to speak again, but the boy knew well enough to simply hold his tongue. And so, he looked away to his flame and considered the story of the dying man and the weight of Cecilia's truth. By the time he thought to look back to Margaret, she was already on her feet.

"T'is strange to think that I have not been here before."

She then stepped as though a ghost to the frugal door of that rickety shack and made her exit, thus: without another word, without another sound.

Sister Margaret's absence about the church the following day was initially ignored for the lady, in her age, had tendencies to nap a good deal. As a result, she was not so often missed. By evening, however, concern was high.

Not a cough was heard since the previous night. Her room proved empty. There was no sign of her at all. From end to end the church was searched and, yet, to no avail.

As night eased into place, it was finally determined that the old woman had somehow furthered herself away. By then, of course, not much could be done. The moon was up, and a frost had set in and a stiff wind was there to support it. There was only to sleep and imagine the old woman stumbling about the market in Adelayde.

It was not until early the next morning when Sister Margaret was finally found, when her snowbound steps were followed into the nearby wood where she was happened upon, sitting calmly, even politely against a tree, eyes to the heavens, as though to reflect upon the sweet mist of her very last breath as it rose ever skyward.

27

Barthalamew stood before a most curious door. It was not so easy to spot. It was positioned to the far side of the pub, purposely shadowed and for a proper reason.

"Where's it go?"

Toby stood over the boy's shoulder, wanting for his own answer but his try was disrupted.

"Ever downward, sir!" from Mr. Dean, who, unlike the former pastor, thought best to keep a distance.

"Don't mind him!" from the very nearby Mr. Doyle. "That just happens to be the finest door in all the kingdom!"

Barthalamew was baffled. Surely, there were a thousand doors better than this throughout Alagood alone, to say nothing of the rest of Kirkland. And yet, he could not help but note Toby's confirming eye. Apparently, there was something to this door, after all.

"But," the boy started, finally understanding that it was not the actual door that was to be questioned, "what's behind it?"

"Your cure, my friend," from Toby, who, by this moment, seemed almost giddy with intoxication.

A hardy pat on the back was extended before the former pastor made his reach for the rusted knob and gave it a twist. Mr. Doyle then stepped forward and descended into the waiting dark. Toby thought to take his own step, but noted Barthalamew's hesitation.

"What was the last thing Sister Margaret said to you?"

"What?" Barthalamew choked, surprised by the sudden mention of her name.

"What did she say?"

The words came up at once, as though it was his heart's want to say before it could withhold. "Something about how she couldn't believe she hadn't…"

The boy was stopped. His tongue held. His mind stepped up. He understood.

"For Sister Margaret, then," from Toby, who was pleased to make his point, off-putting though it was.

Barthalamew accepted the toast, eased a gulp of his waiting rum, then took his first downward step. All hesitation was gone. His mind was now forward. There was only for his feet to follow.

As that threshold was crossed, the boy's soul was halted. He turned quickly and glanced Mr. Dean, who still held to the glorious expanse of that remarkable pub as though a bridled team of wild horses could not pull him to. Mrs. Dean's lesser half then gave a turn of his own and eased back towards the bar with the heaviest sort of step. It is only too easy to say what one may want about a fallen fellow, but at that moment, Mr. Dean was a husband.

The door was then closed. Ever downward was now the course. By the begging light of a singular torch, the width of that stairwell was quickly revealed. As well as being dark, it was unreasonably narrow. Barthalamew's shoulders were somewhat challenged to clear the tiny space as his feet reached for and made for a number of unexpectedly steep strides.

From behind him came the footfalls of Toby, who stepped in kind, slowly, carefully and yet with some deliberation. From ahead, the sounding of a number of voices could now be heard. The boy was now between it all, bounded by the solace of a lone friend and the assurance of some unthinkable cure.

In a moment, the sconce was reached, and a turn was provided. By this final step, Barthalamew then alighted into the slight room which remained every bit as poorly lit as the narrowed stairs. And yet, the shadows about quickly formed and provided for a number of unexpected characters.

To the far wall two gentlemen stood before a shoddy, makeshift bar. They each looked across that quaint room, toward the start of a hallway that was clearly policed by the most curious sort of woman. It was obvious their intent was entry and equally obvious that her intent, for the moment, was denial. And so, each party held its respective ground as patience and impatience braced for its jittery little dance.

Barthalamew's attention was first to those men but his attention was quickly distracted. The woman before the corridor was a curious creature. At first, his eyes were drawn to her overly confident stance, but then it was all about the state of her dress. To the point, she was hardly dressed at all.

An easy guess put the woman somewhere on the backside of middle age, which proved all the more shocking for her daring appearance. As well, her eyes were bold, and her smile easily suggested that she was as pleased as she could be considering her less than spectacular placement in life, being that she was well beneath a pub and not atop it.

The boy could not help but see her. And she, bless her barely covered heart, could not help but see him. At once, the madam's voice sent up.

"Pastor Doyle!" her sound was as alarming as her dress. There seemed rocks in her throat. "What have we here?"

"Madam Emma," from the former pastor, "I have a friend."

The word struck the boy's ears at once. Barthalamew quickly glanced about so as to assess who that friend might be.

Again, speaking as though some legion of gravel had hold of her voice, Madam Emma sweetly inquired. "A friend, you say?"

Her stare did not waiver. Barthalamew now understood. The friend, clearly, was he.

"The lad favors a bit of company," Mr. Doyle pressed and then turned back to Barthalamew with a knowing smile so as to confirm that, indeed, here was his friend and that he did, in fact, favor the idea of company.

Barthalamew glanced Toby, now holding beside him. His eyes begged for some proper understanding. Toby, in turn, only held to his slightly drunken smile.

"Company, you say?" Madam Emma blasted as though two tons of sand now heeded the call. She then made a proper target of poor Barthalamew before the rock salt that was her voice continued. "And, has the boy ever had…company before?"

Barthalamew was stumped! What sort of question was that? Who, after all, had not had company before. To the point, company was being had at that very moment!

"From the looks of it, I believe this would be his first…company," the former pastor submitted.

Barthalamew began to object, but Toby, noting his puzzlement, gestured for patience. The boy acquiesced.

"And what sort of company do you suppose the boy might like?"

Toby could not help but let up a chuckle. As far as he was concerned the proceedings, at this point, were the height of amusement. Barthalamew, however, could barely offer anything more than a slighted smile for all the swimming that was still going on between his ears.

"Perhaps Ms.Trudy," Mr. Doyle then said, "might be his sort of match."

Perhaps? Ms. Trudy? His sort of match?

Again, the boy was baffled. What was meant by any of it and by way of that cramped and ridiculous room? Barthalamew was on the precipice of a proper complaint but Madam Emma's eyes were now fully committed, burrowing deep, deep into his startled soul. His voice seized in the moment. Nearly half a minute came and went before the full throttle of her coarse-grained voice surfaced once more.

"Yes. I agree. Trudy would be a good match for the likes of him."

Ms. Trudy Bishop had the fast appearance of an almost prettied sort of peasant girl. She was fair in a lesser light, less fair in better. Therefore, lesser light it would always be for the likes of her.

As well, Trudy's permanent placement beneath the pub had a clear effect on her appearance. She was a thin and dreadfully pale young woman. There hardly seemed a touch of food or sun or hope upon her.

The dirted floor of her tiny room pushed its hue all about her: a small touch of brown, here and there, attached to her reddened hair and her precious cheeks and the many exposed areas of her lighted skin. Only her teeth, yellowed and unshapely, remained untouched by the constant swirl of filth.

Of course, the boy saw none of this. There was only for him those impossible eyes. The dear girl looked as though the whole of her broken life was somehow packed into those golden, remarkably sized orbs. How could he not dream? How could he not look? How could he not love?

"T'is a small space, but my space," she eeked as though a begging mouse.

The spell was momentarily broken. Barthalamew glanced the tiny room and considered his newly beloved's space. There was but the small door and the closing walls and the bed that fit between them. There was a brittle chair and a table as small as any table could be with a daring number of candles burning atop it. There was a single book, worn and happy, and there was absolutely nothing like a window at all.

It reminded him of his current room. It reminded him of a previous room as well. To be sure, it was all too familiar.

"T'is quite suitable," his calmed reply.

"I'm not so sure of all that, sir," Trudy answered, "but t'is sized well enough for its purpose."

Its purpose? Barthalamew was startled by the word. What could possibly be the purpose of such a room as this. The boy looked again to the bed, as though on the hunt for some clue. It was of the very poorest sort of construction and size, seemingly jammed into that tiny space as though by some remarkable force. As well, it issued a particular odor that was more than unseemly.

"It looks…comfortable," Barthalamew thought to say, for he was in need of only saying kind things.

Trudy put her sizable eyes to the bed and then back to her suitor. "T'is the least comfortable thing of all, sir."

With this said, Ms. Trudy sat upon it and gestured for Barthalamew to do the same. There was some hesitation but what choice had the boy. And so, he sat beside her and once more considered her look.

Oh, how her eyes were the thing. They were almost all the dear girl had to give. And yet, there remained the treasure of her thinly pressed lips and the sound of that light and near heavenly voice. There remained those tiny but dirtied cheeks and all the little, though slightly malnourished things that comprised all of her impossibly tiny charms. Though there was so little of her to see, the more he saw, the more he loved.

At once, the boy begged for some proper coat or covering. Hers was not the sort of dress he was accustomed to seeing. It was barely any sort of dress at all. It was a terribly tattered garment and featured a strange showing of beads and was clearly a tight and uncomfortable fit.

"T'is quite colorful," he thought to say before he realized there was no real compliment to offer in regard to such an unusual attire.

"It serves its purpose."

Again, with the notion of purpose. It was as though the word itself was camped out in that meager room, crowding it all the more. Barthalamew thought to try once more.

"Do you…entertain much…here?" was now his ridiculous question and, at once, he wanted it away.

Ms. Trudy Bishop eased her smile and allowed for her appreciable answer. "Of course. T'is expected. T'is why the room is provided."

"I…see…" he tried with a smile, for it seemed only proper to extend a smile in return.

"Would you like to touch my breasts?"

And just like that, the subject was quite changed. The question struck Barthalamew as though an open palm across his face. To be sure, the boy had no such want! But…didn't he? And, in fact, why wouldn't he?

Barthalamew looked away as he put some serious consideration toward the formation of an answer. Yes! Now that it was mentioned, he wanted to touch her breasts. His heart, his soul, indeed his hands, had a very real want to touch but he was remarkably stilled. The poor, dumb fellow only had want to…

"I am pleased to simply sit."

Never had such wide eyes suddenly become so much wider.

"Is that what you have paid for?"

Barthalamew was astounded by the idea that…

"But, I have not…paid."

Indeed! He had not!

"Well, sir, I have been paid for," Ms. Bishop said with some vigor. "Otherwise, you would not be sitting beside me."

Barthalamew was shaken. His mind was suddenly swimming as much as any could swim and was doing all it could to do to stay afloat. At that very moment, he considered his heart, his want, his need, his words. He considered the room and that colorful but raggedy dress and the ever-widened eyes of the beautiful maiden before him.

He considered Toby's curious glee and Madam Emma's unusual praise and appreciation. He considered the narrowed stairs that brought him below. He considered the dimly lit rooms and the admonishing words of Milford Dean. He considered and then finally understood.

Trudy was not before him to be loved. She was not there to be known, to be admired, to be adored. She was there to be touched. Indeed, she was there for a good deal more than that. Barthalamew's voice nearly failed in his asking for something…less.

"Perhaps, we could sit," he nervously repeated.

"But, we are already sitting."

The boy then tried for a proper rebuttal. "Perhaps, we could talk."

"But, we have talked, sir."

Barthalamew was staggered. What else was there to suggest? He looked crazily about the room. His eyes pounced upon her singular book.

"Perhaps, we could read," for it was his strongest want at that very moment and yet, even as the words left his lips, he knew it was entirely the wrong thing to say. The look on Trudy's dirtied face affirmed as much. Her mousy voice suddenly stressed.

"Well, sir, there is only the half hour that is paid and much of it'is nearly gone. As well, t'is not a good read, sir."

Barthalamew pulled his old hat from his head for he had want to fidget. "But, all books are a good read!"

The boy was anxious now. The rum had found its depth. The lesser light prevailed. The tight quarters pressed. The bed still wreaked.

"I'm certain the books you read are quite good, sir, but mine is just a lot of romantic nonsense."

Barthalamew was stymied. "But, how can romance be nonsense?"

Ms. Bishop proffered a look that suggested something like confusion. Was he jesting? But, of course! His query was meant as a joke. And so, she laughed.

"I appreciate your company, sir. You're a funny sort of fellow."

And yet, her happy words barely skimmed the boy's heart. Barthalamew did not feel funny. He had never known funny and, much to the point, it was not his choice or want to be funny at this particular moment. It was his want to be quite serious. Indeed, the boy was perplexed.

Sensing his unease, Ms. Bishop decided to take the reins. Her nearest hand quite suddenly arrived upon his nearest thigh. Barthalamew's focus was immediately returned. A fast stutter sounded.

"I don't…I don't know what I'm…"

At once it was clear to the girl. The whole of his face was flustered with embarrassment. Truly, he did not know.

"But, sir? How can you not?" she asked, as her hand inched ever toward.

Barthalamew launched from his spot on the bed as though yanked into place by some remarkable force. The boy now stood over the unnaturally wide-eyed Trudy as he grasped for any sense of decorum, but, of course, there was no decorum to come. There was only his gaping mouth and its want for some better word.

Barthalamew glanced about, choosing against her waiting eyes, choosing, instead, for those four closing walls and that wretched bed and the tiny table and it's ridiculous, if not somewhat dangerous allotment of candles. Anxiety was now the rule, and so the boy did the only thing he could think to do. He quickly made a grab for the door and yanked it open. He was out in a flash.

The room was suddenly emptied, save for the most confused prostitute of all time. Trudy could only hold to her spot on that stained and fetid bed, startled by the boy and his absurd state. It was her want, of course, to simply chalk it up to the always silly ways of men but that moment, in particular, was quite—

"Can I see you again?"

Her abnormally wide eyes were drawn once more to the doorway where Barthalamew now stood, hat in hand, as though the most lost sort of child. Silliness, indeed! Trudy considered the oddity of his sudden reemergence and then voiced the only answer she knew to give.

"Your coin is always welcome here, sir."

Barthalamew was immediately affected. The unrest in his eyes surrendered at once. A smile launched across the full width of his face. His voice eased.

"Of course," he said and then dared for the skies as he pushed her blessed name across his waiting lips. "My dear, Trudy!"

Toby's return home was curiously marked by a somber look. He stepped heavily across the threshold and took to a seat at the kitchen table without so much as looking up. He then lifted his hat from his head and crumpled it into his hand and offered not a syllable to the waiting missus in explanation. Something was not right. Something, in fact, was clearly wrong.

Joan knew well enough how much her good husband enjoyed his rare nights at the pub. She knew well enough that he was an honest man who simply sought some proper fellowship for an hour or two outside of his own home. She knew, well enough and much longer than he, of the lesser room below that too easily dared and ruined a proper and, more often, less than proper man, but Toby was not the sort of man to succumb to such mischief. This, she knew, without question.

And yet, there appeared by her husband's look something like guilt. At that moment, Joan was quite worried. She stepped quickly to the table and tried for her query, but her husband beat her to it.

"I took him…" Toby started, but then halted. It was a not his want to say another word, but the words came, for they had to be said. "I took him…below."

Below?

"Below?"

"Below."

Below!

"To the Madam," Toby then concluded with his eyes still low, as though he was speaking only to his shoes.

Joan eased a gasp. After all, it was no gift to her heart to hear those words, to know that her husband purposely visited a whore house or, in that particular instance, a whore basement. Her whole body gave a deep shiver before she realized the full of Toby's statement.

"You…took *him*?"

"Barth."

The name reached with its intended weight. At once, Joan understood. It was a mission of mercy, a last resort. Of course.

The good wife pulled a chair and sat next to her Toby. She followed his gaze to the floor at her feet. It was not ever her want to discourse on the subject of madams and whores and the business of rooms beneath bars, but something was very much amiss. Deep down, she knew the answer before the question was even asked.

"And what of it, husband?"

"I swear to the Gods, Joan! He was only in there for ten minutes."

To her way of thinking, that seemed about right. It even seemed…good, all things considered. And yet, it was clear that there was more to it than that. Joan kept her head low and pressed once more.

"And what of it?"

And with the coming of the first of many tears, Toby let it out.

"He loves her," he choked. "He's in love…with the whore that I bought him."

28

Love, by Trudy's want, was easy enough. She loved simply and without regard or condition, so long as two coppers were placed before the waiting Madam. Barthalamew, of course, found this to be a very curious exchange, but he was only too happy to submit. And so, his offering was made, and, for the full run of a half hour, Trudy granted his heart's desire which, to be sure, was never once quite what she expected.

After all, Barthalamew was a lovelorn boy, much moreso than usual, which, might I suggest, was quite singular considering the usual. As such, his blessed soul never once considered Trudy to be a lesser woman by way of her unsavory trade. In fact, he was somewhat pleased for it.

To the point, Trudy was entirely genuine with her attention, with her smile, with the call of her mousy voice and those ever-bulging eyes. What matter was it to the boy that it was only to be some half hour, for her minutes to him were as though days and weeks added to his previously wearied years of life.

Allow me to take a moment to properly explain. Barthalamew's style of love is best categorized as what some may call unconditional. It has a nice sound to it, of course, but it can be a troubling thing for any fair, or even less than fair maiden, to process. To the point, the notion of anything unconditional generally comes across as more Godly and, therefore, less human. Accordingly, its practice is sadly wasted on the mortal.

And yet, what chance had the boy! That was how he loved. That was how he always loved. And that, dear reader, is why he was as doomed as any thousand men could ever be.

And it is not because love hurts, for surely it suffer its pains, but for the fact that Barthalamew's unfortunate heart never quite achieved its boundaries. His love, after all, still remained for all those many who came before his blessed whore. His soul still pined for Daphne and Dear Jayne, for

Janice and wretched, though still lovable Gretchan and for wicked Becca to boot.

His heart, like a faulted ship upon the sea, was so taken with water than it could barely hold another drop and yet somehow kept its course. The sea, however, would soon make its claim. That, after all, is what a sea is for.

"It's a boat," Barthalamew said by way of his second visit, pointing to an obvious bit of whittled wood on the floor by Trudy's bed. "I've seen them at the marketplace."

"Yes," was Trudy's simple answer.

"It's very nice."

"If it pleases you then it pleases me."

The words darted directly to the boy's waiting heart. The notion that Trudy took pleasure in the things that pleasured him was quite liberating. As well, it had a very unconditional sound to it.

"Of course, it pleases me."

"That is unusual," was her immediate chime. "It is not something anyone has thought to notice before."

"Well, of course, there is much more here to admire than some carved bit of wood."

"Such as!" again her immediate quip, for Trudy was routinely immediate by way of reply.

Barthalamew was quickly pleased for the invitation to say, "Such as your smile. Your eyes are wonderfully kind and my ears so appreciate the sweet call of your voice."

Curiously, Trudy was not moved. By way of her profession, such words were offered up a dozen times a night and not even for the fact that one might have a kind smile or prettied eyes but for what generally resonates as procedural foreplay. Such words to her were more a trap than courtesy. Trudy's smile softened. Her reply was less than immediate.

"I see."

An awkward pause descended as Barthalamew tried to consider and decipher her tone but, of course, he could not, for what man could! It was Trudy who broke the silence as she felt it her duty to press forward with the business at hand.

"I can take my dress off now, if you like."

Without even holding for a response, Trudy was already clutching for the nearest button on her scanty bodice. Barthalamew's voice sent up at once.

"Stop!"

Trudy was checked. It was not a word she was accustomed to hearing. She immediately faulted to another line of thinking.

"Of course, sir, I am sorry. You prefer to undress me?"

"I do not!" Barthalamew persisted.

Trudy was again halted. The boy's words were nearing insulting.

"Am I not...pretty enough?" she tried.

Barthalamew's soul was nearly shattered by the sounding of such a question.

"Of course, you are," he said quickly, but softly, nearly as a whisper. "You are the very example of pretty."

Another word. Another trap. Another man!

"Do you prefer another girl? Josephine is but a room over."

The sounding of that particular name nearly ruined the boy. He immediately envisioned the old and dying sister in ways that were immediately unfit.

"I do not."

"Well, sir, there is a lot you do not want," Trudy quickly pushed, for she had found her rhythm once more. "Perhaps, we might start with what you *do* want."

Yes! Of course! A proper question. Barthalamew thought quickly upon it.

"I want..." the boy said with some hesitation for his request was remarkably personal. "I just want to...hold you. If that is all right."

"Hold? Me?"

Barthalamew was taken aback by how poorly his question was just then returned. It seemed as though Trudy was nearly mocking. His heart stopped. His head bowed. He was

237

hesitant to proceed. His confession came as though a whispered cry.

"I've never held a woman."

Trudy made effort to contain her surprise and nearly failed. Surely the boy was jesting.

"T'is hardly a thing," she returned with a wisp of a giggle, but then noted Barthalamew's sudden apprehension. Clearly, he was as serious as could be. "But," she then said, providing for an accommodating tone, "you are welcome to hold me, sir."

The boy's soul fluttered. Her answer reached his gentle heart as though a feather adrift settling so ever softly upon a desperately waiting ground. Oh, blessed little room! What impossible dreams you spawn!

And so, Barthalamew, mindful of his height and the lesser ceiling above, stood from that dainty chair and eased from his side to her side of the room. The effort required no more than half a step. He then lowered himself upon Trudy's tiny, disheveled and still somewhat rancid bed and outreached his arms for her.

At first, the effort was an awkward and gangly mess. It was far from romantic form. The ensuing entanglement looked as though some wreck of a person upon another.

Trudy, bless her soul, quickly corrected. She allowed her body to better provide for his reach and then instructed the boy to lay back upon her rickety bed. The instruction was gladly received. Barthalamew reclined. She then followed. And by this manner, the girl was properly held.

A calming smile eased across the boy's face. His lanky arms were entirely around her, holding her, cherishing the kindness of her form, of her blessed touch. Not a word was said for nearly that half hour before a quick and familiar rap came upon her door. Trudy leaned up and broke the peace.

"We are done, sir."

Barthalamew was hesitant to rise, but he knew it was his duty to do so. His time was past. His copper was spent. And yet, his very soul could not have been more pleased for its purchase on that miraculous night. The boy's voice lighted upon the air as he stood and offered his parting words.

"I am so very grateful for your gift, my dear! Thank you entirely!"

"But, of course, sir," Trudy said, quickly pleased for the simplicity of his nature. "I'm most happy to oblige."

Barthalamew allowed his eyes one last glance before he turned to make his leave. Her smile remained. It was still there and only for him.

The boy was elated. His heart skipped and hopped and bolted about as though it would never know or find its proper beat again. He felt faint and happily so as he reached for her door, gave it a tug and stepped from her pocket-sized room into the dimly lit hallway beyond.

"Take yer time, do ya!" erupted a curt voice from the shadows.

"Beg your pardon?" Barthalamew said as he turned to the erupting voice.

It belonged to a clearly impatient sort of man, well-aged and quite bothered.

"Get!"

That was all that was said. Barthalamew was pushed aside as the fellow stepped quickly, and rather rudely, into Trudy's room. The door was then abruptly put to a boisterous slam.

It happened in a rush and it was clearly an unkind brush, but what did Barthalamew care about some irritable geezer. His heart, at that moment, was much too high above it all. Not a soul could touch it. No silly old man could weigh it down.

And so, Barthalamew eased his way back into that small basement of a room and up that cramped stairwell. He walked back into the Great Raff Pub and floated out the door and back down Port Street to his simple room and mattress where a thousand kind and proper dreams awaited his young, oblivious heart.

29

Trudy, of course, had dreams of her own. Clearly, hers were small dreams, born from that small room and by way of her impossibly small heart but dreams they were. And while those dreams were only rarely entertained, for Trudy's schedule proved rather constant, a moment occasioned here and there when she allowed herself to consider the notion of life's sweeter things.

Foremost among them was her want for a precious dog. Oh, to have hold of a proper pup, some beast to know her command, to know her wants, to know her voice, to press the absolute want of her heart upon it and to never hold or love but to demand and hurt.

Well, to be sure, that may not strike one as a comforting thought, but Trudy Bishop was not a comforted soul. Pain was all she ever knew of that curious thing called love. Her life was as windowless as the boy's and even moreso for the slaughter of demands that were daily, hourly thrust upon her.

Another dream was to simply know about her father. A mother was remembered easily enough. The wench died of a wretched illness in what was now Trudy's very own room. The father was never mentioned. There was provided no clue or understanding as to who the man was or how he came to be in her mother's life though, given the mother's occupation, being the same as the daughter's, a proper clue could hardly be expected.

And so, Trudy was left to wonder by way of her late, more quieted hours. Her father, she was sure, was a john, likely poor and uneducated and, by simple observation of her own carriage, a smaller sort of fellow. Perhaps he worked nearby. Perhaps at the whitesmith. Perhaps he was married, as so many of her callers were. Perhaps he had a proper beard and a kind face with big happy eyes like hers. Perhaps she would have even loved—

And then a knock would come, and a man would enter and put his drawers to the ground and she was at it once more. Some nameless face. Some hairy fellow. Some fat beads of sweat.

And then another.

And then another.

Mindless grunts became the songs of her night. The ceiling and the floor became her most intimate of friends. She greeted each with a turn and made her faces and pretended on some happy conversation as though it was her party and not his.

And then he was done. With his drawers gathered from her good friend the floor, the john was off with a whisk, so as to make room for the next. And then there was the next and another to follow. And, so on.

And then the most curious sort of knock arrived. And the most curious sort of boy stepped in. And the most curious half hour prevailed.

At the very least, Barthalamew's two coppers briefly spared Trudy from her usual toil and that alone eased her position a bit on how she might handle her imaginary pup.

"Ms. Bishop," for the boy was decidedly formal when in love.

"Sir," for Ms. Bishop was formal without reason.

"I am quite pleased to see you again."

"T'is a pleasure to see you as well."

The answer had a genuine sound, for the answer was true. There was to be no grunting or sweating or mindless indifference. There was to be the boy's silky talk and, most pleasing of all, his complacent heart.

"I have brought a book," he said, holding it as proof. "I have an exciting chapter to share."

Of this, he seemed sure, but Trudy clearly lacked imagination. And yet, Barthalamew's time was paid for. There was only to accept his want to read, his want to give her some proper hold, his want to care which, she had to admit, was purposed with a curious sort of confidence.

And so, the boy happily read. And the girl politely listened. And his time was soon up.

"It is a kind sort of story," was her common issue at the end of so many sessions.

"Yes, it makes for a nice romance," Barthalamew offered more than once by way of reply.

"I don't understand what that might mean, sir, but our time is up."

Barthalamew tried to remain. "But there is no kno—"

The knock then came.

"My next john is readied."

"Next…john?" Barthalamew begged, for the name did seem oddly mentioned.

Trudy realized her error and made effort to explain. "Yes, my friend is always called john."

Barthalamew absorbed this poorly. It seemed an odd thing to call anyone john who was not actually John. He was rather taken by the notion and even thought to press the matter a bit.

"Am I…a john?"

Happily, "A john with a book, sir."

"But, my name is Barthalamew."

"T'is all the same, sir. You are as much a john as the next fellow."

Trudy said this without so much as a wink. Her impossibly widened eyes gave no indication of a wink. Winking was not her nature. Johns, apparently, were.

"But I love…" the boy stopped, but the word was out and already heard.

"Thank you, sir. It is common enough to hear when it comes to this business of men, but your good words are noted."

It was not what was said, but how it was said that struck Barthalamew. Her voice was plain. To the point, it was lifeless. It was purposely unkind.

The boy's heart was stopped. He turned his eyes from hers and stared to her good friend the floor. The realization hit its mark.

"I'm a john."

"We're all a john!" from Milford Dean who seemed entirely assured on the matter. "T'is all you and I shall ever be."

It was a most curious hour at the Great Raff Pub. The room was empty but for Barth and Mr. Dean and Big Red who was busied with his mop. There was hardly a sound in the tavern but the echo of their drunken voices.

The boy turned to his wayward companion and tried for his reply. The rum was there to help.

"That seems...unlike her."

Mr. Dean was astounded by his misconception. "T'is entirely like her, sir!"

Sir! It was no longer a kind word. He wanted it away. He wanted it clear of his breaking heart.

"I am no sir," Barthalamew barked.

"So, let it be said, so let it be done!"

Though Barthalamew's ears were every bit as drunk as the rest of him, Mr. Dean's words seemed more than a bit off target.

"I am not a sir," was now his whisper. "I'm not." There was a bit of a stumble before Barthalamew finally realized what he truly wanted to say. "I wish to the gods it was my actual name!"

Mr. Dean was certain that the boy meant for a toast. And so, a toast was spiritedly proffered.

"Then it shall be!" he said with a raised mug. "To my good friend, John!"

"To John," was Barthalamew's simple but disheartened reply.

And so, the toast was had, and the mugs went up and were brought back down to the bar, nearly emptied. Mr. Dean looked to Big Red, clearly on the verge of asking for a proper refill.

"Big R—" he tried but was quickly halted.

"Get out."

Big Red's reply was firm but begging for volume.

"Perhaps, one for the road. For me and—"

"Tha's the las' call for th' like's a' ya'!" Big Red then yawped. "Goin' on about your damned whores and your names for hours now. Get out, sirs!"

"I am no sir," Barthalamew protested.

"He's John!" Mr. Dean reinforced and with a drunken chuckle.

And now the volume, "Get! Now!"

Mr. Dean was startled. Decorum was clearly at a loss at the Great Raff Pub that night but even in his condition, Milford realized that the better hours had come and gone. It was only proper to make the call. Mr. Dean stood first and made his salutation.

"Good evening, John!"

Barthalamew drunkenly responded in kind. "And to you, John!"

"Johns be gone, the lot of you!" again from Big Red and with a temper still suggesting volume.

"Johns be gone, indeed!" from Mr. Dean who was only too happy to concede, for his want was now for his home even though his home was no longer his own.

And with that said, the estranged husband gave Barthalamew one last, kind look before he humbly stepped from the bar and made his quieted exit. In that brief and telling moment, the boy was pleased. His heart was hurting for another and not just for himself.

"Where does he go?" Barthalamew asked, almost to himself.

Big Red had little care for the matter and said exactly that. "I don't care. So long as he goes."

By his sharp tone, it was clear that the barkeep had no care for Barthalamew either. He was to go as well. And so, the boy tried for one last sip of rum, then reached for Mr. Dean's mug so as to assure both were empty. He then stood and made his step to follow after Mr. Dean but not before turning back to the darkened door across the room.

Oh, how his heart wanted! Oh, how he begged once more to know the feel of those narrowed stairs that led to his beloved beneath that waiting floor! Oh, how he longed to hold her forevermore.

But the whore was no longer his to hold. She was no longer his to love. There was only her memory to hold him now. There was only the haunting of those impossible eyes. And there was not nearly enough rum in all the world to float what remained of his sinking heart.

The boy clumsily pivoted and exited the pub. Port Street then carried him west to Jasmine House where his simple room awaited, where his needful soul was met with silence and where his want for some candle had all but vanquished.

The boy had loved as low as one could love and was rejected, still. It was clear, now more than ever. He was no more than a worthless john. At best, it was all he would ever be.

30

It was despair now that was in advance, that came to roost in the heart of Barthalamew Buckett. It was despair now that kept him so near the ground. It was despair that quit him of his job, that stole the pen from his hand and the words from his soul and forced his eyes from his fellow man as he silently knocked about those cobbled streets of Alagood.

It was despair that put him well behind on his rent and bid him to care not a bit if it was ever paid again. It was despair that all but starved him, that made him a perfect stranger to himself and once again to everyone in town. It was despair that pitched a slow and determined battle for his soul and it was despair that was winning out on all fronts.

But, let it be said, it was also despair that saved the boy when he was most in need of saving. It was despair, you see, that came for him and not a moment too soon, for a thousand deaths were fast at hand and it was despair, on that very particular day, that spared his wretched life.

Well, kind reader, we have reached the part of our story where a number of legends collide and much of it, I am saddened to say, is a rather unpleasant business. Perhaps as the coming pages unfold you will allow yourself a nice brandy or claret. At any rate, that is my counsel but, of course, you may do as you please.

As for myself, another rum is in order. A moment, if you will, while I hasten a splash and heave a toast to that good fellow Theryoung. Oh, there is no more to hear of him but, perhaps the tale of his demise. A thousand deaths on that terrible day and, by Molly, his was the most brilliant of the lot. Why that one is not lionized is beyond me! Now, to proceed.

History kindly notes for us the date, as do so many stones in the bone yards there. Not that anyone needs reminding but if, by chance, one ever did, one would not have so far to look.

Whereas it was a day to end like no other, it began as well as most any could. Dawn gifted an easy sun. A kindly blue sky settled in place. A cool and tender breeze spurred from every nearby bird its most earnest serenade. Summer was fallen back now, was gone by a matter of weeks, and by its doings there remained the promise of a most substantial harvest.

Mid-day's arrival brought about a mad rush to the fisherman's market for not a ship in the fleet came up short by the weight of that morning's catch. Trading was brisk. The wheels of commerce were at full spin. Prosperity, that season, was all but assured. To the point, all was right in the world, as all usually is when the world is on the brink of some hellish tilt.

T'was late in the day, nearing sunset, when there appeared in the sky across the bay a thickening band of clouds. At first, it was not thought a worrisome thing, for a good rain was just then needed, but it did seem, even to the least informed eye, to be quite curiously formed.

Perhaps then, the thought emerged, it was to be some sort of tropical push. Such storms were common enough and what else might that mean, but a bit more rain and what, in all the world, was the worry of that!

Only too late was it realized that the nearby birds with their happy serenades had not only quit their songs but had, by then, been gone for some time. Only too late was the veil put up and the true nature of that awful storm revealed. Only too late did that black towering swarm of clouds appear on the horizon, bruising at will the twilight sky, rolling fast and low, from west to east, rolling as though to menace, as though to press an eager weight into the path spread out beneath it.

It was an autumn witch of a storm, a wicked aberration, and beneath it all, there was no doubt, things would surely die. And that which had the strength or luck to live would not soon forget that dear old Madam Nature, every now and then, must simply have her say.

From the seaside perch of Alagood the worst was fast expected. What few stores were open were closed at once. Streets were quickly cleared. Doors and windows were bolted shut. Families huddled inside their homes. Through westward windows fathers peeked and pondered the storm's approach as mothers whispered worries and children offered prayers while all about them traipsed the scent of some deep and distant sea.

Oh, that wicked autumn witch! There she was to take from them full possession of the night. There she was to steal a bit of life from each and every one. Hopeless was the hour, for what else could those good people do but pray and count the minutes until day came back around.

And as those prayers were muttered, the twilight sky was taken. It was to darkness, then, the spoils. And so nature held its breath, as nature does before a storm, and what an awful sound it was.

And then a flash between two coming clouds. And down came the wind with a banshee howl. And up came the sea to greet it.

And then a crack of thunder ripped the air and shook the town below. And down came the rain, though sideways now, lashing the west end first, lashing the boats of the west end pier, those humbled boats so quickly foundered by those pounding waves and wind.

The west end, of course, was low ground and was at the mercy of it all. It was previously unknown how fast it might all flood, but much too soon the dreadful fact was had. That wretched water seeped then crawled, then ran itself amok and took quite well to everything the west end had to give. Up from the swamped dens of those many artisans and fisherman came a knot of agonizing cries, but it was all so sadly muted, hushed by the roar of the storm and the rush of the surging sea.

T'was worst of all for the scores of hapless beggars, for the very poorest of the poor, those woeful souls, who had no place at all to go, who had no home from which to send up their frantic calls, who were drowned at once and without a sound and gone with the morning tide.

Oh, how the west end suffered. Oh, how it could not be watched, but there was nested, to the east a bit on Port Street, where the middle ground endured, a heedless bunch of hardy drunks who looked on or looked on as best they could. And what they could not see, they heard and what they could not hear, presumed, for presumption was, and always is, a fast and easy rule as it comes to those who may comprise a heedless, hardy, drunken bunch as this.

Their shelter on that fateful night was the Great Raff Pub, where Big Red, bless his Big Red heart, left the men of that heedless, hardy bunch to his wine and ale and to his gin and rum and to something else they could not make out but were only too happy to receive - something as was called the honor system. To be sure, Big Red was good and gone and chasing fast some higher ground.

As for those fellows who remained, they had all the looks and smells of wrecked and wretched men. There were four, each one by now so much a regular that each was, in truth, quite hard pressed to cite an address of his own. And so, they sat about and stood about and talked about. And each happily filled and sipped of their mugs as though to dare the raging storm. The storm, it seemed, had want to dare them back.

"Oh, t'is a mess!"

"Wot?"

"I say'd, t'is comin' down hard!"

"Wot?"

For it was coming down loud as well. Dudley Doyle, the former pastor, not yet the former drunk, watched from the window, watched the pelting rain and the muddied streets and all those forming ponds where ponds had never formed before. It occurred to him to look concerned but by the effort, so unsober as he was, he only looked more crocked for the effort. With a slow hand, he shuttered the window and gave up his post, then shuffled across the room so as to join the others in congress at the bar.

"T'is bad. Never seen it so bad as this," Doyle said with a boozy step and a tipsy lisp. "T'is a rotten mess, I tell ya'. This'll be for my sins, I jus' know it! My sins have come ta' haunt me!"

"Ha!" cried the estranged Milford Dean who was at once unconvinced but who then resumed his drink with a new worry of his own.

Behind the bar stood Pap. Pap, who was old and who, by all recollection, had always been old and who, by all those same recollections, had always been drunk, appeared, at that moment, very drunk and very old and, in fact, as drunk and as old as ever.

Perhaps, you might agree, it was on account of the storm but to that score we must also add the expense of all the gin that came to him, on that particular night and at the aforementioned cost of his honor. It was rather fortunate then, one may conclude, that he had so much of it to spend. Therefore, Pap was given to age and therefore given to drink and not quite like ever before.

By Red's extraordinary absence, Pap was quick to assume full run of the bar and he was much pleased with his role as the keep. And though he was notably kind with a bottle in hand, he did call for coins from Misters Dean and Doyle as they each held out their mugs for another of his generous pours.

It was their reputations, you see, that supervened. Between them, Pap knew too well, there was simply no honor to give. Ergo, the system could not support them. The two were forced to drink without it.

Then there was the matter of the fourth, the newcomer to the bunch. He was thoughtfully provided for as it seemed all but assured that he was much too young a fellow to be too much a fool, much too young, at any rate, as it concerned good old Pap. But, of course, a fool was precisely what he was.

"Gin?" was now the offer from Pap to the fool, with an eyebrow raised, hairy and gray and seemingly on the march.

By the light of a nearby sconce, the fool refused with a shake of his head.

"Ah, my boy, but here's a pretty gin. I do believe it the prettiest gin yet!"

"Bah," the fool then croaked, for he was a mirthless drunk. "Who drinks pretty?"

"Ah," Pap returned, "who drinks honorably?

And here a good laugh was had by Dean and Doyle, but mostly by Pap. Barthalamew, though, remained loyal to his melancholic form and his half-emptied mug of rum. He heard, instead, the crashing rains and the howling winds and the walloping rounds of thunder. He wondered, instead, of the fate of the fisherman's market, of Dear Jayne's bench, of Papa Jack, of all of Bow-Street. He then wondered once more of the last thing said by the haunted Mr. Doyle.

"Seems th' lad doesn' take ta' gin!" Pap said, now lecturing the other two.

"Well, he's young yet," from the scratch throat of Mr. Dean, who knew the boy a bit and even thought to like him.

"Best be on your guard, Barth," cautioned Doyle and with the touch of a knowing smile. "Gin is th' devil and he's comin' ta' get ya'!"

And again, laughter reigned for that heedless, hardy bunch except, of course, for Barthalamew who once more refrained, who only gave a stoic look to his still half-empty mug and who then took it upon himself to say the most unexpected sort of thing.

"And I say the storm is the devil. And here he is now!"

That, as you may imagine, was woefully unfunny. The three onlookers were immediately quieted. In the short silence that followed there was heard by the force of the storm a certain strain on the rafters above and the four walls around them.

"My sins, I believe," Barthalamew resumed and with a cursory glance to the darkened door across the room, "have come to haunt me, too."

Old Pap gave a scratch to his bearded chin and applied a squint to his eye. He reached for a bottle of rum. It was hastily uncorked, and the rum therein was brought to the rim of Barthalamew's waiting mug.

"What sins have ya', my boy?" he then asked. "What sins could ya' possibly have at your tender age?"

What sins, indeed! Dean and Doyle were suddenly all ears for the subject of sin, but of course you know, is the most welcomed subject of all. It is especially a source of song to the ears of the heavily fated, as sirs Dean and Doyle were, as, in truth, every man was, is or soon shall be.

Barthalamew, though, accepted the query in stride. With a touch of patience, he put his mug to his lips and took for himself a drink. His heart was calmed. His tongue was steadied. His answer was quite simple.

"I loved poorly."

At first, this did not stir the men. It barely seemed a sin at all.

"Well, my boy," sputtered Pap with a crooked grin, "As I see it, if lovin' bad is a sin, then all th' world is bound for hell."

Another crack. Another laugh. But then all was halted by the tower bell of High-Street church which just then let out a harsh and frightful note. Across the reach of that wetted night it sounded struck, and struck it was, by a wicked kick of lightning.

In that instant Barthalamew winced for the lowly church on Bow-Street. It had no bell. It had no tower for it. It was as simple a construct as could be constructed, and, at that moment, he instinctively knew it was taking on its unfair share of sea.

To his rum the boy once more attended. To his silence he once more held. And then, he confessed to his pitiful sin.

"I loved a lowly woman."

The words still failed to find root. The men remain unstirred.

"But, Barth," from Mr. Dean now and with a crooked grin of his own, "that's no rare business a'tall!"

"Quite a common sorta business," Pap rejoined. "I'll be bound for hell a good hun'red times if that be any kinda' sin!"

By Pap's good cheer, the three laughed the loudest yet. Barthalamew, though, spared not a sound; he only glanced once more at that dimly lit door. How odd the walls seemed now! How so very much it looked as though they were each on the move and with a groan at every step! And how so curious was the sea, for it was just then beneath the pub's bolted door and pushing its salted way, though at a leisurely pace, to all corners of the Great Raff Pub!

"I love her still, " at last he said.

The laughter abated. At first no man dared to speak, for there seemed no words to say but a curiosity quickly prevailed.

"Which one?"

And for this, the former pastor was nudged and evil-eyed and so the question was fast abandoned, but in that kindly silence, Barthalamew knew, without so much as a look, that the soft whisper of her name was passed.

The howling wind abruptly let up, revealing the intensity of the hard hitting rain. A glimpse of light flashed through the cracks of the shuttered window. A bone-rattling jolt of thunder was quick to follow.

There was heard from the rafters at the far end of the room a jarring crack suggesting some sort of architectural sway but the pub, so far, held its place. It was uncommonly clear that a good deal of danger was encroaching but what did those fellows care for that! They longed only for their gin and rum, for only their gin and rum would have them.

It was Milford Dean who then took his turn and put his sin before them. It felt right, he knew, to say it and so he said it, slow and clear and with a voice not quite his own.

"Aye. I, too, loved poorly. But in a diff'rent sorta way," and here he paused and took his sip. Outside the pub the wind picked up and was on the prowl again. "My dear wife!

Oh, but there's a good-hearted lass. A bit of a looker some say. I say, at any rate. The damned'st smile a fellow could know! A fine cook an' keeper. A woman a' virtue. A woman a' kind spirit. As good a woman as I've ever known, as good as a man like me will ever know. Who am I ta' go off an' leave a blessed woman like that? Who am I, I ask ya?"

But the shallow ears of those muddled men were ill-prepared to field a question of such unexpected depth. No man, therefore, proffered an answer.

"Well, tha's my sin, I suppose," Dean concluded with the start of a tear.

"I think she'd have ya' yet," said good old Pap with a helpful wink and a nudge upon the shoulder.

"I know it. I know it for fact!" was the husband's fast reply.

Barthalamew looked up and spied the man, for he knew it also to be true.

"Then why are ya' here?" said Doyle.

"B'cause I'm a coward," said Dean with more tears than he could possibly hold. "B'cause, I'm scared ta' look her in th' eye. I'm scared a' her seein' th' man I become. I'm scared a' her lovin' a man like me. I don' want that for my dear Lora!"

And with that confessed, the estranged husband loosed his last tear and upped his gin and, in one shot, drank it dry. Pap then reclaimed the mug and filled it proper and this time without a charge, for it was then and there decided that the honor system could indeed support such a man as Milford Dean.

Pap supposed he should go next, but Doyle tossed him for it. And so, a copper piece went up and then came back down and by the tale of its many turns called on Doyle to be third.

Thus, having gripped his mug and, likewise, his heart, the former pastor, not just yet the former drunk, began his confession in what had become, on that fateful night, the customary way.

"I, too, have loved poorly," he parroted. "I have loved so poorly for so long now that I barely remember a time when I loved well."

"Ya' loved well your dear Trilby," said good old Pap of Doyle's young wife who was, quite sadly, dead by many years.

"Aye. She is the love I remember, the love I try to forget. It's not so easy to explain, except to say that..." and here a pause for the sake of a heartfelt sigh. "Gentlemen, it is such torment to not know her, to not have her to love anymore, to not know that smilin' face at the start and end a' my day. T'is a nightmare to the soul, I tell ya'. The only thought is ta' try ta' forget her but that hurts too much, too. So, I try to love somethin' else."

Having purged those words from the very depths of his soul, Doyle pulled his mug a bit closer as though, perhaps, that was his something else. He seemed unable to finish for his lips came to and appeared as pressed together as any two lips could be, but his mouth again opened and out poured the words he was trying so hard not to say.

"An' I try not to hate God! But, then there are days when I want...when I truly want to hate Him, to hate Him right out of existence. But tha's no good either. What does God care if I hate him or not! Hate is like love. Only matters when someone cares."

At that point there was another pause as Mr. Doyle was clearly out of breath and nearly out of heart. Well, I daresay there was some preacher in him yet. His words were richly offered and, to be sure, they were thusly received.

"So, here I stand before the devil's storm," he finally concluded. "Ruined. And drunk. And all alone."

"Well, not so much alone," said Milford Dean with a sympathetic smile.

"Aye," Mr. Doyle conceded with a tiny smile of his own. "Not so much."

And so, the former pastor's mug was taken and filled to the rim and this time returned without a charge, for it was determined just then by good old Pap that there was honor in him yet.

More gin was called for and produced. More rum was poured and swallowed. More thunder shouted. More lightning flashed. More cracks sounded from the rafters above.

A toast then followed, to which each of the four raised his mug and drank to the other and to what remained of their health and to all those many glorious things to live and die for. All the while, the uninvited sea continued to gather at their feet.

It was Pap who spoke next, who spoke up with such swiftness and charm that his confession seemed all but over the very moment it began.

"I kill't a man!"

A fast and discomforting silence descended.

"I s'pose tha's lovin' poorly," Pap concluded and then turned up his mug of gin.

"Well," Mr. Doyle started, for he felt it was his place, as confession use to be his game, "there are times when a man is called upon to properly defend himself, to defend his good honor and home—"

"T'was nothin' so grand as that," Pap quickly rejoined. "I was but a lad. Sleepin' all alone in th' wood. Well, along comes this fella walkin' up the trail, mindin' his own business. He was jus' a whistlin' away, he was. I even remember th' tune," and here Pap took to whistling some age-old mariner's song before continuing with his tale. "Well, as most a' ya' know, I don't care much for people tha' go whistlin' all about. T'is a racket! A damned racket! So's, I took hold a' my trusty pitchfork and jabbed him but good, square in th' chest. Well, tha's all what was needed. Down th' fella went, never ta' get up again."

Once more a weighted and bothersome silence loomed. The old drunk, for his part, eased a fast smile and refilled his mug and said nothing more on the matter, as no one dared ask any more of good old murderin' Pap.

Just then another spray of lightning flashed between the cracks. Another rip of thunder came clapping at its heels. The wind pushed. The water surged. It was high tide at the Great Raff Pub, a fact oblivious to all but one.

It was Barthalamew who alerted. Only he among them cringed at the touch of the sea. Only he paled as he felt the raw, salted waters seep into his shoes and wet his socks. Only he felt the fast chill that ascended his drunken spine.

The boy was then gripped by the icy-coldest of miseries, grasped by the deepest of despair. The words came to him out of nowhere, as though dispatched from the briny deep itself.

"I don't belong here," Barthalamew said rather asudden, though he was quite hard-pressed to suppose where, in truth, he actually belonged. "I have ta' go!"

"Go where?" from the curious Mr. Doyle.

"Where's ta' go?" from the whistler-hating Pap.

Barthalamew's answer seemed wrong at once. "My room."

"Are ya' mad? All tha's left for ya' now is wha's left in this here bottle," from Mr. Dean, who seemed to speak from the very lonely perspective of experience.

"I have ta' go," Barthalamew repeated with his lowest voice yet.

"T'is the sea," Pap then said to his friends Dean and Doyle, "tha's wha's got him! Tha's what scares th' lad. But there's nothin ta' fear a' th' sea, lads. I been livin' on or near it all me life. What's ta' get all bothered about if it thinks ta' step in for a drink."

"Aye," Doyle said with a half-smile. "Give it some gin!"

And with this announced a bottle was grabbed by the former pastor, still yet to be the former drunk, and slung to the ground where the gin spilled into the salted waters now lapping about their feet.

"Perhaps," Doyle then considered and with some regret, "th' sea had only need for a sip."

"Not ta' worry," from Pap who was quick to draw upon another bottle from beneath the bar and uncork that particular regret away.

The boy, however, remained unconvinced. His eyes were low now, to his sinking feet. His heart, he knew, was beneath those wetted planks.

"I'm ta' go."

The walls then brought about another shiver and from the rafters, once more, another wicked crack. Those were now the sounds that compelled the boy onward, that pressed his wearied steps across the gathering waters of the Great Raff Pub and toward the bolted door, seemingly leading him from one certain death to another.

The door was unbolted, and the sea was let in with a devilish rush.

"Shut it!" came the cry that was barely heard among the charging waves.

The boy made his exit and pulled the door to, for there were manners yet in Barthalamew Buckett.

"Tha's a proper fella', there!" from Pap who begged for and received some proper nods.

Indeed, the remaining three were impressed. The boy was brave. The boy was daring. The boy's choice was unique to be sure.

And so, each held to the bar now before them, each dedicated to the very last of their homes, each pleased for the walls somehow still around them. Mr. Dean stepped quickly across the sea-ridden floor and made effort to bolt the door. He then returned to the last of his friends and offered his toast to the blessed memory of that lovelorn, whore-loving boy.

The three men had their sip, then a good deal more until the sea at their knees was all but forgotten. What remained of the hours of that dreadful night in that particular pub is forever sealed in the confidence of that eternally silenced band of fellows! They fared quite well as the hour progressed, but a far less hospitable hour followed. And then there was only the sound of a misting rain falling upon an unsettled sea.

Dawn arose as though a drunken lout who had only then remembered his place. As the sun ambled up and shed its light upon that crooked town, the depth of the storm's imprint was ominously revealed. Port Street was all but wiped clear from the map.

Mr. Dean's sins were washed clean.

Old Pap was old no more.

And the former Pastor was, at long last, a former drunk.

31

Seventeen proved a curious age for the boy. Barthalamew was just then at the start of what would be his eventual form. Height, in the years since Sister Margaret's death, had come into play. It was not so much that he was unusually tall, but that his prevailing thinness readily suggested it.

And yet, it was equally clear that Barthalamew was on the verge of some mannish mutation. This was mostly due to a flourishing run of black hairs that now ran their course. There was also, on the occasion of his more laborious days, the hint of some budding muscular form that, in fact, never actually set but kindly allowed for the suggestion that he was, perhaps, a bit more man than not.

As well, there seemed by the simple show of Barthalamew's eyes some evidence of contentment. Although still awkward and quiet and as unsure as ever, a sort of complacency had made its gains, had gripped the boy well and given him an agreeable shake. He was, after all, at a busied sort of age in which routines are established and kept and well appreciated for the many simplicities they so kindly provided. In short, the everyday life of those ascending years had become so plain as to be almost pleasant for the boy.

By then the sisters were rather accustomed to Barthalamew's ways. Even Josephine's requests were generally made with a good deal of civility. Chores were done quickly and with ease and although little was offered by way of compensation, the boy was becoming increasingly aware of his own competence and worth.

No longer was he tolerated as some slave to the order, but treated, nearly, as one of their own, nearly as though his place among them was somehow assured. This was most commonly evidenced by the softest of smiles that came to him that year from a good many turns and from one turn in particular.

Though just shy of fourteen, Lydia seemed at the precipice of some early maturity. The red of her hair was easing into some lighter shade that told of a ripening grace. There appeared both curiosity and clarity by the crisp green of her eyes that, when combined with her imperishable smile, divined a spirit well advanced of a child her age. And whereas, by her younger years, Lydia's silence was somewhat offsetting, it was more agreeable now, seemed, in fact, a quality most befitting of the heart of the woman whose true beauty was yet to emerge.

The nave was now her castle and the bench before the tavern piano was now her throne. With her nimble fingers so softly and soundly dancing across those faded ivory keys, her purpose was slowly found and secured. Her love of the room, of the music, of the want of music was only succeeded by her love of—

"You're all done?"

Lydia's fingers slipped across the keys, striking some rotten note. The dear girl could not help it. She was, at that moment, distracted from her lessons. She glanced across the nave and spied Barthalamew's entrance.

"Yes," was his timid reply.

From her usual pew, Sister Marihanna eased a kind reply. "Then you will find in the sacristy that the post has arrived today."

Indeed, the year was accentuated with a number of unexpected letters from the southern town of Alagood. At first, the sisters, amazed by this relative flood of correspondence, were equally impressed to learn that every bit of it was directed to Barthalamew. After all, the boy had never seen, much less received a distant letter before.

To be sure he was hard pressed to understand what it meant. That was, of course, until Sister Marihanna took him aside and kindly explained the matter to him. Toby, though gone, was still ever-present.

With the arrival of the very first letter, Toby briefly described his trek towards the coast, laden, apparently, with far more adventure than was expected, thanks to a number of quirky highway characters as were met along the way.

The following letter produced talk of a town by the name of Kent which was described as social and wanting but for strangers and stragglers of which, sadly, Toby was decidedly both. His stay here was unkind and, thereby, brief. With Kent behind him the young nomad continued to the coast, with his eyes and heart set on as sweet a setting as was ever put to words.

Alagood was his destination now, a town renowned for its port and work and general hospitality. Renowned, of course, as it mattered to the residents of Kent, who were only too happy for strangers and stragglers to proceed forth from their beloved township to anywhere at all, and what better way to encourage that than to sanction a million wondrous lies about some distant port full of a million wondrous and distant opportunities. And so, Alagood it was.

Toby's arrival to that awkward and crooked town was quickly met with good news. It seemed the folk of Kent did the fellow some favor after all and by more reasons than one. He was employed at once by a prosperous property owner and given almost right away to the heart of his fair daughter! Her beauty, Toby assured, was unrivaled, was far from the notion of those few haggard women of the order.

Well, to be sure, this news of the world, and all it involved, was most encouraging. And as the many letters continued to arrive, Barthalamew felt as though there was only to revel in these many wonderful revelations. It seemed, from Toby's singular perspective, that love and achievement (but love most of all) were simply waiting, wanting and all but for the taking.

And then came the dispatch of that particular day. Barthalamew stepped quickly to the sacristy to find the most remarkable missive of all. Toby was to marry. A wedding was at hand. A proper life and property was secured.

There was only now for the boy to dream, to imagine his own coming voyage and all it would procure. He adored the idea of some proper love, of some absolute heart and life to share. From that moment on, he imagined her in every possible way. He dreamed of her every night, as though some ghostly beauty quietly awaiting his arrival in some strange and always happy land.

With that last letter read, Barthalamew left the sacristy and returned to his shed where he stumbled across sweet Lydia apparently making her way from the opposite direction. She was quick to glance away, again for the sake of a blush, but also for the sake of some guilt. The dear girl, you see, had nearly been caught.

The boy continued to his shed and opened the squeaky door and made his entry and, at that moment, he was struck by the presence of yet another letter. Atop his bed, it sat and waited.

Well, it was becoming a rather common affair. Letters were all about the boy. What else was there to do but read?

And so, a candle was lit, and the note was unfolded and given a proper eye. Lydia's words were much less about adventure and more about the kindly things that often came to a good girl's heart. She wrote of the changing seasons and about the sweet sounds of birds and of all of that grew about them, of her gardening and her reading.

She sweetly carried on about her love and devotion in regard to her education and the order and the notion that she, too, would soon serve as a proper Sister. She seemingly had no want to know of adventure, of the outside world, of any such dream or hope beyond the singular confines of her simple life. The girl was apparently pleased, and in every possible way, with the idea that she would always be in that crumbling church and before those crumbling women of discontent.

She often asked of his well-being, of his words and thoughts on a thousand matters that seemed a bit silly to him. There were paragraphs of flowers, talk of roses and their better smells. She pressed a want for his notions of bees and summer and...the moon.

To the end she often wrote about her love of music, of her happiness with the piano and how she one day wanted to play something proper for him. She would then suggest that her family was missed and that her life, though good, was spotted with a touch of loneliness.

To this, Barthalamew was aloof. Though the dear girl was slowly placing her good heart before him, she was no more to his own than the coming supper. And yet, a part of the boy was rather struck by her kindly efforts.

After all, Lydia's letters were impeccably crafted. Her words were beautifully chosen. Each and every line suggested a voice of uncommon tenderness. There were moments when Barthalamew was nearly inspired to pen a reply of his own, but the boy was entirely unpracticed in the art of correspondence. It was all a mystery to him as to how one might go about starting, to say nothing of ending, some personal note or thought.

As well, his mind was already overwhelmed by the notion of all that Toby promised. Those letters only provided for a temporary distraction. Love was now a number to the boy, a number that was sweetly considered and, thereby, lessened, by the passing of each day.

As a result, Lydia never received the simple letter she always begged to know. His pencil was never raised to counter hers. His thoughts and feelings and answers to her waiting questions were never left for her to find at the end of any day. And yet, the dear girl was not thwarted.

Hers, after all, was a rare and proper soul. Lydia was not of the selfish sort. It was not her intent to plague the boy or push him in some direction or another. Her precious heart simply had want for a voice and some kind boy to know it.

And so, she persisted. Her letters continued. Her kind words were read and finally known.

And her smile was forevermore.

32

The color was slow to come. There was, at first, a blur, but then it was there. A telling gray. Round. Batty. Orchestral. The words escaped his lips before he had a chance to stop them.

"Am I dead?"

"Of course not, Barthalamew."

The boy recognized at once. The suggestion of Lora Dean's liveliness remained but her voice was curiously sounded. There was a weight to it now, as though it was more to the floor than the air above it.

At that moment, she came into focus. Mrs. Dean looked as she always had, though it was clear her energy was faltered. It was then equally clear that the previous night had left a mark upon her. Her hair, her clothes, her face; it was all a muddied mess.

"The storm," Barthalamew pressed, for it was his fast need for an answer.

"It has passed," Mrs. Dean returned, all smiles, less heart.

The boy then eased a look about the room. At once, he recognized it as Mr. Loydford's office. He was laid out on his back, upon the man's very desk.

"The Hamm?"

"Indeed."

"Mr. Loydford?"

"Well, there's a good man, Barth."

It was not so much an answer, but Barthalamew was satisfied by her tone which easily suggested that Mr. Loydford was still about.

"It was dark…" the boy started as he made effort to remember.

"And wet."

"Quite so," he agreed, realizing now the full stench of the sea.

"You were found just across the way, by the whitesmith's."

"I…was?" and then a hard recollection. "I was at the Great Raff Pub!"

The boy pushed a fast and curious look to Mrs. Dean for he could not help but wonder, by her smile alone, if the pub was, in fact, spared.

"Laid flat," she then said with something nearing a sense of humor.

Barthalamew's apology was quickly at hand. "I am so sorry, ma'am, but your husband was in the pub. I do pray he is well."

"Sir," Mrs. Dean pressed with an unexpected touch of formality, "Let us not discuss Mr. Dean. Ever. Again."

"Of…of course not," the boy allowed, baffled, at first, but then continuing. "But…the storm?"

Mrs. Dean then leaned forward and in the most curious way. It was as though she meant to kiss the boy. Her voice softened and offered a curious, nurturing tone.

"It was a very unpleasant business, to be sure."

Unpleasant? To be sure? Barthalamew was overwhelmed by the notion that his landlord's wife was quite clear of her senses. By her look alone, she suffered but her eyes suggested a different sort of orchestra. They were, in a word, touched.

The boy made effort to sit up, for it was his want to give the Hamm a proper look about. And so, he stepped to his feet and his shoes were instantly re-wetted. Apparently, a bit of sea still coursed the floors and yet those detestable brown bricks remained. The Hamm held to its drunken slump but appeared quite steadied, impressively so.

"How unpleasant?" Barthalamew asked, for clearly it could not be so bad as all that.

"Well, there is some damage about," from the gray-eyed wonder whose smile was now leaning more toward something like a cadaverous grin.

"Some?"

"I won't lie, Barthalamew," Mrs. Dean then stiffened, for the words to follow required a bit of stiffening. "It is not so good a'tall."

Another glance of the Hamm all but assured that this could only be less than true.

"And you say the pub is gone?" the boy challenged.

"Washed out to sea, along with those dreadful bitches that lived below. The town is cleansed."

Oh, how Mrs. Dean's words then found their depth. Such a wicked thing to say, especially by way of that suddenly wicked smile. To be sure, that was a smile to be trusted no more.

Barthalamew stepped forward. He wanted to see for himself what this unpleasant business was all about. Mrs. Dean's hand was quickly upon him.

"Perhaps, you could just stay with me a bit, sir."

Barthalamew was startled by her touch. He looked at once to her crazy greys which, at that moment, were no longer dancing about but disturbingly stilled.

"I need a man to…" she said with a blush.

To what? What might the landlord's lady need from any man aside from rent?

"I need a man to," she halted again and then softly continued, "to stay with me."

The request seemed harmless and so the boy gave a quick search about the Hamm.

"If Mr. Loydford is about madam, I suspect he—"

"He is about, sir. But, he is no longer the man that I need."

Indeed, it was as curious a thing for her to have said as it was for the boy to have heard. Pray tell, what did she mean?

"But madam, I must find…" the boy held his words as he made effort to properly consider them. "I must find…" he tried again and was stopped as his heart regrouped. "I must…" and now with vacant eyes Barthalamew realized there was nothing at all for him to must or find. There was only to beg away from the uncomfortably stilled eyes of that bothersome woman. And so, he begged away.

"But, sir?"

The word, again, struck the boy poorly. The syllable was crushing, unkind.

"Please, let me be!"

"I must insist!"

"I need to see for myself!"

"It is no good, sir."

"Nor am I!"

Both were silenced at once. Even Barthalamew was overwhelmed by the sounding those particular words. For the first time in his life, his own heart felt the touch of some lesser current, of some darker tide. The boy had no want to be kind. He had no need to be needed. There remained nothing left of his soul at that moment but a mounting disgust for the woman before him and, consequently, for the many women now behind him.

Mrs. Dean glanced away as though struck. The boy's sudden tone was most unfamiliar to her ears. His intent was clear and clearly hurtful. She was to be left alone. There was to be no man to hold her now, to know her, to forgive her failing heart.

Barthalamew turned and stepped quickly away. His feet pushed hard against the wetted floor as he made his way to the exit before him. Once reached, he yielded and considered that rickety knob before him. How, the boy wondered, could anything fall without this ridiculous door falling before it?

It seemed nearly half a minute before his grip took hold and gave a twist. The Hamm was then opened to Port Street. There was now only for him to step forward and suffer all anew.

33

Barthalamew's eyes were quickly drawn to the immediate surroundings. Alagood was battered. Alagood was punished. Alagood was all but gone.

Ruin was clearly the rule. What the waters had not fetched, the winds had freely taken. Where buildings once stood, rubble now rested. Directly across, the whitesmith's workshop was expected but nowhere to be seen. There was only a view of the bay just beyond, the touch of a breeze and the push of an impossibly blue sky.

The sight was all the more bothersome by the presence of a telling sort of silence. Not a soul stirred. There was not a step, not a voice, not a man, woman or child about. Only the sounds of the sea remained amid the ominous suggestion of a thousand quieted deaths.

With his eyes then to the east, Barthalamew was wrecked! The Great Raff Pub was entirely lost. The King Robert's Arms, and all its finer renovations, was no more than waste upon the wetted ground. So much of Port Street was wiped clean, as though the finger of God reached down from the Heavens and flicked it all way.

The boy then looked back to the pub, to that once darkened corner where a door once stood but was clearly no more. Among the debris he could clearly see the start of a stairwell that dipped ever downward, some hole in the floor that was still as full of the sea as any hole in the floor could be. Beneath that telling pool, the boy knew, was the flesh and soul of his very last love.

With his heart so low, Barthalamew then carried his eyes a bit further up Port Street where he noted the remaining presence of the High Street Church. Although the angle of the street did not afford the best view, it was clear that the steeple, though beaten, remained. Those of the very highest ground were seemingly spared and that could only mean one thing.

Barthalamew then turned about and his soul was shattered at once. The West End was done. There was nothing but the sea to serve it now. The uncaring tides of Alabaster Bay splashed in and rolled about as though the west end was and had always been its claim, as though its quieted depths had always been for those now well beneath the surge, for the docks and the marketplace and Papa Jack's. And for...

Jasmine House! Barthalamew blinked and blinked once more. His eyes could hardly believe. The building was clearly gone, removed from both sky and ground. Its rubble now rested just beneath the churning waters where Port Street struggled to emerge from the slowly receding tide.

Barthalamew was stopped, breathless, stunned, but then his feet dared him forward. So weighted was his walk that he barely knew how to step and yet, he could not help but do so. At first, there was more debris than road and, soon enough, more water than debris and by time the crossroad was reached, the boy's feet were bloodied, and his knees were clearly wetted and...

By Molly, there was nothing there at all. No wall stood. No brick remained. No common room. No stairs to take him up. No dark and somber chamber with its rotted mattress and keepsake desk. No mantle with its two constantly read books. No poems. No letters wrapped in that wonderfully faded ribbon. No heart. No soul. All that he knew or loved or ever hoped for was forever lost to a hundred million gallons of heartless sea.

There was a want for tears, but the boy was hard-pressed to draw them out. His heart, after all, was too busied begging to breathe and no longer had the proper strength to summon such things. There was only to try and to fail and to simply beg it all away.

Barthalamew looked east again, to the standing Hamm. It was entirely untouched. It stood as though it would stand forever. How in all the kingdom could such a clearly fallen thing not fall? How was it that all of Port Street was put low but for that ridiculous pile of bricks?

The boy's imagination was stumped by the mere sight of it. He begged for some word, for some proper understanding and then realized his imagination would require a good deal more stumping, for another discovery was suddenly at hand. Ruin, apparently, was not done with the likes of him.

A strange and curious sound was just then heard. There was clearly some bit of sloshing about, as though something or someone was approaching by way of that knee-high tide. Barthalamew gave a fast turnabout, both curious and concerned, as any smart fellow would be.

At once, the source was spotted. A large sort of rat was nearing, clearly some awful, wetted rodent that had somehow survived the storm. Barthalamew was quick to wade away, to push east through the water and debris and towards a more shallowed ground.

And so, the boy hastened his steps. He made no effort to look back until he was nearing the Hamm and at once regretted his choice. The rat, it seemed, followed. The rat, it seemed, was determined. The rat, it seemed, was no rat at all.

Oh, that dog! That damned, damned, damned dog!

34

Dark and tired times prevailed. What remained of Alagood was a misery. Though as some soulless tease, the skies above held blue and clear for days and weeks to come. And yet, the lands beneath were as black and muddied and as stilled as could ever be imagined.

Barthalamew's new home was inexplicably the Hamm. His office was eased into something like a room. Aside from his weakened desk, it was now occupied by a moldy mattress and a constantly wetted pillow.

Gilbert Loydford made similar preparations about his own little room. A full bed frame was secured, apparently from his family home which barely suffered the storm. Though his ground was just as wet, he simply slept above it all.

Mrs. Dean kept to her space about the middle. Here she dallied and swept and cleaned as though an ounce of water was a thousand pounds of dirt. Quieted words were tossed from her mouth and flung about the room, but it was clear that they were not meant to be heard. The orchestra in her eyes was clearly retired. The music was gone. A new mania was calmly settling in.

At night, Mrs. Dean took to the driest of corners and rolled herself into a ball where sleep claimed her at once. And yet, the poor widow still had plenty to say. Her dreams were dotted with hypnotic chatter and periodic screams that jolted Barthalamew from his soaked slumber. Mr. Loydford, however, heard not a bit of it. His fatted sleep was heavy and absolute.

To be sure, a number of survivors made effort to gather at the Hamm, but the Gazette was having none of it. The press, after all, still functioned. The paper was still in business and even though there was hardly a soul about to buy an edition, Loydford's conviction was as strong as ever.

"That door is to be chained!" the editor yalped to the Hamm's select residents. "There is proper refuge up the road! We have a business still to run!"

"Indeed, sir!" from Mrs. Dean, whose particular responsibilities as it regarded the business, forever remained a mystery to Barthalamew.

"Are we not to help feed or provide—" the boy started but was at once rebuked.

"We are to help ourselves! And they are to help themselves! That is the way, sir! It has always been and shall always be the way!"

It seemed an unkind untruth, but what could the boy do? He had his room. He had his work. He had more than most at that point. He was at the whim of the master of the Hamm.

"What shall we write about?" was the boy's early query.

"What!" Loydford almost leaped at the insult. "We write, sir, about the storm! We write, sir, about the death and the misery and the wretched ruin of our beloved town!"

Of course, that was obvious by Barthalamew's mind, but his soul was flattened by the idea of any such assignment. After all, it was more than a hardship for the boy to even consider the loss of all that he so dearly loved. There was no word or news of Daphne or Dear Jayne or Janice or Gretchan or Becca or even Trudy, whose room was so close and still so beneath it all.

The mere thought of any one of those beloved names halted the boy's breath. The notion that any or all might be harmed, or dead, collapsed his fragile heart. How could his pen come to any sort of life considering—

A rap at the door!

"Our front page is here!" Loydford snapped.

"Front…page?"

Loydford lit up with a smile. "A stunning story, sir. Heroics and heartbreak and all before the most devastating wave of the storm. I heard of her account and insisted she come by right away. Be a good lad, Barth and bring her forward."

Barthalamew stepped to, nearly uncaring, nearly aware of the thick chain and many locks upon the door, nearly conscience of his effort to undo it all so that some heroic story might step in and bleed all about the room.

In a moment, the locks were off. The chain was dropped. The door was opened. Barthalamew was ruined at once.

"Barth!"

Mrs. Joan Theryoung.

And her three children.

And no one else.

Barthalamew kept a fair distance. It was not his want to know or hear but to leave, he knew, would be entirely rude. And so, he stayed and kept his eyes to Lee Ellen and Amy and to young Jack, who was seemingly past his burning goldfish phase.

In fact, the child had a very different sort of look in his eye. It was clear his youth was gone, murdered in the night. The storm, it seemed, killed more than people.

"And then we couldn't find Jack!" the tears now of a grieving wife and a terrified mother as she relived the moment for Mr. Loydford. "He was in the barn, last we saw."

"The barn that was brought down?" the curious and ever sensitive Loydford queried.

Mrs. Theryoung gave her cheeks a quick check. "Yes, sir. But not just at that moment."

"Of course, Mrs. Theryoung. And then what did Mr. Theryoung do?"

"He stepped from the shelter. He went to find Jack. He made us lock the latch behind him. I never saw him again. He didn't even say goodbye or… anything. There's no sign of his…of him anywhere."

Loydford looked to Jack. There was a clear want in his journalistic eye to know the child, to prod for his story, but even he could see that the young lad was hardly there, was, in fact, quite gone from his senses. The widow's voice pressed on.

"We waited. Hours. It was morning when I unlocked the latch and opened the shelter door. And there stood Jack. Wet. Bruised. But saved!"

"Did the boy say—"

"Not a word," from Mrs. Theryoung with the hard whisper of a broken mother. "He has not said a word since, sir! And I fear he will never say a word ever again!"

Barthalamew put another eye to the woeful child and then back to the girls who quietly, curiously tucked themselves away from Jack and looked by some other direction as though there was nothing more for either of them to see or hear. It was a bothersome sight, for distance was now clearly the Father of that family. Distance it would always be.

And in that moment Barthalamew understood. His future was clear. His want was no longer for love, for family. It was for…Distance.

"The barn," Mrs. Theryoung then said with a coming tear. "It was wiped clear. Gone. Somewhere it rests, with my husband beneath it."

Mr. Loydford eased a hand forward and rested it upon the good widow's shoulder. It was his want to reassure. And so, he did.

"The article will press for volunteers to scour the woods beyond your land. We will find Mr. Theryoung and bring him to the rest he deserves."

Mrs. Theryoung's strength was improved by his words. Her tears were dried. Her eyes were up and upon his at once.

"I appreciate this, Mr. Loydford."

"I will put my star reporter on it. Mr. Buckett will paint Mr. Theryoung's finest hour with a masterful and heroic stroke."

It seemed the finest possible thing said until it was quite suddenly, and unexpectedly unsaid.

"No. I won't."

From Barthalamew's lips, no less. Mr. Loydford was aghast. His voice was quickly stressed so as to carry his point.

"This good woman needs your help, sir! You are precisely the man for the job! You shall take this assignment—"

Barthalamew abruptly stood. He glanced his editor with a flash of contempt. He then looked to Mrs. Theryoung with a broken smile. His words were soft but firm.

"I'll never write another word. Not one more."

As though somehow signaled, Mrs. Dean stepped up from the far back room where she was preparing a small tray of beverages. It was her intent to serve when she realized the obvious tension in the room. All parties were silent, staring at Barthalamew. Even the distant and impossibly quieted children were in tune to the moment. And yet, what could she do but provide her inquiry with those deadened eyes.

"Perhaps, a lemonade to ease the day?

It was her thought that, at the very least, the children would brighten by the invitation, but the children did not. The widow did not. The editor most assuredly did not.

Barthalamew only glared, which caused Mrs. Dean to shrink. And so, gray-eyed widow and her tray of lemonades quickly withdrew from the room. Mr. Loydford then resumed.

"You cannot be serious!"

But, he could. And, he was. And to further prove the point, the boy stepped over the fallen chain and locks and then to the door and exited the Hamm for the very last time. Mr. Loydford was dumbfounded. He put up his apology at once.

"I am very sorry, madam. The boy is acting a fool!"

"The boy, good sir, is the only one among us who is not!"

Barthalamew held his spot just outside the Hamm, seemingly stuck on the notion of a direction. He pushed a thoughtful look to the sunken west end and noted a small number of fishing boats floating about some wayward port.

Life was clearly trying once more but the concept of trying was lost on the boy.

He then eased his look just across Port Street, where the white-smith was expected and still failed to be, where something much worse now held its ground. Dog was patiently upon his hind legs, looking back across the road to the boy as though his little one-eyed, chopped tailed, lice-infested life depended on it.

"I want you to know," Mrs. Theryoung pressed with her sudden presence, "I understand. I would never ask it of you."

Barthalamew was jolted, embarrassed, even intimidated by Mrs. Theryoung's sudden appearance at the door. The widow pressed a smile and then eased herself into the most compassionate embrace the boy had ever known. She then stepped back and, with her quieted children by her side, offered her truest words.

"You were his oldest friend. You were his dearest!" Joan said with effort, failing to hold her tears. "Barth, I had no idea! I was certain you were...I was certain those were...the last hours for all of us."

35

"These are the last hours for the two of us," Sister Marihanna said, failing to hold back the tear that just then started its run.

"Yes, sister," was Barthalamew's timid reply.

The boy sat in his shed, head down, searching deeply for some emotion to step up and explain itself, but his heart remained curiously still, as though it had some true need to refrain. His eyes then took measure of his surroundings one last time.

The shanty he was sure to miss, those four corners of his that would soon be his no more. The blankets. The pillows. The tools, even.

And then there were the many other things that occupied the very whole of his life. There was the roof and the patch and the nave and the sisters and his common chores. They would all soon be gone, to be taken from him and forever dismissed. It was as though his purpose, his understanding of all life and hope, was no longer of use or need. There was only to…

"I am sorry to be leaving," he uttered with a quieted tone.

"Dear boy," Sister Marihanna started but could not finish, for her heart just then swelled to the point of near asphyxiation.

And so, Marihanna sat beside him on his bed, the only true touch of comfort Barthalamew had ever known, and openly wept as any proud mother would.

"Why can't I stay?" his words then came, for he seemed to want to stop her from crying but knew not how.

Sister Marihanna composed herself. "T'is simply our way, Barth. A man cannot live among us. And today, you are a man."

"But, I don't want to be a man today! Can't I be a man some other day?"

Marihanna was pleased to laugh, for the inquiry was sweetly amusing.

"You are a man now. It cannot be changed. And today you will venture out into the world and find the life that has been waiting for you all these years. Just as you have imagined since the arrival of Toby's letters."

Indeed, those letters still inspired, but there was a very real step ahead of the boy. He was to be abandoned once again, to be pushed from a known world to an unproven one. Despite all of Toby's assurances, fear was now the rule.

"But...what if I'm not a man? What if it is not my birthday?"

To be sure, it was a fair question. The boy's date of birth had always been more of a doubt than anything like an answer. Whether he was seventeen or fifteen or even eighteen was all but a guess. However, the matter was decided on some time ago. It was put to a vote and happily secured for the record.

"It is your day," Sister Marihanna assured. "The first day of Spring."

It seemed a kind thought that the idea that spring might, in fact, be his day but the blessed record did not take into account that the first day of spring comes by a different date each year. Well, the Sisters wanted nothing to do with that sort of picking and choosing. By their collective minds, the more vague the better. And so, vague it remained.

Of course, it was a confusing matter by the stretch of Barthalamew's early years but, in time, he simply cast it off. After all, birthdays were rarely noted or celebrated about the order, though Marihanna, from time to time, allowed the boy to return from his birthday chores to find some old volume of tales waiting upon his pillow. Otherwise, he learned to overlook the idea of having any birthday at all until, of course, the slow but inevitable arrival of that very one in particular.

"It is with great sadness," Sister Josephine said with nothing nearing a state of sadness, "that you are removed from us, Barthalamew."

Barthalamew stood, as Toby once stood, just outside the abandoned church. The Sisters lined up before him as though it was the most common of all possible rituals, each now inexplicably holding to some ritual-like candle. A curious sense of religiosity stained the air between them.

The boy passed his eyes from one woman to the next. It started with Josephine and then, seemingly, went from older to younger until Lydia, in her full sisterhood splendor, candle and all, was had. Not a sister smiled for the occasion but her, for the dear girl always reserved a smile for him.

"Today, you are a man, sir," from Josephine again.

Though it seemed a point worth arguing, the boy kept his tongue.

"You are free to the world," from Maribeth, a line as clearly and happily rehearsed as any.

Barthalamew then looked to Marilynn for it seemed her turn. Marilynn, by way of her own style, offered not a word. It was Marihanna who then tried through the throes of a coming sob.

"You are like a son to me."

This was quickly interrupted by Josephine, who thought to put her throat to some strong and effective use. Marihanna was seemingly off script.

"You have done fine work here, sir," Josephine said, improvising now and making effort to cover Marihanna's obvious tears. "We feel as though the roof has been well patched. And the lumber has been well gathered and placed."

Marihanna's sob was escalating. Her volume was quite disruptive. Josephine was hard-pressed to continue but it was her need to make sure that the boy was sent away without any botheration.

"You shall—"

Blubbering now from Marihanna. Josephine pushed a fast glare before turning back to the boy.

"You shall make—"

Loud blubbering now from Marihanna and then the start of a trickle from Marilynn. Josephine pressed on.

"You shall make for a fine laborer, sir, if you serve others as well as you have served here."

Preposterous blubbering now from Marihanna who could hold it no longer. By Molly, the cork was out. Her face was deluged in misery. Marilynn then erupted, followed by Maribeth, who was beginning to crack and, happily, for the record.

Josephine went red. Her temper peaked and yet, it can be said, for it was noted, that she was at the verge of a tear herself as she sounded her very last words to him.

"Damn it all! Just go boy!"

And with this, Josephine threw her candle to the dirt and stormed away as though compelled by the whole of the world. It was a remarkable scene, to say the least. Barthalamew had no idea how to make sense of such an unexpected demonstration.

Nothing looked at all like it did when Toby was expelled. This was a very different sort of scene and the boy was baffled as to what was wanted of him now, except of course, to damn it all and go!

At first, the other sisters were much too preoccupied to notice but as this awkward moment passed, the nature of Josephine's exit seemed a fitting resolution. And so, Marilynn was next. Though her words were not as harsh, her want to be away from the moment was every bit as clear.

"Be well, Barth," Marilyn said as she put her candle to the dirt and stepped away.

Barthalamew then looked to Marihanna, for surely, she might carry the moment. And yet, she did not. Remarkably, Marihanna only loosed her candle to the dirt and stepped quickly away with her hands and, thereby, her tears stuck to her face.

Two sisters remained. The boy was flustered. The moment was simply too much for his unrehearsed heart.

He looked to Maribeth who, for the record, gave no more than a simple nod. She then made a turn of her own and traipsed away, although, unlike those before, she kept a proper hold of her ceremonial candle.

Barthalamew looked to the ground, wondering, even bothered by the dirtied candles, before he realized there remained a sister still before him. The boy looked up and was greeted at once with Lydia's sustained smile. There was a want for words and so he made effort.

"I should—"

But he was stopped by a curious gesture. Lydia blew out her candle and gently put it to the ground. She then reached behind her head and untied a red ribbon. Undone, her hair fell to the back of her shoulders. It was recently cut, clearly so and by way of the order, but there seemed a simple elegance now by her look and effort, a grace that was previously unnoticed by the boy.

Barthalamew was wide-eyed as he watched Lydia hand over her red ribbon. It seemed, to him, the most peculiar sort of gift but it was clear that this ribbon, this simple color was everything she had and wanted to give.

I guess you're the lucky one," he started, uneasy, for it was always uneasy with her. "You get to stay."

Of course, there was no reply. There was only her gift. And so, Barthalamew accepted it and expressed his gratitude.

"I have your letters in my pack," he softly offered in return. "I shall bind them with your ribbon and keep them safe."

Such a perfect gift from such an imperfect boy. Lydia was quickly overwhelmed by the idea, by the notion that her letters were still with him, that they would always be. Indeed, his unexpected sentiment found its depth. The candles in the dirt, the scent of a coming and going breeze, the mere sight of the boy now standing before her, providing his gift in return, were each secured by her heightened senses and put immediately and permanently to heart. The result was the start of tear by way of the most precious green eyes in all of the kingdom.

The boy smiled. The girl smiled. The boy then realized his place. And his place was no longer there.

"I s'pose I should go."

Those were the last words exchanged between Barthalamew Buckett and the Order of Cecilia. Sister Lydia held her smile and, for the sake of her order, held her place.

Barthalamew executed his turn and, for the first time in his entire life, stepped away from that old, abandoned church. His direction was south and then east, towards the waiting city of Adelayde.

36

Life is forever a circle, an absolute universe of unending orbits. From the smallest particle to the largest, it's all a mad business of dutifully going about our laps, one after the other, until the end of time which, by the way, is a circle as well. Indeed, don't get me started on time.

And by this, all of Heaven looks down on all of life with wonder. Hordes of angels with darting eyes, dizzied for all the circling that nature exacts, gaze upon the lot of mankind and each begs to wonder.

Here, after all, and before all eternity, stands man, forever weighted by his past, by his sin, by his unyielding regret; forever burdened by his suspicion, by his lifelong insistence on permanence and conditions; by his assumptions and claims; by his demands and his beliefs and disbeliefs and by his love of self, which becomes, more often than not, so entirely inflated as to be nearly useless, and by his hate, which, by any degree, weighs most of all. How so very separate from the angels he must therefore always be, for not one of these things can any one man do without.

And on that particular night, were an angel to cast an eye to the top of that particular crag, to that lonesome bench where Barthalamew sat, that angel would see, and with particular ease, the slowing orbit of a tormented man. And in that moment, that angel would think to pity, for angels have that in spades, as the boy's fate was clearly at hand.

And then, that angel would push her eyes away and would seek some other circle, some other life, some other coming and going, for even an angel, with so much pity, would rather some better view.

But the boy did not. The view just then before him was precisely his want. It was haunting. It was daring. He knew it was to be his last.

There remained only his bench and the ground before it and the crashing waters upon the jagged rocks far below.

There remained only the murderous dark of that final and uncaring night. There remained only an emptied bottle to ensure it all.

To the point, there would be no more day for the likes of Barthalamew Buckett. All hope was choked from the chambers of his crippled and dying heart. That it was broken, he knew, was not the matter, but that it only lived to be broken again and again and again. The boy could no longer endure the idea of another beat, for what good is one heart without another! It is but a pump, no more, and what need had he for that!

And yet, that silly pump ached! So sharp was the wound and yet so dull. So swift and yet so stilled. Why could not one of those names, not one of those darling faces, not one of those sounding voices, be forever silenced from the unending depths of his memory? Why could he not forget? Why could he not unlove?

Here now was his undeniable fate. Here now remained the obvious truth. Barthalamew had more want of life than it ever had want of him! He was lonesome no more but merely a child waiting, even wanting to die.

There only remained his bottle, his faithful bit of Rum, so curiously constant and pretty. It eased his soul a bit. It made him feel as though he belonged. It cajoled him and offered him tears of a gentler persuasion. It was, he decided, the only true love of his life.

After all, had Rum not always stood where no man or woman would? Had Rum not always lent its cheer? Had Rum not always breached that awful dark of his room and brought him comfort? What a kind friend Rum was to him! What an ever-present friend, indeed!

With the bottle now standing against the side of the bench Barthalamew looked to it as though one might look to his wife or child or his good parent and offered up his breaking voice one last time.

"Why must I only know the endless indifference of those I love?" was Barthalamew's cry.

Rum stood tall, as though to say, but then said nothing at all.

"Why must I always have such a loathsome heart?"

Rum begged to consider but remained ever quiet on the matter.

"How is it that I have so much to give and no one to give it to?"

And to this, it seemed Rum had want to speak but Rum, once more, kept its unkind peace.

Tears to the boy came freely now as he knowingly whispered the fast bulk of his remaining words.

"You are my friend. Tell me to live."

Rum gave not a word.

"You are my hope. Tell me to stay."

Rum shared not a thought.

"You are all that remains to me. Tell me to stop."

Rum held its tongue.

Damned friend, what use have you! Where is your purpose now? Why is your spirit so suddenly silenced?

The bottle was quickly put to hand and tossed to the waiting sea below where it was greeted by the rocky shoreline and died a dark and lonesome death. Barthalamew braced but satisfaction never came. Only misery remained.

How had it come to this? Why was he standing on that damned cliff, always and forever alone? How was it that he came into the world as some discarded baby in a bucket and devolved into something less?

Was his own heart the enemy? Was his own want his ruin? Was his own breath his doom? What other answer could there possibly be!

Barthalamew put down his good hat and wandered to the edge of the crag. It was not his wish to look down but to look onward, for onward, by that moment, was exactly the point.

The sky was overworked. The clouds covered all signs of the angels and heavens above. There were no stars to count. There was no cosmos to answer back. There was no blessed moon. There was only…

Barthalamew just then realized he was not alone. Dog, in its perpetual state of uncaring, was nearby, comfortably seated beside the bench, in moonlit wonderment of the boy's many curious words and actions. Though it made effort to scratch and beg away at its own constant infestation, the beast seemed clearly mindful of the boy's inexplicable passion.

To the point, Dog was clearly focused and happily so. The streetwise mutt seemed entirely at rest with the idea that it was to live forever and as an absolute nuisance to the proper or broken hearted. Such is the way of any and every possible demon.

And yet, the demon noted, only too late, Barthalamew's changing glare. Something turned. Something was failing. Something was remarkably different.

The boy's eyes were sharp now with purpose. It was a most curious look, even a sickly look. It was, sadly for Dog, a very determined look.

"If I am to go, I am not to go alone!"

Those were the last words of Barthalamew Buckett, but it was not his last action. In one fell swoop, which could not have been more unexpected, Dog was scooped into the boy's arms and together the two were given to their first and final flight.

37

You must not be taken in by the lore of that land that tells of Oglethorpe's haunts. Be well assured that Oglethorpe is not haunted. Pay no heed to those hooligans who, for so many coppers, will happily provide all the dramatic accounts of visions seen, most often in the fall and early winter months and almost always by the brush of dawn, when all the thickest fogs roll in from the sea and fill up the town until High-Street is reached, until the mist runs up and over the stones, under which those quieted residents lie.

Here, the pretenders will say, are the curious ghosts of Alagood's past, coming about to the site of their rest, to count the flowers if there are flowers to count, to spy the churchyard, perchance to seek out the face of a loved one or to look over the progress of their cherished town and of all they so sadly left behind.

It is then said, for an extra bit of coin, that you will be allowed your choice of stone and that a flower will be placed there for you and in your good name, so that the ghost of that particular grave will see your gift and know to bless you for it.

T'is quite a pretty little trap, as far as traps go but, then again, perhaps the word is unfair. I suppose the ruse is harmless enough so long as you grasp the very simplest of truths, which is that no ghost is for real that is for sale.

To further the point, you will discover rather quickly, as so many do, that neither your gifted flower nor any flower at all, is allowed to favor the grassy green of his blessed ground, except, of course, as are those placed there on that very specific date and by those very specific hands. So, do not expect, as a prize for your visit, any sort of blessing from him, for even if Barthalamew's blessings were real, it is all but implied by the townsfolk that his blessings are not yours for the expecting.

I shall spare you the task of asking around or taking up a count for yourself and tell you that the pastoral field of

Oglethorpe is home to precisely three hundred thirteen very un-busied souls. There lies, and with some splendor, the great aristocracy of Alagood's dead, the great names of Alagood's humbled past, a great many men and women who were, at a time, all pride and wealth and status to boot but who have since become no more than a nearly forgotten box of bones. Well, that is, after all, what it means to share sod with a saint.

Not that the many who went before him had much choice in the matter, but these days it does seem as if those fair men and women were buried thrice as deep. It should, therefore, not surprise you to learn that no one chooses to be interred there now. No one has for some time. And that is just as well, for I suspect the church would not allow it, preferring to think, I do believe, that it was their idea to begin with.

With the boneyard thus prefaced it is now our business to poke around it a bit. I pray you don't mind, but I am rather of the opinion that some introductions are past due. However, I do recommend that you keep to the path provided. It is the caretaker, you see. He is unreasonably touched and more than a bit particular about his lawn. Having said that we have only to step past Oglethorpe's celebrated gate to begin.

And so, we are underway. In a clockwise manner we are met at once with a most honorable set of stones. To our immediate left lies the largely recognizable family name of Alagood. Michael B., properly noted as a devoted husband and father, is little known for anything else aside from the lending of his name to so much crooked ground. To this minute, I daresay, there are those who will not forgive him for it. Still, he had a better heart than most and gave as good as he got. That no worse can be said of him is respectable enough.

To his side we find Tracy, his eternal wife. It is said that she was rather pretty by her youth and just as graceful be her age, a very dear lady who enjoyed a wondrous stretch of life and who is remembered to this day by the fame of her smile which, legend still contends, remains without equal.

And to her side is found Johnathan Michael, the good couple's unmarried son. Here lies a fellow who is every bit as rested now as he was in life, for resting, it seems, was his particular gift. To the point, the last of the founding line was as lazy a man as any ten men could be and appeared, by all accounts, to have napped away all of his fifty-two years. This one died just as he lived, that is to say, he went in his sleep.

Other men of politic follow the row. Lord Mayor Joseph Kent is stretched out nearby. He was well known as a loud and snobbish man of considerable height though, I suppose, we may now call it length.

Captain James Harper is just down from him. The good fellow also served as Lord Mayor but, being the very proudest of seamen, he never answered to anything less than Captain.

Lord Mayor Gramm Powell and his dear wife Anna are just past. Now, there was a man of considerable charity. The poor lad died insolvent and charity, it seems, has yet to forgive him for it.

Behind him we have Lord Mayor Hightower, Lord Mayor Sanford, Lord Mayor Wrayford and so on. Lord Mayor Hundley and his family, if you must know, are buried at his former estate, which is more than a bit odd for the fellow who lives there now. He swears of ghosts. Very pretty ones, I suspect.

Stepping further up the path, keeping to our left, we find a good variety of names, entire lots of families, worthy by their wealth and beneficence but not so much remembered as they would like to be. The Marshalls. The Charlotts. The Iveys. The Bradleys. All fine names as far as each was concerned, but all abandoned now to time and so much dirt.

Tell me, if you can, what has become of all those dreams, of all those hopes, of all those smiles and tears, of all that passion, of all that love and hate? What, do you suppose, has History to say to all that now? The answer may well surprise you. It tends to surprise them all.

Oh, but here is a valuable name. Here is Mr. Hamm. Edward Hamm, that is. All by his lonesome. Not a brother to be found. Not on this side of the boneyard, at any rate. Theodore lies at a distance, in the far southeast corner. It was thought upon and then decided that the brothers, even in death, should be no closer. The remaining Hamms, what few there were, set off long ago for lands unknown.

Another two rows and we are before a number of Loydfords, Gilbert the truth-slayer foremost among them. Fate saw fit to age that fellow poorly, to retire him rather quickly and then to strike him both deaf and blind. Can there be a greater curse than this for the likes of him? I think not, therefore I say not.

The wretch could not read. He could not be read to. He was dumb to all that was said and done. What a blighted soul, indeed! A queer sort of smile, it is said, sprang up with the letting of his last breath, suggesting, you may presume, that he was quite pleased to be on his way.

Here, yet another row, and we light upon the Littletons. A good scattering of Robs, you see, alongside a few other names, but nothing in the way of a Janice. The family men persevered. The reestablished King Robert Arms still thrives.

As to Janice, well, one may say she persevered as well, but in a more perverse sort of way. The finicky gal did finally meet her man and he was, by her wish, the very paragon of virtue, the most impassionate man, in fact, as could possibly be met.

She married that pitiable fellow at once. And then left him for another. And then him for another. And him for yet another. And, so on. Where she lies now and by what name is anyone's guess. Well, anyone's guess but mine, of course, but there really is nothing more to say on the matter. Her mark in life, I must insist, was rather poorly made.

In truth, not one of Barthalamew's former loves is here. Ms. Davison lies in Adelayde. Dear Jayne is at rest, as aforementioned, within the confines of the former family estate. Ms. Coopersmith was quieted, it is presumed, in the great flood, along with Rebecca Foxworthy and Trudy Bishop. Lora Dean, though not quite a love of his, ate gobs of poison and died with such a glaring lack of dignity that the only place for her was an unmarked grave somewhere on the outskirts of town.

To the northeast corner we now come and turn south, so as to begin our stroll back west. Not much to see or know here. Just a number of folk who lived as well as any but who lay just as forgotten, perhaps even moreso, than all the rest. Still, the stones are rather handsome though, it must be said, this is more to the credit of the stone maker than the stone haver.

Of course, there is the matter of the Theryoungs, buried just ahead here alongside the heroic patriarch. Joan lived such a full life, raising each of her lovely children into adulthood and prospering entirely on her own, with only the love of a memory to guide her.

The children each married well and lived a life of quiet wisdom, as was their good father's way. Dear Amy, though, it is sad to say, fell weak just before her wedding, never to know her strength again. She was quite short on life, thereafter. The good, it is said, die young, and sweet Amy shall always serve as considerable proof of that!

Nearing the gate once more we bring the tour to an end, for it is his stone that we now see, so charitably placed at this good spot. What a kindness it was to put him here for the boy had no more than a copper to his name.

All that he owned, which was, but you know, hardly a thing, was put to sea and without so much as a raft. So, you may be sure, this was not at all the sort of spot he could even think to afford.

And yet, here he lies, ahead of so many others and so nearing the Oglethorpe gate. How, you ask, did this come to be? Well, it was the wealth of his reputation that afforded him the means.

But what reputation, you might now think to ask? Yes, well, I suppose it is time we get to that.

Welcome then, good friend, to our illustrious third act. Herein lies your reward for such patience. Herein is found the curtain behind which lies all of the most unexpected truths.

Forward, then, shall we.

38

T'is a long and jagged stretch of rock that awaits the sea at the foot of that now infamous crag. T'is no place, you may well assume, to stand or sit on, God forbid, to fall upon and not once had any one of those things happened before that fateful night. And, not once, had any such thing since occurred.

The seafaring folk of Alabaster Bay knew then, as they know now, the push and pull of the daily tides and the lack of depth on approach to those wrecking rocks. It only took, in the early years, two ships to be claimed, the second to rescue the first, before the prevailing decision was made that nothing more than a dinghy was to come that close again. And no more than a dinghy has.

It was Anthony James who first spotted the bloodied and broken lump. Mr. James, a short and ugly man of more warts than skin and of twice as many arms than legs (having lost one in a wayward duel) was a miserable sort of captain aboard a miserable sort of boat that was designed exactly for the purpose of fishing but, by reputation, did little more than float about and miserably so.

By the early hours of the following morn, the boat happened by, trying here and there for its usual catch and failing in all of its usual ways. James, for lack of any actual charge, stood upon that dull ship's bow, with his stumpy little leg of wood and all his warts in tow and, by use of his monocular, put his interest on that jagged shore.

Such was the captain's way. No matter his duty to ship and crew his interest was always elsewhere and on that particular morning it was on that particular rock and, specifically, on that particular lump where there was seen a curious bit of unexpected color.

To be sure, there was a peculiar, even familiar sort of form. Beneath so many odd shades of red it looked almost like…almost like…

"A man!"

His voice was forceful. Forceful was called for. The first mate was nearby.

"A man what, sir?" his eager reply.

"A man on that rock, there," Captain James said, now with the added benefit of his pointed finger.

"Wha's he doin' there?" the nearby thought to ask.

"By Molly, he's dead," James concluded. "He's as good and dead as death itself."

"But how'd he get there," for the nearby was not so bright.

"He fell," said James as he aimed his monocular to the top of that considerable crag.

"Fell from where?" for the nearby could not at all help himself to anything nearing wit.

"From the cliff, a' course."

"From the cliff..." the nearby said and with a fair amount of awe as awe was a common response for those so limited as he.

"Get Heavy in the dinghy!"

And with that said, Heavy, who was, at that moment, not so aptly named as he was sickly as of late, was placed in a dinghy and put ashore before that jagged rock. And it was here that was found not just man, but man and dog, the latter stiffened against the other with as much a look of surprise as anything like a dead or dying dog might have.

Heavy was quickly grieved for it was a heart-rending sight and, at once, he knew this, above all, would be the tale he would be telling for what remained of his sickly life. His eyes and soul begged to divert but his work was now before him. And so, he lifted the stiffened pair into the dinghy and returned them to the waiting vessel.

Once arrived, Barthalamew and his guest were then carefully boarded and brought to a temporary rest at the port bow of the ship. The small crew gathered. To be sure, it was quite a sight.

"Now tha's quite a sight!" the captain said so as to assure that it was, in fact, a sight.

"I think I seen this fellow about," one of the crew then murmured.

Indeed, it was true. He had. The murmur was then pursued as others considered the notion of that nearly familiar face.

"Tha's th' fella'," another voice started but then stopped, for he was unsure how to continue.

"Bu'," from another who then stopped as well, for he had no idea and realized, rather quickly, that he should simply hold on this almost needless syllable before making it any more needless.

A telling silence then prevailed as the fishermen looked from the deceased and then to one another. Clearly, they each had want to know the man. Clearly, they each made effort to say as much. Clearly, not a one of them did. Their attention was then put back to the spectacle before them.

"The' dog does look a bit suspicious," as it now seemed relevant to consider the poor pup.

"Aye. Ratty little fellow."

"With just th' one eye!"

"Perhaps the fall took it!"

"Perhaps the fall made a mess a' that ragged tail."

"Seems odd," from Heavy, who was more than curious now.

"What's odd?"

Heavy looked back to the cliff, leading the others to do the same. His eyes then followed to the rocks below and then back to Barthalamew and Dog.

"Seems odd that he fell with that dog in his arms."

"Seems odd to the dog as well."

"Whaddya supposed happened up there?"

"I'll tell you' what happened up there!" from Captain James, who suddenly caught hold of his kindly imagination. "This here man came…

"…across that there dog upon the cliff. The dog, being impaired in one eye, had no notion of his proximity to the edge!"

A crowd was gathered about the makeshift wharf of Alagood where a marketplace now stood and made effort to succeed. Upon the ground before the many gathered remained Barthalamew and the one-eyed pup, still wrapped so tightly in the boy's arms. Captain James's voice launched over the body and into the crowd with an emotional pitch. His simple tale was something akin to a performance.

"And this good man stepped to the dog in an effort to save it. The animal was nearly spared, but then the fellow slipped and fell to his doom upon the ragged rocks below!"

The crowd was shocked by the notion of such drama. To be sure, it was exquisite. Indeed, it was heroic. In fact, it was entirely false. But what care has anyone for truth before a story so wonderfully crafted as that!

"I know that chap!" from the audience. "There's a good fellow!"

"A proper man, to be sure!"

"Proper, indeed!"

"Neve' saw him go anywhere without tha' dog."

This was a different thing said. At once, the crowd turned and tried for the source, but the voice could not be accounted for. Another voice then surfaced in support.

"Never saw the two apart!"

More stares as the crowd turned from left to right to left again. The source, once more, was not obtained, but there was an obvious truth to what was said. The boy was seen before and almost never without that dog! A slow realization was curiously forming. And then, finally, a voice that knew!

"That's the writer fellow! A' the Gazette!"

Eyes pushed and found, at once, Mr. Fearnhead. Well, there was a reliable source, a good man among the many who was only too happy to put his face forward and say as much.

"I knew him well."

It was a half-truth, but, as far as truth is generally concerned, half is better than most.

"Aye," now from another who stepped forward to say as much. "He wrote a' the fellow, the painter who made the portrait a' the Prince."

"The Hundley Ball!" another then shouted.

"It was a lovely bit of story," from an affected woman who recalled the article well enough.

The crowd hushed. The crowd remembered. Eyes were then put back to the dog. It was all quite macabre and then, suddenly, rather beautiful. For the full run of nearly a minute not a soul thought to speak, but then a soul emerged.

"He saved that dog!"

It was a kind thing said until another thought to counter.

"Obviously not!"

"But he risked his life to do so," from Captain James, who just then reclaimed his voice. "And tha's what makes the man proper!"

Indeed! How could it be doubted? The proof was in the dead fellow's arms. There was the personification of charity. There was a man in love with his fellow being! There was a heart as large as the world and willing to risk all for the smallest and least of all things.

The crowd was clearly moved, clearly touched. Murmurs were passed back and forth and back again, all in support of the dead man's obvious sacrifice.

"He deserves a proper spot!"

The voice was deep and, at once, convincing. Not a head turned. Not a head needed, for all heads understood. A hero deserves a proper spot.

A petition was drawn up and quickly circulated among the storm survivors. It was resolved that the boy was to be granted some better soil. He was to be honored with a suitable place of rest and Dog, bless his flea infested soul, was to be honored along with him.

It was a wondrous suggestion by those who decided that they, above all, were in the know. The petition was approved

298

by everyone who received it. A meeting was had. Plans were made and quickly realized.

For the first time since the advent of that murderous storm, the beleaguered folk of that tattered town came together and committed to some new and kindly purpose. Even for me, it is an unusual thing to suggest. In death, the boy was finally given to life.

And yet, allow me to say, and I do speak from experience, that no grave ever put to ground has known so much spinning as that of Barthalamew Buckett.

39

High-Street was chosen.

It was unanimously decided. The boneyard there was a more respectable place for such a fellow and his beloved dog. The groundskeeper was approached and pointed out a very kind place to the front, nearing the gate.

With the spot secured, a number of spades were then put to the task and a proper depth was quickly reached. The boy's grave was dug. There was only for him to claim it.

Barthalamew was given to a better box than most. It was donated by a wealthy fellow who had a love for dogs and, by consequence, a love for those who loved them. His kind generosity eased to the surface upon hearing of the boy's fate. His charity also extended to the High-Street Church as the pastor was not so shy about asking for some coin for that precious plot of land that was so quickly and all but forcefully acquired.

Barthalamew was also generously prepped. Mrs. Theryoung donated her dead father's suit once more and for the very last time. The boy was cleaned, dressed and given to his best haircut, all before being placed into his slightly smaller new home.

Dog was then placed atop him just as he was found, across Barthalamew's chest, grasped by the boy's loving arms. A good deal of hammering then commenced. The box was thereby sealed.

A notice was then sent to the Gazette. Loydford, in mourning, made sure that the ad was placed with prominence. The Gazette went to press and was then delivered to market.

It is, and always will be, a curious historical note that Barthalamew's service was quite well attended. Hardly a soul about Alagood ever made any sort of effort to know or care for the boy, but the suggestion of his love for that previously thought unlovable beast was the very sort of thing that inspired a crowd.

And so, a crowd, led by the very saddened Mrs. Theryoung, gathered at Oglethorpe and looked on as Barthalamew's box was lowered into the ground. There were tears, to be sure, from a number of the ladies who Barthalamew most assuredly would have loved without question had he ever the chance to know or care for them.

And then there were words, such kind words as were spoken by the High-Street Pastor who also had no knowledge whatsoever of the boy. But this did not prevent him from loving him dearly, as though his own son.

"Today, we commit unto God our dearest brethren Barmalew—"

"Barthalamew, sir!" quickly from the nearby deacon.

"Barthalamew," the Pastor then corrected, "Buckens."

"Buckett, sir," again from the deacon.

"Buckett," the Pastor corrected. "We ask upon our God that he be accepted into the eternal life that he so richly deserves for he stood among us all as a man of compassion and unending love, for his fellow man as well as his fellow animal."

Murmurs abounded for clearly the point was most kindly made.

"God on high, we ask that you embrace this man's good heart, that you appreciate his many worthwhile deeds whilst he shared his time among us. We ask that you—"

A rumble.

It was only a slight sort of rumble, but it clearly registered among those in attendance and, especially, among those nearby along Port Street. The Pastor stopped, considered his place and started once more.

"We ask that you forgive his good soul of his transgressions and admit him into your good graces—"

A rumble.

To be sure, it was only a slight bit more of a rumble than the previous rumble and, yet, it left its mark. The Pastor was stopped again. He gave a glance to the deacon as though to beg of an answer. By all the devils of Bazre, what was being such a bother to his vivid and blessed performance?

The deacon had no clue and could only say as much. He simply provided for a quick shrug of his shoulders and then proffered a glance down Port Street way as though to suggest that it was the result of some lesser folk who were up to some untimely mischief.

The Pastor quickly tired of this.

"Bless his soul. Amen," he said with haste and then signaled the grave digger to commence with the dirt.

And so, the grave digger scooped up a shovel's worth and tossed it into the waiting grave. The dirt struck the box below at the exact same moment as—

Rumble.

Another shovel of dirt and another—

Rumble.

This time that slight rumble made effort to be much less slight. It was, in fact, something a bit more than what it was before. The ground provided a considerable shake. Those good people in attendance of that historical ceremony could not help but wonder of this incredible—

Rumble.

And now it was far more than slight and markedly more sustained. Each of the attendees looked to the direction of Port Street as the rumble continued unabated for a full half minute. Something dreadful was amiss. Something foul was about. This concern was quickly augmented by a number of screams that could now be heard sending up from that very direction.

A curious cloud was then spotted, charging for the horizon. It was quickly deemed a bothersome sight as it surely suggested some tremendous misfortune. And yet, as no one about the ceremony had ever witnessed such a thing, there was some question as to what it was that was actually being witnessed.

But then, it was realized. After all, that was no ordinary cloud. It boasted a very unfavorable hue. It was, in fact, a rising fog of the most unpleasant shade of brown as any had ever seen. At that moment, it was considered and then quietly affirmed.

The Hamm had given notice. The Hamm had said its peace. The Hamm was down and never to be up again!

40

We now reach a moment that has been well anticipated, for if there is anything about Barthalamew's life that is not distorted or lost to so many second-hand accounts, it is the tale that is to come. It is the legend of the Lady of Oglethorpe.

Oh, blessed reader, here we unveil a curious truth. Here we bring to the page the absolute love of poor Saint Barthalamew's wretched life. And with this chapter we shall quickly and clearly end the mystery.

The dear Lady appeared, at first, as though something on the wind, something like a scent that stepped up and let loose its gift without so much as a sound in all the world. She was a stranger to all of Alagood. As well, she was clearly a woman of less than modest means. Her simple apparel said as much and clearly promised of some distant home.

And yet, there was no sense of burden. The Lady seemed to float more than walk. She appeared to smile more than not. She looked as though her heart breathed as much as her lungs ever could. She was beauty without a word, without a thought, with merely a glance. She was entirely a Lady.

It was exactly a day to the year of Barthalamew's death when she first appeared. Her form stepped from the West End and then up Port Street where, without any notice whatsoever, she eased across to the High-Street Church beside which the cemetery was found. The Lady then slipped into Oglethorpe as though an angel upon some worthy cloud.

To be sure, it was a most remarkable moment! Indeed, History took note! As many poems as could be written have been written. As many books as could be crafted have been crafted. Some of the mightiest pens in all the world have efforted this very moment.

And yet, who among them knew so much as the good woman's name? Well, to be sure, not a one! She was only the simplest of all possible women who, in time, became a worthy angel who, in time, became the Lady of Oglethorpe.

Joan Theryoung saw the Lady first and, by right, all but claimed her for her own. It was Joan who first noted her on approach to the cemetery. It was Joan who first spied the presence of that white rose in the Lady's hand. It was Joan who simply gave a nod of respect as the woman stepped by, for Joan was there to provide her respects as well.

And yet, it was instinct that made the widow look again. It was curiosity that pressed her eyes from her husband's grave and once more to the hooded figure. Though she was cloaked from head to toe, Joan sensed the stranger's confusion.

"May I...?" the widow tried but then stopped as she was rather unsure of how to proceed. "If I can be of—"

The Lady turned. The cloak, the hood and all now stood before her. Joan tried for some sense of recognition, but it was all so much more thread than flesh.

"If you're looking for someone...?" Joan tried but, once more, was unable to finish.

The Lady then stepped to the widow and extended her hand. Joan looked to it and quickly realized the simple pale of her skin. It was not the sort of pale that one often sees in a coastal town. And yet, it was not the tone of the woman's skin that alerted the widow. It was the curious parchment that was at the Lady's fingertips.

Joan kindly accepted the note and opened it. At that moment, her life was entirely changed. There was only the one word for her to read, handwritten and carefully so.

"Barthalamew."

"Barth!"

Joan was stopped. Her breath, at once, left her body and made no promise of its return. A gasp, therefore, prevailed. "Ya' mean ta' see Barth!" she then rejoined, touched for the prospect of this kind and most unexpected visitor.

The Lady gave not a hint. She said nothing in return.

"Yes. He is nearby. You have walked just past," Joan said, gesturing back towards the gate, back towards his nearly forgotten bit of rock.

But the Lady held. Her attention now kept to the marker that stood before them. It seemed, by Joan's imagination, that this obvious stranger glimpsed some recognition of the name inscribed on her husband's stone. And then, in a moment, it was gone. The Lady righted her gaze and acknowledged the path back to the gate.

Joan stepped up as though to lead the stranger, but the Lady quickly gestured that the widow should remain, that it was her intent to see for herself. And so, Joan allowed the woman her peace as she put her own attentions back to her beloved, as she kneeled before Toby and whispered her smiles and...

But how could she concentrate! How could she even pretend to ignore what was unfolding right before her! How could she not beg to look over her shoulder, to watch what was so clearly forbidden for her to watch!

She could not! She would not! There was only to peel her eyes away from her beloved so that she could spy upon another's. And by that quieted effort, Joan Theryoung witnessed for herself the historical, inaugural visit.

By way of the many decades to come, it would play out exactly the same way. There would be no variation for the full run of forty-one years. It would only be exactly as Joan saw that fateful day.

The Lady stopped and stood over Barthalamew's stone for half a minute, no more. She said not a word. She gave not a tear. She then kneeled and offered her white rose and then stood again. At that moment, it was done.

The Lady then turned to leave and made her steps toward the gate. Oh, how curious it all was to Joan and, in time, to an entire kingdom! How could she not look now? How could she not be rude?

And so, she looked, she stared, she gawked. She put her eyeballs all over that cloaked and hooded guest, all but daring the Lady to look back. Where did she come from? Why was she already gone? Who was she to poor, lost Barthalamew?

Look at me, she yelled with her eyes! What do you want of him, she dared with a glare! And, as though the Lady had the strength to hear these unsaid things, she stopped at the gate and gave a turn.

And in that moment, Joan's good heart skipped, for there was, by that Lady's silent reply, all the gratitude and peace in the whole of the world. How heavenly her gaze! How blessed her smile! How so impossibly green were the eyes of that adorably freckled face!

But, of course, now you know.

41

The next sighting, of course, was a year to the date. Joan was once more tending to her beloved's stone when the hooded woman with the pleasing green eyes approached the boneyard fence and made her entrance. The widow was enthralled, absolutely overwhelmed. The Lady was returned.

"Ma'am," she offered, for she was quickly in want of offering.

But the Lady gave no reply. She simply entered the boneyard and stepped to Barthalamew's uncelebrated stone where she stood for nearly a full minute before placing her blessed white rose. The Lady then turned and made her exit without so much as a whisper and was gone in a flash.

Joan was stunned, was amazed, was well beside herself. To be sure, she was caught in place, begging for some way back in time and then for some way forward. It was rather obvious now that there was only to wait another year.

And so, another year was waited. And another sighting was had. The Lady appeared again and by the exact date. Indeed, the quieted woman was a force, was a blessed and remarkable energy and Mrs. Theryoung could not have been more delighted.

"Ma'am," she tried again and with a full year's worth of practiced pleasantry.

And yet, the Lady said nothing. She simply placed her gift, turned and was gone.

Another year. Another try. Another white rose.

Joan was rather stumped, but then suddenly charged. Here, after all, was a proper mystery to be solved. And so, she made effort to properly solve it. Mr. Loydford was consulted at once.

"A what?"
"A white rose!"

The words sprung from Joan's mouth and launched about the walls of that wretched basement where the boy's last love was plucked from the waters and then tossed into a nearby unmarked grave.

Yes, dear reader, it had come to this. That formerly scandalous room was now home to the Gazette and, to be sure, Mrs. Theryoung was very displeased with the notion of her descent into that once unkind space.

"And this rose is for who?" from the editor-at-large who was now as large as ever.

"For Barth!"

Silence.

"For...Barthalamew? Buckett?"

"Indeed!"

Ridiculous.

"Ridiculous!"

"But, why?"

"How do you mean?"

Well, it seemed a proper question and Mr. Loydford seemed pleased to press it.

"Why would she not?" was Joan's rebut, for she could think of no other.

"But, who is she?"

Indeed! Mr. Loydford was finally upon a more reasonable line of inquiry.

"I have no idea, sir. I have greeted her four times now and she won't say a word. She simply places her rose and steps away."

"Well, that seems rather silly!"

And now, it seemed, Loydford was falling away from the point. Joan quickly lured him back to center.

"I believe she approaches by way of the north-west road. She comes up Port Street and then leaves by the same route."

"North? And west?" centered now. "By Molly, that suggests a proper mystery!"

"I believe it a most worthy one, sir!"

"I do, as welll!" from the deadened eyes of Mrs. Dean, who was seated in a corner pretending on some task, quietly holding her deadened green eyes to the waiting floor.

At first, it was Loydford's want to quiet the woman, but a thought quickly stepped in. It had been years since a proper story had surfaced. It had been a good while since the Gazette sold out, since anyone thought to care of his flailing press. And now, a real story was at hand, a true and proper riddle.

The editor was suddenly struck by the potential and then bothered by the idea that his star reporter was not up to the task. Barthalamew would clearly be the most suited for the story and, yet, because of the very fact that the boy was no longer among them, he was now, in fact, entirely the story.

Oh, yes, here was something quite exquisite! Here was some romance for the many disheveled! Here was the Alagood Gazette surfacing in its finest hour and by way of what very well could be its very finest headline! Loydford turned back to Mrs. Theryoung and committed at once.

"I have time, then?"

"Well, sir, if the good Lady holds to her schedule, then you have a year, minus today."

"Then I shall spend my year minus today raising our boy from below. This is the sort of news the good people of this town needs! This is the sort of story that will have the Gazette pulling some coin once again."

"I am not certain profit is the point here, sir."

That elicited a quick chuckle from the nearby Mrs. Dean. Mr. Loydford snapped a hard glance in her direction. The green-eyed widow was silenced. Her head turned sadly away to once again note the darkened corner that was now and forever the rest of her life. The editor-at-large then returned to Mrs. Theryoung with a consoling smile.

"Of course, of course. I simply mean to suggest that all of Alagood benefits from a properly restored economy as well as an inspiring story of hope and...and...suspense."

"Love, sir," Joan plainly corrected. "This is a story of love."

"But, of course. I could not agree more. Hope and love. And suspense."

To be sure, Mr. Loydford simply could not help it. He wanted to be in agreement, but experience all but assured him that love was hardly the thing to harvest a profit. In support of that theory, he only had to consider his protege. Love was precisely the boy's currency and yet the boy lived the most unprofitable life of all.

"But perhaps hope and suspense to lead the way, madam?" he tried, for he had to try.

There was only for Joan to concede. She had no more want to be in that awful room and before that strangely desperate man. Her alliance was struck. It was now her want to simply be away.

"I suspect you are right, sir," she offered lightly. "T'is the mystery that begs me to you. But our dear friend's legacy is at hand. I only ask that you treat it accordingly."

And with her peace then said, Mrs. Theryoung stood and eased herself back to the narrowed stairway and ascended from the infamous pits of the Gazette.

"Of course!" Mr. Loydford called after. "I will see to it personally. The boy will be adored every bit as much as his Lady!"

But what Mrs. Theryoung heard, he was not sure. As well, he had no care. Mr. Loydford's mind was now running as though a mad hamster upon its wheel. His story was at hand and, by Molly, he meant to seize it.

"I shall unveil this freckled beast!"

Mrs. Dean could only assume that he was speaking to her. "But, of course, Mr. Loydford."

"But before I do, I must make sure I give her a proper welcome!"

"Of course."

"I will praise her. I will invite the public to adore her. All of Alagood will step out and watch her approach and then I will expose her! And the mystery of this so-called Lady…will be vanquished."

"But, what is there to expose, Mr. Loydford?" Mrs. Dean then inquired, for she was rather confused by this approach.

The question struck the editor as oddly familiar. "By Molly, you're worse than the boy ever was! There is to expose the…the…woman, of course!"

And with this said, Mr. Loydford turned from the dead eyes of Mrs. Dean and made a grab for some parchment and a pen. He then charged that narrowed hallway, for a proper charge was needed. After all, the aging fellow was as nearly as wide as that narrowed hallway. As such, more momentum than usual was needed.

Once ascended, Mr. Loydford stepped through the new construction that was, again, the Great Raff Pub where he was greeted by Big Red before reaching the door to Port Street. He then turned west as his nose for news directed. It was his intent to query as he went, to press what remained of the West End.

But the good folk circling the marketplace had no answer for him. No one about witnessed anything like a hooded woman pushing up and down Port Street with white flowers in hand. And even so, what of it! A woman in a hood was hardly a thing to note, much less remember. The fat man with his waiting pen and parchment sounded more than a little crazy.

Loydford then carried a bit more westerly until the limits of the town were reached. Here the city guard was stationed, and so, he thought to ask among them. And yet, not one of the guards had any recollection of a passing woman from the day before. To be sure, the mystery deepened.

To the cemetery then! Indeed, that would be the place. Some unturned stone, some clue, some ghostly witness was sure to emerge, but Mr. Loydford was dumbfounded. It was silence all about. There were only the many quieted stones, as gray and empty and as unfeeling as ever. There was only the ground and the wrought iron fence and the many long since forgotten at his feet. There was only—

The Lady's gift! It was not so notable at first as the white rose had given a push from its original spot. It was just off now to the side of the boy's grave and almost turned over. And yet, it was there, exactly as promised.

Mr. Loydford took a knee and put his face nearly to the ground to better observe it. His want was to reach for it, to better scrutinize its presence and yet, his old, dumb heart recognized the reverence of those failing white petals pushing now towards the dirt.

It was for Barthalamew. It was for his friend. The rose, above all, was to be respected. And yet, what a proper clue!

The was the evidence at hand! Joan's words struck true! A woman unseen made her way up and down Port Street in the full light of day before an entire population. The Lady had done so for years now and all for the sake of placing that singular gift before the grave of the most unvisited man in all of Kirkland.

By God, who was at the root of this remarkable mystery! Then and there the question burrowed deep into Loydford's dizzied head where it seeded and sprouted at once and plagued the poor fellow's mind until his dying day.

And, allow me to suggest, well beyond.

42

A year passed. The days and weeks and months were dutifully counted. The fifth anniversary of Barthalamew's heroic death made its slow but inevitable approach.

To be sure, the Gazette provided for the announcement and, to be sure, hardly a soul about Alagood made effort to care. Though he was a remembered fellow for the sake of his sacrifice, the citizenry simply had other, perhaps even better things to do. And so, better things were only too easily considered.

But one fellow among them could not have been more pleased by the dawning of that particular day. Mr. Loydford awoke from his small cot in what was once the very room where Trudy Bishop was born and, in fact, the very room in which she died. Though it remained a hauntingly small space, every bit as cramped and dark, the editor-at-large had come to call it home and, in fact, awoke that very morning as though it was the most pleasant little room of all.

"The Lady arrives today!" he chirped to Mrs. Dean as he emerged from his modest space and with little care as to the failing state of his dress and hygiene.

"I suppose she does," her distant reply.

"Yes, she does!"

Loydford's exuberance could not be contained but Mrs. Dean was exactly that. She handily held her tongue and kept to her corner where she was now consumed with a considerable amount of aggressive knitting.

It was Mr. Loydford's want to properly excite the woman and bring her some sense of joy, but the widow simply had no need to care. Her eyes, like her soul, were eternally dimmed and lost to some lesser cause.

The round fellow quit the matter and quickly proceeded to dress. His finest threads, though only just barely fine, were adorned and, indeed, he felt all the more remarkable for it.

The editor-at-large then reached for his pen and parchment but stopped. An unusual thought was upon him.

"You say it is usually mid-day, madam?"

"Yes, Mr. Loydford."

Mr. Loydford stood beside Mrs. Theryoung, sans pen, sans parchment. He was clearly prepared to take on the notion of the Lady by way of his senses alone.

"Should I...Should...maybe I should stand somewhere else?"

"T'is no matter, sir, where you think to stand. The yard is the yard and the Lady is the Lady."

"I...see," for clearly the editor did not. "Do you suppose that I should—"

"Hush!" was Joan's sudden demand.

At that moment, there was heard a pull on the cemetery gate. Loydford turned at once and saw the most remarkable thing. A hooded Lady was arrived by way of Port Street. Her head stayed low as she managed her quieted approach. In her hand was held a single white rose.

Loydford was stunned for the sight of her. A full year was waited and here she was, a ghost fashioned into form before his very eyes. The Lady of Oglethorpe was real!

And, per the promise of Mrs. Theryoung, the Lady was remarkably quiet. Hardly a sound issued from her impossibly soft steps as she walked to the nearby stone. No word emitted. No breath given. No tears fallen. It was as though the whole world of hearing had stepped aside in obeisance of her presence.

Mrs. Theryoung blindly reached for Loydford's arm in an attempt to curb his unrelenting gasp. The scene begged for more silence, for some proper respect and, yet, the editor was as though a lapping dog.

The Lady, of course, made no effort to note or acknowledge the audience before her. She simply went about her business as though her business was all she knew. Her rose was at hand and then it was lowered and given to Barthalamew.

Oh, blessed be that remarkable sight. The purity of that very moment could not ever again be unseen by those two bearing witness. The widow realized a fast tear and made no effort to wipe it away.

Mr. Loydford was equally entranced. His gasping was stopped, but a nervous energy was on the rise. His heart was failing. His soul was pounding. And when his voice finally surfaced, he sounded as though a man struggling with a new language.

"Madam!" was his awkward try as the hooded woman stood from the boy's stone as though to leave.

The Lady was shaken. It was, by her good ears, an unexpected voice, an aggressive voice. Quickly noting the offense, Joan pushed Loydford back and quickly tried for amends.

"My apologies miss. We do not mean to intrude."

The Lady eased. The voice, the kindness of Toby's good wife was quickly a comfort. An awkward nod was then provided.

"Did you know...?" Loydford started.

"Be quiet, sir!" Joan chirped and with some venom for the Lady's nod alone was sacrosanct and the man seemed only there to spoil it.

Loydford was checked. Though he begged for the chance to press for her story, he was simply too much in awe to do anything but concede. Mrs. Theryoung turned back to the Lady and amended once more.

"My apologies, miss. It's just that," Joan pushed and ever so lightly, "Barthalamew was a friend of mine, of my husbands. He was...a friend to all..."

The Lady was visibly jolted. Joan held, worried that she had committed some offense. She then glanced the editor who could only glance back. After a moment, she decided to try again.

"Clearly, you must know..."

But Mrs. Theryoung's sentenced failed and for very good reason. The Lady raised her head and gave her eyes to Joan. A kindly smile then followed. In that moment, Gilbert Loydford's heart nearly burst through his fatted chest.

"Dear God, save me!" was his begging whisper.

It was as though all of Heaven was descended. Here was no freckled straggler. Here was no random stranger. Here were eyes so wide and soft and so green as grass, so pure as to stop a man's soul in its tracks and cause it to cry for some quickened Mercy. Here, Loydford knew, was the mask of a thousand silent angels.

Joan conceded. Loydford was halted. No words could be found, much less said. There was only to look on as the Lady turned about and made for the gate and Port Street beyond. In a blink she was gone!

"That, sir, is the Lady of Oglethorpe," Joan then offered by way of introduction to the clearly affected Mr. Loydford.

"Yes, Mrs. Theryoung. She is, indeed!"

43

Another year. Another twelve months! Oh, how Loydford's heart beat and skipped for the full course of those impossible days. He was certain that the memory and, moreso, the mystery of that mysterious Lady would take a full decade from his life.

But what care had he for his life or any other save hers! What choice had he, after all, but to commit entirely to her lure, to her beauty, to her absolute profitability! She was now his absolute passion and she would remain so until his dying day.

And he could not have been more thrilled. Loydford's pen was now sharpened. His ink was enlightened. His muse was now the very purpose of that fatted man and he could not have been more delighted.

"Mystery Lady of Oglethorpe!" was his fatted headline the day following her previous visit. The edition sold out.

"Lady of Oglethorpe Expected!" was his headline the week before her coming arrival. The edition was gone in a flash.

"Our Lady of Oglethorpe Brings Her Rose Today!" was his headline upon the anniversary morn. The edition all but evaporated off the press.

And on that particular day, just before noon, Port Street was alive with expectation. A proper crowd was gathered. From the lowly stretch of the marketplace all the way up to High-Street, a parade of spectators awaited. The Lady was eagerly anticipated.

For his part, Mr. Loydford could not have been more satisfied. It was his doing. His name was all about it. Were it not for his efforts, it would simply be another day when some quieted stranger walked among them without notice. His pride was clearly on his sleeve.

Mrs. Theryoung, however, was altogether apprehensive. The crowd upon Port Street was begging with curiosity, to

318

say the least, and she was sure it would upset her anticipated guest. Joan looked to Mr. Loydford with some unease, wondering now if she had overshot the mark.

And yet, what could she do? What was done was done. There was only to hope and wait. And, soon enough, the wait was ended.

It was early afternoon when the Lady arrived. Her head remained low as she stepped softly about the fisherman's market as though it was it was no more than a thing to step about. She then found Port Street and began her ascent before the many gathering voices that quickly surrounded her.

At that point, many made an effort to greet her, but the hooded Lady paid no mind. Her focus was certain. She simply held to her single white rose and pressed her steps as though she was married to each and every last one.

All of Port Street was impressively silenced. The many before her were humbled by her quieted nature and dedication. Nothing more was said to or around the Lady from that moment forward. Silence quickly became the rule that day and it remained the rule for the many years and decades to come.

Upon her arrival at the cemetery gate, the Lady was quietly greeted by Mrs. Theryoung who made no effort to talk or approach but who only bowed before her hooded guest. Though a kind gesture, it was awkwardly received.

To be sure, the Lady was confused. At that moment, it seemed as though she had want to say something, but the words never came. There was only to step forward and take a knee before the boy's waiting stone.

And so, the Lady made her step and a quieted reverie was underway at once. She seemed entirely at peace with her task until Mr. Loydford decided to intervene. His hand, you see, was extended. His voice was sudden and jolting. Though he meant otherwise, he was quite suddenly disruptive.

"Excuse me, my Lady, but I would like to ask—!"

Mrs. Theryoung was on him at once and with a telling violence. "Mr. Loydford!" was her strike, for clearly some offense was at hand. "Don't you dare lay a hand upon this blessed angel!"

To further enunciate her claim, Mrs. Theryoung swung hard upon the editor-at-large, clipping his arm in such a way that caused a fair bit of harm. His reach was suddenly retracted. His voice was suddenly ended. His eyes looked to Mrs. Theryoung as though to call for mercy.

Bearing witness to this spectacular event, the Lady gave pause. It was clear that she was struck by such curious aggressions, but she had not a clue as to how to accept the scene before her. There was only to acknowledge, which she kindly did, and then to place her rose.

She then stood, gave a turn and was gone.

With a wounded arm, Mr. Loydford returned to the Hamm, typed, prepared and then presented his story. Though he was denied his chance at an audience, his re-creation of the moment was heartfelt. It was, in truth, one of his finest efforts.

The edition sold out twice for Loydford was wise enough to print both at the start and the end of the following week. He then settled into his simple routine while quietly awaiting the chance to try again for the ever-mysterious Lady of Oglethorpe.

Another year. A slightly larger crowd. The Lady stepped up to the boneyard and gave a fast eye to her immediate public. Joan and Mr. Loydford simply held their place and quietly acknowledged her gift.

No words. No threat of violence. Mrs. Theryoung's presence all but assured a proper assembly of respect. The Lady allowed a simple nod, lowered her gift and gave her turn.

Another year. And then another. The crowds thickened with every pass. The spirits flowed. The tales broadened. The truth weakened. The tourists succumbed to the unusual suggestions of the natives which, of course, were entirely designed so as to assure the coming of more tourists.

"T'is said she is an angel from above!"

"T'is said she is a ghost from below!"

"If ya' speak while she passes, God will take your tongue!"

"If ya' speak while she passes, the devil shall take your soul!"

"If ya' value livin', ya' won't dare look at her directly!"

"Look to her eyes, an' ya' lose your own!"

"A dozen men can no longer speak!"

"A dozen men have died trying!"

Folly. It was all such impossible folly. And yet, any such folly so profitable as that is the sort of thing that quickly becomes fact. And so, fact it became.

The Gazette pressed on! It repeated everything in spades and as often as it possibly could. The yarn became tale. The tale became truth, and, in time, the truth became something like legend. And then, the most unthinkable thing happened.

A man with a big hat arrived on the scene.

It was not just any big hat and it was not just any man. He was a fellow with a title and his title was Bishop. As the next year stepped to, another man arrived, another sort of hat and he called himself arch-bishop. Another year, more hats, bigger hats, more titles and, each, all the more curious of Barthalamew's story.

Well, to be sure, what could be said! The man beneath the stone was heralded. He died as he made effort to save the life of a loved one. A renowned building of architectural might collapsed into a heap upon the very moment of his burial. A beautiful ghost visits his grave every year.

The many big hats were positively impressed. They stayed and observed the crowding street as the Lady stepped to. They were amazed by the uncommon display of reverence. They were overwhelmed by the silent woman's gift, by her turn, by her departure. So much effort for but a minute of kindness! Indeed, this was the very sort of thing that was worthy of their attention.

And so, the many hats attended from thereon. And they did so under the strict supervision of Mrs. Theryoung who, religion or no, enforced her rules of absolute silence and respect and with a telling snap of her eyes. The hats kindly acquiesced for silence was often their rule as well.

It was upon the fifteenth anniversary of Barthalamew's death that a rather large number of proper Cardinals chose to see this particular event for themselves. To the point, the church suddenly found itself entirely invested. The notion of the boy and his dog and the many remarkable things that were now attributed to them were more than compelling were, in fact, nearing the suggestion of miraculous.

More questions were then begged from an unrelenting number of pontiffs and priests. More answers were given from a continual stream of lies and fabrications. After all, no one really knew the boy from a hole in the wall and, in fact, knew the hole better. From start to finish the nature of his life, his heart, his soul, was all a guess. And so, those fine folks of Alagood simply guessed Barthalamew into fact.

And what impossibly lovely facts they were. He was an orphan, assured Mrs. Theryoung and with great authenticity. He was raised by nuns. He was blessed with a proper soul and a God-given talent. He spread love and hope to all those in need. He cared for the animals as though the animals were his blood. He attended High-Street Church with strict regularity and, in fact, was an honorary deacon.

He was adored and loved by as many women as could be, but, despite the times and temptations, he remained celibate. He never smoked. He rarely drank and only rum and only on the rarest and most celebratory of occasions.

He was the most pious man all of Alagood had ever seen or known. Oh, how he was adored, how he was a champion of the community! Oh, blessed boy, what a constant and unrelenting gift you were!

And just like that, it was all true. Every bit of it. None of it could be, nor would be denied or retracted. Barthalamew

Buckett was heralded as a favorite son, a cherished fellow, a kindly and worthy savior. He was beloved by all.

The many hats could not have been more pleased. The boy's tale was remarkable, was proper, was, in a word, sellable. And so, it was properly packaged and sold. Almost at once the Lady's annual appearance was deemed a miracle and it was the want of the many hats to simply know of two more.

The fall of the Hamm was then considered. The details of its collapse were scrutinized and properly investigated. A hundred witnesses gave of their irrefutable testimony, of the matter of the dirt striking the boy's box at the very moment of the Hamm's demise. Well, that was simply beyond coincidence. Miracle, indeed!

The boy's compassion for animals was then regarded. Clearly, he loved well beyond what might be considered ordinary. To the point, Barthlamew loved and chose to care for a flea-ridden one-eyed street mutt with a broken tail, the smelliest road rat that might ever be acknowledged by the book of life. Few could or would even think to accept such a pet, to take in such a wretched stray as this. And yet, Barthalamew, by his almost always sober and remarkably celibate ways, not only adopted this impossible beast, but forfeited his own life for the sake of its wellbeing.

The hats required no more. The church was decided. Three miracles were attributed! The proclamation was decreed.

And so, before the advent of the following anniversary of Barthalamew's death, the often drunk and heartsick boy who was mysteriously left to a mop bucket outside of a nearly abandoned church and then raised by a scattering of generally unkind women who were remarkably mistaken for nuns, and who was then shoved out into the world where he was generally dismissed and forgotten entirely by the book of life, was canonized, was, in fact, glorified, was praised and adored and forevermore by those many hats and so many hats to come.

The boy's name was now held on high. His pedestrian stone was amended. His annual Feast was formally declared by the highest order of the church. That sad sack suicide who never even suspected the scent of a proper friend or love was now and forever known by the most impossible title of all.

Saint Barthalamew of Alagood.

44

Forty-two years. That was the count. The Lady of Oglethorpe made her proper visit forty-two times.

By the stretch of those many decades, the good folk of Alagood simply gave up on the idea of who she was or was not. For all but Mr. Loydford that mystery had long since lost its appeal. The mere idea that she was there at all remained the prevailing wonder.

And so, by the turn of each anniversary the humbled citizenry waited and watched as the Lady of Oglethorpe made her quiet march up and then back down Port Street. And once her departure was witnessed and announced, a proper feast was had and the whole of the town offered its toast. That was the way it was. That, it seemed assured, was the way it would always be.

In the years to come, the Feast of Saint Barthlamew began to acquire more attention than could be expected. Following the church's proclamation, the Feast, of course, was a common cause throughout the kingdom, but the streets of Alagood were soon overwhelmed. As the anniversaries gathered moss, the crowds thickened. In no time at all, that crooked town was swarmed.

Tourists flocked to High-Street Church and to where the Jasmine House once stood and, most of all, to the waiting bench that sat upon that one extraordinary cliff. They listened with serious intent to some Loydford or another, spouting newly beloved names and tales invoking his beloved name. And then, they would line Port Street upon a very specific hour and a vigil was begun.

Lookouts were posted on the road coming into Alagood and, upon sight of the Lady, messengers were sent and alerted the marketplace. A bugler then turned his horn toward the ascent of Port Street and sounded his notes. At that moment, the whole of the city held its breath. There was now only the reverence of absolute silence.

Out of true and proper respect, it had long ago been decided that there would be no beverages or food served during the hours approaching and, to be sure, during the actual event itself. And so, the town corked its barrels in observance of the Lady's arrival and only uncorked when she was decidedly retired from the scene. It was a simple law among the revelers and it was accepted, respected and dutifully enforced by the locals.

And for this, the Lady's visit, brief as it was, was always as quieted as she. There were only her slight steps to be heard as she ascended and then descended that lofty street. And once she crossed the west side and made of her exit, the bugler sent his notes back up Port Street for all to hear. And that marked the start of the Feast of St. Barthalamew of Alagood.

The Lady's forty second visit was deemed to be the same as any of the previous. For nearly a month the townsfolk braced for the many tourists. For nearly a month, the marketplace readied itself.

The pubs were overstocked. The artisans were overjoyed. Everything was in its place as the crowds happily descended.

And then, the day and the hour arrived. Port Street was bursting with life. From west end to the east end, there was hardly a place to stand or see, but clearly the Feast was at hand. There was only to wait for her approach.

And, then it happened. A rider stepped to the marketplace and gave his signal. The bugler sent his lone note up Port Street. The Lady of Oglethorpe was nearing. A strict silence thereon was enforced.

Very soon after, the Lady eased into the marketplace. Her face remained hooded. Her white rose, though lilting, was easily noted. Her pace was simple, measured but then, in a moment, it was not.

There was a pause. Those of the west end took fast note. The Lady held for nearly a full minute as she looked up and forward and then down again. It was unusual for the fact that she was never once known or accused of a halt, but there it was, for all to see.

The Lady then pressed onward and upward, and, in that moment, it was evident that the upward part was the cause of her hesitation. Her steps were now meticulous, chosen as though thoughtfully planned. The street's daring ascent had a fast and obvious effect. The result was something more like a crawl than a walk and it was a dreadfully painful thing for those many in the crowd to see.

It was, of course, presumed by the advancement of these many decades, that the Lady was old, but it could not be predicted that she was so old as this. After all, hardly any had ever seen her face or anything like a lesser pace. It was and had always been decided that she was some youth eternal. She was sacred. She was blessed. She was forever up to the task. And yet, there she stood and walked as though on the verge of some great faltering.

The crowd looked on, quietly, of course, as quiet was demanded, but the many hearts began to weep with the slow pressing of her each and every step. In no time, the grade of the road proved to be too much.

Her steps slowed all the more. A heavy breath was let. All about her now were the witnesses of one of History's lesser moments.

As the Lady neared the historical marker that observed what was once the Jasmine House, she stumbled and took a wicked fall. At once a gasp sent out from the crowd and surged its way up and down Port Street. A hundred folk nearly launched forward, but that worrisome group kept.

After all, it had never been considered that any among them might do as much. For decades the rule held. There was to be no approach, to be no word said, no effort to advance. Her space was decidedly divine and, as such, only to be observed.

But the Lady was down. The Lady was hurting. And the crowd was begging for some kindly intervention. It would take a bold effort to correct the situation and so a bold effort was made.

History kindly records that a noble fellow of Bourg by the name of Sir Charles Magruder broke rank, rule and all sense of decorum and made his hurried approach. He had to. He was sure of it. And yet, it could not be a more daring choice.

The crowd was in awe. Here was clearly a man of wealth and standing and yet, his presence on the scene that day was something very much estranged.

"Madam," his fast words as he neared. "Can you proceed?"

And in that moment, the life of Sir Magruder of Bourg was immediately and forever changed for he was before the greenest, loveliest eyes of all creation. The Lady simply looked up and smiled and ruined that man's good heart forever with a kindly nod.

Sir Magruder then offered his hand and the Lady was raised and thankfully so. There was a want for a fast round of applause and it nearly began, but for the notion that silence still remained the absolute rule. And so, silence held.

The Lady started again. At once, she efforted a better step and the crowd was quietly appeased. But as she passed yet another marker, the one announcing the placement of The Hamm, her legs, again, came up weak.

The Lady stopped and took a knee. The crowd again sent up a gasp. Sir Magruder, still near, tried once more for her hand, but then a familiar face was quite suddenly on the scene.

Mrs. Theryoung was alerted by the Lady's first fall and launched from her position nearing the bone yard. Though an elder herself at this point, her life and her love was now devoted to the moment. As such, her feet were as the wind. At once she was upon the fallen.

"My Lady!" was her voice, as sharp as a knife and yet every bit as loving.

Lydia looked up and noted the familiar face. In that blessed moment a proper smile was shared. Joan understood. There was but a want for some assistance.

The widow happily extended an arm and the Lady took hold and together the two stood amid an audible sigh of relief. The two ladies then turned to face the rising street and took their steps together. And just like that, Lydia's walk was once more renewed.

Her steps were easier now. Her effort was lighted. High-Street was soon in sight and, by the matter of a few more steps, was finally at hand.

At the wrought iron gate, the Lady gave a kind eye to Mrs. Theryoung before she stepped into the boneyard and eased her way to Barthalamew's waiting stone. She then held her gaze upon his now glorified rock as her hooded figure took a knee and placed the white rose upon his dirt.

It was as had been done for forty-one years now. It was a heavenly sight. Do believe, dear reader, that those in view of that very moment were hastily moved to tears. And then, the most miraculous thing!

The Lady stayed!

For the matter of the ceremony, the boneyard was considered privileged ground and only a very select dignitaries were allowed. And what that better folk saw on that particular day was something nearing extraordinary, was, in fact, historical.

To the point, the Lady was typically there and gone, but gone, on that day, was clearly not her choice. It was unexpected. It was not tradition.

Even Mrs. Theryoung was stunned. The dear woman stepped forward and then back, forward and then back. She was absolutely caught by the notion of proffering some sort of help, but the Lady never called for it, never provided a hint or want of it. And so, the widow kept.

A quarter hour passed, and another threatened before the Lady finally stood before that impossibly quieted crowd and made her way back to the gate where Joan kindly awaited.

The two women again shared a smile and, for the first time in all these many years, the widow was afforded a considerable look upon Lydia's freckled face.

Joan's heart warmed. Her tears seeped. A seed was settled and made its quieted suggestion. The Lady's prolonged visit was for a very specific reason. It was for the fact that it was to be her last.

At that moment, all tradition was lost to the wind. The Lady reached for Joan's hand and, once secured, she lowered her hood and revealed her aged face to all. A gasp erupted and then subdued. The Blessed Lady of Oglethorpe was now in full view and was as loved as a thousand blessed angels could ever be.

No one dared a breath. No one dared a word. Many bowed their heads to quietly pray. Only Joan held her gaze and offered her voice.

"My Lady, would you allow me the honor to see you past the market?"

Of course, the Lady said nothing in reply. She only assented with a kind nod. And so, Joan eased her forward and together the two made their pleasant walk west.

The now hoodless Lady was met with genuine awe and reverence. All of Port Street looked on, wide-eyed, overwhelmed by the flow of the Lady's brilliant red hair, by the presence of her evergreen eyes, by her freckled cheeks and kindly smile, by her absolute and unending beauty. She was a sight for the ages. Indeed, the Lady of Oglethorpe did not disappoint on that miraculous day.

By way of that historic walk no words were spoken between the two ladies. No voice, nor sound stepped up from the thousands in constant observance. There was only the touch of their feet upon the downward pavement as the two made their way to the waiting west end.

Upon reaching the Market, the Lady separated and gave a kindly smile to Joan. A nod was exchanged. According to the ever-telling journal of Toby's widow, the dear woman loosed a tear and made no effort to clear it. It simply eased its quieted way down the stretch of her cheek and disappeared into the dirt at her feet. The Lady of Oglethorpe then made her turn and stepped westward for the very last time.

And then a year. Autumn was again upon Alagood. The crowds returned. The feast was happily at hand. The drunkards were in force. What chance had a thousand kegs of rum!

And then, at the appropriate hour, the kegs were corked. The crowds were stilled. The horsemen gathered upon the road leading to town. The bugler happily held to his instrument, pleased for his role before the masses.

Tens of thousands held their sacred spot on Port Street. Tens of thousands held their breath, held their hearts, held even their sobriety. Tens of thousands awaited that historic call.

But the call never came. The riders never sent forth. The bugler never sounded his note. The day came and went and without so much as a sound upon the air.

Evening set in. The sun made its dip. The hours ever so quietly passed. There was no Lady upon the road. It was as Mrs. Theryoung expected. And yet, the widow could not help herself.

From her mark atop Port Street she turned sharply to the boneyard, as though some hooded figure might have snuck by but there was no such figure, no hooded Lady. There were only the many stones that stood above those many bones and the church that shadowed it all.

There was only the quieted crowd of dignitaries who now stood before her with all the most curious faces. There was only her slow breaking heart as she began to understand the coming of the midnight hour and the passing of that dreadful day. There was only her duty as she suddenly saw fit.

And so, a nearby deacon was summoned to her side and proper instruction was given. The deacon disappeared into the church at once as the many still in waiting lit candles along Port Street to better provide for the Lady's walk on the notion that she was simply running a bit late.

But Joan knew better. With the midnight hour nigh, she looked one last time to Barthalamew's stone and wept for the boy. His mysterious Lady had missed their date and would miss it forevermore.

Midnight then pushed. The deacon committed to his task. The silence of that woeful night was quite suddenly shattered as the High-Street church bell breathed and gave its toll.

Forty-two times.

Just as it would every following year, in perpetuity.

The Lady of Oglethorpe was never seen again.

The Lady of Oglethorpe was…

45

Home.

T'was a practical day with all its practicalities in bloom. The sun spun its pretty web across the bluest of all possible skies. Nary a cloud dared. The blue was simply not having it.

Just past the western limits of Adelayde, across a large and empty field and just above the lonesome rise of that familiar hill remained the old church. Time had come and had its play and seemingly left for some other day. To the point, and from that perspective alone, it looked as it had always looked.

It was a matter of architecture, you see. The old church was of a simple build and thereby firm. The result was something more like a statue than a building. It was stout and centered and featured a strong sense of purpose. Even though it was unpretty to the eye it stood as though a force against all of nature's tempers. It stood, seemingly, forever.

And yet, a good many things were different. To start with, there was an obvious population. There were many children now, all about and each happily tasked to a number of gardens or some other delightful chore. The old church was surrounded on all sides and by all hours of the day as the children tallied and toiled and made their way. Clearly, there was a sense of community here and it was all overseen by the remaining and beloved Sisters of the Order.

To date, there was but the two. There remained Sister Lydia, who was, at that moment and by way of nearby Adelayde, returning from an early journey. And there was Sister Maribeth, clearly aged now, though still very pleased and very much for the record!

It was she who first noted Lydia's presence across that easterly field. Her step, for her years, was rather impressive. And so, she stepped quickly to her very dear friend.

"I trust it was a pleasant visit."

Lydia's reply, of course, could only come by way of a pleasant nod. Maribeth's heart erupted.

"It was just announced in Adelayde. Can you believe! Our Barth! An actual Saint! I suspect Josephine is spinning all about her miserable little grave."

Lydia's smile was wide to the point of breaking. Maribeth wrapped her arms around her remaining friend and gave a tight squeeze. The order had never known such perfectly happy times as this.

And then, from a distance, a cry of many sent up.

"She's home!"

The two sisters released and looked across the field. The nearby children alerted and began their charge.

"Well, it seems a proper welcome awaits you, Sister."

To be sure, this was the most treasured moment of Lydia's travels. The children were on her at once. The varied lot of them encircled her, each reaching for her, holding her, providing for her last steps before the waiting church and then into the nave where she was directed to the altar.

The orphans counted just past a dozen now and by a variety of ages. The youngest was nearing five and the oldest was just past fourteen. And the lot of them adored dear Lydia and in ways she could never have possibly imagined by those many years of her own quieted youth. She was now a mother and to every one of them and to the order above all and this, alone, had become her purpose.

"Play!"

It was the common call of the many children upon her return to the altar where the piano remained and impeccably so. It was, after all, the direct call of the order, and by way of Cecilia's still plentiful funds, that that the piano be perfectly maintained.

And so, it stood, as the church stood. It held, as the church held. It was, as the church was, beloved.

And yet, nothing about the nave was truly changed. The scattered pews remained just as scattered. The dirted floor was just as dirty. The walls and the ceiling and especially the patched hole in the roof above were all as they were and would always be.

It seemed by either sister that Toby or Barth or even Marihanna might step in at any moment, that some call for dinner or the minutes of some past meeting might quickly sound. Everything about that unusually poor room seemed infinite and simple and beautiful above all.

"Play," again the call and by a dozen unrelenting voices.

It was clear that Lydia was more than a bit worn for her travels, but she loved that dear piano almost as much as she loved her blessed children. And so, with a humbled heart, she stepped to the bench and took her proper seat and placed her hands upon the waiting keys.

At once, the nave filled with the sounds of joy. The many notes and chords of that blessed piano were now the voice of the Lady and her many words sang out with a telling and lively passion. Here now was Lydia's conversation, her thoughts and wants by way of the most melodic sentences and paragraphs. She no longer kept to the sheets of music, but simply played from the heart, where all the love in the world simply begged to be heard.

And so, her heart was heard.

The dozen or so orphans slept well that night by way of a number of well-fortified buildings that lined the back acre of the church. These were not sheds full of tools and holes and weathered miseries, but well-built rooms for the many loving children who now made up the future of the order. And it was, from a very particular view, that the Lady of Oglethorpe watched over them all.

Each and every night Lydia stepped up that creaky bell tower and made her way onto the roof and stepped sweetly across to her waiting place, next to what was clearly the most thoroughly patched bit of roof in all the kingdom.

From here, all that she cherished was visible; the homes of her good children, the fruits of her own labors, and the shine of that lonesome, but magnificent moon.

That old bug!

Made in the USA
Middletown, DE
01 November 2018